The Oath of Blood & Roses

by

C. M. Hano

Hearts of Dalaria, Book One

The Oath of Blood & Roses

Contact Information: info@thewildrosepress.com

Cover Art by *Lea Schizas*

The Wild Rose Press, Inc.
PO Box 708
Adams Basin, NY 14410-0708
Visit us at www.thewildrosepress.com

Publishing History
First Edition, 2024
Trade Paperback ISBN 978-1-5092-5433-0
Digital ISBN 978-1-5092-5434-7
Previously Published:2021 C M Hano Books

Hearts of Dalaria, Book One
Published in the United States of America

Dedication

To my Husband, who sees the beauty in all my scars.

Part One: Blood Oath

Chapter One

Clover

My room is a mess of fabrics and perfumes.

The lacey material irritates the healing marks from my last visit in the room.

I am standing at the center, keeping my posture as perfect as I can while the seamstress pins and marks the silk skirts of my crimson gown. The aching in my legs and lower back is from the extended time forced to wear needlepoint heels. Today marks the day that I become engaged to a prince from the outlying territories.

The treaty demands it.

A tattooed parchment, decorated with the symbols from each kingdom. A dragon's head for Greveil, a sword and shield for Shuang, and Thornwarf: a rose mounted in the center of a crown of golden antlers.

Created by all three rulers after the Dragon Wars finished three centuries ago, the treaty demanded the Princess of the High King marry a prince from one of the lower-born territories. Before my birth, my ancestors only sired sons. My great-grandfathers sought various healers. Hoping for some kind of remedy to aid in the consummation of a daughter. Magic has been gone since the end of the war. The only hope was to keep praying to Emnera.

Goddess of Earth and Nature, and our kingdom's past, present, and future. That is what Mistress Seigel continually preaches about during our studies.

"When magic returns, Emnera will return. The flavor of ash will fill the mouth of her reincarnated form." Mistress repeated this at the end of each lesson.

When I was born, the kingdom rejoiced, but all the prayers since have gone unanswered, making me question their existence altogether. Why didn't they hear my screams? Come to my aid every time that blade touched my skin?

Since the treaty mentioned a daughter, the peace between kingdoms has been on a thin line. King Deka, my father, promised King Tywin of Greveil and Queen Iliana of Shuang, that on the day of my twenty-third birth year, a royal ball was held in honor of the royal engagement.

To keep the peace, whoever the king didn't select would have the chance of choosing any eligible high-born maiden they considered worthy of becoming their next princess. I don't have the freedom to choose who I spend my life with.

The queen established everything down to the golden cutlery. The gown, the ball, the royal suitors, and then the wedding. Once that happens, Mother and Father will relinquish their titles as High King and Queen and go somewhere far away from me. If they don't do it on their own accord, I will just convince my new husband.

"Stay still, princess," Vivian, the Royal Seamstress, pleaded while under my skirts, pinning the inside, and I felt highly uncomfortable. The silk slip Mother made me wear covers my scars, but can Vivian still see them? If she does, what will she think?

"My knees itch," I grumbled softly that only her ears could catch it. Mother, also known as Queen Malian to others, was sitting across from Mistress Siegel at the round wooden tea table, chatting while eating small biscuits and sipping on black tea.

I had her eyes, the deepest shade of blue from what Father would always say. "You look just like her." It was true to a point since I was a younger, shorter, and quite scrawnier version of the queen. That was about the only thing I inherited from her. She is the epitome of royalty. Her sun-kissed skin and honey-colored hair are perfectly flawless. Not a single patch of uneven skin or a single strand ever out of place. But don't let that perfectly crafted appearance deceive you—her bite is far worse than her bark.

"Scars will do you good, my flower," she would say anytime I've disobeyed her. "They remind us of our trials and successes."

After my most recent painful lesson, I've gone out of my way to avoid any further attacks that would enable me to be punished and thrown into that damned room once again. Instead, I stand on the polished marble floor, with arms hanging loosely by my sides and legs trembling in pain, while Vivian continues to wrap multiple shades of red and pink fabrics around my body.

I didn't dare ask why she didn't just use one of the various statues of earlier queens as her pin cushion instead of my body. But, as logical as it seems to me, I would surely regret trying to suggest that to her.

"My darling Clover," my mother started, with her high-pitched tone filling my ears and making them painfully ring. It didn't help that she also pushed back on her chair, causing the wood to screech loudly onto the marble floor while she approached me. "Doesn't she look exquisite, Siegel?"

While circling me, she fingers the fabric along my waist and gives me a white smile. Scrutinizing every inch of me and the gown for anything that seemed misplaced.

No one is as vile and torturous as her. She would force guards to intimidate me into giving in to their desires. Let them touch me or seduce me into inviting them into my bed. I never gave in, and that was the only time my mother ever said she was proud of me.

"As beautiful as a rose, Your Grace," Mistress Seigel delicately replied. The people respected my mother, but they also feared her. That response became warranted these past thirty years since she became Queen. Beheading someone for looking at her or Father the wrong way, sending servants to the room for punishment, some got to go home, but others—

"Ouch." I winced as I felt a small needle poke near my ankle. I involuntarily looked down and then froze in that position. Coming out from the various layers of my skirts, Vivian's violet eyes were widening with fear, and her right hand holding a needle with a small bead of crimson on the end, was trembling.

"My apologies, Your Grace… I didn't mean to." Vivian was on her knees, and before I could tell her it was all right, my mother snapped her fingers, and the two knights jolted her onto her feet. I would expect an expert seamstress to wear something nicer, but since she was not highborn, she could wear nothing other than the simple brown dress and leather boots she bore.

It was the color of horse dung. They forced all servants to wear such a boring color to stand for their low-born status. The plainness allowed them to blend in the background, allowing us high-born and royalty to shine through the crowds.

"You hurt the princess." Mother snatched the needle from Vivian's trembling fingers and examined the pointed end.."And you drew blood." Her lips twitched at the corners, while a tremor raced along my spine when I noticed what she was looking at.

At the sound of her tongue clicking, I wanted to move, to speak, to do something, but fear and the consequences of action against her kept my mouth shut. "Do you know what happens to servants that hurt their princess?" I heard Vivian sob and plead for forgiveness, but I already knew it was too late.

My attention immediately shifted to the two men standing on either side of the frightened seamstress. Dressed in bright crimson tunics, expertly tailored black breeches, and darkened boots, they were a frightening sight to see. Each guard had two swords strapped on either side of their waists, in which a hand always rested against the hilt, ready for action. A blackened headpiece shielded their entire face and neck, leaving only their eyes to be seen. The one on the right had eyes the color of warm chocolate, while the other one bore eyes the shade of forest green trees.

There was no trepidation, regret, or any other emotion in either of their gazes. Just like their queen, only emptiness filled their pupils as if their souls were no longer housed within their robust bodies and it left a mere shell in its place. Being a part of the queen's guard could do that to a person.

Mistress Siegel was standing to my right, a portrait of obedience and mimicking my mother's expressions. That was who the old crone was. A brown-nosing, snitch, wicked woman that would do anything to stay on my mother's good side. She is the main reason so many scars littered my skin. Although she would never lay a finger on me, no, she would run to Mother about anything and everything that went wrong during my lessons with her. Everything from her silvery hair to the wrinkled skin, and thin pale lips screams a mean old spinster. I bet she never married because of how presage she was toward people that didn't have deep pockets and power. Not that she needed the connections being middle-born.

"Forgive me, Your Grace, it was an accident." Vivian was sobbing and my aching legs wanted to run to her and save her from the inevitable fate that was about to be given upon this poor woman by the queen.

"Hush now, Vivian. It will be over soon. I mustn't let anyone hurt my child." Chills filled the air as I watched in terror, a sinful grin forming on my mother's bronzed face as she grabbed a fist full of Vivian's black curls in one hand, and then took a dagger from a guard in the other. Stabbing it right through Vivian's right eye. Repeatedly, with each shriek, blood spurting into her tanned hand, a mix of red and brown. I couldn't move. I have seen and been on the receiving end of my mother's temper before, but I have never seen her kill anyone. Bile crept up into my throat and it burned to keep down my last meal.

Vivian's eye was hanging from the end of the dagger, her body slumped over, blood spilling onto her brown dress, and her breath was gone. Paralyzed with fear, I watched Mother wipe her bloodied hand onto Vivian's dress and gave her next command. "Feed her to the pigs."

Once the double-floral pattern doors of my chambers closed, Mother approached me. She cupped my chin with that murderous hand, painting it with the leftover blood, and poked her sharpened nails into my skin. Blood, Vivian's life source, was splattered across her face, making her look more menacing than usual.

"Not a word of this, my dear."

"I don't know what you're talking about, Your Grace." My voice was so steady, which surprised us both, considering the murder I just witnessed.

"Good girl. Mistress Siegel," she stated while letting my chin go. I still didn't move, and I was sure my legs down to the tips of my toes had disappeared or just went numb. "Have the maids clean this up and, Clover, darling."

"Yes, Your Grace." I was still standing poised and perfect in the same spot.

"You may change your clothes, go see Hilda about your ankle, and then meet me in the throne room." As soon as they exited my chambers, I ran to the chamber pot in my bathing chamber and emptied my stomach into it. Of course, those gods forsaken heels came off before I ran. How could she kill her in cold blood, over a simple needle prick?

I have never seen my mother kill anyone before, but I have attended the beheadings that she ordered the executioner to carry out. The first time was when I was five and completely terrified. Father was away on diplomatic business elsewhere, and I was too young to have any privy to the knowledge of where and when he would return.

No matter. Mother told me it was part of being the High Queen, to maintain order and discipline executions are necessary. I don't agree with that one bit but, I can't say that to her.

I unlaced my gown, removed everything until I was just in my ivory silk undergarments, and then sat on the cold floor to examine my right ankle. There was a small scab already formed from the spot where the needle made contact—it wasn't an accident. There was nothing on my ankles that needed any sewing or pinning. But I don't remember doing anything to anger Vivian.

Did she want to die? She must have known what Mother would do if she, even a simple prick of a needle, hurt me. That is how possessive and controlling Mother was. My hand explored up my calve, to my inner thigh where the first set of scars was.

In a blackened room, lit only by a few burning torches, I was in just a silk night slip strapped down by my wrists and ankles to a table. My legs spread shoulder length apart, arms bound above my head. The room was hot, and it was difficult to breathe because at ten years old, the thought of what my Mother was about to do to me, scared the hell out of me. She dressed in her regal emerald gown, perfectly primped as if she were not about to punish me for eating a pastry when I was told not to.

"My sweet child, do you know why I have brought you here?" She deadpans.

"Please Momma, I didn't mean to... I just."

"Just what? My little Clover just wanted to taste a sweet treat and become fat ruining the perfect body the gods blessed her with. Not my daughter. No, you have a

duty to the realm to become the perfect wife to a noble prince so the Treaty of Peace will not falter. And so, as Queen and your mother, I must punish you for disobeying my orders."

My eyes widened in terror when I saw the dagger in her hand. When the blade hovered over one torch, I cried. It didn't matter how much I begged and pleaded with her that I was sorry. And when that heated blade touched my skin, I screamed so loud that I could barely hear my burning flesh, but I smelt it.

Hilda tended to my wounds a day later to prevent infection. Mother wanted them to stay unattended long enough for them to scar so I could remember what the desire to eat pastries resulted in. I have eaten nothing sweet since that day.

After I cleaned myself up, I changed into a well-fitting purple gown, with my not-so-high heels on, I placed the unfinished ball gown on the bed and then left to head toward the throne room. Eyeing it now, I could clearly see how beautifully crafted the gown was. Vivian was highly skilled.

The narrow halls were not as appealing as one would think for the High King's castle. Floral patterns extending from the ceiling straight down to the marbled floors added a more feminine charm. Mother was obsessed with the gardens; especially since the royal crest had a rose as its focal point.

Though I am named after a flower, I don't share Mother's unconditional love for the dreaded plant. Just to spite her, if I ever have any children in the future, I will name none of them after flowers.

There were knights stationed at every tenth column, standing erect, and straightening even more as

I passed them. All dressed in that hideous uniform Mother made them wear. For managing the castle, Father had no part in it. He managed the rest of the realm and left everything else in the hands of Mother. There were times I was not so sure they even loved each other. I have never once seen them display any kind of affection toward one another and they barely speak to each other when I am around.

Father was usually away on business or with the council discussing diplomatic issues. Or at least that is what Mistress Siegel would tell me when I asked where the king was. It soon got to a point where I would just stop asking and if he showed up, then that is when he showed up.

If he knew what she did to me would he stop it? Would he kill her for how she has treated me? Do I care? Because if my father genuinely loved and cared for me, then perhaps he would be present in my life on more than one occasion.

"Your Highness." I stopped mid-step, only a few feet from the vast oak doors that led into the throne room. I turned and saw my dear sweet friend walking up to me. Alma Hagar, best friend, and personal guard to me. She was the first female allowed to become one. On the day of her trial, she bested more than half of the other recruits in her class. Alma impressed Mother and Father with her fighting skills and assigned her to guard me. Little did they know she was more than my protector.

"Alma," I said in a cool voice. Maintaining professionalism around each other was part of the facade because if my parents found out just how familiar we had become, they would send her away or

Mother would have her executed. She was beautiful, strong, and someone that I admired. Her dark skin was imprinted with different sigils from her homelands.

Intricate swirls of silver across her arms and legs, complementing her exquisite dark-skin. Her beautiful golden eyes matched the color of my hair, and her face was flawless. A head of white hair, braided into a ponytail sat atop her head, except for the shaved sides above her ears. The uniform she wore differed from the rest of the Royal Guard. Her ivory blouse, with green embellishments of clover on the sleeves, matched the emerald pants and black boots she wore.

She bowed in front of me and then stepped to my side, our shoulders barely touching, she whispered, "Are you all right?"

I nodded and turned toward the doors. Alma opened the one on the right, and I walked in. A burst of frigid air danced across my skin, making it raise, as I stared in shock at the sight laid out before me.

Standing center of the polished floor was a man, with a shadowless face hidden behind the cover of a hood dressed in a black robe. He held a bloodied ax above his head as pools of crimson flooded the floor where two bodies lay, their heads placed gently on the two pompous thrones at the center front of the room.

The thundering of boots and blades rushed in behind us as I faintly heard Alma shouting and trying to pull me out of the room, but my feet merged into the floor.

"Princess Clover," the shadow man said in a pitched voice. Alma stepped between him and me, her double-edged swords out and ready to strike. My heart was shockingly calm as I stepped toward him. I heard the guards fighting with the intruders, but I couldn't feel any kind of emotion developing inside of me.

Alma charged at him with her swords, cutting and slicing through distant shadows. He was gone and all I could focus on was the fact that my parents were dead. Instead of feeling sadness or anger, I felt relief.

Two hands gripped my shoulders.

She was shouting at me.

"Chloe, we need to get you out of here now," Alma begged.

Chloe, the nickname Alma gave me when we first met.

I pushed past her, staring down at the decapitated bodies of my parents. Their wrists and ankles were bound behind them like wild hogs, their blood painting the white tiles red. My gaze fixated upon their paralyzed expressions. Both of their eyes and mouths were open with their last shout of protest as their heads were removed from their bodies. Whoever killed them, did it to send a message, placing their heads gently on the throne and leaving it out on display.

Then, I saw it.

A silver needle sticking out of both of my mother's eyes and just when I thought I had emptied the entire contents of my stomach before, I vomited all over her head.

"Vivian." That was all I said between heaves of vomit as Alma's arm came around my waist.

"We need to leave now." I nodded. My episode of paralysis melted away. The hall was filled with dead guards as the shadowed men dissipated. Alma ordered guards to come with us as she ushered us out of the throne room.

I was expecting to see more bodies outside, but it was clear of any evidence of that. How did they get inside?

"Magic is back. Emnera is coming back. I can't believe Siegel was right," I started as Alma rushed us toward my chambers, flanked by guards to the front and the rear. We made it into my chambers, but something was off. None of my torches were lit, my balcony doors were shut, and all my curtains were closed. My room was pitch black.

"Something's wrong," I whispered to Alma. I felt her grip tighten on my wrist.

"Get those damned torches lit," she ordered.

"Come now, we won't bite."

Chapter Two

Calian

Sweat gleamed off the side of Eli's face, his blonde hair sticking to his forehead as the High Sun beat down on us both.

The training yard was clear except for the two of us. He preferred it that way. I didn't mind because it gave me a chance to beat him without his mentor giving me a disapproving glare. I never understood why they'd want the crown prince of Greveil to think he won every fight. Out there, in the real world, an assailant will not let you win based on your status as a human. You're nothing but flesh and bone.

I blocked his strike, kicking my leg out to knock him to the ground with a grunt.

"Ease up, Cal. I'm meeting my fiancé tonight," he said while rubbing his sore bottom, jumping to his feet.

"And how do you feel about that?" I ask. The question I've been hankering to ask since we got the notice two weeks ago.

He brushed the dust from his pants and walked over to his waterskin, taking a long swallow before answering. "Honestly, if I were in the position of High King, I would have the power to send out armies further beyond the boundary."

"You think there is more outside?" I ask, picking

up my water to drink. My throat dried out a few minutes ago, but I would've kept going if he wanted to.

Eli wiped his forehead with a cloth."I know there is. The map isn't complete, is all. There has to be more than just our two kingdoms and Thornwarf. Think about it, Cal, where do you come from?" He looks at me but I don't answer him. I have no knowledge. "I'm sure if you ventured out, beyond the mountains of Shuang, or past the Great Sea, you would understand."

"I mean, those are dreams. You know your father would never allow it," I remind him.

"My father may be the king of Greveil, but he isn't High King, is he?" He smirks, knowing he has a point.

"Your Highness." A guard rushed out, catching our attention. "A letter has arrived from our scouts along the borders." He handed a rolled parchment, bearing the symbol of House Gian; Hog's head.

I watched in anticipation while the prince broke the seal and scanned the writings. "Prepare the armies." He ordered after a moment, looking toward the guard. Without hesitation, he bowed and obeyed.

"What does it say?" I asked, his change in demeanor concerning me.

"We never told you this, but Sir Reginald and a few other council members have been planning for an attack." The council met? Without me? He must have noticed my confusion because he elaborated. "Around four months ago, the Great Barrier fell. We don't know why or how, but the sea grew larger and birds, ones from none of our territories, made their way here. Our spies were sent on covert missions to explore those new lands and they discovered a dark tower in a territory covered in sand.

"An army of beasts was being led by a man bearing the shadows of the realm itself. They called him Emperor Rai. My men came back petrified, because if he could conjure magic as dark and powerful as that, then that meant only one thing."

He didn't have to voice it, because I felt it. The flavor of ash filled my mouth around the same time, but saying something was pointless. I am not the creature I was born to be.

"Magic, Cal. It's back, and I believe he has the means to destroy us all. And now, we have the location of his first attack."

"What do you mean? How could you know this?"

"Because we infiltrated a flank of his army, the ones not made from his dark powers but animals that walk and talk like you and I."

"Eli, what are you intending?" The mischievous look dancing in his ocean eyes had my heart rate beating with growing concern.

"You will take your legion of men and a few of my own, go on a discrete mission and rescue the High Princess of Thornwarf. Bring her here to me. Unharmed but by any means necessary."

"You want me to kidnap her? That's…" I snarled.

"Not kidnap. Haven't you been listening? Rescue. There will be an attack tonight and you must hurry so you can reach her in time." He made his way back inside the palace, leaving me with orders that go against my moral code.

****

"No one asks questions. I'm your commander, and if you disobey me, then you won't be returning home tonight," I tell the men gathered on horseback around me. We all dressed in black, to help us blend in with the night. By the time we arrive at the palace, the White Sun will have reached its highest peak.

We begin our hasty ride to the High King's castle with one thought running through my mind: How the hell am I going to convince a spoiled princess to come with me?

****

We arrived just as the White Sun's beams illuminated the backside of the fortress. There was no evidence of an army approaching. Looking toward the higher points, I blinked twice to bring on my nocturnal vision but still saw nothing. My ears twitched as I listened for the sound of metal clashing or boots crunching in the snow, but all I picked up was the call of night owls to one another. Jumping down from my horse, I walked him over to the nearest trunk and tied off the reins before pulling an apple from my side pocket to feed him.

The men followed my lead, something I've never had to worry about. But that didn't hold true for the two men Eli sent with us. They eyed me curiously, and I gestured for them to do the same as the rest. Reluctantly, they followed my silent command.

"It's quiet," one of his men whispered as he walked up to my right side.

He was right.

I waved my hand in a forward motion indicating to my men we were approaching from the back. We fell in one behind the other, close to the wall, using the shadows to hide us instead of letting the White Sun reveal our position. I'm not sure where the princess' bed chambers are, but I approached the closest balcony and entered.

Snapping my fingers, one of my men ran up with the grappling hook. He wound it around a few times, took aim, and tossed it over the side, securing our means of entrance. One by one, we scaled the wall until we were outside the open doors of a bedchamber. I moved first, scanning the area from just inside the curtains for any sign of life. A few torches were lit, but my Ashana eyes saw through the dark just as well as the day.

I signal the all-clear, clicking my tongue twice, and we flood inside, the last man shutting the doors quietly, another dousing the flames that would reveal us.

"What do we do now?" the same man from earlier whispered.

"Remain here. Stay quiet. Unseen." I ordered and left.

Making my way down the narrow hall, I heard the shouting chorus of guards accompanied by the thundering of boots against the marble. "To the throne room! We're under attack!"

"Get the princess to safety!" a woman shouted.

Quickly, I made my way back inside her room, gave the signal to be ready, and positioned myself on the edge of the bed. Something told me we were about to come face to face with the High Princess of Thornwarf and her royal guard.

Chapter Three

Clover

I sucked in a sharp breath at the husky voice. My hand reached out to Alma's thigh, gripping hold of the hilt of her extra dagger. She didn't stop me. In a blink of an eye, my room lit up, and then we saw them. Another flavor of magic hit my mouth. Am I only able to taste this? Ten men dressed in all black, their faces covered except for their eyes, holding swords in their hands. Some held two, with jagged blades meant to tear through skin and bone.

"Get out," Alma snarled. Our backs were toward each other, with the circle of three guards around us.

"We will, once you hand over the princess." The man, I can only guess to be the leader for speaking up, sat at the edge of my bed, picking at his nails with a dagger, completely calm.

"Your master has already left with the rest of your army. I suggest if you don't want to die, then you should vanish too," Alma said. The man's eyes gleamed with the challenge and the men closed in on us.

My room was large enough for ten ladies to have a comfortable teatime in but not large enough for a fight to happen and any of us to escape with our lives.

I couldn't think of a way out of this that didn't involve fighting. But I knew I had to do something. I didn't want Alma to die. And she would if they started attacking. Ten against six and me. Helpless, useless me. I didn't even know why I was holding this stupid dagger, acting as if I knew how to use it. If I go with him, then maybe I could save us all from more bloodshed. They killed my parents, broke into my home, and if they fight, no one will leave this room alive that I care about.

"If I go with you, promise me you won't hurt them."

Alma turned to me. "No." She scowled at me.

I ignored her.

"Promise me, we will walk out of this room, and you will leave her unharmed and alive." I stepped toward the man. My gaze fixated on his chest. He is a head taller than me and smells of spices and leather. "Swear it."

He was now inches away from me; I didn't avert my eyes; I held my ground, looking into those deep greens of his. The surrounding skin bronzed, which told me he spent a good amount of time out in the Sun.

"Reach out your hand, Princess," he asked me.

I never broke my gaze, never trembled to show the rising panic inside of me. "I will give you two options. We can seal this with a kiss—my preferred option—or with a blood oath."

I raised my eyebrows and then glared at the smugness of his voice.

My parents are dead. I can be free if I go with him. Even if it means being bound to him until death. Alma will be safe. She is brave, selfless, and I know she will take care of the kingdom. This was a chance for me to get away from here. I won't give him the satisfaction of kissing me. I will learn who that shadow man was and why he killed my parents.

A sacred bond that can only be enacted by using blood magic. That confirmed the suspicion that magic had come back to the realm and our goddess will be reborn again. There was a lot I didn't know about this oath, but what I knew was that once I agree to it, I won't be able to lie to him, kill him, or betray our original vow. That was the full extent of my knowledge of this oath, but he didn't know that.

"Blood oath," I spat.

"This will hurt, which is why I preferred the kiss." He held out his right hand and then ran his blade across his palm, then across my right. I didn't wince, and I saw the flicker of amusement on his face. I have withstood far worse pain in much more sensitive places on my body.

"Intriguing," he said.

"Chloe, you don't have to do this," Alma pleaded, reaching for my left hand.

"It'll be all right," I told her. I am not a ruler or leader. Mother burned any chance of that out of me the day she made the first cut. But Alma, she is. That is why my next order can be said so easily.

"Once we leave, you will assume the throne. Cancel the ball and inform the other kingdoms that the entire royal family is dead because of an unforeseen accident. This man will let me make an official document having you take the throne because of my death. This is an order and not a request." Snagging my left arm, she turned me toward her.

"Don't do this," Alma begged.

I jerked my arm from her grip, handed her the

dagger, and then turned back toward the man.

"Get on with it."

"As you wish." We joined our cut palms, blood mixing, and then he pulled me into him. One hand gripped my waist, and I felt the hardness of his body against me.

"Do we have to be this close?" I asked. Completely ignoring me, he began the oath, and my mouth filled with the flavor of magic as our joined palms burned.

"Under the rights of the *Blood Oath*, I swear we will leave your people unharmed if you come with me willingly and without complication. If you break this oath, your people will pay with their lives. Do you swear by it?"Our gaze didn't falter.

"Under the rights of the *Blood Oath*, I swear to come with you willingly and without complications, and you will leave my people unharmed. If you break this oath, you and your people will pay with their lives." It came out a lot easier than I thought it would.

"Sheathe your swords," he ordered his men, our eyes still locked onto each other.

"Lower your weapons," I ordered. "Leave these quarters and don't follow us. Don't come after me, if any of you disobey me, you will be executed."

"Chloe." Alma sounded defeated, and it broke my heart.

"Draw up a parchment willing the kingdom over to her and then stamp it with the royal seal," I ordered the man.

"You heard her." The entire time, our bloodied hands, bodies, and eyes never faltered from their positions. I knew he was trying to intimidate me into submission, but I have been through worse with

Mother.

Alma and the guards left the chambers. The man stepped back from me, our embrace broken, but not our eye contact. One of his men brought over the parchment. He examined the message, and then went over to my stationary and sealed it with the royal crest that belonged to me.

"Bring that to the one called Alma. We need to get going." He then approached me. "You are a very brave woman." He snapped his fingers and one of his men brought over some rope.

"Is that necessary? I just swore to you I wouldn't escape."

"I don't want you getting any wicked ideas about stabbing me, Princess."

I held my head up high before he could ask me to and positioned my wrist in front of him. He let out a laugh before binding my wrists. Then the unexpected happened. A cloth bag came over my head, and my world was black again. I tried to calm that rising panic, and focus on my breathing. Of all the lessons Mother made me go through, this one was the one I always failed. I hated being in small, dark places, unable to see where I was or what was around me. My world was collapsing on me.

"Please." I heard the trembling in my voice. "I am being compliant, the bag isn't necessary."

"Shut it." I heard a different man speak right behind me. And then two hands were on my shoulders, pressing down onto me, making my body fall to its knees. The different man laughed, and then the bag came off my head. I felt the tension in my chest ease a little, but then, standing in front of me, that different man began to untie his pants. I glanced around to see where their leader went but I didn't see him.

"What are you doing? Where is your leader?" I demanded.

"I'm going to piss in your little pot." I swallowed the bile rising in my throat. The other men had vanished, and all that was left were the two of us. I averted my eyes as he made his way past me toward my bathing chamber. The flow of his urine almost made me lose control of my reflux. I closed my eyes, knowing that something like this would happen by going with savages.

"Open your eyes." I didn't obey. Didn't move, but I felt his fingers prying my eyes open, as his foul breath assaulted my nose.

Refusing, I felt his fingers prying my mouth open. Thrashing, kicking, it wasn't enough—he overpowered me and shoved me to the floor. I was powerless again. I couldn't let this happen, *Blood Oath* or not. Instinctively, I jerked my head forward as hard as I could, until I tasted iron in my mouth. He fell backward, cursing me when our heads made contact.

I shook the fog from my head as I stared into his devilish eyes. Before he could hit me again, a blade stuck out of his mouth from the back of his head. Blood splattered on my face as a small whimper escaped my lips when his body fell to the floor, and I saw *him* standing there. He helped me to my feet.

"Did he hurt you?" my captor asked, feigning concern.

I spat in his face. "As if you care."

He took a rag from his back pocket and wiped my face before cleaning his own. "I made an oath to you,

Princess. There is a lot more than words when it comes to one of those."

What else could he be talking about? "What do you want from me?" I asked.

"We don't have time for this." I could tell he was smiling at me, but I didn't care. "Did he hurt you?"He repeated his question, apparently not believing my first answer.

"No." I then looked at the dead man, his blood spilling out of both sides of his head.

"Good. We're leaving." He grabbed my arm and proceeded to my balcony doors that were opened, realizing at that moment just how they got into my room undetected. A large metal hook wrapped around one of the stone columns and a rope was dangling from the side. My eyes widened in shock because a drop from the third level would surely kill me.

"Don't be afraid, I won't let you fall."

Now was not the time for me to show fear. I swung my legs over the ledge one at a time, gripped the rope between my bound hands, wrapped the rope around my right leg, and shimmied down. The movement chafed against my bare thighs, but again, it was not the most painful thing to happen between my legs. I had the scars to prove it. As I made it to the bottom, firm hands wrapped around my waist, and when I looked to see who it was, I was surprised to find it to be him."How did you get down here so quickly?"

"The time for questions is later, Princess." He hoisted me up onto a horse and then sat right behind me. Glancing around, I looked for any posted guard to come help, but all I saw were his men on their horses. There was nothing on this side of the castle except the forest and a path in the snow, which I assumed was made by these men.

It was dark outside. The White Sun had risen. There were no lit torches. I felt blind, and a bit foolish for agreeing to this. I wanted to be free, yes, but what price did I just pay for it? I won't be truly safe until these bindings are off me and I can escape this group of men.

His thighs rested on either side of me. I gripped the rounded leather part of the saddle while he held the reins and motioned for the horse to run. The ride, something I wasn't used to, because I never left the palace walls, was rough.

The snowfall was soft, but my dress didn't prevent the icy breeze from piercing my exposed skin. A wool cloak was draped over my shoulders, putting more material between my body and the harsh weather. The only time I ever experienced winter in Thornwarf was when Mother forced me to walk the gardens. I used to smile when we would find dead flowers, but I stopped after she burned a rose petal into my thigh.

Gallivanting through the Evergreen Forest, a mix of snow and dirt tumbled in the air behind the horses as we hastened the pace. I'd never been in this forest and had no idea which direction we were headed, but I couldn't help but admire the beauty splayed out before us.

A man-made path shot through the never-ending trees. With his men on all sides, I felt somewhat free. It was unbearably cold, so I welcomed the warmth of his body pressed against mine.

The White Sun was bright in the sky by the time we stopped. I had no clue where we were, but I knew we had ridden for a couple of hours. Usually, once the White Sun started to rise, it was time for dinner, a bath, and then bed. I was never up at this time of night. When morning came, the High Sun was a beautiful display of auburn.

"We will camp here for the night."

"In the middle of the forest?" I asked as he jumped from the horse and then picked me up off it like I was nothing.

"Are you scared?" he teased. I shook my head as he laid out a bedroll he pulled from the saddle. I looked around and noticed it was just the two of us. "Don't worry. My men are posted on all sides. No one will come near us undetected."

"Do your men not sleep? Or are you just that cruel?" I scolded.

"You assume you know me, Princess."

I rolled my eyes at him. One of his men approached from the shadows with an arm full of branches. He kneeled and started to build a fire, as I just stood there, again, observing. My captor removed his face covering, drank something from his waterskin, and then handed it to me. I took it from him, admiring the chiseled features of his face. There was stubble left over from a recent shave, matching the chocolate color of his shortened hair. His face was as I suspected, beautifully bronzed, and in that moment, I determined that he was the most beautiful man I had ever gazed upon.

I sat on the hard ground, sipping at the water, and then handed it back to him. I wanted to ask him what his name was, but what was the point of getting to know a man that kidnapped me?

"You must have lots of questions, Princess, so go

ahead and ask. I will answer three tonight, and then we get some rest." I did have about a thousand questions boiling over inside of me, and didn't think it was that obvious.

"Who are you?"He smiled at me, and I couldn't stop the way my stomach flipped at the sight of it. But I didn't dare lessen my prestigious posture. He stood up from where he was sitting and came over to sit in front of me. Our knees mere inches away from touching. I wasn't sure if the heat wave was from the fire or from how my body was beginning to react to him. But it was unsettling, unwanted, and most definitely unwarranted.

"You may call me Calian." Have I heard of him? It was something to think more on, but I also didn't want that to be my second question.

"Why did your master kill my parents?" I asked, not breaking my emotionless face.

"That man was not my master," he said. *But that doesn't make any sense*. Yet again, I didn't let the shock of his answer affect my composure. I need to think of a good question because if I am going to escape without invoking the wrath of the blood magic gods, I need to know something useful.

"Which route do I take to get back home?" Not what he was expecting me to ask. His brows furrowed and he cleared his throat, rubbing the back of his neck with one hand. I gleaned on the inside because my question appeared to rattle him.

"Through those trees over there, toward the constellation of Naga." I turned to look, and I saw the beautiful outline of the legendary War Horse. Naga was the first horse, to Killian the god of War. I remember a lesson in history about the gods. Killian made an appearance to try and stop the last war but somehow was not able to.

"Your turn, Princess."

I gazed right at him. "No," I said. There was no way I was going to have this conversation with him and reveal things about myself.

"Why did you agree to come with me?" he persisted

"Because I didn't want Alma to die, and I have wanted to run away for most of my life."

"Interesting." He smiled at me again and I just knew his next question was going to be even more devious. "Why didn't you cry when you saw your parents had been slaughtered?"

"How did you know that?"My palm started to burn from where our bloodied hands had joined. That was pain, enforced by magic I couldn't handle.

"Answer my question first, Princess."

"I was abused by Mother and Father. While an excellent Father to the people, was an absent one to his own flesh and blood." In that moment, with disdain in my voice as I spoke of him, I realized my feelings toward the late king were not far off from how I felt about his queen.

He didn't smile this time. And I investigated those pools of green, expecting to see sympathy, but all I saw was anger. He leaned into me, our mouths mere inches away from each other, and I prayed that he would not ask me that tantalizing question. A smirk of amusement came across his lips.

"Do you want…" He paused, oh gods. "…to sleep on the ground or the bedroll?"

Not what I was expecting him to say, but I

answered truthfully. “The bedroll.”

Backing away from me, he got to his feet and then helped me to mine. I walked over toward the bedroll and then laid down on it. It was not as comfortable as my bed back home, but it was better than sleeping on the cold ground. I watched as he lay down across from me, the flickering fire between us. Rolling over, I couldn’t face him. After all that had happened today, sleep was something I didn’t want to welcome. Because when I sleep, all I see was her.

Chapter Four

Calian

The High Princess of Thornwarf is nothing at all what I was expecting.

Proposing a Blood Oath, and her accepting it…showed she had more hardened steel than any of these men possessed. Her soft breaths tell me she's fast asleep, something I heard her trying to fight for the past hour. But, witnessing the fall of your queendom, the death of your parents, and leaving your home does seem to be exhausting. Her hair is soft and falls in waves against the snow-covered ground.

I'm tempted to reach out and run my fingers through it. Her scent is something I've never smelt before. Not that the woman back home I've shared a bed with is privileged enough to afford whatever soaps and perfumes she can. It's a different kind of smell. Something my inner beast recognized the second she stepped into her bedroom.

Being the only one of my kind, based on the teachings of the family that took me in, there is little known about Ashana. When I was old enough and able to get a job inside the palace, I scoured the library searching for answers but could find none. From what I've discovered on my own, we have retractable wings, control over fire, incredible strength, and the ability to shift human eyes to the slanted eyes of a dragon.

That's the closest animal I could compare them to. Out of curiosity, I walked over to the fireplace in the Great Hall one day and stuck my hand directly into the flames. I was prepared for the pain, but when it didn't come, I couldn't help but feel relieved. I looked into the abilities of extinct beasts and read more about different kinds. Each could control an element depending on which colony they were born into.

"Mother, please…" The princess's pained whimpers caught my attention.

"Princess?" I whisper.

"Stop! I didn't mean to." She shouts, her body violently shaking as she sleeps.

On instinct, I crawl over to her, wrapping an arm tightly around her waist. There isn't much for me to grab but that doesn't concern me nearly as much as how frozen her skin feels.

"You're freezing. You may hate me for this, but I'll stay long enough to calm you and warm you," I whisper against her ear.

As soon as her chest hits my back, I rub a comforting hand up and down her arm using my internal heat to pass onto her. It takes a few moments, but her shivering halts. The murmurs in her sleep continue and I decide to try to comfort her. Let her know she isn't alone but also wanting to know what she meant about her mother abusing her. How? Why would the High Queen want to hurt her daughter? Questions I suspect will soon get answered the more time I spend with her.

The soft wind blows around us. The loose strands of her hair dance along my nose, tickling me and causing an involuntary inhale. *Rose blossom and...something I can't pinpoint just yet.*

Something deep inside of me rears its head up. A flash of crimson, the roaring of an extinct beast, and the surge of fire course through my veins.

My Ashana is speaking to me.

The sleeping beast begins to awaken after being dormant for so long.

Why now?

It has to be the return of magic. The fall of the great barrier and the rise of this Emperor. Because the latter, the one reason I don't care to voice, is currently coaxing me into a deep sleep as my body has never been more relaxed than it is at this moment.

Chapter Five

Clover

"How many times must we go through this, Clover?" Mother asked as she played with her necklace. It is always there, and she is obsessed with it.

"What have I done this time? Look at someone when I wasn't supposed to?" Walking up to me, her precious dagger in hand, she peers down at me.

"Did you think I wouldn't notice how you and Sir Leon look at one another? It is not proper for a princess to look at a man of lower status. Especially the way you were."

I scoff in disbelief. "I just look at him the way you look at your precious gemstone."

Then came the snarl and the melting of my flesh.

My eyes fluttered open, the beams peeking through the canopy of trees causing a strain on my adjusting vision.

A small buzzing in my ear, the smell from the embers, and the feeling of the hard ground beneath the wool blanket made me remember just where I was. In the middle of the damned forest with a stranger that took me from my home. My right side ached with the pain of sleeping on it all night. I rolled onto my back, and then I felt it. The breath of someone sleeping next to me, the weight of a thick arm wrapped around my waist, and another under my neck.

Looking over, I saw two green eyes looking intently at me, and then a sly smile appeared. “Morning, Princess.”

“What do you think you’re doing?” I asked him. He removed his hand from my waist, and brushed strands of hair from his eyes.

“You have nightmares,” he whispered, and then pulled his other arm free before standing. My wrists were still bound, and my skin was raw from the rubbing of the rope. I sat up, stumbling while attempting to rise. Two strong hands on my torso balanced me until my feet planted.

“You must be mistaken,” I said as he let go of me. I brushed the dirt off my skirts.

“I don’t think so,” he argued while standing in front of me, moving at that incredible speed again.

“What do you want?” I know he can’t lie to me. I didn’t want to wait any longer for more short answers.

“You,” he smugly said, and before I knew it, my bound fists curled into balls and I tried to rip the rope apart.

Calian pulled the rope taut, withdrawing his dagger and freeing me.

“We may have made the *Blood Oath*, but I will never be yours.” I turned my back to him, headed toward the horse, and then foolishly tried to get onto it.

“What do you want?” I snapped at him again. “And you better not say the word ‘you’, because there is more to it. My parents were murdered, I was taken from my home, and now I don’t know what the future of my kingdom will be because the treaty will not be fulfilled. As I am sure you are not aware of, or if you are, you just don't care. So, since we clearly can't lie to each other, tell me something. If you didn't kill my parents, who did?" I paused but I was too angry to let him answer.

"Better yet, why didn't you just kill me? Why didn't you let your friend finish the job? None of this makes any sense to me. You will answer me with more than just simple, short words." The space between us was full of tension, and I wasn't sure what he was going to do. Smack me, kill me, punish me for speaking my mind. I don't know why I spoke so freely with him. If it were Mother, I would be back in that *room*, strapped down, and then gods only know what kind of punishment she would give me. He is the enemy, so I will not back down from him. Another skill my mother instilled in me. Something I've been realizing as of late. She may have had a heart of stone, but at least some of her lessons have been useful. I'm not sure how I should feel about that.

"The people who killed your parents were coming to kill you next. I saved you."

"Saved me? You are so full of shit!" My voice trembled. He closed the distance between us in two short strides. I raised my chin to meet his blazing eyes.

"I can't lie to you. You said that yourself, the oath doesn't allow it. And as far as my so-called friend, he wasn't one of *my* men. As soon as I left him alone, I waited to see what he was going to do to you." His breath was heavy, and his eyes were full of rage. "But I got distracted when my men were speaking with your guard. By the time I saw what he was doing, I lost it. None of my men will touch you or force themselves onto you. Especially now."

"You used me as bait?" I asked. Everything else he said, whether reasonable or not, went through one ear and out the other.

"I didn't think he was going to try and kill you. I just knew something about him didn't seem right. I needed to test my theory. Guess I was right." He shrugged, as if putting my life in danger was part of his everyday routine.

"How?" How did he know so much?

"We need to get moving." He went to grab my waist to place me onto the saddle, but I stepped aside.

"I'm not going anywhere until you answer my questions."I crossed my arms over my chest.

"We don't have time for this, Princess," he growled.

"I think that is your new favorite saying." There was more he needed to say. I know it and I was going to give him hell. He took me from my home and although he can't lie to me, there are ways around the whole truth. He reached for me, but I stepped around him. A glinting hilt from the dagger strapped to his outer thigh was enticing and the next time he goes for me, I am grabbing it.

"We don't have time for whatever games you are trying to play." He let out a frustrated breath.

"I told you, I'm not going anywhere with you until you tell me everything."

He bit his bottom lip, sucking his teeth in exasperation. I smiled on the inside, knowing that I was winning this argument. Before I knew it, he was on me. An arm wrapped tightly around my waist, the other hand gripping the back of my neck, and I took my unbound hands and brushed my fingers along the inside of his thigh. Making him take a deep breath in.

"What are you doing?"

"Brushing my fingers along your thigh," I said, which was true. I just didn't tell him that my hands were now wrapped around the hilt of his dagger. "Isn't that what you want from me?" I teased.

"If you pull that dagger, I won't be gentle." He pushed me up onto the saddle of the horse, unsheathing his dagger at the same time. I gripped it tightly in my hands. One small setback in my plan—I didn't know how observant he was. "I cut your bindings, but just know that if you run or fight, or stab me, the blood magic will enact that betrayal."

"All I want are some answers." Calian hoisted himself to my rear, with the dagger now in his possession, and then eyed my wrists.

"I'm sorry," he said, glancing at the rope burns on them. "It was never my intention to cause you any pain. But you must believe me when I tell you that all your answers will come to you once we make it to our destination."

"It's fine, this isn't the worst—" I started and then stopped. He was gently rubbing the area with his thumbs. Then suddenly, he grabbed the reins and then kicked the horse into a gallop. Leaving the remains of our camp behind. I had no clue where his men were or why he decided we didn't need the bedroll, but I assume it is due to us making it to some type of housing before nightfall. Another question that I desperately wanted to ask.

"Where are we going?" I asked.

"Home." That was all he said, and I was starting to get irritated with the mystery behind Calian. I've heard of that name before. I'm sure it has something to do with the other kingdoms. There was a legend of a *hooded mercenary*, stealing from High-Born, killing them if they didn't cooperate. I can only assume that with the way he and his followers dressed, and the fact that he kidnapped me the day before the ball. When my royal suitors would be attending it. It was too much of a coincidence.

"So…" I started. "About our pact of honesty."

He hummed.

"Right. Have you heard of the *Hooded Mercenary*?" He let out an annoyed sigh. "I'm going to assume that is a yes. They say the attacks are High-Born, holding them for ransom or other nefarious means."

"Sounds interesting." He deadpanned.

"I mean, that's what this is about. Isn't it?" The horse stopped, and I knew I had struck a chord with him. I leaned back as he moved to face me.

"You think I am him?" he asked, with sarcasm in his voice.

"It makes the most sense."

He lifted a hand to my right cheek. I felt the warmth behind the callouses. I didn't flinch, which was surprising because I'm not used to a gentle touch.

"And what if I was this hooded man? What are my intentions with the Princess of Thornwarf?" He was toying with me.

"Steal her away the day before her engagement so her royal suitors will pay her ransom." He chuckled and it sent a flutter through me. I couldn't help but smile at his laugh. The fact that I made him laugh was new to me. I've never made anyone laugh before, never got the chance to. His smile was alluring and beautiful.

It sparked a new feeling within me. Something that I buried a long time ago when I thought I knew what it was to feel some kind of emotion for another person.

"That's not why I took you, Princess." Then my smile faded, and anxiety fluttered, reminding me once again that he was the enemy. I cleared my throat before speaking again.

"You said you didn't kill my parents. You say you are not a hooded mercenary. Who are you and why did you take me? Please don't say you wanted me. Tell me the entire truth." I was stern.

"Why do you want to know so bad?" That anxiety turned to anger.

"How can you not answer right away? My palm is burning by avoiding your question." He smirked. "Are you insane? Why wouldn't I want to know the truth? I don't know anything about you except your name. And that you don't know what personal space means."

His chuckle vibrated through my entire body. "I will play this game. If you agree to the conditions."

"What conditions?" I worried what his answer would be.

"A truth for a truth." He gestured for the horse to start walking again. I faced forward.

"Agreed."

He pulled me back against him. I welcomed the warmth.

"Tell me a truth that only you know." That damned cut on my palm started to burn with a warning.

"I have a higher pain tolerance than the average person," I said.

"That explains some things."

"What about you?"

"I'm terrified of the dark." I scoffed. He cannot be serious. "I am." There it is again.

"Why did you agree to the Blood Oath?"

I didn't answer right away because I wasn't sure it would be the entire truth. "As I said, it was to protect my people." He pinched my side. "All my life, I was groomed to be the perfect bride and queen just like my mother. I felt as though agreeing to it would be something my mother would not approve of. But something my father would've."

"You seem to have been close to him."

"No. I wasn't." We were silent for a while. It was true that my father and I were not close.

"My father and mother are with the gods too," he responded quietly.

"I'm sorry." I truly felt sorry for him. I didn't feel my parents' loss. Not like I imagine he must have.

"Don't be. I never met them." Now I felt even more apologetic.

In the silence that followed our conversation, I took in the sights before us. The ground was glistening with the recent snowfall complimenting the beautiful green of the forest trees. I have yet to see any other animals, but I sometimes heard the rustling of branches and something that sounded like a bird.

I have yet to see a single flower in this entire forest, which satisfies me in a way that only I could ever understand. Flowers and my mother go hand in hand. I hate flowers and I hated my mother.

"Look up, Princess." I heard him whisper in my ear, not realizing my eyes had started to close and my head started to droop low with exhaustion. My eyes widened at the breathtaking sight before me. Settled on the peak of a grove, a beautiful township with ancient statues of dragons bustled with townspeople. We needed to cross a narrow bridge over a steep drop and my heart skipped with every sway of the flimsy bridge. But it didn't falter.

"Don't worry, Princess, this bridge has never failed me yet." Calian's reassurance was comforting.

"And that is supposed to bring me relief?" I heard the quivering in my voice. Heights and small spaces are two of the fears I haven't been able to overcome. Calian started to move his thumb in small comforting circles on my hip. I shifted my weight slightly at his touch—it was too gentle, and something I wasn't familiar with.

As the horse took the last step off the bridge and onto the paved road, the tightness of my chest eased.

"Told you." I heard the smile in his voice. I couldn't help but roll my eyes and then a deep laugh of amusement came from him. As we entered the town, it looked a bit rough, with its muddy ligneous rooftops, faded sandstone walls, and a randomly placed cemetery. The atmosphere was alarming.

"Welcome to Timbervein, Princess."

"What is this place?" I asked. My eyes darted side to side, as the people watched us meander by.

"This is the village right before my home. Just past those last two buildings, we get back on a narrow pathway that leads up to the castle gates." Castle? What castle? I wanted to ask, but then I saw it. Six thick tetragonal towers dominated the skyline of a massive fortress, connected by high, thick walls made of dark stone. Misted windows were strewn here and there around the walls in equal patterns, along with trivial holes for archers. Something to keep in mind when needing to escape.

"What kingdom is this?" I had no idea if any of the other kingdoms were this close to my home.

"This is the Castle of Greveil, ruled by King Tywin and Prince Eli." I twisted to face him, giving him a look of disgust and anger.

"Greveil?" I yelled louder than I should have. "What the hell is wrong with you?" Before I knew it, I leapt from the horse's back and took off in the opposite direction. I made it to the bridge before he stopped me.

"I will explain everything to you once we are inside. But right now, you need to control yourself because if the king sees you hitting me, he will ask questions. Got it?"

Liar. This man has been lying from the start and I was a fool to believe that the *Blood Oath* prevented him. Just because it had prevented me. He must have used some type of magic to alter it. I don't know how. It doesn't seem logical.

"Let go of me." I snarled at him.

"Are you done?"

I was expecting to find anger in his green eyes, but all I saw was concern and regret.

"Welcome home, Sir Calian." A man's voice came from outright. I hadn't even noticed the guard that was dressed in a pointed helmet with no face guard, but a thick scarf that hid the face beneath it. Two bright blue eyes peeked out of slits in the fabric decorated with several layers of black feathers.

An interesting uniform for a guard. I noticed the finer details of his armor. The shoulders were oval and overshot them slightly. They were embellished with the

Royal Crest of Greveil, which is a dragon's head. His upper arms were protected by round, layered metal armbands which sat perfectly under the shoulder plates. Braces with a dragon claw attached to the outer sides covered his lower arms.

The breastplate was interesting, made from many horizontal layers of leather with squared edges. But I didn't think it would stop a blade. It covered the entire torso, and the attachment straps left the sides under the arms exposed. His breeches appeared to be made of thick animal hide, but still, not enough to protect him from a fatal blow. The lower legs were protected by leather boots, with the shins plated with steel.

Greveil appeared a bit lax in its ability to fully shield its guards. I know the guards inside the palace walls of Thornwarf didn't always dress in their protective shields and metal plates, but the guards posted outside dressed in their full suit.

"Thank you, Sir Reginald." Calian escorted me back to where we left the horse.

"The king and prince are in the throne hall waiting to greet you," Sir Reginald said.

"Now I understand." He shot me a questioning glance. "You may have been telling the truth about you supposedly saving me from the assassins who killed my parents, but that was just a bonus to your kidnapping scheme. Your prince ordered you to take me so I would marry him." I waited for a response. "Your silence confirms it then. Fine, I will see your cowardice prince and his father. Just know that what they have done is not to be forgiven or forgotten. They violated the treaty and will have to answer to the gods for it."

I flinched at the sound of clapping coming from

behind me. When I turned to look, my body quickly went from solid to liquid.

"You are a quick one, aren't you?" Dressed in all-black, with hair the color of charcoal trimmed to just above his ears, and honey-colored eyes that glistened in the High Sun's ray, stood the most beautiful man I had ever seen. Even more so than Calian. My knees started to buckle, and I was not sure if it was from the sight of him or the long journey. "She's going to faint."

I felt an arm at my back.

"I'm fine." I straightened myself up and marched right up to him. "You have got some nerve. Do you know what you did by taking me?"

"I believe my men saved your life, Princess."

"You couldn't wait one more day? A few more hours and my father was going to choose my husband. You threw it all away, and when Queen Iliana finds out, there will be war."

"I retract my previous remark. The girl may be smart, but she suffers from selective hearing." I heard laughter coming from behind me. Mother told me to never raise a hand to another Royal, but today I considered making an exception. "You will not strike me, Princess."

His eyes looked deep into mine, burning at my core.

"Why shouldn't I? Did you order Calian to make a *Blood Oath* with me too? Knowing damn well if I violate the vows, my people will suffer?" I saw his eyes dart from me to Calian.

"Cal? What is she talking about?" A nickname? *Those two must be close. It is not unheard of; Alma and I are that close.* Royal protocol aside. By the sound of the surprise in the prince's voice, I would say striking that deal wasn't part of the plan.

"It was the safest and least difficult way to get her to comply." Calian approached us, whispering, "By any means necessary."

The prince nodded. "You know what that means, don't you?"

"What are you talking about?" I asked, getting annoyed they seemed to be talking about me while I was standing right in front of them.

"It means you two are bonded until death."

Chapter Six

Clover

There wasn't much said on our walk to the throne hall. My mind was buzzing with unanswered questions, and I wanted to run away the first chance I got.

The Throne Hall was quite impressive, with bright braziers at the bottoms of each of the six ivory columns, illuminating the entire hall. There were paintings of vast landscapes on the bowed ceiling that danced in the flickering light, while sculptures and monuments looked down upon the granite floor of this extravagant hall.

My worn-down heels quieted while I walked onto the crimson rug sprawled from the throne down the center and stopped just before the doors. Tall, stained glass windows depicting gods and goddesses were slightly hidden by fabrics colored the same dark pink as the banners. The curtains were adorned with elegant black tassels.

A stately throne of hardened material, almost identical to dragon scales, sat atop a tall, elevated platform, adjoined by two similar, but less ornate seats for the king's family members. Something Thornwarf didn't have. I was never allowed inside of the Throne Hall unless summoned and where I sat was never next to the King and Queen because I wasn't allowed to sit at all.

Much like now, I was standing shoulder to shoulder with Calian, right in front of King Tywin. He is much older than I had imagined. No color in his silver hair, no reminisce of youth on his face, and his eyes were glossy. I could have sworn I saw a small droplet of drool leaving the side of his lip. He looked non-existent.

"Father, may I present Princess Clover of Thornwarf." I felt a small nudge from my right, and I took it as a sign to curtsy.

"Princess Clover." His words dragged and were soft. It was like it was exhausting just to speak.

"Your Grace, might I just say—"

"She is delighted that we offered her sanctuary after the brutal assassination of her parents. The High King and Queen of Thornwarf." I shot Prince Eli a glare, and he gave me a look as if to ask me to play along.

"Please, Princess," I heard Calian whisper beside me.

"I am honored and grateful for the sanctuary of Your Grace." I guess all those years of learning how to be proper with Mother paid off. Again, using what she taught me, seared into my brain and onto my skin, just didn't seem right. I felt sick to my stomach realizing I was behaving just as she would want me to.

"Come closer, girl." I did, and I got a better look at him. His eyes were not just glossy, they were pure white. And that only happens when–

"I'm blind, Princess. Please, let me touch your hand. I promise I will not bite." His smile was sickening. Full of yellow and decayed teeth. Bile crept up in my throat and lately, I've come to realize that I don't have a strong stomach for such things as these.

His hand was as cold as I imagined death would be. It wasn't smooth at all, and he smelled as if he hadn't bathed in a month, still reeking of his last attempt at the chamber pot. It took all my strength not to vomit on him.

"How long are you staying with us?" His breath nearly knocked me over.

I shot a questionable glance at the prince, and he nodded his head for me to answer.

"Until it is safe for me to return home, Your Grace."

"Who have you chosen to be your husband?" Another wave of foul breath and decay. This man was dead or dying.

"The Engagement Ball was intended for today, Your Grace, but due to the unforeseen murder of my parents and kid—" I heard the prince clear his throat before I could ramble on about how I was captured.

"The daring rescue of your men, I now assume that it is postponed."

The King placed his scratchy lips on the back of my hand, and I wanted to bathe for a week.

I was more than grateful when he let it go. "It was supposed to be the celebration of your twenty-third year, wasn't it?" I had completely forgotten that I was now in my twenty-third year of life, and all the things that came with it. A ball, a husband, the entire three territories. I started to feel lightheaded.

"Clover." I heard the Prince call my name as I fell back into the familiar arms of Calian.

"I'm fine," I whispered. My eyes were slightly

open as I looked closely at the man holding me.

"Take the princess to the prepared quarters so she can rest. I will come to see her once I am done speaking with the king." I faintly heard the prince order Calian and before I knew it, I lifted from the ground and was being carried out.

My consciousness stayed slightly intact the entire trip to where I would be staying. I was taking in deep wafts of Calian's scent, just to mask the horrid smell of the king. Pine needles and sweat, smells far better than feces. I wanted to reach up and touch his face. Feel it, memorize it, but I stopped, reminding myself that he was in part to blame for me being here. Although, he was just following orders and there is a sense of loyalty and respect in that. I was curious to know what would happen to us now. Would he simply just go back to wherever his earlier assigned duty was? Or would he stay with me?

"Would you want that?" I heard him ask and I was confused again. Can he read my thoughts? But that is impossible. Only those with magic can do that.

"I didn't say anything," I calmly said. My head nuzzled deeper into his hardened chest. My hormones must be going crazy because I started to wonder what it would feel like if there were no clothes between my head and his chest. I looked up at his face and saw a small smirk appear. I jumped from his arms, and he stopped mid-step. "You can hear my thoughts, can't you?"

"Took you longer than I expected to figure it out," he said. I walked straight up to him, the toes of our shoes touching, and then the embarrassment hit me. *Oh, gods.* I saw that smirk turn into a full-on smile and his tan skin flushed slightly. "I don't mean to. Sometimes, it just happens."

"It just happens? What is that supposed to mean?"

He ran a large hand through his hair and rubbed the back of his neck. "When my thoughts line up with a person I am in close contact with or touching, it sort of just happens. Like they are speaking aloud."

"So, what was the last thing you heard?" I dared to ask. He leaned forward and I didn't back away.

"You're worried that you won't see me again and you wondered what it would be like if there were no clothes on between us."

I flushed with heat at the accuracy of his words.

"And so, what if I did?" Why did I say that? I should not be acting like anything could happen between us. He is not a prince, and the treaty demands a prince. I started stepping backward and he followed until the cold stone of a wall pressed into my back. He placed the palms of his hands on either side of my head and leaned into me. His lips were mere inches from mine, nothing but the rise and fall of our chest and breath between us.

"I'm going to ask you the question I wanted to ask last night," he said, staring into my very soul. I swallowed. "Do you want to kiss me?" My palm started burning for me to answer. I wanted to lie so badly. Needed to, but that pain, the burn of blood magic, was too much.

"Yes." It was due to the sheer physical attraction I had toward him. "But I also would like to rest and it isn't appropriate. You're a knight and I'm a princess."

"I see. Then we shall continue to your rooms, Your Highness."

My feet stayed on the ground as I followed him in silence to my room.

We approached double oak doors, both with two metallic handles forged into the shape of dragons' wings. Calian opened the one on the right and a burst of warm air welcomed me as I walked in. The room was beautiful. A canopy bed with white linens neatly made sat at the center of the back wall. Next to that was a marbled fireplace, a settee, and a small tea table.

"The bathing chamber is through there as well as the wardrobe," he said, and I realized that we were alone in this room. I turned to face him, but before we could say a word about what happened in the hallway, a knock on the door stilled us. The door opened and in walked Eli.

"I see you have settled in okay," he stated more than asked as he entered. He turned to look at Calian and gave him a nod, to which Calian responded with a bow of respect, and then exited the room. Utter disappointment washed over me. "How do you like your room?"

"It's beautiful," I spoke. It was awkward, way too awkward.

"Good." There was silence between us for a moment. "Look, Clover, may I call you that?" I nodded. "We got word of the assassination attempt days before I sent Calian to get you. We were supposed to get there before your parents were killed, but we didn't make it in time, and for that I am sorry."

I couldn't tell if he was lying, but something about the way he spoke just didn't sit right with me.

He walked over to the crimson-colored settee and then gestured for me to sit next to him. I obliged, hoping he'd tell me everything I wanted to know.

"The *Blood Oath* wasn't part of my orders, and I will speak to Calian about that after this."

"No. It's no big deal." I didn't want to sound too eager.

"Do you know the true meaning behind the oath?" I shook my head. "Blood magic is very sacred and should be used sparingly."

"I thought anyone can make that kind of bargain?"

"That is correct. But you can only make one *Blood Oath* your entire life or until the other person dies." He paused. "There is a lot going on that I'm not sure you know about. The assassination attempt was sent by a dark and dangerous new threat. A wizard who's mastered shadow magic."

"I didn't think any were still alive."

"This one is, and he has built many followers through the last century. It appears, since the Great Barrier fell, we've spotted his massive armies marching all over the territories." I cocked a brow, unsure if I believed him. "I don't mean to frighten you but he does have a name. His generals call him Supreme Leader Rai, but we call him Jarhead." I giggled and didn't mean to because it all sounded ridiculous.

"Jarhead?"

"He decapitates his victims and collects them in jars, putting them on display for all to see." That explains my parents' heads put on display for all to see.

"I'm sorry but this is all too much. Why would a Supreme Jarhead dark wizard thing want my family dead? What is in it for him?"

"It doesn't have anything to do with your family. It has to do with you," he responded, far too quickly for comfort.

"What?" I gasped.

"Did your mother ever give you a green gem? Told you it was a family heirloom that needed to be protected at all costs?" he asked.

"No." I lied. Why would I admit that I knew exactly what he was talking about? Because I don't have an oath with him, I can lie all I want. Mother taught me how, which brings shame and guilt coursing through my veins.

"Clover, this creature is searching throughout the realm for these gems. They are immensely powerful, and if he gets all of them, we will be his slaves."

"Tell me more about the consequences of the *Blood Oath*." I changed the subject, partly because I wanted to know what I got myself into and because I didn't want to hear more stories from him.

"The rules, which I'm sure you have figured out by now, are no lies, no killing each other, and you mustn't break the original vow. When you bound your blood, you didn't just combine hands. Your souls are now bound together for life."

"Which means?" I asked, and I could tell he was getting frustrated.

"Which means that if you were to share a bed with another, marry another, without Calian's blessing, it would be a betrayal and the blood magic would enact the consequences of that betrayal," he responded, sounding strangely enraged by this.

Oh, gods.

"Does the magic make you want the other person? In that way?" He smiled at me.

"Gods, no. It doesn't wield it but, if the pair

becomes intimate with one another, that solidifies the bond, and even death itself cannot break it."

We were quiet for a few heartbeats. I don't know if I wanted to be bound to Calian like that. I barely knew him. But I couldn't deny the attraction.

"I should let you rest. Calian will come to get you for dinner. You will find a wardrobe full of clothing that should be your size. If not, our tailor can alter them."

Eli left me to rest, and I welcomed the moment of peace. I was still coming down from the turmoil of emotions I was feeling for Calian. I can't let that happen, not with anyone. Would Calian even bless a marriage? What would happen if he refused? *Stop.* There is no need to be worked up over something like that.

My feet ached as I pried them out of my ruined heels. The cold-stone floor sent a calming sensation, easing the pain. As I entered the bathing chamber, I was surprised to find a porcelain basin, big enough for two people, at its center. There was water already in it, and I ran my fingers through it, welcoming the warmth. When I looked up at the sink, I noticed something strange about my reflection in the mirror. My honey-colored hair was matted with dirt and leaves. The dress I'd been wearing since last night was filthy, with minor tears in it.

I didn't recognize the woman staring back at me. There was no polish, only flaws that Mother would surely point out if she were here. But then again, I wouldn't look like this, or even be here if she were. She was dead, and the honest truth—I was relieved. That's when it hit me. His small touches, the gentle way he's been treating me. It's having a new effect on me physically because I'm used to Mother's harsh words and punishments. There was no pain, no criticism, and no coldness.

The water eased the ache in my thighs and my womanhood because of the long ride here. My upbringing didn't allow me to learn how to ride a horse, so my body wasn't used to that. I'm sure if *she* thought it was important, then I would have been a master at it. The soap smelled of spices and pine. Unlike back home, our soap was made with flowers from the orchid. I would be happy if I never smelt or laid eyes on another flower again. It's bad enough to be named after one. Not that I don't want to go home, but I won't lie and say I'm not enjoying being outside of those walls. Away from that *room* and all the painful memories.

I dried off, slipping into a silken black robe left hanging off a hook for me. It felt exceptionally smooth on my skin. There was a red dragon embellished above the right breast, and the threading reminded me of a ruby. This felt like a betrayal to Thornwarf, but what does that place have besides a harsh past? Alma knew what the queen did to me, but never once offered to help. I welcomed this new symbol and the meaning behind it. If I am to marry, I would rather become a dragon than stay a flower.

The bed was as comfortable as it looked, and I sank deep into those sheets and welcomed sleep for the first time since I could remember.

Chapter Seven

Calian

I wait just outside the Princess's chambers, waiting for Eli to make his exit. Should I be spying on them? No. Is it appropriate? Not really, but I don't care. Something about the eagerness in Eli's demeanor, actions, and otherwise reaction to her Highness unsettled me.

If his intentions were honorable, why would he be badgering her with questions about some gem her mother may or may not have given her? Everything about this up-and-coming new evil has my hair on end. I intend to find out exactly what is going on and what it has to do with Clover Celestia.

The doors finally open and the prince makes his way out, turning in the direction of the Council Chambers, instead of his own. Following him goes against all my training, but he's up to something. Besides, it's not like I haven't done this before, using my gifts to move undetected.

I follow him all the way to the chamber doors, passing the kitchens, armory, and library until finally coming to a stop. He looks behind him, those bright eyes scanning for something. Or someone. *What are you up to, old friend?*

A half-smile pops up in the corner of his mouth

before he says, “You can come out now.” My brows furrow. That’s not possible. “Cal, you’ve lived here since we were boys. I know all your tricks. You aren’t nearly as quiet as you think you are.”

With a low growl, I step out from behind the pillar to face him. “How could you detect my presence? You know what I am.”

“Clearly you need to study more about the architecture of this place and less on extinct beasts.” He laughs. “Iron. It has the nastiest effect on beings created by magic.”

“Iron? I see. This place is made of stone. The only iron I’ve ever seen is in those torches,” I state.

“Come on. It’s time to tell you everything. Sir Reginald and the rest of the Council are assembled.”

“I’m invited, this time?” I scoff.

“Of course. My best friend and personal guard won’t be excluded from one of the most important strategic meetings that Greveil has ever had.” He pats me on the back, walking me through the door while continuing to whisper my praises. It’s something he does when he’s offended someone. Thinking that false compliments earn their forgiveness. The prince isn’t a saint, but he isn’t a bad guy. He’s human, after all, and they have flaws. We all do.

“Our number one concern should be the Eastern Front. This army is massing in the desert, marching across that side of the continent,” Sir Thoran of House Blian argued, throwing his on the painted table to add emphasis.

“What about the Great Sea? They’ve already taken the High Palace in Thornwarf, next will be the ships,” Sir Reginald argued.

"Gentlemen," Eli said, catching their attention. They bowed before we all took our places around the world map. "Now, I think that we should be prepared for negotiations. Every ruler has something they value, something they would be willing to give up in order to keep their people safe and maintain the crown on their heads."

I don't like how this is beginning to sound. He can't be suggesting the princess, can he?

"What do we have that a creature of magic could want? He controls the shadows. Forgive me for being outspoken, Your Highness, but we have nothing," Sir Thoran explained.

Eli hummed before looking down at the unfinished map. The scent of fresh pain hits my nose and I could see a slight wet spot on the Eastern border of Shuang. The color is amber or light brown, matching the color of the sands on the beach of the Great Sea.

"It's true that a man, and I assure he is one, who can control those shadows shouldn't want anything us non-magic users could potentially have. However..." He paused, looked at me, then winked. "I happen to know that he is looking for something. Five magical relics known as Dragon Hearts."

"Impossible." Sir Reginald snorted.

"They're a myth. A part of the bedtime story we told our children when they asked us about the dragons," Sir Thoran chimed in.

"That is what we, meaning the royal family, have always told you. But I have it on good authority on the location of at least two of the five," Eli stated. We all waited with bated breath while he walked over to one of the shelves, pulled a lock box down from the top, and placed it at the center. He reached under the collar of his tunic and pulled out a key before unlocking it. I caught myself leaning forward, watching as he slowly opened it to reveal a glistening ruby shaped just like the image of a dragon's egg.

Round, smooth, and absolutely breathtaking.

Take it.

A deep growl rumbled in my head.

Take it. Ours.

I shook my head, taking a step back before Eli snapped the box shut, breaking whatever trance we were all in.

"This gemstone is believed to hold the magic of the fire-breathing beasts. Rai wants this one and the other four. If we could get to them before him, we just may have the power to stop him before he enslaves us all," the prince explained.

"But where are these other four? And how do you know that thing isn't just another ruby?" Sir Reginald inquired.

"I don't, but we should be able to find someone who can authenticate it. Someone born of magic." He didn't look at me but I could feel his elbow brush my arm. "Finding that said person won't be difficult, we need to find the other stones. And I already know the location of the emerald that contains the powers of the nature dragons."

"Where is it? We must get to it," Sir Thoran demanded.

"It's right here, in this palace. Our very own Calian has brought it here with him. I'll get it, one way or another. Princess Clover Celestia has no idea what she's just walked head first into." A sneer, one that I could only describe as twisted, formed across his face.

I raced out of that room as quickly as I could. Running directly to my chambers, stripping down until I was neck-deep in my cold bath water. The thought of him hurting her, killing her, doing anything but respecting her had my nails elongating into talons, my teeth sharpening into fangs. Eli may think he knows the true nature of an Ashana but he's never seen me transform.

My palm was burning where our skin had touched, the blood magic calling me to protect her.

The only way to secure her and find the truth of these stones is by taking them and leaving this place. I closed my eyes, and a flash of a dragon's head reared up at me as my beast spoke.

It's time to free me, Calian. You can't face this evil alone.

"You're a monster. You hurt people, kill them. That's not who I am."

If you wish to save your Princess, then you will call on me to help you. Become one with me and we will be unstoppable. You will see.

My eyes snapped open, steam emanating from the bubble popping all around me. The ice-cold water had nearly burned completely out of the tub. Standing, my skin was sizzling as it dried. I rang my fingers through my hair before walking into my room, grabbing my slacks, and making my way to the door.

I went to open it, but a knock sounded before I could. On the other side was Eli, still in his day clothes.

"Ah, Calian, might I come in and have a word with you?" He put on that debonair smile but I couldn't refuse his request.

"What can I do for you?" I asked, with no enthusiasm at all because I had a sinking feeling he was going to ask for help in manipulating *Her*.

"I'm here to talk about your unusual behavior these past two days," he said, taking a seat on my settee.

"My unusual behavior?" I questioned.

"Using blood magic? You didn't have to do that. But, I'm willing to overlook that if you do one small favor for me." I sighed, rubbing the back of my neck. I'm not going to like this. "The princess can't lie to you. Get her to admit she knows about the emerald, then I'll take care of the rest."

"And that's it? You just want to know the truth?" I'm weary of his true intentions but if he swears it, I'll obey.

"I swear." He held out his hand, and I took it in mine, the one opposite of the oath I made with Clover, and we shook.

"Then I'll find out if she's lying or not. And you must promise not to harm her. You know that I can't." I squeezed his hand harder, ensuring he knew what I would do if he broke his word.

"Yes, I understand." He nodded. "I'll leave you to it. Dinner will be ready within the hour. Go wake the princess. "

"Yes, Your Highness," I mumbled as he exited my room.

A breath of smoke left me as thoughts of her filled my head. She's just one thick wall away. I could use my enhanced hearing to check on her. Without further delay, I close my eyes and listen through the walls, passing the field mice racing to find rotten cheese until I envision her.

"No! Get away! Please, stop!" A growl rips through my throat as I race to her room. Whoever is hurting her will pay with their life.

Chapter Eight

Clover

"Do you know what this is?" Mother asked while holding up an emerald, caressing the smooth surface. In the meantime, while she was loving a jewel, my body was strapped down to the table. Its cool steel presses into my bare back as the leather straps hold me down tightly by the chest, waist, and ankles.

"An emerald, Your Grace."

She let out a pitiful laugh. "No, my child." She walks over to me, holding the gem to my eyes. "This is the most precious and powerful item in all of Thornwarf. And we have a duty to protect it."

"Why would anyone want to steal a small green stone?" I regretted the question the moment it spilled from my lips. Then the burning heat on my right side told me I was right to regret it.

"Wake up," I heard Calian's voice. "Wake up, princess." My eyes snapped open, and I felt the weight of him on my shoulders. Those two pools of green were looking deep inside of me. Concern and fear swallowed me. His shaggy hair hung loose, and I had the urge to brush it back. His grip went from my shoulders to the mattress on either side of my head. I brushed that silky hair back, cupped his smooth face, tracing a finger along his jawline, down his throat, and then placed my hand on his chiseled chest. He was warm and I could feel the rapid beating of his heart.

"Are you okay?" he finally asked. My eyes wandered down his body, all the way to the waistband of his leather breeches. The top button is undone, and I can see little fine hairs poking out, making me blush. "Princess?"

My gaze returned to his face, and I saw that humor had replaced the concern. "I'm fine."

My hand started to have a mind of its own, falling lower until it stopped right below his navel. I saw the restraint was killing him, waiting for the permission he so desperately wanted. Not today, not after what Eli revealed to me about what would happen if we went there. If we crossed that line, there would be no turning back. I felt his knee inch closer, spreading my legs slightly further apart. Nothing but the sheets between my sex and him.

I moved from under him as I noticed the disappointment cross his face.

"Are you hungry?" He got up from the bed and turned his back to me. Gods, it was just as alluring as his front. A tattoo of dark wings covered his entire back from the top of his shoulder blades down to the two dimples at his back. I wanted to trace every single line and soon realized that I was hungry, but not so much for food as I was for him to be back in my bed.

"Yes. But first…what does your tattoo mean?" I asked, pulling my sheets tightly around me to avoid him seeing any of my scars.

"Dinner will be ready soon, and the tattoo has to do with my family," he answered over his right shoulder.

Why hadn't he asked about my nightmare? The

fact that he was in my room, shaking me awake, told me I was screaming again. Which is funny because when Mother disciplined me, there was a point when I became numb to the pain, and I didn't scream at all. Or it was because I learned very quickly what happened when I did. She never touched my face, and said it was my prettiest feature. The scars on the rest of my body wouldn't turn my husband away because he would only be interested in pleasuring himself with my sex.

What would Calian think of my scars? Would he turn away in disgust? Just another reason not to cross that line with him.

What would Mother say about me wanting to kiss a man that wasn't my husband? What would she say about him being in my bed? Nothing, because she is dead. I've got to stop thinking about her, wanting her approval from the grave for some reason.

Slipping out of my bed, my nightgown flushed with my ankles, hiding all my imperfections, and I approached Calian. It was like he was waiting for me to come to him. Letting me touch him, worship him, and tease him with my own body. It was wrong, but it was fun, having control over someone clearly stronger than I was. I should stop. This is exactly what made my mother so vile.

I don't want to be like her, try not to be, but when something is physically and mentally burned into your body and soul, it does something to you. And he's awoken an unexplored desire inside of me. I don't know when it happened, or why, but something tells me the insatiable need to be with him won't go away by ignoring it.

"Where is your tunic?" I asked. Balling my hands

into fists, not to touch him. I didn't want that to be us. Didn't want that to be me. Horny virgin girl that wanted to have a taste of what could be and now can't control those urges. I know I was groomed for breeding, but that is not who I want to be. I don't want to be the tool Mother tried to morph me into.

"You think you're the only one who needed rest?" he asked. Still facing away from me. No doubt his way of controlling his desires.

"How loud was I…?" That heat started to dissipate at the memory of why he was in my room in the first place.

"I thought someone was hurting you." His tone had a mix of fear and frustration.

"Oh." I turned away from him. Our backs now to one another. I didn't want him to turn and see the embarrassment I felt.

"What happened to you?" I felt heat on my back and realized he was no longer turned from me. My back was to him and there were barely any inches between us.

"I…nothing." That stupid cut started burning again with my lie. Trying to bring the truth forward but I held onto it for as long as I could. He stepped around to face me. A large hand interlaced with my right where the burning was. He lifted it toward him, and I felt the soft brush of his lips, while his eyes bore into mine.

"I revoke my question." The burning stopped at once. I didn't know about that. I am such a novice. "If I ask something that you're not ready to answer, then tell me. I don't want you to be in pain. That was never my intent when we made the oath."

"Why did you choose me?" I asked him. "You only

get one *Blood Oath* each lifetime and you wasted yours on me all because you were afraid I wouldn't come willingly to save my people."

He let out a sigh before speaking. "Revoke it."

What? I am stunned, not expecting that response. Then I saw his right hand where the cut we made started to turn red. He didn't want to answer me, and he had just offered me the opportunity to not discuss things I wasn't ready for, and now—

I grabbed his hand, kissed his palm, and my left hand ventured to his face, then to his hair. Then immediately stepped away, creating space between us before I did something we would both regret. "I revoke my question."

My kiss must have a paralytic effect on him, and it made me gleam inside. We stared at each other for gods only knows how long. A silent conversation of admiration and understanding. It was a knock on my door that broke our connection.

"Princess, it is Prince Eli. I've come to escort you to dinner."

"I will be out in a few moments," I answered, my eyes never leaving Calian's. He smirked at me while stalking toward me. My eyes went from his face down to the sway of his hips. They moved like I imagine a mountain lion did when stalking one's prey. With delicate ease. I put my hand forward, pressing into his hard chest.

"Stop," I ordered.

"Shall I help you dress, Princess?" He was being charming, and I heated at the thought of my body exposed entirely in front of him. Not just my shoulders and arms, but the bare skin of my scarred torso and legs. Especially the one at the apex of my sex, right above the clit. A shiver ran through my body, and his eyes went from teasing to apprehension.

"I think you should leave before anyone gets the wrong impression," I whispered.

He grabbed my wrist, moving it out of the way, and pulled me into him. A hand wrapped tightly around my waist, the other let go of my wrist and fisted my hair, pulling my head back. "What impression would that be? A guard looking out for his princess?"

His lips brushed my neck, catching my breath. "The fact that you only have breeches on, and I a nightgown could make one question our honor." The words came out as smooth as ice.

"We haven't done anything to disgrace our honor, Princess." He let me go slightly, only holding my hands low, brushing against his hips. "Nothing yet, I mean."

With a wink, he vanished.

Still bewildered at the sight of Calian vanishing right before my eyes, I washed quickly, fastened my hair into a loose bun atop my head, and then dressed in a lilac gown. My choice of shoes was simple. They had heels matching each dress, or a pair of knee-high leather boots. I slipped those boots on easily over the stocking and then exited my room.

"You look beautiful, Princess." Eli was dressed in a simple crimson tunic, brown breeches, and knee-high boots. A sword was strapped to his right side and a dagger's hilt was sticking out of his left boot. His blonde hair was loosely combed, and his eyes were as bright as ever. Like two small oceans glittering symmetrical in his face. The sun-kissed skin was just as tantalizing as those plump lips. I now knew what it was like to be kissed with lips like those. Even though they belonged to another.

"Thank you." He reached out an arm and I interlaced mine with his.

"Happy birthday, Clover," I heard him say.

"Thank you, Eli." I smiled at him. We walked with our arms interlocked, silence filling the air of the vacant halls, until we turned a corner and I saw *him*. Calian, dressed in all black just like the night we met, and his eyes were on me in an instant. Slowly moving to where mine and Eli's arms locked together. He bowed before us, and I couldn't take my gaze from him. It was highly inappropriate to do in front of the prince, but I couldn't help it. Something about him was pulling at me. It could be the influence of magic. The whisper of the kiss he left on my neck was still teasing me.

We entered through open doors into a great dining hall. Crystal chandeliers hung from the domed ceiling, painted with memorials of the past war. Soldiers fighting alongside dragons. A large stone fireplace was centered on the back wall and in front, a long crimson-painted table with two chairs at the head.

"Is your father joining us?"I asked, breaking the silence.

It was proper for me to ask, although I hoped he wouldn't. I don't think I could eat around someone who smelled as horrid as he did.

"No, it will be just us. I informed him I wanted some time alone with you."

I blushed and then glanced behind us, praying Calian didn't see.

He wasn't there, and a mix of relief and disappointment filled me. Eli pulled out one of the chairs to the right of his and gestured for me to sit. It was cushioned like a settee, soft, and comforting. The display laid out before us was glistening golden plates and cutlery. Flute glasses filled with champagne and the display of food was appetizing. A servant placed some fletching, bread, and greens on my plate.

"To you, Clover, on your birthday."

I raised my champagne glass and sipped on it. We ate in silence for a few minutes. I took a few bites before realizing he was gawking at me. I checked to make sure my cleavage wasn't showing, but my dress covered it well enough.

"What do you plan to do with me?" I asked after wiping my face. I wanted to know if I'm to be forced into marriage or if he was just keeping me safe until we could march into Thornwarf, ensuring it to be safe.

"Whatever do you mean?" He sipped his drink. So, he wants to play a game. Fine. I reached out my right leg until it brushed against the inside of his calves. I saw him gasp at the gentle touch.

"Am I to be your prisoner, bride, or redemption?" I leaned forward, using the table to ease the tops of my breast, noticing his eyes drifting to my chest. Mother was right about one thing—men couldn't resist a woman's touch.

"Which one do you want to be?" he teased as he leaned forward, moving my leg further up his. He was playing too. Now I just need to win and get back to my people.

"Like I have a choice," I started, sipping on my bubbly.

"There is only one thing I desire more than for you to be my bride." He trailed a finger up my arm to my shoulder. I was expecting the same reaction I had with Calian but instead, there was nothing. Except a feeling that I was betraying him letting Eli touch me.

"What's that?" We were inches from each other and any concern I had about his breath being as foul as his father's quickly faded. It smelled of mint champagne.

"I want…" He reached out. Fisting one hand into my curls, and the other onto my hip, he lifted me from the chair onto his lap. My legs went to either side of his waist, straddling him. The hard feel of the table pressed into my back. That was not the only hardness I felt. He pulled my head back, so my throat felt taut.

The steel cold blade of his dagger teetered at the very edge of my neck. My breath caught in my throat, not due to fear—blades don't scare me anymore. Because he could kill me or take advantage of me. I tried to get control of this, relying on what Mother taught me, but it backfired. Stupid. I was foolish to remotely think I could use her knowledge to my advantage.

"You can't seduce me. I want that gem and I will get it one way or another."

A chill in the air suppressed the heat in the room. I wasn't going to allow myself to be intimidated by him. A deep voice, cold as death itself, came out of the dimming light of the hall.

"I suggest you release her at once, my prince."

It was Calian. I didn't move, aware that the blade could slice me with the slightest movement. I watched as Eli's gaze shot from me to the space behind me. I saw a smirk form on the prince's face, and then he did as Calian had suggested.

"We were just having a bit of fun. Weren't we, Clover?"

Once I was free of his blade and grip, I kneed him right in his cock, smiling as he doubled over in pain.

"*That* was fun." I smirked.

Holding my head up high, I walked past Calian, out into the hall, and then ran to my quarters. Slamming the door shut, I rushed to the chamber pot and emptied my stomach. During a break between heaves of vomit, warm hands pulled my hair back and then rubbed comfortingly along the arch of my back.

When I was done, I rinsed my mouth out with some lemon-mint water and then went to the settee and sank into it. Bringing my knees to my chest, placing my forehead on them, I held back all the tears of anger and regret.

"Did he hurt you?" I didn't lift my head to answer. Didn't even speak. My palm started burning, but I welcomed the pain, because pain was my friend. It helps me forget where I am at times; helps me become numb to all my emotions. Every slice or burn Mother inflicted on me only hardened my skin deeper.

None of my scars were warranted or necessary in my opinion. I never asked for it or did anything to get punished on purpose. One small bite of a pastry and Mother gets this insane idea to cut me every time I disobey her or do something to piss Mistress Seigel off.

I felt a gentle touch of warmth on my shoulders, and I knew if I didn't answer him, he would just keep asking.

"Why do you care?" I asked as I lifted my head. "You are his loyal guard." My words lit a fire in those green eyes.

"Are you serious?" His tone increased, and it surprised me. "You think that for one second I would let him harm an innocent, let alone an unarmed woman?" I didn't answer, and my silence hurt him worse than words. "For fucks sake, Clover, you have known me what, two days, and you can intently look at me, touch me, but you can't trust me?"

He was right. None of it made any sense to me either.

"Cal," I started, "I'm sorry." That was all I managed to say. He studied me. "He didn't hurt me, but he could've. It was my fault, anyways. I…I was trying to get information out of him the only way Mother taught me, and it backfired. I didn't think the prince would react the way he did."

"Clover…" He kneeled in front of me. My legs straightened, the palms of my boots pressing into the floor as I leaned down closer to him. His eyes didn't shoot down to my chest but remained on my face.

"I'm sorry. I should have never brought you here. It's just…" He shook his head. He wanted to tell me something but was holding back.

"Cal,"—his head snapped up to look at me—"what is going on here? Our bond is far too strong. Your prince is cruel and will torture me if I don't give him what he wants. What are you?"

He let out a sigh of defeat. Scooting closer to the edge of the settee, I cupped his face, pulling him closer to me. "Tell me everything," I whispered into his lips. "And then I will decide if you can have me."

A rumble of desire came from deep within his chest. I broke away from him slightly. He rose from the floor and pulled the chair closer so he was sitting in front of me.

"The prince received word from his spies that the Supreme Leader Rai was sending assassins to dispose of the High Royal family in Thornwarf. And that there was a stone in your palace walls that he wanted. I didn't find that out until after we were already here."

He paused for a moment to see if I would speak, then kept going.

"It's a stone of great power, and there are five in total. It was a result of something that happened in the Dragon Wars. The Super Leader or Dark Wizard wants the stones back to enslave the world. The prince did send me and my men on a mission to rescue you, but when we got there, your parents were dead, and the assassins had their eyes set on you.

"That was when I made the plan to hide in your quarters and then make the *Blood Oath* with you. I was trying to save you, but now I fear you will never leave this place."

"What else do you know about these stones?" I asked.

"I know there might be a place to release the magic that binds them. *If* it's all true. It is said that in this place, the souls that were used to create it will return to life anew." I stood, soaking all the information in about this stone. The Prince wants it, which must mean he wants all of them and knows what they can do. Then that means he will use the power to become the next High King. Oh, gods.

"Cal, do you know where the rest of the stones are?"

"No. But I think I may know someone who might," he answered with furrowed brows.

"Good."

"What are you planning, Princess?"

Something devious, disastrous.

"If we don't get those stones and set things right, Eli or that Jarhead wizard man will enslave our world. My people, the ones that I am to protect, will suffer. I can't let that happen." I started for the wardrobe, scoffing at the dresses upon dresses. I needed breeches and tunics for traveling. "Do you know where I can find some breeches and tunics?"

He was now on his feet. His thick arms crossed across his chest and his eyes watching me as I paced in a storm of panic and excitement. "Why do you need those?"

"I can't travel the world in a dress, now, can I?" I grabbed a leather pouch and started to fill it with random things. Useless for this journey I was planning in my head. Calian approached me, and I didn't realize he was turning me to face him.

"Calm down, Princess. We need a plan." With his words, all my panic flushed out of me.

"Tell me more about the *Blood Oath*. Is the blood magic so strong that we are aroused when we are near one another? I know you have magic, so tell me how? I was told magic died a long time ago…"

"What makes you say that, Princess?"

"You vanish and reappear without effort. You have unnatural speed, and you can read my thoughts. Your strength is anything but normal, so tell me what you are."

"If I answer your questions, Princess, will you let me kiss you? Will you be mine for all eternity?" I sucked in a sharp breath. I couldn't deny these feelings, but I needed to know if it was influenced by magic.

"Depends on your answers." I shrugged. I stepped out of his hold, walked over to the edge of my bed, and sat. Eyeing him from head to toe. When he started to prowl toward me, I put my hand up and said, "Not until I give you permission."

A low growl escaped him, and I knew from that sound alone, he wasn't human. "You tease me, Princess." I crossed my legs, giving him a daring look. "Blood magic only strengthens the natural bond two souls have to one another. So, if there was no natural bond or attraction, the Blood magic wouldn't have any effect on that person." He took a step forward, and I laughed at his eagerness.

"I didn't say you could move, Calian." He smirked at me. "If I am to understand this, even before we met, there was a natural bond between us and when we made the *Blood Oath*, it strengthened it."He nodded.

"That's why you can't keep your eyes off me." What a smug thing to say. I took a boot off and threw it at him. He let out a laugh, and I knew I was blushing.

"Continue, Calian. It's been a long day and I would like some rest."

"I am what you call Ashana." Demi-god.

"Your parents are gods?" I said, louder than I expected.

"Only my father. My mother was a mortal. At least that's what the family that took me in told me. They only knew what they did from a single letter given to them by whoever left me on their doorsteps."

I cupped my mouth. "If that is so, then when you said your parents were with the gods, did you mean—"

"My father was killed trying to save my mother."

"But I thought gods couldn't be killed?"

"Unfortunately, someone figured out how." I wanted to hug him. To give him the same comfort he's gracefully shown me and apologize for something I had no part in.

"Cal…"

He didn't wait another second. He was on me in a split second. Leaning over me, placing his hands on either side of my hips, sinking into the mattress, making my back arch. "When you call me that, I don't think you know what it does to me." His voice was deep and full of restraint. "Tell me, Princess, are you mine?"

If I do this, if I let this happen, there will never be another. The *Blood Oath* demands it. I wanted him, but our bond felt old. Some sense returned to my brain when I realized the gravity of the entire situation. Whether I wanted him or not, now was not the time. And this certainly was not the place.

"I can't." My palm was on fire with the avoided answer. "Revoke it," I whimpered. The bond was calling to him and me. Begging me to solidify it.

"As you wish, Princess." He stayed true to his word, kissed my palm gently, and whispered sweetly into my hand.

I saw the lust for me in his eyes and it filled me with unsatisfied hunger. Sitting up, my legs straddling him, I soon became aware of his hardened length, and blushed at the thought of it inside of me.

"I can still read your thoughts, Princess." He grunted.

"I know." He smirked but waited for my answer and so was the *Oath*. "Calian, if we cross this line, there is no going back. I have never been with a man before. I am inexperienced with all this stuff. And to be honest, terrified to let it happen, plus with all the other stuff going on, it doesn't seem like the right time. We barely know one another, and if I choose to spend my life with you, I really need to know who you are on the inside."

There was an unmistakable slump of disappointment in his shoulders. "Before you met me, you would've married a stranger. What makes me so different from them? Because I'm not a prince?"

"Your title has nothing to do with it, and I was doing that as a means to an end. How do I know that once we cross this line, solidifying our bond, it won't backfire? What about the prince? What will he do if he finds out about this? He will use you to get to me, just so I can reveal where the stone is."

"You know where the stone is?" he asked, and I noticed a sudden shift in him that was alarming.

"Yes. I mean, I suspect," I whispered.

"You told my prince you didn't."

"I can't lie to you," I said with ease.

Realization just smacked me in the face. Calian said, *my prince*. This was all a game to him. I began distancing myself from him bit by bit, but he held me tight. "Calian," I warned.

"You don't know how badly I wanted you to be mine. Because then I wouldn't have any choice at all." His face was hard.

"Choice about what?" He pressed his forehead to mine and the hairs on the back of my neck rose.

"I wouldn't have been able to follow through." My world began to spin, eyelids growing heavy, and I reached for something to hold onto, but I felt myself clawing at air.

"What's…happening?" I was no longer in control of myself as I fell into the pit of darkness that was my unconscious.

Chapter Nine

Clover

"Clover, my little flower, focus." Back in this damned room again. Strapped down, awaiting my punishment. This time, it was for rolling my eyes at Mistress Siegel. She was going on and on about how I needed to walk with my shoulders back and chest forward. "Why did you disrespect Mistress Siegel?" A rhetorical question, but one that needed answering.

"She was annoying me." At this point, after ten years of this, I was numb to the pain she would inflict. Answering honestly wouldn't make it any worse.

"I see." Mother walked over to a wooden bucket, grabbed a piece of ice, and then over to the open flame of a torch, heating the blade of her dagger. "I thought by now you would be better, but unfortunately for both of us, my dear, you will be punished for your actions."

"Another scar, Mother. What will my future husband think about the uneven flesh of my skin? What will the kingdom think once I am queen and reveal to them just how vile you are?" The words flooded out of me like a river breaking through a dam. The tapping of her heels across the tile floor was soft. She always walked with such grace.

"My sweet flower, there is no one in the entire realm who will believe you." The smell of burning flesh

came before the pain and then increased tenfold as she replaced the heat with frost.

My eyes opened instantly as I screamed from the painful memory across my navel. The room was hot, dark, and I still thought I was dreaming, but then I heard him.

"Cal told me you have nightmares."

Prince Eli.

Jerking my head side to side, soaking in the gravity of my situation, I was back in another dark room. But this one was different. My wrists were bound by metal bracelets connected by chains to the wall behind me. Standing on my feet, I calmed my rising panic, noting that my body was free of restraints everywhere else.

"What is the meaning of this?" I demanded. A deep chuckle came from somewhere in front of me. Then a snapping sound echoed through the room and with it came lit torches. I could see him and the small room. There was a cloth with metal devices laid out on an oak table where he was leaning.

"Tell me, Clover…" He took a few steps forward, then stopped in front of me, the toes of our shoes touching. "When you were about to fuck Cal, did it ever occur to you that was part of my plan?"

I swallowed hard. What a fool and naïve person I was to have believed a word that came from Cal's sinful lips.

"Are you jealous, Eli?" The one advantage I had in this situation was that, unbeknownst to him, I've been trained to withstand torture. Instigating him would just make it more enjoyable for me when he realized that I can't be broken. He scoffed at me, leaning down, leaving only an inch or two between our foreheads.

Which was his first mistake.

The sound didn't do the pain justice as I thrust my head up and into his nose. A curse of pain came from him as he stepped away from me. I smiled when I saw the blood pooling from his now broken nose.

"That was a warning, Eli. Next time, it will not just be that little nose of yours. Let me go back home and I will consider forgiving you. Based on your stupidity alone."

He charged at me, those narrowed eyes turning into molten pools of rage. Drawing his dagger, he held it up to my neck, and I glared at him.

"You stupid bitch. Cal should praise the gods for not having to deal with you anymore."

I spat in his face. He wiped it off with the cloth he had been using to stop the bleeding from his nose.

"You know, he told me that he was going to do it with or without your permission if I said so." He was trying to get inside my head. *She* did the same all those times before. And just like the past, it went in one ear and out the other, not affecting me one bit.

"Gods, you *are* jealous, and this is the result of a temper tantrum because I didn't choose you. Piss off, Eli. And after this little stunt, you will never be my husband. You will never be High King, and you will never win." A feline smile came across his bloodied face. Not the response I was expecting.

"Tell me something, in all your intimate conversations with him, didn't you find it strange how excessively lustful you were toward him?"

"Yes," I answered, a little too honestly. But what was the harm in that?

"And you never asked him why that was?" I went

to speak but he silenced me with a finger. "Oh, yeah, that's right, he told you something about being soul mates and the Blood Magic only intensifies it." I didn't answer. "Oh, and I love the part where he played you about not being able to lie to one another. Yet, he told you about his powers and you believed every single word. You stupid child."

It cannot be true. I felt that pain in my hand, and I saw his hand turn red when he didn't want to discuss a certain topic. If this was true, oh gods. "No, you're lying."

"He played you for a fool." He went to touch my face, but I tilted my head further away, noting he still held the dagger to my throat. "I can punish him."

"What?" Now I know he is insane.

"For attempting to assault the princess." The sound of a bolt caught my attention directly behind Eli. The doors opened when two guards came dragging in a man with a bag on his head and bound wrist. Dropping him to his knees. *Please don't be him, please don't be him.* "Would you like to see the criminal?"

"You're bluffing." I held my ground. To let myself feel anything for Cal was stupid. Eli gripped the bag, tearing it from the prisoner, and my heart dropped to my stomach. The shaggy brown hair, deep green eyes full of regret, and that sun-kissed skin, and plump red lips. Those lips that had caressed my skin, leaving their mark on me forever.

"Cal?" I felt a burning sensation in the back of my eyes, struggling to keep the tears back.

"Whatever he said to you, I can explain." A lump formed in my throat and then the image of my mother appeared in my head. And I heard her voice. *Block it out, flower. The pain, the emotion, is the best way to fight*. And so, I did. The worry on his face told me it had worked; that my face was now emotionless.

"I think you broke her, my friend," Eli said as he ruffled Calian's hair as if he were a pet. "This is how this is going to work, princess. You tell me about the Dragonheart, and I let you both live."

"And if I don't?"My words, like ice, rolled off my tongue. Eli dropped the dagger he pointed at me the entire time and cut down the center of Calian's tunic. Dropping it down to where it hung from his bound wrist, revealing that chiseled physique that, if my emotions were not off, would be sending heat and dampness between my thighs. That wicked smile came back on Eli's face as he held the blade to the spot right above Calian's heart.

I didn't notice before, but he bore no scars on his upper body. Which was weird, considering he was a soldier. But then I remembered he was an Ashana. Which also brought the question of why he was letting these mortals handle him like this? I shot a questioning look at him and he gave me a nod.

This is part of the manipulation. He was doing this to get to the prince. But why?

"Where is it?" Eli's eyes narrowed menacingly, the blade held against Calian's chest, and the other hand gripping a fist of that beautiful chocolate hair. Just like when Mother killed Vivian, I stood there like the poised, perfectly useless statue of a woman. No movement, except the rise and fall of my chest. My eyes locked onto Calian. I watched the emotion fade from him as Eli pressed the sharpened edge of the blade into his chest, crimson coating that perfect bronze.

"You don't think I will kill him, do you?" I heard Eli say, but again, I didn't respond because, from the look Calian was giving me, Eli couldn't kill him. Even if he tried, and Eli assumed I didn't have that kind of knowledge. Or Eli was the uninformed one on the powers of a demi-god.

"Fine." He feigned upset.

The prince stepped away from Cal and right up to me. "I didn't want to do this, but you leave me with no other choice."

I felt the cold blade as he placed it between the fabric of my dress and my skin, slowly cutting it in half, and dropping it to the floor at my feet. With nothing but my silk undergarments on, covering my breast and sex, I still didn't budge. This was how I was tortured, and from the look on both the prince's and Calian's faces, they saw the truth of my life laid out before them. A map of what life was like for the High Princess of Thornwarf.

All my scars connected; it was as if Mother was slowly, painfully imprinting a tattoo along my body. Starting from under my right breast, down in a curve to my navel, then dancing along my right hip, into my inner thighs, and around my calves. Both sides of my body matched the other in the exact pattern of raised pink skin. To them, it would appear as one torturous moment, but to me, it was thirteen years of punishment delivered by the late queen.

"Gods." I heard the disgust before looking up to see Eli grimace at the sight of me. That had no effect on me, but when I shifted my gaze to Cal, those emerald eyes were now green flames of rage, and that snapped me out of my emotionless stupor. I heard a low growl coming from the demi-god, as his eyes trailed my body.

"Who did that to you?" His voice was like death itself. The palm of my right hand started to burn at my silence. But I refused to answer him. I now knew that everything he said to me was either a lie or close enough to it just so he could manipulate me. Let it burn. Burn the memory of everything we ever shared. Not that it was much, but he was the first man that I opened myself up to. Felt vulnerable. Magic or not, I have a feeling it still would've been that way with him.

"Calm down, Calian." Eli clicked his tongue. "It's a shame. Your face is divine, but the rest of you are pitiful. I should kill you just to end your suffering."

"You think you can break me, Prince?" He was looking away from my body, and I knew it was because he was disgusted. "Look at them. That should tell you that I don't break. No matter what you come at me with, you will never get anything out of me." I spat on the floor.

"And you!" I glared at Calian, who was still steaming with rage. "You have no right to ask me that. Revoke your question or I let the prince cut my hand off, right here, right now."

The rage in his eyes started to dissipate, and I saw the guilt seep in. "Bring me to her," he said in a low soft voice. The guards didn't move. "Bring me to her."

His tone was deeper, and my palm was now on fire. And as those tears slowly dripped down from my eyes, I still didn't beg. Did not plead. I remained calm.

"Eli, please. You know what will happen if I don't revoke it."

"I know." Eli was going to try and use the oath to break me. My hand will turn to ash before I let that happen. The burning was the most intense pain I'd ever felt before, and I bit down on the inside of my cheek so hard I could taste iron in my mouth. I saw Calian's gaze shoot to my right hand and widen with shock. At first, I was scared to look, but I turned my gaze and what I saw was impossible. Bright green and red flames were dancing around my hand. The burning was easing and a strange sensation, something I couldn't explain, was there in my palm.

"Not possible," Eli said and charged at me. Calian growled and broke free from his restraints and guards. Grabbing Eli by the back of the neck, he slammed him onto the ground hard.

In a threatening voice, Calian snarled, "You don't get to touch her. If you do, I will rip your heart out and eat it." A shiver went through my body at his words.

"I am still your prince and your friend," Eli said as he struggled against Calian.

"I don't give a fuck because she, *she* is bound to me, and I will protect her until my last breath. Even if it means killing a sadistic royal ass. You don't touch her without her permission. You don't look at her or speak to her until she says you can. I am Ashana, Eli, and your little facade of me being your prisoner is over." Calian let go of Eli and turned to me. He ripped the chains from the walls, freed me from the wrist restraints, and then took a step back. The ball of fire was still dancing around my right hand. I thought my arms would be stiff after being in that position for so long, but I felt energized.

"I apologize for my part in all of this, Princess."

"Fuck you. You can't just betray and manipulate me and then betray him. Figure out whose side you're on." I stormed past him, stopping just before where Eli was sprawled out on the floor, and did something foolish. In a split second, I was on Eli, straddling him, and the look of surprise made me laugh. I turned to stare at Calian. "I will never be yours." Turning to Eli, I moved the flame to his face. Gripping his jaw with my other hand, I said, "You will let me leave here without any interference. If you don't, this little fire will be the last thing to touch those little lips. Understand, Eli?"

"You wicked little whore." He smirked at me. Bringing my hand down to his face, his smile remained, and his sapphire eyes filled with desire for me. With my sex on top of his, I felt his hardening arousal. It made bile creep in my throat and I was tempted to let it out.

"Do we have an agreement, Eli?" Sweat beads erupted on his face from the heat of my flame. I could see he was debating on calling my bluff. When he didn't answer, I did something even more foolish. With my free hand, I grabbed his fallen dagger, stuck it right through his breeches, until the tip was grazing his cock, and he let out a cry of pain. I heard a feral growl come from where Calian was. I shot him a glance. "Are you serious, Calian?"

"We have a deal if you stop." Eli was completely useless against me, and I was feeling powerful. For the first time in my life, I was the one in control. Not the prince or his men, not even the powerful demi-god that could destroy me with the snap of his fingers.

"Goodbye, boys. I pray to the gods I never see either of you again." I got to my feet, and walked over to Calian, the ball of fire still dancing around my fingers. "Revoke it."

I placed my hand in front of his lips. He was angry

with me. Good. Because I hated him and now, I hurt him as bad as he hurt me. “Revo—”

I didn’t finish my words as his lips crashed onto mine, an arm wrapping tightly around my bare waist, pulling me against him. Claiming me. I didn’t fight as our tongues danced with each other, scraping teeth, and I felt his arousal on my leg. It was longer than Eli’s and that made me flush with heat. He broke away from me before speaking. “I revoke it.”

Chapter Ten

Clover

The warmth of the bath eased my muscles, and I scrubbed every inch of my skin that touched either of them more than once. My palm didn't bear a mark anymore. It was as if the fire burned it away and I felt an ambiguous mix of relief and disappointment. After everything I just did with both in a matter of a day, I questioned my sanity. This was all a dream, and my nightmares of Mother's torture were reality. Where did that flame come from? I have no magic and they seemed just as surprised as I was.

I needed a plan.

Step one: get the hell out of here. Step two: find the stones. Step three: figure out what all this means. Gods, I would give anything to have answers to these questions.

"I know someone who can." The voice came from out of nowhere and in my head.

"Who's there?" Have I gone mad?

"The only person who can get into this pretty head of yours."

"Cal?" I sank lower into the bath, trying to hide my breast. As if he could see me. "Get out of my head. Didn't I make it clear to you I was done with you?"

"Straddling Eli to make me jealous or try and hurt

me only made me want you more."

Is that what I did? Gods, I didn't even know how I knew what to do. It was just instinct.

"Fuck off, Cal." I heard the deep rumble of his laugh, and like so many times before, it aroused me.

"I heard what you were thinking when you compared mine to his." I was blushing now. "You can still find out. All you need to do is ask." The arrogance.

"What do you want, Calian?"

"To help you." He sounded sincere.

"I don't trust you. Just leave me alone. If you care for me at all, leave me alone." I got out of the bath, dried myself off, and dressed in my night slip, waiting for a response. But nothing came. Until a knock sounded on my door. Like an idiot, I opened it. "Can't you take a hint?"

"Hear me out." I hated him. With those pleading eyes, that shirtless body was teasing me. I looked down to where the blade had pierced his skin before, but it was already healed. His hair was wet and that just told me he had just bathed too. "Give me five minutes. If you don't like what I have to say, then I will never speak to you again."

I was going to regret this. "Fine. Five minutes."

He came in and shut the door behind us. I sat on the settee, and he sat on the matching chair across from me. "I know you plan on going after the stones. I know you want to know why a fireball formed in your hand." He paused.

"Four and half minutes."

"Blood magic can be weird. I think when our blood mixed, some of my power transferred to you. When you refused to answer my question, instead of your hand turning to ash, it turned to flame." He cleared his throat before speaking. "Let me help you find all the stones before the Rai does. And I promise to sever the bond of the *Blood Oath.*"

"You can do that?" I asked.

"There is a way it can be severed, yes." If one of us dies.

"Death is the only way it can be severed." I shook my head from side to side in disappointment. There would be no other way.

"Not true," he started. "Those stones don't just have the powers of the dragon souls. They have individual unique powers to each tribe. Since I am a descendant of the god of dragons, I can use the stone to sever our bond without killing either of us." If what he is saying is true, then I would be completely free. But can I trust him?

"In the last sixty seconds, you better give me a good reason to trust you. Don't you dare kiss me again!" He smiled, making my heart skip a beat. Getting up from his chair, he walked over, kneeling before me. We were at eye level now as he raised his right hand and placed it on my chest, then gestured for me to do the same to his. I obliged.

"I, Calian, do solemnly swear that if I betray you, lie to you, or harm you in any way, my heart will stop immediately and without warning." My body went loose at those words.

"Why would you make that kind of vow?"

"Because the fact that I hurt you so badly, that pain I felt in my soul when I watched you nearly lose yourself, is something I regret and swear to never do again." I wanted to pull him into me and tell him I was sorry for the pain I caused him. I didn't move but sent a message to him, and he lifted himself toward me. My arms wrapped tightly around him as I buried my face into the warmth of his chest. I let myself feel for him again, praying I wouldn't regret it.

****

Packing for the journey wasn't as difficult as I thought it would be. A brown sack made from deer hide held a couple of changes of clothes Calian brought from the local seamstress, a bedroll, and food. Cal packed the food and waterskins, while I went to the stables to grab the horse. The stable was large, with twenty stalls divided in half, smelling of muck and hay. I wasn't sure which one I should pick, since I had no clue how to ride one. A beautiful mare with a chocolate coat walked toward me. Reaching out, the horse rubbed her long snout against the palm of my right hand, allowing me to pet her.

Her fur was soft, and she was unique with her white mane and tail.

"What's your name?" I asked as I looked for a nameplate.

"That is Oreo." I heard Eli's voice from behind, making me reach for the handle of a nearby shovel. I expected restraints and even an attempt to take me prisoner again, but nothing happened.

Eli reached down and grabbed a horse's brush and stood on her other side.

"About last night," he started, and I stopped. Panic rose in my chest. "I know why you have to leave, but I don't wish it to be on such bad terms. I don't know what came over me when I kissed you without your permission and for that, I am most sorry."

What? I furrowed my brows, confused at what game he was trying to play this time, but from the look on his face, he was being sincere.

"Please forgive me, Princess Clover," he pleaded, and I was confused.

"Eli, I don't think—"

"Princess, may I have a word with you before we depart?" It was Calian who interrupted me before I could finish my sentence.

"Excuse me." Eli nodded as I walked over to where Calian was standing. Exquisite as ever in his all-black leather, matching the same he wore the day he came for me.

"The prince doesn't remember anything from last night," he whispered.

"That's impossible. How?" I asked.

"I might have influenced his memories." With that confession, I curled my fist, I wasn't sure how to react. He looked amused at my slight confusion.

"You were so insecure that you had replaced the memory of what I did, with making it seem as though he came on to me without my permission." Calian smirked. "You are an ass."

"You should be grateful. Because after our conversation, when I walked out of your room, Eli and his guards were approaching your door to murder you." He gritted his teeth before speaking again. "He's lucky I didn't kill him for plotting your murder."

"Thank you, I guess." I didn't know what else to say. Everything about this man was confusing. He helped kidnap me, plotted to manipulate me, violated my trust, and yet when it became clear his magic was in me, he turned the tables and suddenly wanted to kill everyone that threatened me? My head hurt.

"Princess Clover, give my regards to the people of Thornwarf upon your safe return home." Eli came up to us, his patience spent.

"Thank you, Prince Eli. I bid you farewell. Tell the king I hope he favors better in the future." The politeness tasted sour on my tongue. Part of me wished Calian had followed through with his threat. I wish I had killed him for taking me prisoner.

What's happening to me? Wishing people harm, speaking out of turn, wanting someone dead? This isn't who I am. Or maybe it's who I'm becoming. Being free of the chains of the life I lived before Her death. I should embrace this new me.

Due to my lack of experience riding, mounting Oreo proved challenging. Naturally, Calian lifted me with ease onto the saddle.

"Would you like me to ride with you?" he asked with a wink. Knowing he was trying to get his hands on me again, I ignored him. "Well, if you fall, I will catch you."

"Just get on the damn horse. You can pine for me in silence on our way out of this hell hole." That stupid smile appeared on his perfect face, and I had to look away to hide the pink I was sure appeared on my face.

"As you wish, Princess." He bowed at the hips and then mounted his horse.

The sound of hooves hitting the path brought some ease to the tension in my muscles. This past week was the worst I had ever experienced in my entire life. Starting with seeing the murder of Vivian, the planned assassination of my parents, being stolen away, making a *Blood Oath* with an impeccably handsome Ashana, and ending it with the Prince of Greveil nearly torturing me. The gods must either hate me or are using me to entertain themselves.

Riding through the market, we slowed the horses' pace to a walk. The entire place was busy with people buying, selling, and trading goods. It smelled of spices, food, and leather. Some eyes watched as we passed and others didn't seem to care who we were, only paying attention to their next coin.

Their culture is unbothered by our presence. I don't have much experience with people, so not acknowledging me doesn't bother me at all, nor does it seem to bother him. I don't stop to take in the sights of this kingdom because yet again, it's just left me with more bad memories. Not even what happened between me and Calian was real.

Once we were on the outskirts of the town, Calian stopped and waited for me to ride up next to him.

"Is something wrong?" I asked. He stared at me. I saw that untainted desire lingering in those mesmerizing green eyes of his. It was almost primal, like I did something to make him want to bite me or take me right on that horse.

"Cal?"

A low growl rumbled in his throat before he spoke. "Princess, we have three options here."

"Okay."

"Option one, we take the path back to Thornwarf, retrieve the stone of Ziran, and you reclaim your position as High Queen. Option two, we ride on to Cypress Grove, where a friend of mine can tell us exactly what we need to do once we find all five stones." He paused.

"And option three?" He cleared his throat, and I suddenly became nervous. He stayed silent and the suspense was killing me. "What is option three?"

"We go to Shuang and tell Queen Iliana what has happened. Hopefully, prevent war for the treaty not being honored with the death of your parents and unfortunate disappearance of their princess."

"Kidnapping. In case you forgot." I glared at him, and he just smiled right back at me. "If I go back home, there is no way in all of creation Alma will let me leave again. I'm not sure where Cypress Grove is, but the stories about that place don't make it sound very friendly to outsiders. And gods only know what Queen Iliana will believe."

Pondering the options; none ensured my kingdom of safety. Tracking down all the stones could take months. Besides, I suspected the location of Ziran, but what about the other four?

"Are you sure you know where they are?"

"I am," he said. Not surprising. In the past week, I have learned quite a lot about Calian's abilities as a demi-god. Teleportation, telekinesis, and magic. The ability to manipulate memories. I should be afraid of that kind of power, but I felt the complete opposite. "The health, ice, and death stones are in unknown territory."

"Which means?" I questioned, gesturing for him to get to the point.

"Which means, I don't know the dangers that lurk in those parts of the world."

"Where exactly are you talking about?" he rubbed a hand on the back of his neck. Then shuffled through his sack, pulling out a rolled parchment. "This is the map of the realm. We are on the Western side. Up North is Shuang country, and then across the Great Sea is the unknown world."

"I've never seen a map like this before." It was true. On a day when Mother showed me the War Room, there was a map, but it didn't go beyond the Sea. There were only the territories: Thornwarf in the middle between Greveil and Shuang.

"I believe that on the other side of the sea, or in that mountain range across from Shuang, is where we find the other three stones."

"Three?" I asked.

"Ziran, the nature stone is in Thornwarf, and Huolong the firestone," he paused, then pulled out a necklace with a large ruby on it from underneath his tunic. "It's right here."

"Where did you get that?" It was beautiful. Cut into the perfect shape of an oval, it glistened in the rays of the High Sun. Reaching out to touch it, Calian placed it gently in my palm and it sent a strange sensation through my body. It almost felt alive. "Is that a heartbeat?"

"Yes." The stone was no bigger than a small potato and looked even smaller in Calian's palm. "That is why they are called Dragonheart."

He placed his warm hand under, helping me hold the stone, and the feel of his skin on mine was electrifying. Our gazes locked, and I felt myself lean into him, not realizing the space between our horses. Before our lips touched, Oreo moved away, and I nearly fell from the saddle until Calian caught me. Grabbing me by my hips and then placing me in front of him. My legs hanging over his thighs. He was so fast, my breath caught.

"I told you I would catch you."

Gods, he was right. "Thank you," I said, and he leaned down. I thought he was going to kiss me, but he placed his forehead against mine. We just breathed in each other's scent for a moment.

"Princess," he started.

"Cal," I answered, and the low growl rumbled through him. I wanted him to kiss me, to claim me again.

"You need to get back on your horse before I do something you don't want me to do."My imagination went haywire with the thought of what he was thinking.

"And what's that?" I asked.

Placing a gentle hand on my cheek, the other on the back of my neck, he tilted my head back. Exposing my neck to him. Brushing his lips across my skin, he whispered, "Do you truly want to know all the things I want to do to you?"

Gods, I did. But he manipulated me. Used my lack of experience to get information out of me. But I hated the thought of those sinful lips never kissing mine again. Fisting the front of his tunic, I pulled him onto me. Our lips touched softly at first, then I claimed him for myself. Our kiss deepened, this time, he wasn't holding back.

"Princess," he growled out.

"Cal." I gasped as his hands trailed my body, cupping my rear.

"What do you want from me? Tell me and I will give it to you."

The question surprised me, but I knew exactly what to say to make him regret ever betraying me. My lips brushed against his neck, then I nibbled his earlobe before whispering, "I want you to worship me, and I will make you regret ever betraying me again." Before he responded, I jumped down from his horse, landing hard on the ground, and then walked over to where Oreo had wandered to graze in the grass. Satisfaction radiated through me for what I'd done. Mother would be proud of my attempt at trying to manipulate him. But little did I know playing with a demi-god had its consequences.

I didn't feel him on me until the ground was distancing itself from me and I realized I was in the air. "I'm flying? What the hell?"

Then I felt something hard against my rear, two arms wrapped around my waist, and flapping of wings. Turning my head…"Oh gods, you're flying."

I dug my nails into his arms, trying to hold onto him so I wouldn't fall. I hated heights and I know he knew that since the day we crossed that bridge. "You see, Princess, when you play games, I will always win," Calian whispered in my ear.

"What do you want, Cal? Scare me into fucking you? Is that what you want? To take my virginity and claim it?"

He stopped mid-air, turning me in his arms so I could face him. The look of desire, anger, and need was so powerful. I knew if he wanted to, he could kill me. Let me fall to my death. But the vow he made would prevent that. I cupped his face. "What do you want from me, Cal?"

"I want you. I want you to want me. Do not play with me or seduce me. I don't want to fuck you because you're a virgin. Because when that time comes, you will not be that to me. You will feel passion and love when we come together. It is what you deserve. But until you make that choice, I don't want you to touch or kiss me unless you accept everything I am and everything I have done. Once you do that, you will get your wish."

Gods, he meant every word. I did want him, but I still couldn't bring myself to say it.

After all the hell I went through with Mother, he broke a piece of me that he started to glue back together. Closing my eyes, I relaxed in his arms, letting myself trust him. The feel of the cool wind through my hair was tantalizing. But I knew if I opened my eyes and looked at him…Knowing he was so close that all I had to say was yes, I would be lost to him. It frightened me more than the height itself.

"Open your eyes, Princess." I didn't want to. "Trust me." My eyes fluttered open, and I hadn't realized, but he had placed me on Oreo. I looked at him with questioning eyes. "I pray that one day you will not hate me so much."

"I think we should go with option two." It was too much for me to continue the subject of us. "We can circle back and get the stone from Thornwarf once we meet with your friend and figure out what we're supposed to do exactly."

I watched as his shoulder sagged slightly and his wings disappeared before I had time to examine them further. They were black, but I didn't pay close enough attention to their size.

"As you wish, Princess." He bowed, defeated, before mounting back onto his horse. Guilt. That was what I was feeling while toying with him. But it was also for me. I knew what I wanted, but now, I was too afraid to act on those desires.

We rode in silence over the next couple of hours, Calian only speaking when there was a tree branch or spider web in the way that I needed to avoid. There were times when I thought he wanted to talk, but I knew he felt just like I did. What would we talk about? We couldn't get past this tension between us to have a friendly conversation. I could ease it; I knew all I had to do was tell him what I wanted. Fear and regret kept me from owning it.

A tree snapping brought me out of my head and I looked up to see Calian gesture for me to remain silent. It was times like these I wish I knew how to fight. Mother said there was no need for it. That was what the guards were for. I almost found myself begging Alma at times to train me, but she just repeated what Mother did. Calian dismounted his horse, drawing his swords, making his way over to me.

"What is it?" I whispered. The cracking of branches grew louder. I dismounted my horse, ungracefully and almost face-planted, before Calian wrapped an arm around my waist, helping me balance myself.

"Do you know how to use this?" he asked, handing me his sword. I took it while shaking my head from side to side. "The pointy end goes inside the bad guy."

That much I knew. He let the hilt go completely. I was surprised at how light it felt. I had never held a sword before in my life, but I knew that it tended to be heavy due to the material of the blade.

"Who dares trespass the Grove of the Cypress Queen?" a thick, raspy voice came from ahead of us.

Cal stopped in front of me, putting space between me and whatever was speaking. "Don't be rude, answer the question."

"Calian, son of Tika, god of dragons." Appearing from behind the shadow of trees, a towering beast with a long tusk, gray moss atop its round head, and large body tramped toward us. It had to be over seven feet tall, seeing how much larger than Cal it was.

"And the girl?" It gestured toward me with its branch-like digits.

"I am Clover, High Princess of Thornwarf." The beast had no face that I could see under the flowing moss.

"I heard the princess was killed some nights ago. It appears I was misinformed. What are you doing in my Grove, girl?"

I gave Cal a worried look, but he nodded for me to answer.

"We seek knowledge on the Dragonheart." I kept my voice steady, although my insides were in a fit of panic.

"The girl may enter and seek council, but you,"—it pointed a long branch toward Cal—"Ashana must stay here."

"Not going to happen." He snarled.

"The girl will come to no harm; I promise you that."

Cal stepped in front of me, but I grabbed his arm, squeezing tightly. "It's okay." His eyes were full of concern and anger. Stepping out, I walked toward the beast.

"Know this, Queen, if any harm comes to her, I will burn your entire Grove down and dance upon your ashes."

My heart did that stupid flutter at his endearing words. Gods, I wasn't sure how much longer I could have this need for him. No one ever protected me so fiercely before and I loved it.

The Grove was hidden behind low-hanging branches that moved out of the way on their own. Knowing that their master was passing through. I kept a tight grip on the hilt of the sword, praying that I didn't just fall into another trap. In the middle of a clearing, two cups, and a small cube are displayed on a large oak trunk. The queen kneeled on one side and gestured for me to do the same on the other. I obliged.

"Princess Clover Celestia, named after the flower and raised in the kingdom of thorns and roses." Her voice shifted to a normal one. Human-like and then all the nature on her dissipated to reveal a beautiful woman. Red wine hair flowed down her body, touching the forest floor. Crystal blue eyes reminded me of the clear skies above, and her charcoal skin was untainted and smooth. I blushed at the sight of her nakedness. Her hair was the only thing keeping me from seeing her plump breast.

"You're—"

"Not what you expected?" she asked before a decanter appeared out of nowhere on the trunk. "I know, that is the disguise I use to challenge intruders who enter my Grove."

"It is quite alarming," I stated.

She smiled a pearly white smile. "I know why you're here, princess, but I can only answer three questions."

Damn. "Only three? Why is it always three?" I

asked.

"It's the rules of the game." Game? Cal never mentioned a word about a game. And where was this so-called friend of his?

"I beg your pardon, what game?" I asked in my most polite manner.

"I want you to guess the number of dots that are on this small cube. If you get it right, I will answer a question." She raised the small cube and then placed it under the chalice in front of her.

"And if I get it wrong?" I daringly asked.

"You must speak one truth to that boy upon your return. No holding back." I gulped because I knew that whatever she was, she knew more than I ever could imagine. "But, by the time we are done playing, I'm sure you will do that whether you lose or not."

"How can you be so sure?"

She stopped me. "The game hasn't started yet, princess. First, I need to hear you agree to the terms."

"Agreed." I was more than eager to get my questions answered. Although I had a lot more than three. So, I needed to think of the best three that would give me the most information.

"Very well. The max number is twenty dots and the lowest is one. I place the cube in my empty chalice, shake it, slam it on the table, and then you guess. Only one guess per turn. Understand?"

I wasn't daft, so I nodded my head, letting my confidence take over as Mother taught me to do. Separating my emotions was a skill I had mastered long ago.

She did exactly what she said she would, and as soon as that chalice hit the wood, she waited for me to guess.

"My first number is ten."

She smiled as she lifted the chalice, looking at the cube, and then showed me that I guessed right. "Smart or lucky. No one ever guesses on the first turn. Ask your question."

The first question blurted out of me before I could think it over. "What does this mean?" I held up my right palm, hoping she would understand what I was hinting at.

"*Blood Oaths* are derived from old magic. During the first days of life, the gods and goddesses created magic within all living things. The plants, the animals, and all humans. There were other species created. Elves, dwarves, and manticore colonies, along with the dragons. Each wielding their own source of power. Blood magic was used to strike treaties and peace between different lands. It was what they knew but,"—she paused, letting out a sigh, caressing a dandelion on the floor beside her— "like all things, there is a balance. With all the good came the bad. Hiatus, God of the Shadow Realm grew cold, greedy. He wanted more followers. People worshipped him more than the rest in the Temple. He got inside the minds of the most vulnerable and started wars with members from each colony until he had his own company of Shadow Wizards.

"The gods and goddesses decided then that the best thing for our world was to take all magic away. Only those blessed enough to be true descendants of a god could use this power. Since Calian is the direct bloodline of Tika, he can use his magic. But, that wasn't always possible. Blood magic is dangerous and sacred in our time and should never be used with anyone other than one's true mate."

The answer shocked me more than I realized. She could be lying, just telling me what I wanted to hear. "Don't doubt my words, girl. I can never lie; it's a gift bestowed upon me by the gods themselves. I see into the very soul of every living creature, and I know their truth better than they do."

"I'm ready for the next turn." I didn't want to waste any more time or questions here. She repeated the move and I guessed wrong this time.

"You must tell Calian how you got your scars." I sucked in a sharp breath because telling him meant I had to relive each one of them. "I will know if you didn't, girl."

I wanted to ask how, but knowing just how powerful she seemed, I doubted I would get away with avoiding it. "Let's continue."

"You must agree that you will tell him. That's how the game works."

"Fine. I will tell him about my scars. Please go again." She obliged and this time, I won. I didn't waste my question on Calian or what she said about true mates. I needed to think of something more important that we could use to our advantage.

"When I have all the Dragonhearts, what am I to do with them?"

"Once you retrieve all five, you must go to the Temple within the dragon colonies, place each stone in their pillar of creation, and then recite the words to free the souls."

"What–" She held a hand up to stop my next question.

"You must win once more before I answer that one, girl."

"Fine. Get on with it." I also needed to know where and how to get all the stones and where the dragon colonies were located, but I couldn't fit all that into one question. I had to be smart with my last one.

"You lost again, Princess." She smiled, and I could tell she was enjoying my losses much more than my wins. "You must confess to him what you truly want from him."

"Agreed." I hate her so much. She shook the cube once more and I lost again.

"For this confession, you must tell him what you are afraid of and why." I was afraid of telling him all this and being rejected. "Ready for another turn?"

"Agreed. Continue." She obliged and this time I won.

My last question.

I felt my insides churning as I thought it over. It had to continue from the previous. Fill in whatever gaps I could on these stones. My relationship with Calian wasn't as important as saving the entire realm from being enslaved. "For my last question, I would like to ask…" I paused. Thinking about it more than I should've. "Where are each Dragonhearts located?"

"Are you sure that is what you wish to know?"" She was giving me a choice? So, I reworded my question.

"I know where one is located, and suspect where another is, but I need to know where the other three are exactly. If you please." She smiled a knowing smile and I realized she gifted that to me. Appearing out of nowhere, much as the decanter did, a map of the realm etched itself into the trunk. All the territories were labeled, and I didn't know any of them except the three I grew up with.

"Across the Great Sea, in the Kingdom of Orion, the queen owns the Shuang and Heise Stones. To the far north, in the Jian Mountains, the Dark Wizard owns the Jian stone."

"The Dark Wizard, as in Rai? How are we supposed to travel to an unknown kingdom and ask a queen for magic stones? Also, we can't face Rai without having more people. I don't have access to Thornwarf's forces. Greveil is…if I don't have to ask Prince Eli for anything I won't, and I've never met Queen Iliana. If Rai is a powerful wizard that has magic influenced or inherited by the god in the Shadow Realm, what do we have to stop him? Surely Calian isn't strong enough to take him and his entire army out." My chest was tight, breathing fast, and the words kept flowing.

She put a comforting hand on my shoulder.

"What have I gotten myself into?"

"This is your fate, child. Without you, the Rai will take over our entire realm and enslave us all." Her words sank deep inside of me, like a boulder falling into a river. "I will give you one last gift."

I looked at her, and she held out her hand. The small game cube was in her palm.

"Thank you," I said as I reached for it. When my fingers closed on it, her hand clasped over mine hard.

"Once you fulfill your end of the game, and you confess to Calian, this cube will answer one of your many questions."

"Why are you giving me this?"

"Because I saw into your heart. You are full of untouched passion and love. Once you release that building flame inside of you, nothing will stop you."

Part Two: Goddess Awaken

Chapter Eleven

As I exited the grove, I found Calian sitting on the forest floor, Oreo and his horse nuzzled up next to him. Are they sleeping? My gaze drifted up to the skies, and the White Sun was at its highest peak. Noting that I had spent over twelve hours in the Grove, but it didn't feel like that at all.

I wasn't sure if I should wake them as I approached, but the cube vibrated in my hand, and I knew it was time. Gently tapping the bottom of his boot, I tried to wake him, but he didn't budge.

"Cal. Wake up," I whispered.

He still didn't awaken. Lifting the cube to eye level, I spoke to it. "If I confess everything now, does that count? Or does he need to be awake?" It sends a small electric shock through my fingers. "Thought so."

Kneeling, I leaned over him, so my eyes were level with his. He slept so soundly; it was rude to wake him. I gently pressed my lips to his, then his jaw, then his ear, before whispering, "Wake up."

In a split second, I was on my back with Calian straddling me and a dagger to my throat. "Princess? When did you get back?"

"Just now." He felt so huge on me. "You mind?" I gestured to the dagger at my throat.

"Sorry." He removed it and then got up from me, reaching a handout to pull me up. He held me close to him for a split second and then stepped away, clearing his throat. “So, tell me what happened.”

I fumbled with the hem of my shirt, trying to find the words to begin. There was a lot to tell him, so I avoided my confessions until I informed him of everything the queen told me. “And she told you this out of the good of her own rooted heart?”

I knew I couldn’t lie, not if I didn’t want all those answers revoked. “No, it was a game.”

“A game?” he asked. I turned my back toward him and took a few steps away.

I explained about the small cube and her rules.

“And if you lost?” he asked, and I heard him take a step closer.

“If I lost, then I had to reveal the truth to you.” We were both quiet, and I swallowed hard.

“And you didn’t lose?” he asked after a moment. Turning to him, I noted there were about four paces of space between us. A good distance for what I was about to say.

“No, I lost more than once.” He was trying to mask the smirk but I caught the corner of his mouth twitching. I knew he was gleaming on the inside. Dying to hear my secrets.

“What did she tell you to reveal to me?” He took a step toward me.

“Don’t. When I am done, then you can move. It will be a hell of a lot easier if you stay over there.”

“As you wish, Princess. There is nothing that you say that will make me think any less of you.” He was sincere, and it made this all so much harder. Why was this so hard? Why do I even care? The cube vibrated more, sending me the message that I needed to tell him now before it was too late.

"You once asked me how I got my scars." I paused. My breath came out heavy as I let out a deep exhale, calming myself before continuing. "For thirteen years, my mother punished me for anything and everything that she deemed wrong. She would lock me in a dark room, strap me down to a table with just my chest and sex covered, and then teach me a lesson." I took a breath before continuing.

"She had this dagger that she used. I remember every detail on it. The hilt had an emerald at the center and was twined with golden thread. The blade was made from steel and sharpened on all sides. She would take the knife, hold it over an open flame, heating it until she saw the purple resin, and then pressed it into my skin." I felt the tears starting to drop slowly, and I was too afraid to look at him.

"It hurt the first couple of times, but then my body became numb, and my mind would fade out. Mother said that scars would build character and that she was just doing what was best for me and the future of the realm. It was complete bullshit because no husband would want a scarred wife in his bed." I wiped my damp cheeks. Daring a glance at Cal, I saw fire in those eyes, not disgust but pure utter rage.

"The sad part is, I think my father knew what she was doing and didn't help me. No one did, not even Alma. That is why when I saw them dead, I didn't care. I felt relief swarm over me. Then shame for not fighting her. Not fighting for my body. It's too late now." I let out a small laugh. "But then you showed up. I felt something for you the moment our palms touched, and it scared the shit out of me. Because once upon a time, I loved my parents, trusted them, and they betrayed me. Alma, I love her, but she didn't protect me from myself. And then when I started to feel something for you—the stranger that stole me away, but secretly rescued me—I felt pieces of myself coming back.

"When we shared our first kiss, I knew I wanted you because I thought if he kissed me with this much passion, gods, he must feel that connection too. But then I found myself chained to a wall in another dark room. All because I let myself feel for someone again and they hurt me, again. Even after everything, I have tried to convince myself that what we have, what I feel is impossible. There is no such thing as love at first sight or soul mates. But then, I lost again, and she told me to reveal my truth. What I genuinely want from you."

"And what is that, Princess?" He spoke for the first time, his voice soft, and body tense with restraint.

"I want you to claim me. Possess me and worship me as yours because what I feel for you is hate, lust, and love. It's killing me to not unleash it all on you." He still didn't move. "Then I lost again, and I must tell you why all of this is so frightening for me.

"Because I know that if I give into this passion, this unclaimed love, it will break me. I will lose it because it will be the one thing in my life that I have claimed to be mine, and if I lose you…" My voice was breaking, and I fell to my knees, hitting the grass with a soft thud. Cal was kneeling right in front of me. His knees brushed up against mine as his hands laid gently on my shoulders. "If I love you, and let you love me, and I lose you, I fear the consequences that come with our union."

"Clover." That was the first time he said my name.

The name I hated more than anything else in this world, and he said it with such diction. "Look at me."

I lifted my head, tears pouring down my face. "Don't fear me. For the love of the gods, what I vowed to before this trip, I take to my very last breath."

"What's wrong with me?" I asked, and he pulled me into him, my face buried into the crick of his neck. Welcoming the warmth of his body.

"There is nothing wrong with you, Princess. What was done to you, gods, if your mother were not already dead, I would kill her." I let out a giggle and then lifted my head to his, resting my forehead on his.

"Now you know all my secrets. You see how damaged I am."

"Look at me." I did as I was asked. He wiped my tears away and then kissed each cheek softly. "From what I saw this past week, you're not damaged. You're strong, powerful, authoritative, and courageous. Eli tried to break you, and you shut off your emotions, calling his bluff. You know what I would give to have that kind of restraint?" I smiled. A real one for the first time in so long. "It takes every ounce of my power to not take you when I want to. Because I don't see the damage, I see power and beauty."

"Cal,"—I looked at him— "if I say yes, what is going to happen?"

A feline smile came over his lips, and my body flushed with heat. "Oh, Princess, how I have waited so long for you to ask me that question." He leaned down and I thought he was going to kiss me. "I need your permission to show you."

"Okay, but on one condition." He sank back on his haunches. "From now on, you must call me Chloe." He cocked his head to the side and then I said, "Yes."

"First…" He leaned over me, pressing a kiss softly on my lips, making my heart flutter. "I will kiss you until I take your breath away."

"That seems deadly," I stated. When his lips brushed against my neck, the scraping of his teeth made me gasp. Did I want him to bite me?

"After that, I will undress you, then explore your body with my mouth until I hear you scream my name." A moan passed my lips. He kissed me again, deeper this time. I parted my lips, inviting that sinful tongue of his into me. My hands started to explore as that kiss intensified. Running my fingers through his silky hair, he lifted me onto him, and my legs wrapped around his waist.

I slipped one hand underneath his tunic, touching his chiseled abs, and then down further to his waistband. Both of his hands cupped my rear as I sank further until I felt his arousal brushing against my knuckles. I wrapped my fingers tightly around it, and I suspected before, but now I know he was bigger than Eli, and that intimidated me.

"Lay on your back," I whispered.

"As you wish, Chloe." When he said my name, it ignited my desire further. I fumbled with the tie on his breeches, then pulled them down, exposing his full length. My hand ran down from tip to root and he let out a moan. Then, I got the urge to taste him. Pressing my lips to his head, he let out a sound that made me wet.

"Fuck."His back arched when my mouth sank deep down onto him. I wasn't sure I could fit the entire length in my mouth. His hands found their way into my hair, fisting it, guiding my head up and down. As his cock hit the back of my throat, his hips started rolling, and I held on until his release came. It was hot and tasted of salt, but I swallowed it, licking my lips as my eyes met his.

Sitting up, our lips met again, as his hands reached for my waistband. "Stop."

"Let me worship you," he pleaded, his eyes locked on mine.

"I don't want my first time to be in the middle of the forest outside Cypress Grove."

He let out a sigh. "You didn't have to do that."

"I wanted to, and I have decided that I am not letting anything or anyone hold me back from what I want anymore." He kissed me softly. He was still aroused, and it was teasing me. "Was I okay? I mean, did I do it right?"

He shot me a smile and kissed me again before saying, "You were perfect." At that moment, I felt the happiest I had ever been in my entire life.

We stayed cuddled like that for hours. Soon, I fell asleep in his arms and when I woke, I felt the warmth of his body behind me and his arousal touching my rear. I feel more rested than I have in years. "No nightmares," I whispered to myself.

He pressed against my back.

"Cal?" I wanted to know why he was aroused this early in the morning.

"Good morning, Chloe."

"Why is—" I cleared my throat, trying to think of the right words. But instead, I turned over, placed my hand on his covered cock, and asked, "Were you dreaming about me?"

"Oh, darling Chloe, it is common for a man to wake with a boner. It isn't because I dreamed about my cock inside your mouth again, although a pleasant memory. No, it is because I need to piss."

"Oh." I didn't mean to sound disappointed. He kissed me softly before getting up to go relieve himself. My mouth felt tart, and I realized I went to sleep with the taste of him last night. Getting to my feet, I grabbed my waterskin from the sack and downed it in two gulps. I still can't believe any of this. Part of me is afraid I will wake up and this will all be over, and I'll find myself back in that dark room. Gods, how I wished I could just erase all those memories, but Mother ensured I would never forget.

"Are you ready, Princess?" Can he be more beautiful?

"Chloe, we are friends now." I smiled as he wrapped me tightly in his arms and kissed me softly.

"We are a bit more than friends." He winked at me, and I couldn't help but kiss him back.

"If you two keep that up, you'll never save the realm." The queen's voice came from behind us. We both looked at her, blushing. She was in her normal form. Well, normal for whatever she was.

"Thank you," I heard Cal say. "For your wisdom."

"We are all in danger, including my Grove." She approached me. "You fulfilled your part of the game, and for that, I give you this. Hold up the cube." I obliged. Placing her hand over mine, and closing her eyes, she recited an incantation. A bright light began to shine between our hands.

"What are you doing?" I asked as the glow grew a bright green and I could feel the cube growing in size and weight. When she stopped, the glowing receded and she removed her hand. In the center of my palm was an emerald stone, and I felt the smallest pulse radiating from it. “How did you—?”

“Like calls to like, my dear. I am the Queen of the Cypress Grove. Ziran, the nature dragon, was a dear friend of mine before she was taken from this world.” Her tone was somber.

“But I thought Mother had it.”

“What your mother had was a regular emerald. Nothing special about it, but that didn’t stop her from boasting about it anytime she could. That’s why she got herself and your father killed.” I don’t recall a time when my mother boasted to others about a gem.

“You knew my parents?” I asked, examining the perfectly cut gem in my hand.

“Yes. And I am sorry for what was done to you.” She was sincere. “Enough of that. You two need to be on your way. The stones have all been awakened, and no doubt Rai will be hunting for them.”

“Where do we start?” I heard Cal ask her.

“You have two paths; both will test you. Traveling toward the Great Sea means you have to travel back through Thornwarf.” And seeing Alma again. “But that could cause delays in time you don’t have. So,”—she paused and pulled out a map from her robe. Rolling it out so we could all three look at it— “You are here, in Cypress Grove, just outside the border between Thornwarf and Greveil. If you stay north of the palace, continue up the path until you arrive at Helm’s Harbor.”

“That is the major trade port between kingdoms. If I walk in there, I will be recognized,” I interjected.

“Don’t be so sure, Princess. From what I know, no

one except royal dignitaries has ever laid eyes upon the High Princess of Thornwarf. Since word spread of your disappearance and possible death, I'm sure no one will recognize you."

"And if someone does, they will either report me to Alma or Queen Iliana in Shuang. Is there no other way?" Not that Alma would do anything to hurt me, but Iliana, I'm not sure. Since I technically didn't uphold my end of the treaty.

"Life is full of difficult choices and now that you are free to decide, this will become a constant battle. But I have faith that you will surprise yourself the further along you go on this journey." Her blind faith in me didn't ease the pressure I felt. "Ashana."

"Queen," he said.

"The girl will need protection, not distraction. So, I suggest you both keep your hands to yourselves until your mission is complete." I wanted to protest, but Cal did instead.

"If Chloe wants something from me, I will not deny her. But I will not force her either." The queen let out an incredulous laugh.

"Thank you for everything you have done for me." I couldn't help but reach out and hug her. It was clear she wasn't used to being embraced by another because she hesitated and then closed her arms around me.

"Be well and free, Princess."

Chapter Twelve

With two stones now in our possession, the decision to cross the Great Sea was the best route to go. Knowing that neither of us knew what would happen if we went into Jian and tried to steal the Health stone from the Dark Wizard, otherwise known as Rai. The idea of him decapitating people and keeping their heads in jars is petrifying and if that were truly him in the throne room, then maybe I should be more afraid.

We have been riding north for hours, only stopping to rest. I had to keep telling Cal to keep his hands to himself or we would never make it to Helm's Harbor.

"I can't help myself. You're so damn beautiful, and I still need to repay you for last night." He leaned down and kissed me softly.

"There is another time for that. For now, we keep moving until we reach the Harbor." He gave me a look of sadness. I patted his cheek and then mounted Oreo, on my own this time. I have gotten better at this, figuring out the necessary hand-eye coordination needed to get up there. Cal still kept his hands behind me, claiming that he would catch me before I fell.

"Gods, you're beautiful." I blushed.

"Get on your horse before I leave you here," I muttered before kicking Oreo into a gallop. I heard Cal curse through gritted teeth, and then the thundering of his horse speeding up to me. Encouraging Oreo to go faster as he rides up next to me. Teasing him, I wink at him and then nudge Oreo to move even faster. My hair flowed behind me, and I ducked several times to avoid low-hanging branches while Oreo jumped over fallen down trees. It's exciting and has been the most fun I have had in my entire pathetic life.

Looking over my shoulder, Cal nears, but I plan to beat him. To where? I have no clue but will keep going until Oreo stops on her own. Amid my teasing, I don't see what comes next until I am knocked off my horse, hitting the hard ground, and my breath caught.

"What the—" Coughing sharply, I feel the dust settle around me. Two large black boots stand on either side of my head.

"Hello, Princess." I don't recognize the voice. It sounded like a man. I struggled to my feet, but I couldn't move as he braced a knee over my sternum.

"Get the fuck off me," I scream as I try scratching and kicking at him.

"You have a dirty little mouth for a princess," he muttered, leaning down and licking the side of my face. Bile crept up my throat at the smell of rum and smoke.

"I'm not a princess." Where is Cal?

"You see, I don't believe you. Someone with deep pockets sent me to take you to them. They said you're the High Princess of the realm. And you match the portrait perfectly, although it doesn't do you justice."

Spitting in his face, I yell, "If you don't get off me, I am going to slit your throat."

"Don't make promises you can't keep, Princess. I love a feisty piece on my cock and a little birdie told me you are a virgin. Shall I find out?" He was vile and looked even more so. With missing teeth, the others yellow, and I don't think this man has ever bathed.

"Try it and I'll cut your cock off and feed it to you." He laughed at me and yet again, I'm insulted. He was heavier than he looked. His weight was pinning me down and there was nothing I could do.

"I was paid to bring you back alive, not a virgin, and you are just too mesmerizing for me to pass up. When I make you bleed, you will scream for more. Begging me not to stop until you finish all over me. Then, you will know that you wanted it.'' He started to reach for the tie at my waist, but before he could even loosen them, he was thrust off me.

Calian was standing over me with fire in those emerald eyes, beautiful black wings, like the ones I had seen on dragons, and his dual swords out. I got to my feet and didn't say a word. The man was getting back to his feet, looking for whatever it was that interrupted him.

"That's my princess," he said without an ounce of fear in his eyes. Even at the sight of Cal in his full form. Gods, he was beautiful, powerful, strong, and it made me want him more. Calian charged at the man, still standing his ground. He drew a sword and they engaged in a fight. Metal clashing with metal, the man was highly skilled, and even if he had been drinking, it didn't seem to have any effect on his fighting ability.

He even managed to knock one of Cal's blades out of his hands and I grew worried, but then remembered that Cal usually holds back when it comes to mortals. He likes to fight fair and although he is in his true form, due to the fire burning inside of him. The thought of this man trying to assault me and take me from him. No one has ever cared for me like that. Not even Alma and it hurts me to realize that if she absolutely loved and cared for me as this man did, she would've died trying to prevent my *Blood Oath*. To save me from *Her*.

Cal cut off the man's free hand, and I watched as his blood-curtailing screams filled the air as he fell to his knees, blood spraying onto the ground. The man dropped his other sword as Calian grabbed the bleeding limb and then put a ball of fire to it, cauterizing it to stop the bleeding. The man screamed until he went unconscious.

"What…" I stammered. He is powerful. I am both intimidated and aroused. What's wrong with me? Without him saying a word, I grabbed some rope from his horse, not knowing where Oreo went after I was knocked from her, and handed it to him. In the silence, he tied the man's wrist to his ankles like a hog over a fire. Looking at me, those two green flames in his eyes not dimming at all, he approached me.

"What did he do to you?" He wasn't gentle about his words, but demanding.

"Nothing," I whispered, not realizing how terrified I sounded. He reached out to cup my cheek and I flinched slightly, which made him upset.

"Don't fear me. I am true to my word, Chloe; I will not hurt you. Gods, please don't fear me," he pleaded, and I saw the fire in him start to cool. Stepping forward, I cupped his face, and then on my tiptoes, I kissed him.

"I'm not afraid of you. Thank you for saving me." He leaned down and kissed me deeper, wrapping me tightly in his embrace. I broke away slightly. "What are you going to do with him?"

"He touched you, tried to kidnap you, and someone paid him to do it. First, I am going to cut off his other hand for daring to put a hand on my woman. Second, after he has told me what I need to know, I'm cutting out that tongue for licking you." Every second those words passed between those lips, warmth spread to my belly and I felt the throb between my thighs ache harder for him. Gods, no one has ever cared for me this much. "Then, because he even dared to mention sticking his cock inside of you, I'm going to do just what you said you would."

"What's that?" I said breathlessly. I heard a feral growl come from his throat. I knew he understood what his words were doing to me.

"Cut it off and stuff it down his own throat. Make him choke on it until he dies from sucking it." Oh, gods.

Something is seriously wrong with me because the idea of him torturing him should scare the hell out of me, but it doesn't.

"Then what?" I asked, and I saw a feline smile come across that perfectly blood-spattered face. "You tell me, Chloe. What do you want to do? I mean, I can guess, but that would take the fun out of it," he smugly said.

Before I could answer him, the man, now our prisoner, stirred awake. "Hold that thought. I'm sure it has something to do with me." He winked.

The backside of those wings was breathtaking. Glistening dragon scales, bouncing off the rays of the High Sun, with a talon at each curved top and bottom. The urge to touch them was overpowering, but balling my hands into fists was slightly helping.

"Before I cut your other hand off and remove that filthy little tongue of yours, tell me who hired you to take her?" Cal's voice was hard and demanding.

"Fuck you," the man sputtered. Blood-coated drool spat with each spoken word.

"No thank you. That is reserved for her." He tilted his head in my direction.

"You're a fucking whore," the man said as he looked at me. That was the wrong thing to say in the presence of Calian.

"Cal," I warned, "if you cut out his tongue, he won't be able to answer us."

"Do you know what I am, mortal?" Cal asked, glaring at the man like he was his prey.

"An Ashana."

"Then you know what I am capable of." The man nodded. "So, you know how this will end then?"

"I am friends with the God of Death," the man said with a crooked smile.

"Well, the God of Death is my uncle, and when your filthy little soul leaves your body, he has a special place for rapists like you. And I assure you, it will be worse than what I'm going to do to you."

I swallowed hard, suppressing the fear I had for him. He is not going to hurt me, I know that, but the power illuminating from him was that of a god.

"Do what you will. I've been tortured worse. You won't get a word out of me." I heard a sigh come from Cal and just before he went to cut out the man's tongue, I didn't have time to stop him.

Screaming. That wouldn't stop until tears were rolling down the man's face. Calian held the pink thing up to his eyes, then turned it to ash in his hands. Touching the man's head, he closed his eyes, and I realized now what he was doing.

"Queen Iliana." Calian snarled the queen's name. From the betrayal of my parents, Alma, Prince Eli, Queen Iliana, every lie that I was ever told, it all burned through me, and before I knew what I was doing, my fists were connecting with his jaw. I beat him until Cal lifted me off him.

"Now you're hurting yourself more than you are him," he snapped.

"I don't give a fuck," I said, crying. Cal turned me toward him. I almost punched him, but he was faster, grabbing me by the wrist, softly, but keeping control.

"Look at me, Chloe." My name. He said my name. "Damn it, open your eyes."

Were they closed? They fluttered open and the image of betrayal washed away, replaced by Cal. My kidnapper, savior, protector, friend, and lover.

"I'm sorry," I said. He let go of my wrist, brushed the hairs out of my face, before kissing me.

"You have nothing to apologize for." He calmed me, soothed me, and I wanted to feel that love he so desperately wanted to give me. I craved it. I needed him. So, I took what I wanted. Pulling him onto me, I kissed him deeply, my tongue parting his lips as I took control. One of my hands gripped the back of his hair and the other trailed down his body, landing on his bulging length. He grunted my name.

Hoisting me into the air, I wrapped my legs around him as he laid me gently on the grass. Kissing my lips, my neck scraping his sharp teeth across it. He was still above me.

"I need to take care of him first," he whispered against my lips.

"Okay," I replied, stuffing my hand down his

pants, stroking his length once, and smiling as he growled. “Hurry back.”

He scrambled to his feet, then I heard the slice of the man’s neck. Cal was done playing the game, and now he was ready for me. He straddled me, leaning down to kiss me. “Are you sure?”

“I’ve never been surer in my entire life.” I ran my fingers through his silky hair, across his shoulders, sitting forward slightly so I could reach the inside of his wings, and brushed them. They were hard like a muscle, but smooth and alluring. He shuttered at my touch. “Make love to me, Cal.”

That was the permission he needed. He kissed me again, wrapping an arm tightly around my waist and then the nape of my neck. His hands trailed my curves and then under my tunic. Breaking away from me so he could pull it off me. My hands fell to cover my scars, but he moved them out of the way, leaning down, kissing them, worshiping the strength that I had to endure it and survive. His mouth trailed to my breeches, and he pulled them and my undergarments off with ease.

I lay exposed, the grass itchy on my rear, but before he could place his head between my thighs, I said, “We need a bedroll.” I sighed.

“As you wish, Princess.” He smirked, standing and I saw just how badly he wanted me, and it made me wet with desire for him. He came back and laid the bedroll on the ground, then lifted me into his arms with ease, and set me gently down. He pulled his tunic off, and I gasped at how perfect his body was. Basking in the thought of it being all mine.

“You’re mine,” I said as I touched right over his

heart. "And I'm yours."

When I spoke those words, he tore his breeches and my bra off, and then I felt him stopping right outside my entrance.

"Do you know what this means?" he asked.

"Yes." I scooted closer to him, begging him to enter.

"Chloe, if we do this, there is no severing the *Blood Oath*. You understand that you will be mine forever. There will be no one else." I didn't answer him with words, but gripped his rear and plunged him inside of me. Screaming at the pain, not realizing how small I was compared to him. He let out a roar. "Fuck, Chloe."

He didn't move, as small tears fell from my eyes. He kissed them and licked them. "I'm sorry."

"Don't be. I can handle it," I said, and he smiled at me.

"I know but I want this to be pleasurable."

"If you don't start, I will take over."

He leaned down and kissed me, his hips rolling, moving in and out at a slow pace, letting me get used to feeling him.

"Faster," I moaned, and he obliged. My legs wrap tightly around him. This was better than those ladies from the brothel explained it. With each thrust, he went faster, harder, plunging in and out of me until I was soaking wet. I never had an orgasm before, but I felt something, pressure building inside of me, and I released it with a scream of his name on my lips. Then, when I thought it couldn't get any better, he placed his thumb on my clit and circled it.

"Cal," I moaned. It came again, and he was still going. It was his turn to pump inside of me. With my arms wrapped around the nape of his neck, I pulled him down to me so I could kiss him deeply. Then, with some unknown force, we rolled, and he was on his back, plunging deeper inside of me.

"Gods," he rasped.

And I responded by rolling my hips like I was shown, riding him, then I played with myself, rubbing my clit and nipple. "You aren't faking it, are you?"

"No," I yelled as another release left me shuttering on top of him. He gripped my hips, thrusting inside of me. "Come for me."

"As you wish, Princess." He roared as he pumped his seed inside of me, pulsating and thrusting through it. His voice was so loud the birds fluttered from the trees. And we stilled, trying to catch our breath, bodies sheened with sweat. Sitting up, him still inside of me, he kissed me so softly. Like I imagined a lover would, and that was what we were now. "Hold out your palm. The one you said the oath with."

I did, and so did he. What I saw happening to our palms was amazing. A red dragon was imprinted on my palm with a circle of roses dancing around it. Looking over at him, it matched, solidifying our bond and oath to one another forever.

"Is this what I think it means?" I asked. Still in awe of the new brand.

"It means,"—he started tilting my chin up so I could be at eye level with him— "It means that we are one. You're mine for all eternity and I'm yours. Nothing, not even death can break our bond. And that symbol, the red dragon, is me because my father was the god of dragons, and those roses stand for you. For your family crest."

"I hate flowers."

"Why do you hate flowers?" he asked, his fingers interlacing with mine.

"Because my mother named me after one and it represents all the bad in my life," I answered honestly. For the first time, it felt natural.

He smiled at me.

"Well, now you have a new crest. One that includes me. *Dragon & Rose*."

"Don't you mean *Rose & Dragon*?" I corrected.

"Whatever you say, my mate." He kissed my nose. We were still together, and he didn't soften the entire time. When I moved, he twitched inside of me. "Round two?" He grinned.

"I don't know if I can handle it. Plus, it has passed mid-day and I feel like your roar was heard throughout the entire realm. Curious people will start to wonder where it came from, and I would like to keep my naked body away from others. Don't need you cutting out innocent eyes." I kissed him gently. "My mate."

"As you wish, Princess." He kissed me deeper and out of instinct, my hips started moving again. "If you don't stop, then I'm not responsible for what other people see." Gods, how could I want him again so soon? "Fly," I ordered, and kissed him deeper.

"What?"

It shocked me as much as him, but something about being up there, with him in control of our lives, had me on the verge of release.

"Take me in the air and let me ride you. They won't see, and I want you."

He smirked. "I've never." He paused and I stilled. I wasn't his first and I know that, but it still hurt. Without another word, we shot to the skies, with him still inside of me. Once we were high enough, he turned so his back was to the ground. "As you wish."

I rode him until we were both shuttering again. I wasn't afraid of being that high because my mind was only on pleasing him. When we finally caught our breaths, he pulled out of me, our releases leaking down my legs, and held me tight.

"Don't look down," he said. "You're safe with me."

"I know." He looked down, ensuring there was no one there when we landed, and slowly descended. My legs were wobbly, and he held me until I got my balance. "Thank you."

"Keep looking at me like that and we will never leave this forest," he said as my eyes trailed his body, taking in the full beauty of him. Memorizing him because now, he was imprinted not just on my hand, but in my heart.

And that was dangerous.

After using rags to clean ourselves, we dressed, and he insisted on him doing it. However, I knew if I let him anywhere near me, I wouldn't put my clothes back on. Cal found Oreo while I packed the bedroll.

"Where was she?" I asked while petting her mane.

"Just a few yards away, grazing in the grass." As he hoisted me up, I winced when my sex hit the saddle. "You'll get used to it."

"Easy for you to say."

"You could ride side-saddle," he suggested.

"I barely know how to ride normally. How do you expect me to do that?"

"Ride with me. Tuck your rear between my legs,

while your legs hang over the side, and I wrap my arm tightly around your waist. There may be foreplay involved but that makes it more fun." He winked.

"As tempting as that sounds, Cal, I'm fine." Then I gestured for him to come closer. I leaned down, and fisted the front of his tunic, pulling him into me. "Save that thought for later, however. We still have to save the world."

"Shame I have to share you." He kissed me softly before going to mount his horse. I was surprised Oreo didn't run away at the sound of Cal's roar. But the horse knew we were mating and was not afraid. Gods. Did I just say mated? I chuckled, and Cal looked at me.

"Get out of my head," I said.

"It's called sex, love. We aren't animals."

What an ass.

Chapter Thirteen

We made it to Helm's Harbor just after the White Sun was rising. The darkness offered us some cover, making it harder for anyone to recognize us. The Queen of Shuang put a price on my capture. No doubt about the Treaty being violated with my parents' murder and my disappearance. I thought Alma would've sent word to try and keep the peace, but something unsettling came into mind.

The Harbor smelled of sea and fish. The salty air was cooler here and I welcomed it. At night, there wasn't much to look at. There were so few torches lit that I could barely make out the rooftops of buildings. Cal, on the other hand, could see in the dark. Bastard.

"The Inn is over here." He gestured and I followed. We left the horses strapped to a post, with some other livestock. There was hay and water. Making it clear that this was for patrons only planning to stay a short while.

As we entered, the lobby was in a fit of music and games. There were wooden tables filled with drinks, food, cards, and patrons. All either talking, eating, gambling, or drinking. The bar wench waved us over. Cal had hidden his wings before we left the forest. Appearing just like any other mortal.

"What can I get you?" the barkeep asked, and her eyes cut right to Cal. Soaking in his body from head to toe. She leaned over, pushing her cleavage out, and a surge of anger hit me. Cal gripped my wrist tightly before I raised my dagger to the woman's throat.

Easy, Princess, he said inside my head. I looked at him, confused. *It's part of our bond. I'll explain later.*

"You can have me if you want. What will your sister be having?" She didn't even acknowledge me. *Let me handle this,* I said with a hint of anger.

As you wish, Princess. But play nice, I would like to sleep in a bed tonight. I felt a soft caress with those words. As Cal sat, I jumped up, straddling him, taking in his surprise as I shoved my tongue down his throat. Grabbing one of his hands, I placed it on my breast and squeezed, directing his other hand on my rear. Breaking away, I saw that lust in those emerald eyes and felt his cock hardening under me. Still, on top of him, I looked at the barkeep.

"We would like one room, two drinks, and two plates of your best food," I cheekily said as I gleamed at the shock on her face. She was just as bewildered as Cal. "I can pay, of course."

I reached down, gripping Cal's ever-hardening cock, and said, "Oops, that's not the coin purse." I forced a giggle, feeling slightly foolish, but it was preferable to gouging her eyes out. Gods, I never wanted to hurt someone so bad. I was very possessive of him, and I wanted everyone to know.

After I placed a few pieces of coin on the bar, she cleared her throat, saying, "Coming right up."

As she turned, I felt Cal's grip on me tighten and I leaned forward. "Was that nice enough for you, my love?"

"I'm going to—" He was cut off by the abrupt slamming of our drinks and plates.

"Take it upstairs. There will be no fucking on my bar or in my lobby." She was angry, and I smiled.

"Thank you. But–" She paused, and I got down from Cal, raising my dagger ever so slightly. I gestured for her to lean forward, and she was big enough to hide where I placed my dagger right on that pulsating vein on the side of her neck. "He is mine. Next time I see those little eyes check him out, I am cutting them out. Understand?"

"I'm sorry," she stammered, nearly crying.

"Good. And one more thing—if I want to fuck him on your bar, then that is what I'm going to do because no one tells me what to do. Not even him." I was speaking low enough for only her to hear. "Be a good little wench and see your patrons."

I let her go, turning to Cal. His face was taut with restraint, and he was adjusting himself again. Just because I was enjoying this newfound feeling of power and control, I sat on his lap the entire time we ate. Teasing him as I rolled my hips painfully slowly.

Why do you tease me so, Princess? he asked.

Because it is so much fun. And haven't I told you to stop calling me that? I added pressure to my next roll, and he coughed on his drink as he twitched under me.

As you wish, Chloe. Or do you like it when I say, my love. Wrapping his arms around me, his hands cupping my front, he whispers in my ear, "My love."

"I don't think we are getting any sleep tonight," I responded, leaning back into him.

"Hmm." He hummed in my ear, nipping my ear. "Ready for bed, my love?"

I nodded. He lifted me, cradling me, not caring about the cat-calling, and hollering from the drunk crowd as he carried me up the two flights of stairs, and then into our room. Gently, he placed me on the edge of the bed.

It was a small room, with just a bed and then a door leading to a bathing chamber. The mattress was small and sat on a wooden frame. I chuckled at the thought of breaking it tonight, and that must have gone to Cal because he pounced on me. The bed made a loud creaking noise and we both laughed. "Do you want to sleep tonight?"

"I'm exhausted," I answered.

"Then I shall sleep on the floor." He started to get off me. I pulled him back onto me, kissing him. "Don't, you dare. We can sleep together without losing control."

He smirked. "Chloe, if I have you in my arms, on a bed, there is no way that I'm not making you wet. Whether it is with my mouth, my fingers, or my cock. I have little control when that head takes over." I chuckled and flushed at it. "You're too damned beautiful and I know since we solidified the oath, you have started feeling just as crazy as I have. I'm not so sure you could resist me."

"Someone's feeling a bit egotistical," I murmured, but he was right. Gods, I wanted him to do all those things to me and more. "Cal?"

"Tell me what you want, and it is yours." I knew that was true. If I said no, he would restrain himself. And if I said yes, he would take me over and control me. I was so tired from everything, and I needed sleep, but the damn bond was driving me crazy for him.

"Wash me." The words came out smooth and seductive.

“As you wish.” He kissed me before carrying me to the bath. I let him undress me, trailing my body with kisses, and I knew we were not sleeping. Not yet.

The bath filled with warm water, and it was barely big enough for the both of us, but we stood as he washed me, and then I returned the favor. Before leaving the bath, he sat down, and I straddled him, sliding him into me, slowly. His head threw back as he moaned and with my first hip roll, my back arched, and his mouth clamped down on my breast. Sucking and nipping at me.

“Cal” I gasped.

“My love,” he rasped, and I kept my pace. I didn’t want it to be fast. I wanted to make love to him and that is what I did. Our bodies became one, full of passion, desire, and I felt my soul connecting with his. I didn’t say the words and neither did he. It scared me. I didn’t know if I should say them, but when our releases came, it slipped out.

“I love you.” And then I cried.

The bathwater turned cold, and my knees were aching from rubbing against the bottom. I tried to get up, but he held me tight and then stood. The water dripped from us as my legs fell loosely. I couldn’t feel the floor because he held me at an angle, still inside of me. Our eyes locked as he walked us to the bed. Laying me gently down, the sheets soaking with our wetness. “Cal.”

He silenced me with a kiss, and I felt it.

Then he said it. “I love you too.”

He made love to me until we fell asleep in each other’s arms. His warmth washed over me. He tucked his wing over us, and I played with it until my eyes finally shut.

Chapter Fourteen

When I awoke, Cal was swirling fingers above my navel, and his hardness pressed to my rear.

"Good morning, my mate," he said as he kissed me sweetly. Rolling over, I kissed him back, running a hand through his hair and down his body, stopping right at his hip.

"Cal," I started, "I know last night we were in the heat of the moment when we said,"—I cleared my throat— "those words, and I understand if—"

He shut me up again by getting on top of me, knocking my knees to the side, and thrusting inside of me while kissing me deeply. *Oh, gods.* He thrusts until we both come. The bed didn't break, thank the gods. Then, when he pulled out of me, I slapped him across the face.

"Bastard," I said.

"You loved it."

"Still, I wasn't ready." I lied. I had a sex dream about him, and it made me wet.

"I love you, Chloe. I meant every word and I hate that you doubt it because you were hurt and betrayed by your parents who have said it to you before." He paused. Still hovering over me. "You have my heart, my body, my soul. It has been yours since before we made the *Blood Oath*, and it will be for all eternity. I'm yours."

"I love you, too." He smiled at me, and it was so real, I smiled back. Before he could take me again, I informed him we needed to get down to the docks and seek a captain out to journey to the other side of the world. Of course, he protested.

"We can't stay in bed all day. We will never leave. Besides, as much as I want you, repeatedly, I'm sore and need a break."

"As you wish Pr—" I glared at him. "Chloe." He kissed my nose, rose, and we cleaned up, got dressed, and headed down to the lobby. It was filled with patrons again, and the smell of meat filled my nose, making my stomach growl with hunger. We walked hand in hand to the bar, a different bar wench this time. She was blonde, with blue eyes and pale skin. She is smaller than the other one and, without us saying a word, she placed two hot plates in front of us.

I went to scarf it down, but Cal stopped me. Placing his hands over the food and whispering some words I didn't understand.

"It's safe."

"What?" I asked.

"It isn't poisoned," he answered.

"Your powers can detect poison too?"

"You don't know the extent of my powers yet, love." He kissed my cheek before eating. "But no, they can't."

"Smartass."

"You are the one that scared off the bar wench last night." We laughed and continued to talk through breakfast.

I paid the bar wench, and we walked outside. Blinking, as my eyes adjusted to the light, we discovered our horses were missing.

"Someone stole our horses? Weren't the gems in our bags?" I asked, whispering.

"No." He pulled me to the side of the inn, looking around to ensure no one was watching, and pulled them out of his breeches pocket."You don't think I would let something so important be left unsupervised, do you?"

"I need to work on my situational awareness skills," I said. "But what about the map?"

"We don't need a map." Then he tapped on his temple while he said, "I memorized the locations, and I'm sure I can steer a ship in the direction we need to go."

"Have you ever sailed one before?" I asked. Genuinely curious. He smiled at me.

"Of course, love. When you are as old as me, you do a lot of things mortals can only dream of." I forgot he was older than me.

"Just how old are you again? I don't remember asking."

He kissed me softly before answering, "Two-hundred and twenty-eight. Don't I look amazing?" Did he ever!

"Come on handsome, we need to get going." As I walked past him, he smacked my rear, making me yelp and I heard a chuckle come out of him.

"I will pay you back for that."

"Looking forward to it."

The docks were buzzing with a large crowd. Cal had stolen, I mean, borrowed a cape to hide me from wandering eyes, as we walked through the masses. I wasn't sure who we needed to speak to, but Cal seemed like he did, so I followed.

Stopping at the end of the pier, a beautiful ship from aft to bow, the thick wood was delicately crafted with each board shaping its hull. The three erect posts, the one in the middle with the mainsail, slightly taller than the rest, were connected by a rope and pulley system. Used for controlling the speed of the ship. The sails were tucked away on their post, and the deck was busy with workers.

"Is this your first time seeing a pirate ship?" he asked, and I flinched, forgetting he was next to me.

"No," I said, then corrected myself. "I mean, I read about them in historical text. Aren't they dangerous?"

"Are you afraid?" he teased.

"There are few things I am afraid of in this world, and pirates are not one of them," I firmly said.

"Calian, is that you?" A thunderous voice came from the vessel. "Come here, you big oaf."

A large man with a thick black beard covering down to his chest, wearing a three-point black hat, and an eye patch over his right eye, walked toward us.

"Rob, you crazy fat bastard." They embraced each other like I imagined brothers would. Cal seemed closer to this man than he ever was with Eli. "How have you been, brother?"

I was mistaken. They are closer than he ever was with Eli.

"Tell me that pretty little lass is with you?" I saw the pirate's chocolate eyes zero in on me and I walked over to them.

"Rob, was it? My name is Chloe." He took off his hat and gave me a bow, kissing the top of my out-reached hand. "Manners. Well, that makes one of you."

I shot playful eyes at Cal. He leaned over,

whispering in my ear. "Forgive me, love." Pressed a kiss on my cheek. I ignored him as I stepped between him and Rob.

"Tell me, Rob, is that your ship?" I asked, smiling as I felt Cal brushing against my backside.

"Isn't she a beaut? Names Petunia." Another flower. Can I ever be rid of them?

"And you're the captain?"

"I sure hope so. There is not a lad in this entire realm that can sail Petunia. She needs to be handled with strong hands."

"Can you teach me?" I asked, stepping to the side of Rob as we started walking. Ignoring Cal as he did to me when Rob called out to him.

"Forgive me, lass, but it's bad luck to have a woman aboard a ship. Brings bad omens from the gods." I scrunch my nose up. He stopped in his tracks, and I knew he was watching as I marched right up the plank and onto the deck of the ship. His deckhands stopped mid-work to gawk at me. "I like her."

"You made a mistake, brother." I overheard Cal say. I couldn't hear this well before. It was strange but the less tense I was, the more my senses started to clear up.

"What do you mean?" I heard Rob ask.

"She will learn how to sail whether you teach her or not. So, I suggest to you, if you don't want to see your precious Petunia at the bottom of the Great Sea, oblige her." I smirked and was in awe because Cal knows me so well already.

"Who is she?" My face went taut as I waited for him to answer. Because I wasn't sure what I was anymore.

"She is the one that controls my heart. My mate." My heart skipped a beat. I felt love radiating down our bond. "Give her what she wants, and you will be happy."

"Does that work for you, brother?" I turned my head sharply to them. Making sure he knows I was listening.

"Every damned time." Smart man.

"Alrighty, lass, I'll teach you," I heard Rob shout.

"Rob," Cal started, and I suddenly became nervous because I knew what he was about to say. "I need a favor."

"Sounds serious."

"It is." Then Cal and Rob stepped out of earshot as they murmured together. I gave up trying to listen and then went to the helm. The crew went back to work, and I just couldn't get over how real this all was. I only ever dreamed about ships and pirates. I heard horrible things about them, but of course, everything Mother said to me was a lie. So, my new outlook on life included forming my own observations about things.

It started with Cal, and I intend to continue for the rest of my days. Running my fingers along the wood, it was smooth, except for minor nicks from what I can only assume were caused by weather damage or fights up on deck. There were two upper decks. One for the helm and on the other for the tether for the anchor. There were stairs on either side of the raised decks that led to the lower level where I entered the ship.

Walking down it, I veered over to the right, and I saw a set of black doors leading to the Captain's quarters. There were no doors on the other side of the ship, just an opening that most likely led to lower levels. Where the crew slept, and the kitchen would be.

"You like what you see?" I heard Rob say from behind me. I turned toward him and Cal. He was standing so far away from me; I was not used to it since we became one.

"Yes. It is more than what the books show," I said as I approached them.

"I will set sail and, when it's safe to do so, I will teach you how to captain a ship. But first, we three need to talk," he said under his breath. "First mate," he yelled.

A scrawny-looking man with blonde hair and a cloth tied around his head came up to us. Not what I was expecting a first mate to look like. He wore all black, matching Rob's wardrobe, but he was skinny to Rob's fat.

"Set sail," he commanded.

"What is our heading?" the first mate asked.

"East." With that, the first mate started yelling orders and Rob ushered us through those black doors, locking them not to be disturbed.

Inside, there was a round table with the world map and trinkets all spread out. A large window graced the back wall just above a smaller desk with parchments and coin purses. On the right side, there was a bed big enough for Rob to sleep on and nothing else. To the left was a cabinet full of rum. Not what I expected a Captain's quarters to be, but I appreciated how simple it was.

"Sit." I heard Rob order and I raised a brow at him. "Please."

"Since you asked so nicely." Calian pulled out a chair, but I ignored it and pulled out my own, earning a chuckle from Rob.

"You are something else, Princess."

I glared at him and then at my mate. "You told him who I was?"

"Rob is a friend, he can be trusted."

"He is *your* friend."

"And I'm yours. You trust me, don't you?" I saw concern in his eyes.

"Yes," I said.

Then we heard Rob clear his throat.

"Well don't stop on my account. I love a good show." Sick. Men are such pigs. But am I any better? Would knife play be fun during sex?

"Since Calian has informed you of our mission, I need to know why?" I spoke.

"Why what?" Rob asked.

"Why did you agree to help us so willingly?"

"Cal's been like a brother to me for over ten years. Has not aged a day, the Ashana bastard. Plus, if what he says is true, which I believe him to be, then I want to help save the world from darkness. If I am a slave, how will I sail the seas? Fuck who I want when I want. I like control."

"Okay. Have you ever sailed to the other side of the sea?" I asked. Then Cal placed a hand on my thigh. Caressing it up and up, I let my legs fall open. No doubt this was him punishing me for ignoring him. He cupped me and squeezed, making me jump a little. Rob ignored it as he continued about the course of action and everything Cal told him. Which was everything except about us, but that was clear to any with eyes.

"Cal," Rob started, "let the lass go so she can pay attention, then when I leave, you can fuck her till your heart's content." Gods, how did he know? Right, I started making noises and squirming.

"Sorry, Rob. She is just so damned irresistible, and the *Blood Oath* bond is so damned powerful." Cal didn't release his touch. He kept going, gods, he wanted me to come right in my knickers.

"How long?" Rob asked.

"Two days ago," Cal said. I was on the verge of pouncing. Then Cal stopped, leaning into my ear, and whispered, "Not yet."

Bastard.

I stomped my foot down hard on him and he released his hold on me. I stood. "If you'll excuse me, Rob, where is your chamber pot?"

He chuckled, pointing over to a door that led to a bathing chamber.

"Over there, lass. Don't be too loud or I might join you."

I glared at them both, but Cal's smile turned to fire at the thought of Rob joining me, and it gave me a wicked thought. Instead of going to the bathing chamber to finish what Cal started, I headed toward Rob. Prowling toward him, my eyes never left Cal's. He knew exactly what I was going to do. So did Rob because he got to his feet.

"Don't put me in the middle of this, lass. I know what happens when a *Blood Oath* is solidified. Nope, you are beautiful but not worth losing my life. Besides, Cal was teasing. I'm sure he will pay for it later, just don't involve me." He put his hands up and started for the door.

Guilt and shame washed that arousal right out of me. God's, what is wrong with me? "Rob, I'm sorry.

Please continue. We need to discuss business. Cal and I will behave. Won't we, Cal?" I said glaring at him.

"As you wish, my love." I sat back down, closer to Rob and far away from those sinful hands of Cal's.

"When we reach the docks outside Orion, I will take a crew and ask around about their queen. Hopefully, seeking an audience with her won't prove difficult."

"What's it like over there?" I asked.

"It's,"—he appeared to choose the right words—"an entirely different world. They speak in a funny dialect that is difficult to understand, but they are friendly."

"How long has it been since your last trip?' I asked.

"About a month. I first discovered it about two months ago when we were in our usual fishing spot on the east side and then suddenly it just appeared. A small harbor full of people." How is that possible? "It must have been magic because, in all my years sailing this sea, that harbor was never there until two months ago."

"Like it was invisible or shielded from us?" I asked and then looked over to Cal, who was looking at me with lust in his eyes? Not paying attention to a word we were saying. "Cal, focus, dear. Do the gods possess that kind of power?"

"What?" He snapped out of his stupor. "I don't know but maybe. I wouldn't put it past them."

"What god do you know can do that?" Rob asked. Cal's eyes were on my chest. "He isn't listening to a word we are saying. You broke him, lass."

"Sorry, Rob, once my other head takes over…well, you know how it is."

"That I do." Rob got to his feet. "Get it out of your system. Then we can talk."

"No, Cal can leave, and we can talk," I stated. Cal smirked at me.

"Would you like that?" Cal asked. "Knowing I'm in there thinking about you, pumping me off with my hand. Imagine it was your mouth."

"Get out." I was pissed. Gods, he cannot control a damn thing. "Now."

I heard a whistle from Rob, stopping mid-way while my glare shot to him.

"Damn you, Cal, now she's pissed at me." Without another word, Rob unlocked the doors and left, locking us in.

"Now look at what you did," I yelled, rising, ire fueling me. "You can't control that cock long enough for us to create a plan."

He prowled toward me as I continued to reprimand him. Calling him out for being immature, my words started to trail off as he reached me. Toe to toe, I turn to walk away from him, but a hand gripped the back of my neck. I'm turned forcefully toward him, his lips crashing onto mine. Heat floods me and I try to resist him, but I fail as I'm hoisted up onto the table, my breeches ripped from me. I did the same to his. I don't have time to prepare as he thrust into me, making me scream. He was in control, and I let him remain in control as our release came loud and fast.

Panting, our foreheads touching, he kissed me. "Don't ignore me again. I can't handle it."

"I'm sorry, my love. It won't happen again."

"I love you." He smiled, kissed me hard, and then reciprocated his feelings.

Chapter Fifteen

I never thought being aboard a ship would make me so sick. I've been chewing on an herb that Rob gave me to help with what he called "sea-sickness," but it just made me stay in bed. Preventing me from learning how to captain and sail the ship. Cal came in to check on me now and then. Holding my hair back as I vomited into the chamber pot, giving me water, and trying to get me to eat something.

"You need to eat, my love. It has been two days."

Two days already? Gods, how did I lose track of time? I know how—I have been sleeping because I am too weak to do anything else.

"Are we almost there?" I could hear the fatigue coating my voice.

"Rob says another day, as long as we don't run into a storm." Cal patted a damp cloth on my sweating head. I've never been sick before. Even during my monthly bleed. All that included was stomach pain and mood swings, which also meant multiple lessons with Mother. I should just let her go. She is not a part of my life anymore, or anyone is, for that matter. She is dead, so I need to stop remembering her.

Cal has taken better care of me these past couple of days and weeks than anyone else in my entire life. He doesn't judge, doesn't question, he simply just cares. His love for me has been proven repeatedly, not with just words, but with his actions. I know it started badly, but, gods, I cannot help what I feel for him. Since we solidified the *Blood Oath*, since he agreed to that commitment, knowing what it meant for him too, I cannot help but fall deeper in love with him.

"I love you," I said.

"I love you too, Chloe." Leaning down, he kissed my cheek, then my nose, then my lips. "Hurry up and get better. I have missed you terribly."

"I will get better once I can get off this ship and back on land," I snapped. The nerve of him to ask me that when he has seen my illness.

"Land ho. Land ho." A loud knock came after.

"Put it back in your pants, boy. We will be docking soon," Rob yelled, and we both chuckled.

"Jealousy is an unbecoming trait, my friend," Cal called back. "You don't have to get dressed if you don't want to, love."

"You want me to walk around naked? So all those lonely men up there can gawk at me?"

He snorted. "On second thought, no, because then I would have to kill them all." I kissed him softly.

"Come on, I need to get off this ship before I die of sea-sickness." Cal chuckled.

I know Rob tried to describe this world, but he didn't do it justice. I have never seen a sky bluer than the one above me; the High Sun's rays beaming down upon the harbor before me. Formed on the eastern side of a field, the port is home to buccaneers and foreign travelers. Which would include us. With blackwood rooftops, oakwood walls, and swarms of tradesmen, this place had an otherworldly atmosphere.

The main attraction was the large marketplace,

busy with patrons shouting at one another, some even throwing fish at one another.

"What did you get today, mate?" I heard one patron ask another.

"Catfish and eel." Their dialect was strange, and I had to strain my ears to make out what they were saying. What was a catfish or eel? I only ever eat herring. Before I got the chance to ask, we were ushered into a building. A long wooden bar, stretching from one wall to the next, was occupied by twenty or so men. Three bar wenches working on their drinks or food. It was a massive hall, reminding me of the banquet hall back home. There were round tables and chairs spread throughout, all occupied with drinks, cards, food, and gossip.

"What are we doing here?" I whispered in Cal's ear.

"We need a place to stay, get information, and food. Especially food since you barely ate on the entire trip here." He brushed a soft kiss on my head, interlacing his fingers with mine. We followed Rob to the front. A woman with olive skin, honey-colored hair like mine, and bright green eyes, dressed in a simple brown dress, approached us.

"What can I get you?"

Before I could speak, Rob took point. "We are travelers and would like to seek an audience with your queen." Straightforward and to the point. Gods, I hope Rob didn't just ruin things. I looked at the bar wench, who didn't appear to be bothered by Rob's question at all.

"All right. Well, you head west, past Sumter, and you land right in Orion Fortress. It is about a three-day ride from here. If you hit snow, you've gone too far." She so easily gave that information up to strangers. Did these people have no threats? Did the Dark Wizard not target them? The Cypress Grove Queen said their queen has two stones. Could she have been mistaken?

"Do you have any rooms for the evening?" Rob sounded so proper—it was hard to believe he was captain of a pirate ship.

"We have two. That will be six gold coins for each." We forgot about the money. Cal only had money from our land. I am sure they would not accept it here. Before I could speak, Rob laid out twelve gold coins and the bar wench accepted them without any questions.

Our room was much more lavish than I expected, which told me this world had more money. A porcelain tub, large enough for two, was central in the bathing chamber with a matching sink and mirror. A large canopy bed was set in the center of the back wall, lined with pearl white sheets and not one, not two, but four pillows. A crimson settee decorated the front of a stone fireplace made of quartz. The floors matched the beautiful colors of the quartz.

"This is…" I paused, looking around like a wide-eyed fool.

"Beautiful. Unexpected." Cal finished for me. His arms wrapped around my waist. My back to his chest. "Just like you, my love."

"You are too sweet, Cal." His lips brushed the crick of my neck, sending heat through my body. "Behave," I said.

"Do you want me to?" he teased. "You know what I want to do to you here?"Gods, I could only imagine but I was too hungry for sex. Too weak. I pulled from his arms.

"Later. I am famished and we need to focus on the mission." I heard a groan of disappointment come from him. "You have me for all eternity, remember?"

"Right," he answered, acting as if he somehow forgot.

Rob met us back down in the lobby, holding a table for us.

"What's this?" I asked as we sat down. Over the top was a large parchment. It looked like a map, but something was off. There were four quadrants, marking off the entire map.

"Four months ago, there was a large battle fought here. They haven't updated the maps since."

"What are you talking about? This place acts as if it has no threats," I asked.

Rob cleared his throat, leaning in, and whispered, "I spoke to a couple of the locals, and they told me quite a bit about this world. There was a powerful emperor that put a plan in place for the Kingdoms of Orion and Zoldir to go to war with one another.

"The worlds were divided by a magical barrier set forth by him after the Dragon Wars. Once the princess, now queen, and her kid sister found the lord, the emperor's plan went into action. He sent off these dark creatures known as the Drakere to kidnap the lord and bring him to the dark place of the Hallow Realm. There, the lord had to stand trial for the crimes of his greatest grandfather. He was rescued by this elf."

"Elves? Thought they were extinct with the dragons?" I said.

"According to the locals, they are. They are from a

land called Dalaria, and they aided their princess, now queen, with the defeat of the Zoldirian army and brought peace to the realm. The barrier fell, Zoldir was destroyed, and now the Orion's and Zoldirians live in harmony."

"What about the Dragonheart?" I asked.

"I didn't ask. I figure he would mention it if it were told. I don't think their queen would want the people to know she owned powerful elements," Rob said before taking a swig of ale.

"What's the plan?" I asked.

"Well, I say we go to the queen. You talk with her, royal lass to royal lass, go from there," Rob suggested. I looked over at Cal. His face was taut, and I could tell it was because he was thinking about everything Rob just said.

"Cal?" I squeezed his hand.

"We are foreigners in this land. We don't know whether this queen is a tyrant or not. I know the harbor is full of warmth and appears to be flourishing, but what about the rest of the kingdom? I can't put you in any danger."

"You're an idiot." My anger was swelling inside me. "This isn't about me; it is about the entire realm. We have to release the stones before the Supreme Jarhead Dark Wizard guy gets them and enslaves everyone."

"It *is* about you. I can't lose you." With that, I smacked him across his face, the pain and heat going from me to him.

"You can stay here. Rob and I will see the queen." I got to my feet and left the tavern. Walking out onto the busy streets, the High Sun was down for the evening, and the White Sun took its spot in the dark sky. Cal was being overprotective and over-possessive. I must put my people first and so does he. But what if he is right? What if I entrap myself when we go meet the queen? This town doesn't seem to be ruled by a tyrant murderer, but it could be a facade to what lies beyond those treetops.

"Hello, pretty lady." The smell of alcohol hit my nose before I saw where it came from. "What's a pretty thing like you doing out here all alone?"

"Back off," I spat out. I still couldn't see where the voice was coming from, so I kept moving, but I was stopped suddenly when an arm wrapped around my waist, and my wrists were thrust behind my back."Get your fucking hands off me."

"Such a foul, pretty mouth. One to fill my cock with." There were three men from what I could tell. One pinning my arms behind my back, another in front of me, and the third moved to face me.

"Get your vile hands off me before I cut them off."

"Keep talking dirty to me, lass, and I won't make this fun. And it can be fun. Have you ever taken three cocks at once before?" He leaned in, sniffing my skin like it was a flower and then licking it. "No, you taste like a virgin."

Dumb and dead.

Before I was taken by them, I heard a loud, feral growl. Then a scream of pain from one of the men.

"What is that thing?" I still didn't move. Didn't believe he was here, even as he tore out the hearts of the three men with his hands. His beautiful black wings spread wide, that deep feral growl that made me wet between my thighs. Nothing those three could ever get from me.

"She's mine. You touched her and now, I eat your hearts." He did just that. Ripping each of their hearts from their chest and taking large chunks out of them. They all dropped dead, and when he was done, he prowled toward me.

Those dark green eyes were two burning bright flames. Blood dripped down his chin, neck, and down to his bronze chest. It was only then I realized he didn't have a tunic on.

I nearly fell, but he caught me, wrapping me tightly in his arms.

"What did they do?" He was angry.

"Nothing." My palm burned with that lie.

"Don't lie to me, Clover." He wasn't just angry at them but at me.

"They didn't stick their cocks in me if that's what you worried about." I shouldn't have said it the way I did, with sarcasm and frustration. Truth was, he saved me again. He didn't say anything, just picked up, and then took to the skies.

It was cold, but the warmth of his body shielded me from it. "You saved me."

"I heard you. Saw what they were doing to you. I shouldn't have let you go out alone." He was angry at himself. Cupping his cheek, his bright green eyes were full of sorrow.

"Cal, it isn't your fault."

"I swore a vow of protection and they hurt you."

"No, they didn't," I argued back.

"What did they do? I must know. I have to make it right."

I sighed.

We landed on the top of a hill.

"They just scared me," I said, without any emotion. He dropped his head, letting his shaggy hair fall forward. "Look at me."

He lifted his head and I saw tears swelling in his eyes. I kissed him softly, then licked each fallen tear away. "I love you."

"Cal. It isn't your fault. I am fine, you know that I can turn my emotions off if I need to. That's what I did."

"My strong, beautiful, powerful, Chloe." He kissed me softly and then harder. Before I allowed this to get where we both wanted it to go, I broke away from him.

"We will meet with the queen and produce a plan. The only way this works is if you behave and trust me. Can you do that?" I asked. He leaned down and started to kiss my neck, grabbing a fist full of hair, I pulled his head back. "Cal, I still haven't eaten, and you haven't answered me."

"Gods, you are so beautiful. So insatiable. So demanding. You can have anything and everything you want, my love. Just let me love you." I released my hold and let him do whatever he wanted with my body.

"Cal," I gasped mid-lap of his tongue on my sex, "answer me."

"As you wish, Chloe." He licked, nipped, and tugged, erasing all trace of those men from my body. When I climaxed, screaming his name, he gave me no chance to recover before plunging into me. It was a hard, possessive fuck. He bit me, leaving marks so he could show the world that I was his. When it was time for his release, his roar was so loud, it shook the trees, and his wings went erect.

"I love you too, Cal."

Chapter Sixteen

The next day, I didn't want to get out of bed. It didn't matter how many times Cal and I had sex, I never tired of it and last night, he made love to me three times. This morning, he brought me breakfast in bed and I ate while he tried to eat.

"No. I need a recovery period and I know if you start, we will never leave."

He pouted at me. "Please, my love. I'm starving for the taste of you."

I blushed, of course, biting into my biscuit. "No. Go pack." I was firm with him because I knew it would work.

"As you wish, my love." He kissed my nose before going off to pack.

"Cal, teach me to fight." He stopped mid-pack at my statement. "I have been beaten, tortured, assaulted, and nearly killed. I need to learn to defend myself."

"Is this about last night?" I heard him ask in a deep voice.

"It is part of the reason. I mean, I grew up without learning how to fight because Mother said that is what the guard was for. It was because she and Father became complacent." He didn't say anything and continued to pack. He can't seriously argue with me on this, can he?

"As you wish, my love. But, under one condition."

He turned toward me. "If you need me, you still call for me. And don't run off and play hero by yourself. It takes months to train."

"Let's start with hand-to-hand," I said, holding up my fist.

He chuckled. "No, you need to condition first. So, instead of riding, you will run."

"What? How is that going to help?"

"It will build up your endurance so you can last longer in a fight." Damn, I want to know how to defend myself, but running? "Then after conditioning your body, we will build your strength up so that you can wield a sword and then eventually archery."

"Archery? Like a bow and arrow? How hard can that be?" He offered that grin I so loved.

"You'll see, my love. It takes a lot of strength to be an archer." We packed our bags and headed out the door.

Rob was waiting outside with a couple of horses.

"What about Petunia and the crew?" I asked as I mounted my horse.

"First Mate will take care of her and them. You have my sword and my loyalty, lass. Plus, I am eager to meet this amazing queen they keep talking about. Maybe she isn't married." I shot him an incredulous glance. "It will be worth a shot."

I heard a chuckle come from Cal and it made my heart flutter. When he laughed, I mean really laughed, or smiled, it made all the bad memories go away, replaced by the warmth of his love and only that.

"Lead the way, Rob. I want to get there before three days." The forest was large, radiant, and distinct. Its canopy was a mix of assorted colors and trees not like the ones back home. Ample openings allowed the light to seep through, revealing the mosaic herbs that crept up the trees. Various flowers complimented the green shrubs that lined the forest floor. Running was difficult at first, but when I understood the rhythm, I embraced the beautiful scenery before me.

Cal had my horse striding with him behind me, while Rob took up the front. After about one minute, I was ready to stop. So, Cal suggested a routine—walk for ten, run for however long I could. There was no way to tell time, but we just assumed it after I was ready to move again. I kept that up until my legs felt wobbly and I could barely move.

"Here." Cal sat on the ground next to me and held out a closed hand. I opened mine and felt the weight of something fall into it. It was the Ziran stone and a rose.

"I hate flowers."

He smirked at me. "But you love me."

I rolled my eyes, put the rose in my hair just above the ear, and then examined the stone. I could still feel the faint pulse of a heart. Noticed a green flicker within the crystal walls.

"It's alive," I said while stroking it lightly. Out of the corner of my eye, I saw Cal take the red stone out of his shirt. It was fastened with a rope to wear as a necklace.

"I would presume that is why they are called Dragonheart," he smugly stated.

I looked over at him, examining the ruby he was holding. It was so small in the palm of his large hands. The same hands that made me feel. I was so used to cutting my emotions off that it almost didn't feel real. The way his warmth melted my ice.

"Teach me how to defend myself." He looked up at me. "I know you want to take this slow, but with Queen Iliana's betrayal, the way Prince Eli chained me up, and the impending doom, war is inevitable."

"I know. And I want you to be able to defend yourself because, although I am an Ashana, I can still be killed." He said that matter-of-factly.

"What kills you?"

He smirked at me. "Planning my death already, my love?" I socked him in the arm. "Anything made of a dragon's bone." I gave him an incredulous look. "Think about it. My father was the god of dragons. He was killed by a sword made from dragon bones." Thank the gods there are no more dragons.

"Does that mean, if we—"

"When we," he corrected me.

"Right, when we free the souls, when one dies, your enemies will have access to the weapon that could kill you?"

"Essentially." He smiled.

"What happened to the sword that killed your father?" His head fell low at my question, sending a shiver down my spine. "You don't know, do you?"

"I have no idea when and where he was killed. If I did, I would have killed them and destroyed that sword long ago." There was guilt, pain, regret, and anger in his tone. I can sense them flowing down our bond.

"I'm sorry for your loss, Cal." I cupped his face, turning him toward me. I planted a kiss on his lips. Suppressing those dreadful emotions, hoping to replace them with the love I feel for him.

"Get to your feet." He stood up fast, my hands still in the air, my lips still pursed. Not the reaction I was expecting. "You want to learn to defend yourself, get to your feet."

"Morally gray topics make you cranky." I got to my feet; they were still a little wobbly from my run. Placing the stone in my tunic pocket, I crossed my arms.

"Block your face." I put my arms up. Then Cal came over to me, slightly lowering as I watched him, then he placed two fingers under my chin, turning my head to look straight. "Focus. Protecting your head is essential to not getting knocked unconscious." He adjusted my arms so they were square with my face, and then twisted my hips so my feet were equally balanced. The stance felt powerful and new.

"Good. Now," he started, holding out both palms to face me. "Punch left, then right."

"How is this going to help?"

"If you are going to question everything, there will be no time left to train you. I am limited enough already."

"Sorry." I rolled my eyes.

"Strike." By the time I was done with my lesson, my arms were hurting so bad I forgot about my legs.

"That was good for day one. Tomorrow, we move on to blocking." He smirked, and then tried to embrace me.

"No. I am sweaty and disgusting."

"Then we shall bathe." While Cal and I were busy training, Rob had taken the time to set up camp. We didn't make it extremely far today, and I knew it was because of my request from Cal.

"Tomorrow," I said while sinking low in the cool river a few miles from camp, "we start at dusk, so we can ride the rest of the day. I want to train but we also need to stick to the mission."

He floated closer to me, closing the space between our bodies. "As you wish, my love." There he was, melting my ice a little at a time. Making me feel loved and safe. Something I had never felt before.

"Cal, you saved me." He brushed a wet strand out of my face. "Before you came into my life, my emotions were off most of the time. All I knew was pain. You came in and yes, we started with pain, but look at where we are now. On the other side of the realm, journeying to free dragons." I couldn't help but smile. He took me into his arms, and I wrapped my legs around his waist.

"You saved me too, Chloe." I paused to get his heartfelt confession. He must have known it was what I wanted. "Before I met you, I had sworn off love. I saw what it did to my parents. So, I chose to not bed anyone until I met the right one." Did he just admit he was a virgin? "Before you ask, yes, you are the first woman I ever bedded and will be my last."

Knowing we were each other's first and last, I melted into his arms. "You are highly skilled."

"I am Ashana, my love. Plus, I went to brothels to learn. I never touched, just watched. I learned what women like and don't like. What men like and don't like, and I vowed that I would be a better lover to the woman I chose." My heart fluttered. "So, my love, how did I do?" he whispered seductively into my ear while one hand cupped my breast and the other cupped my sex.

"Perfect." I gasped and then felt his erection underneath my rear.

"Would you like me to show you what I learned?" he asked against my neck while rubbing that bundle of nerves and pinching my nipples.

"Yes." He was teasing me, and I wanted him. He placed his hands on my hips and in a split second, I had twisted around on him. Before I could say anything, he plunged into me.

"Say it," he demanded.

"I'm yours," I squealed. "Gods, Cal."

I begged for harder and faster and he obliged. We both released in utter bliss. I didn't even know I could be stretched like that.

"That was…" I was still trying to catch my breath when he gently unwrapped my legs from around his waist. I was off-balance but his hands stayed on my hips to keep me upright.

"I know," he said, just as breathless as me.

The next day and into the night, my body was sore from yesterday, but this morning I learned how to block and strike. I could tell this was a clever idea because when Cal tried to hit me a couple of times, I blocked each one.

"Good work." Then he swept my feet out from under me, catching me before my back hit the ground. "Pay attention."

"If you two are done beating each other up, I suggest we get moving." Rob has been good company so far. He didn't ask too many questions and he was an excellent cook. I could tell from the size of his belly. Last night, after Cal and I returned from our bath, he had dinner ready for us.

"Thank you, Rob," I said with a smile on my face.

"Wait till you taste it, lass. Ask Cal, my hog stew is

the best in all the realm. Including this place." And he was right. Somehow, the broth was creamy, spicy, full of carrots, and then shaved ham. It was delicious.

"So, Rob, do you have any family?" I had been wanting to get to know him, but not had the opportunity until now.

"My crew *is* my family," he said after taking a bite. "But if you mean before them, both parents are dead. Killed over a loaf of bread. I didn't have any siblings. The earlier captain of Petunia took me in and raised me. Then, when he died, he left everything to me."

"Is Rob your real name?" I had heard somewhere pirates used aliases to keep their identity secret.

"No. And I'm not telling you, so don't ask." He was stern so I didn't pry.

"My parents were decapitated and then I vomited all over my mother's head." I looked at both of them, and there was only silence.

"Gods, lass. I wouldn't have expected that reaction. Not from a princess." Rubbing my arm, suddenly cold and uncomfortable. I know it is not Rob's fault. He didn't know what my parents did to me. Only Cal, Alma, and an erased memory Prince Eli did. He would not get to know. "Did I say something I shouldn't?"

"It's fine. I'm tired." I placed the bowl down and went to my bedroll. A few moments later, Cal's warm body was behind me, and I was in his arms.

"You okay, my love?"

I whispered yes, and then we drifted to sleep.

****

"How much longer until we reach Sumter?" I heard Cal ask as Rob examined the map. We had been traveling for half a day. We were in a cleared area, so there was no shade from the heated rays of the High Sun.

"We should reach it by nightfall." Thank the gods. I was not used to traveling. That is another thing to hate Mother for. She left a permanent mark on me, and I feel as though I can never get rid of her.

"Chloe." I snapped out of my stupor and realized I had stopped. "You, okay?"

Looking over at Cal, I smiled and then motioned for the horse to move again. I knew he would ask again later and there would be no avoiding it. I figured he would not pry until we found shelter again. None of us wanted to sleep on the hard ground again. The bedrolls were not that thick, but at least they were something. It also helped that Cal kept me warm.

We rode for hours, with occasional chit-chat now and then. But I welcomed the silence. Not that I was getting bored of Cal or Rob—no, I enjoyed listening to the rustling of leaves. Trying to figure out which animal made a certain sound. Cal was concerned. I could see it every time he shot me a glance. I would just nod and send a message of reassurance down the bond.

I remember when that first happened. It scared me, the feel of magic. It was overwhelmingly powerful, and I now cannot remember what it was like to not have it. I caught myself staring at the imprint on my palm where our *Blood Oath* had been solidified our first night together. It was beautiful. The way the roses danced around the dragon. It was life-like.

Just like the stone. Taking it out of my pocket, I examined it again. That heartbeat still pulsing into my hand and the small green flame.

Like a fool, I whispered into the rock, "Hello."

You're insane, Chloe. You're talking to a rock. I thought. But then, I felt a rush of magic, and the world around me changed into a bright green light. Opening my eyes again, there was no forest or blue sky, only a prism of green glass.

"Princess Clover." A bright young voice said my name, but I couldn't see where it was coming from.

"Hello," I said, my voice echoing. I was still on my horse, thank the gods. At least I didn't get taken alone.

"Oh, let me move closer." In a heartbeat, a large green dragon was sitting in front of me. Dark ivory eyes sat sunken within the creature's horned, hard skull, and they were looking, judgingly, at me. "I should probably explain what is going on."

The dragon spoke, but I was too fixated on the massive beast sitting in front of me. Several main horns sit atop its head, just above its long, cat-like ears. Large fan-like skin and bone structures ran down the sides of each of its jawlines. Its nose is large and has two long, curved nostrils. A few large fangs poke out from the side of its mouth and show a glimpse of the horror hiding inside. Those teeth could eat me in one clean bite.

Its head is covered in wide scales and rows of small wave-like growths down its spine. Its bottom is covered in raw skin and colored slightly lighter than the rest of its body. Four muscular limbs allow the creature to stand commanding and tall. Each limb has four digits, each of which ends in strong nails made of bone.

Grotesque wings extend from just above its shoulders until its hips. The wings are arched, the inside entirely see-through, especially when viewed from a distance, and rough edges at the bottom almost give it a fledged look. At the end of its graceful tail, a single tendril, covered in the same wide scales as its body.

"Are you listening to me?" It snapped my attention toward it. "Of course not. Shall I start over?"

"I'm sorry, but how is this possible? Where am I? And who are you?" The dragon put a large green claw to its face and shook it displeased.

"My name is Ziran, I am the dragon of this stone. You were transported here through magic and it's possible because you are bound to the son of my god." I know I must look ridiculous to the creature; I mean Ziran.

"What do you want from me?" was the only thing I could think to say. I felt like I was kidnapped again.

"To free me." It was a female. The voice was too feminine to be a male. "And to heed my warning."

"I'm sorry, what? What warning?" I crossed my arms; I was still sitting on my horse unaware of where we were.

"On the night you meet the wizard, one will betray you, and the love you found will be lost." Great, a riddle.

"Ziran, that doesn't make sense. I don't plan on meeting the wizard."

"How do you expect to retrieve the Jian stone?"

Damn. "Do you know who is going to betray me? Because it cannot be Cal, it will kill him…and me," I whispered at the end.

"No. I just know that you will be betrayed, so please use caution." Before I could talk any further, I was whisked away and back into the forest. It was as if I didn't leave at all. We were further along than when I left, and Cal didn't notice. The High Sun was falling, and smoke was billowing out from the other side of the treetops.

"If you need me, call out to me. Just say my name."

How long was I out for? I should tell Cal about what Ziran said. Should I trust the words of a dragon whose bones could kill my love? I wonder if he gets called away into the red stone or firestone, I don't remember what it is called. I just pray that what Ziran says is not true. Or if it is, it doesn't come to pass. Because one thing is for sure, I am one more betrayal away from becoming worse than my mother.

Chapter Seventeen

Entering the village, my thoughts still heavy on what Ziran told me, I didn't notice how quiet it was. The entire place was asleep. Only a few lit torches every few houses, giving life to the faint outlines of buildings. I followed Cal closely, knowing he was able to see in the dark, but something felt off. No town was this eerie unless no one was home. But there are lit torches.

"Cal, something is wrong," I said as I shifted in my saddle. He stopped, and I mocked his movement. Looking over my shoulder, I saw the faint outline of Rob. We were all still here. Grabbing the hilt of the dagger Cal gave me, I was ready. Or at least I tried to be. Without a second beat of my heart, I was snatched from atop my horse with an impeccable amount of force.

"Chloe," I heard Cal roar, and then the sound of his wings expanding. Two arms were wrapped tightly around me, and I jabbed at the person's side. They jolted forward, and we went tumbling. Scrambling to my feet, I lost my dagger but held the stance Cal had taught me.

"Come on. I'm ready." There was a small rustling coming from behind me, slowing the pace of my heart. My ears tuned in to the two soft steps, and then before I was hit, I crouched low and swept the feet out from underneath my attacker. In the distance, I heard grunting and the clanking of metal. Cal and Rob were in the middle of their own fights. It was still too dark to see anything, even with my eyesight adjusting. I could barely make out the person in front of me. Not knowing if they were a man or a woman.

"What are you waiting for? An invitation?" I challenged and the pain that burned through my jaw, when that fist connected with it, had me tasting my own blood.

Leaping forward, I knocked us both to the ground with a hard thud. My punches began connecting with the clothed assailant. A hard force pulled at my hair, and I was jerked off the person.

"Going for hair is a cheap shot," I spat out.

They were silent assassins, and I knew I needed to keep fighting, or I would die. That meant, so would Cal. I let them drag me by my hair, taking my legs. I kicked one toward his feet and as he lost his balance; my other leg kicked straight into the other's back. The hold on my hair was released. There were several of them now. I was outnumbered, and I started to turn my emotions off. Just like I did in any dire situation.

Refusing, I gripped the stone in my pocket and called out to the dragon within. It began glowing brighter and I was able to see four assailants circling me like a shark around its prey.

"Share your power with me," I asked Ziran. When I felt that power surge through me, it was electrifying.

The crunching of bones in my back rippled through me as I felt my shoulder blades tear through my skin. Two sharp stabs of pain pounded the top of my head, reminding me of the feel of that dagger, shooting out from the sides. What is happening to me?

"What the—?" I heard one of them say. I opened my eyes, not realizing I had closed them, and saw I was on fire. No, that I *was* fire. Midnight-colored flames danced around my body.

"Who sent you?" I asked. My voice was much deeper as though possessed.

"Kill her and take the stone," another shouted. I didn't fear them because I was given a gift from Ziran, the nature dragon. I used that gift, and one by one the green flame consumed them. Turning them into ash right before my eyes. I was power and it was addicting. Now that I tasted it, I was not going to let this go. I flew to where Cal and Rob were circled by ten more men. They all locked eyes on me.

"Who sent you?" I asked this group.

"Emperor Rai," one of them croaked.

"How did he know we would be here?" My voice was commanding, and I even feared it.

"The Dark Wizard knows all things," another said.

"Leave and tell your master what you witnessed here today. Tell him that he should be afraid, but if he gives up the stone of Jian, I will let him live." There was silence, then laughter.

"The master isn't afraid of some girl, a bat-boy, and a fat sailor. He will eat you all for breakfast." Anger ripped through me. I let it out on all of them except one. All turned to ash, with one single command of the flames around me.

"Run, boy. Tell your leader what I said." The man shot off in a hurried sprint.

"Chloe," said a familiar voice. Then I saw him. "It's me, Cal." That name sounded familiar to me. "I know what you're feeling right now. All the power of the dragon. It can be addicting, alluring, and even blissful. But you need to let it go."

"No," I heard myself say. Let me go, Ziran. It didn't feel like the dragon I met. This was dark. "Cal." I felt like I couldn't breathe, like I was drowning. Claws were gripped tightly around my throat. I scratched and kicked. I was useless, yet again.

"Poor little princess, no one talked about the darkness within the stones, did they?" the voice sneered in my head.

"Let me go." I gasped. Still struggling against its hold.

"That was fun. I haven't killed mortals in decades."

"What are you talking about?" I heard it snort.

"You called on the power, and power is what you got."

"I called on Ziran. Not whatever you are." The claws loosened on me.

"Ziran was too slow. That's what happens when you are the soul life force within the stone." My vision went from Cal's face to only seeing the darkness speaking to me. "Now that you have had the taste, you can't go back. I won't let you."

"You're wrong. They were trying to kill us."

"Are you sure?" It was trying to make me doubt my actions. "Have you ever killed anything before? And don't say that criminal that you helped your pet kill."

I hadn't. Not until today.

"Thought so. You are, well, were mortal, so you have never known true power. Now you have. You don't have to give it up. We could take on the wizard.

Take possession of all the stones and combine the powers. Imagine, all that power," it whispered seductively in my ear.

"No one will ever hurt you again. You will be the one leaving scars on others. You will be the High Queen and kingdoms will fall to their knees before you." I saw it. Everything it was saying to me. I saw it and I wanted it. But something soft and warm was pulling me back to the light. I went toward it willingly. The smell of cinnamon grew stronger as I walked toward it and then I felt lips upon mine. Wet cheeks pressing into my face, and warm thick arms wrapped around me.

"Come back to me. Don't leave me, Chloe."

"Cal," I croaked, and I saw those green eyes widen in surprise. "What happened?"

My head felt like an anvil was hitting it.

"You turned into a Drancae," Cal said. His voice was still trembling.

"A what?" I rubbed my temple.

"It's when a mortal shifts into a dragon. Neither one nor the other."

"Like you?" He helped me to my feet.

"Not exactly. The power of the dragon's magic shifted you into one. You had wings of pure white, black horns, and a black tail. You even had elongated canine teeth." He sounded amused.

"I felt it. My body, it was changing. It was worse than what my mother did to me. Worse than when the blood magic burns me if I try to lie to you. There was this darkness." I sipped on water Rob handed me. "It tried to take over my body. It said Ziran was not stronger than it." Where is the stone? "Where is it?"

Panic flared in me.

"Right there." My eyes followed where his finger pointed. The glowing emerald merged itself into my chest, right in the valley of my breast.

"How the hell are we supposed to get that out?" Gods, this is bad.

"We will figure it out." He hugged me tightly."We need to get out of here. This town has been deserted. More than likely the work of those men."

"To see the queen," I said.

"Are you okay to ride? Do you want to partner up?"

I started to feel stronger. "I am fine. Let us just get moving. It's time to meet this queen."

We rode all night, into the middle of the next day until we arrived at the edge of the massive fortress. Large pendants with a stallion imprinted upon them danced with the wind. Six ivory towers, connected by thick walls, house archers ready to strike. Striding up to a large arched gate, with two guards posted outside.

"What is your purpose here?" one of them asked.

"I seek an audience with your queen," I firmly said.

"Who are you?" A feminine voice came from behind us. I looked over my shoulder, my gaze landing on the figure of a young woman. She had long brown hair tied to the back of her head and deep-sea blue eyes. She was dressed in a brown tunic, blue breeches, and sported a bow and quiver full of arrows.

"Who are you?" I asked, watching as she walked toward the gate.

"Name's Abby, and if you want to talk to my sister, I suggest you tell me who you are and what you are doing here." She looked much younger than me, but she was poised and hardened.

"I am Princess Clover Celestia, from the Kingdom of Thornwarf." I held my head up high. "I am here to discuss the business of the Dragonhearts with the queen who possesses two of them."

She sucked in her teeth. Something I would not expect from a princess.

"You're from the other side of the sea. Explains the accent." She signaled to the guards, the metal bars on the gate opened, and a drawbridge cranked down. "Follow me."

They are very trusting here. I sent that message to Cal.

Should they be distrusting?

I was expecting a little more resistance, but it appears to me there is no real threat to these people.

Abby led us over the bridge and into a large courtyard. She ordered servants to take our horses from us and then ushered us to follow her inside. The courtyard led straight into a vast throne room. It was not what I expected to see from a queen. There was a massive wooden round table with chairs lined all around it.

The rest of the hall was barren. Again, not what I expected to see from a throne hall led by a queen. A woman with a long brown braid, wearing a red tunic, black breeches, and knee-high boots, was speaking to a tall, broad-shoulder, bronzed man. He was about a foot or two taller than her. He was dressed in all black, it complimented his trained body. Turning toward us, they both smiled.

"What do we have here?" She was most definitely the queen. Speaking with such a smooth tone.

"Sister, this is Princess Clover from the other side of the sea." I saw the queen look at us. Clearly in disbelief. I took a step toward her; the man took a step toward me, with a hand on the hilt of his sword. I heard a growl leave Cal.

"Your Majesty," I started, and then curtsied. "As Princess Abby said, I am Princess Clover from the kingdom of Thornwarf. I have traveled a great distance to meet you."

Mother would be proud. There was silence and it felt awkward. My cheeks heated.

"Welcome to Orion Fortress. I am Queen Kaliegh, this is Lord Rowland, and you already met my sister. I assume that you didn't cross the Great Sea just to meet me, has nothing to do with me, and everything to do with that glowing Dragonheart within your chest," she said matter-of-factly while pointing at my glowing chest.

"Straight and to the point, I see. You are correct. I know you are in possession of two and we need all five to release the souls within before the Dark Wizard takes over the entire realm." I watched as all three of them looked at each other. Speaking silently with their eyes. "You have them, don't you? You know about the Dark Wizard and his plans?"

No answer and I was growing impatient.

"This is the Great Kings of the past doing their work again." What are Great Kings? "Princess, we were preparing to voyage across the Great Sea for the same mission you are on. It seems that fate has intervened, and you journeyed to us first."

"So, you will give me the stones?" I asked.

"No," she said, and then gestured for everyone to

sit at the table. We obliged. "We will journey with you to the Temple within the Dragon Colonies to free the souls." I feel a bit coming on. "The Dark Wizard is in possession of one of the other stones and I can only assume you have two of them. Otherwise, you wouldn't have traveled so far."

I would have. I was going to before Cal revealed he held the Huo Stone. "And we are supposed to just trust each other?"

"It is either that or I lock you in my dungeons until you hand me the stones you have. What do you say, Princess?" She was very charismatic. Different from the way Mother acted in that same position. There was something else about the look in her eyes. It was trusting and I could sense she was not the betraying type. Ziran's words still filtered through my head, but it could have been that darkness. Trying to persuade me from ever trusting anyone again.

"What's the plan? How do we get the last stone from the wizard?" I asked and then Cal's hand grabbed mine. Squeezing tightly and I didn't know whether it was in approval or not.

"The last known location of the Dark Wizard was in the Jian mountains. But unfortunately, four or so months ago, we had a run-in with one of his followers. So, he could be anywhere."

She was young, closer to my age than Abby.

"If we travel north, I can have the Dalarian army flank east, and the combined armies of Orion and Zoldir can flank west. We can take it by force."

"This man is supposed to be all-powerful. I mean, have you heard of his nickname?" I asked. Rob and Cal were unusually quiet, and it made me nervous.

"Supreme Leader Jarhead." Abby chuckled as she said his name. She was picking at her nails, her feet propped up on the tabletop. Very lax. "We have faced worse."

"Tell me something, Princess," Kaliegh started as she leaned forward, folding her hands on the table, "have you been to war?" I shook my head. "Because we have. And what we faced, what we all had to endure to survive, there is nothing that man can throw our way that we aren't prepared for."

"Cocky much?" I stated.

"We have something I am sure the Dark Wizard doesn't have."

My curiosity peaked. "What's that?" I asked the princess. But it was Lord Rowland who answered with a smile on his face.

"Dragons." Cal's grip tightened, but I didn't break my eye contact with the lord.

"Dragons? They have been extinct ever since the Dragon Wars." I heard Rob speak up for the first time. His voice gruff and incredulous. Breaking my eye contact, I shifted my gaze between the three foreigners across from us.

"And I thought pirates were outlawed," the young princess commented. Her eyes were like shards of glass shooting toward my friend. Rob's hand went to the hilt of his sword, Cal let out a feral growl, and I knew if I didn't get a handle on the tension in the room, this would not go the way we needed it to.

"Queen Kaliegh, may I have a word with you in private? Leader to leader?" My voice was regal, matching Mother's anytime she ever spoke. Including the time she killed Vivian in cold blood. The memory sent a shiver down my spine.

"You are all dismissed." That was the first Queen-like tone I heard leave her mouth. There was no interjection, no protest, just obedience. "Rosalie will show you to the guest quarters." That was the last thing she said to Cal and Rob as the throne hall's giant oak doors closed.

Send a message if you need me, Cal said down the bond along with a loving caress. "Thank you, Queen…"

She put a hand up in interruption. "Please, just call me Kaliegh. There is no need for formalities here." That was very mature, and she was even more unexpected than I thought. But all I had to compare her with was my mother.

"Kaliegh, thank you. You may call me Chloe." A pearl-white smile formed on her beautiful face. It appeared to be without any flaws, except for a small scar on her right cheek. Besides that, her chocolate-colored hair complimented her beautifully bronzed skin. She was small, but I could see the defined muscles in her arms.

"I understand we have a lot to discuss," she started as she got to her feet, walking over to a smaller table with a decanter and chalices. Lifting the decanter, she continued, "The stones are incredibly important. I have seen their magic at work, and I can only assume so have you." She assumed correctly as she poured a violet liquid into two chalices. Handing me one before continuing.

"We have dragons, large armies, and allies in the far Eastside of the continent that I know will help." She took a sip, and I sipped mine, leaning on the back of a chair while I listened. A position Mother would highly disapprove of during what she would have more than likely called a diplomatic meeting. “I don’t know you; you don’t know me. My people have just recovered from a very devastating war. I am not keen on bringing another one back home with me again.”

“I don’t intend to start a war. I just want to see the realm safe.” Her gaze softened and I saw an old soul behind those eyes. Even if I was older than her, she clearly had been through her own kind of torture.

“That is very honorable. The war I started was because I was trying to save my people from a man that turned out to be the love of my life.” Her gaze dipped down to the liquid in her cup. It was a sweet wine. Fruit I never tasted before, but it was delightful.

“Did you lose him? In the war, I mean?”

Her head snapped up and her brows furrowed. “No. You actually met him,” she said with a smile and gestured for me to sit with her.

Pulling out a chair, I sat and listened intently. “Lord Rowland.”

“Are you two not married?” I felt like this was inappropriate talk for two strangers, but there was something about Kaliegh, as though I knew her. It was the magic of the stones we carried.

“Not yet. We only just settled down recently in the aftermath of this war. His home was demolished, and his entire kingdom moved here. Zoldir is now a wasteland.” Her voice went soft with pain at the end.

“I’m sorry about your kingdom. But you must understand that I cannot let that happen to mine.” She reached her hands out to touch mine, but I moved away.

“I will make you a deal,” she said, leaning back and then sipping from her cup again. “Meet my friend

Azula, and if she trusts you, then we will defeat this Dark Wizard together."

It was a strange deal, but how was someone named Azula going to know if I can be trusted? Unless they were a seer? Or like Cal? But what choice did I have? We must pass through her kingdom to complete our mission.

"And what happens if your friend says otherwise?" That was a daring question, but one I desperately needed to be answered. Cal and Rob needed to be prepared. I needed to be prepared for any attempt at an attack or imprisonment. The kingdoms back home were on the verge of war anyway with what happened in Thornwarf.

"Then you hand over your stones and be on your ship back home." Her tone was respectful but firm. "Do we have a deal, Princess?"

"Do I have your word you will let us walk away?" Another reassurance I needed. Because if they truly had dragons, would Cal be able to fight them? I barely know how to fight and if this queen has been to war and only came out with a scar on her cheek, then she has skills I don't. Perhaps if this goes well, then she can train me.

"On my honor as Queen of Orion." She put a fist over her heart, and I knew she was being sincere.

"Then we have an accord."

Chapter Eighteen

"Wake up, my flower." Mother's voice was strained, and boney fingers ran along my cheek, sending ice through my veins. "It's time for another lesson." My eyes fluttered open. The room is pitch black, with a smell of iron, and has the faintest ambiance glowing in the light of two torches mounted to the wall. The leather straps across my chest, torso, and waist were no longer brown. They were now stained crimson. Mother was dressed in a violet gown, tight at the torso, but flowing at the skirts. Her hair was double braided atop her head, pinned with her golden crown adorned with violet gems in a bizarre design. Those bright blue eyes gleamed with anticipation as she warmed her blade over the fire.

"What did I do this time, Mother?" My voice was weaker than normal. I couldn't understand why.

"Do you know what an empath is?" What was she talking about? The fumes must be getting to her.

"Like a druid? They are all extinct, along with all the magic of the past." I heard a clicking of her tongue. Striding toward me, more like prowling as stealthy as a wild cat hunting a mouse. She gripped my chin with sharp, pointed fingernails.

"You know nothing, my sweet flower. But someday, even I won't be able to protect you from what you will inevitably become."

My eyes fluttered open, two strong arms wrapped tightly around me, and a hard, bare male chest pressed into my back.

"Are you okay?" He was awake? But of course, he was. Every time I have a nightmare, I wake him. I haven't had one in a couple of days, and it was nice considering I used to have them every night. Reliving my torture over and over. I had to double the cosmetics to hide the forever shadows under my eyes.

Turning over to face him, I pressed my lips softly to his.

"I am now," I said onto his lips. I felt safe in his arms. Then the realization of whose bed we were sleeping in hit me. Sitting straight up, breaking his loose hold on me, I took in the room before me. A large canopy bed with four wooden posts with three violet-colored curtains tied back surrounded us. The silken sheets matched, with embellishments of gold, showing the wealth of the kingdom.

One balcony, with floor-to-ceiling window doors, looked out into the woods where we had entered yesterday. There was a stone fireplace, with two crimson settees, a tea table, and then a bathing chamber with a porcelain tub. It was very lavish. Something home would never be able to compete with.

After the queen and I made our deal, she showed me to the guest quarters, and of course, like I suspected, Cal never left the outside of the throne hall doors. But neither did Lord Rowland. It appeared as if they were staring each other down when we exited. Only snapping their gazes to acknowledge us.

"Are you two all right?" I asked, and they both cleared their throats, mumbling an incoherent response.

"Kaliegh was going to walk me to our quarters if you would like to join?" There was a pause as Cal's gaze shifted back to Rowland.

"Unless you would rather keep his sheets warm tonight," I snapped. Earning a chuckle from Kaliegh.

"Sorry, love. Of course." We walked down a vast corridor with barren walls, except for every few feet or so, a mounted torch. It was welcoming since all I was used to was floral patterns.

"I know the palace isn't eye-catching, but we prioritized re-building. The cosmetics can come later." Kaliegh's voice was somber.

"It's quite lovely. Back home, all the walls have floral patterns and after twenty-three years, it becomes boring." We both chuckled. I hoped admitting my age would get her to admit her age as well, but she just continued rambling on about the plans for memorials of the fallen heroes from the war.

"This spot will be particularly special." I heard the pain in her voice again. It was clear to me she lost someone close. Was it her parents? Or another sibling? I didn't want to pry on a very personal subject. There were things about my past I would never want to relive either. Especially my scars and what they stand for.

A knock sounded on the oak doors to our quarters. It was the maid Rosalie inviting us to breakfast in the banquet hall—that was the throne hall, and war room.

"This place is strange," I said to Cal as I put on my blue tunic, brown breeches, and boots.

"Missing your floral patterns?" he playfully asked me with a wink. I considered throwing a pillow at him, but instead, I just walked out into the hall, leaving his question unanswered. He would get the message.

The oak table was filled with six plate settings, all cutleries made of gold. I expected nothing less from this place. The smell of roasted meat filled my nostrils and made my stomach rumble with hunger. Fruits of all shapes and colors were on display, some I knew, peaches, honeydew, pears, but there were small reds, greens, and purples of which I was unsure. Still, I wanted to try everything. I was waiting on a servant to fill my plate, but none showed but noticed the others serving themselves.

"This place has no protocol," I whispered to Cal.

"Not everyone rules the same," he whispered back and then kissed my cheek.

"Not while I am eating." I heard Abbygale scoff. "I would like to enjoy my breakfast. It's bad enough I have to watch these two gawk at each other."

"Might I ask if the young princess has a suitor?" The room fell deadly silent as all manner of scooping and drinking, any chatter amongst servants stalled; making me deathly afraid I said the wrong thing. My eyes went to the Princess, and I saw pain and anger light like blue flames. Just like Cal's did when those men tried to rape me. "Gods, I'm sorry."

Abbygale got to her feet and stormed out of the hall, slamming the doors behind her. My gaze went to Kaliegh and spotted the tears running down her cheeks. "Kaliegh."

"It's quite all right. Just don't speak on the topic again." That was all the explanation I needed to never bring up suitors in front of the young girl again. I could sense she had lost someone during the war too. Someone she loved like I loved Cal and Kaliegh clearly loved Rowland. Kaliegh had been close to that person as well. I don't know how, but I can just feel what they are feeling. It was a burning flame, much like the way Mother's blade felt upon my skin.

"Are you ready to meet Azula?" Rowland asked, breaking the moment of silence.

"I guess so." Rob and Cal yet again were very silent. I nearly forgot Rob came with us.

"Don't worry. Azula is eager to meet you too." Rowland chuckled and that made me nervous. They already told this person about me? Gods.

"Captain Rob," Kaliegh said this time. The pain faint in her voice, hiding underneath intrigue. "How long have you been sailing the Great Sea?"

Rob was mid-bite into a large sausage at the question. I watched as he swallowed and wiped the grease from his beard.

"Nearly all my life, Your Majesty. Petunia and I are like an old married couple. Fighting on which way we want to go." I heard a gruffer laugh come from him.

"Is that the name of your ship?" she asked. Her eyes brightened with wonder. "I've never met a pirate before."

"Thank the gods for that, lass. Not all are as charming and good-looking as me." He winked with his one eye. That got us all laughing and the tension in the room eased.

"Calian," Rowland started, "what is your position in your trio?"

"Cal is my partner." It was the only word I could think of without giving too much information.

"Partner? Are you two betrothed to one another?" Rowland pressed.

"That is a very personal question," Cal snarled.

"Apologies, it just isn't customary practice that a princess shares her bed with someone she isn't married to." What in the hell happened between them? They hated each other and I needed that not to happen for this plan to work.

"We are soul bound," I said quickly, squeezing Cal's thigh.

"What does that mean? Like soul mates?" Kaliegh asked.

"Yes. Back home, we have an oath that can be made to one another. Once that oath is consummated, it is like marriage without all the ceremonies and tithings," I answered, blushing.

"That sounds lovely. And you worship gods?" Kaliegh asked. "As in the old gods?"

"We worship the only gods. You don't?" I asked.

"We worship or pray to the Great Kings of the past that watch over us and guide our lives." Quite unusual indeed. It was quiet, almost awkward at the revelations that were made. It is to be expected that two separate parts of the realm be exactly that: different.

"When do I meet Azula?" I asked. My appetite was dying along with the conversations in the room.

"Right now," she said with a smile. Jumping to her feet and taking me with her. I heard the scrapping of chairs as the men followed suit and we exited out of the side door that we first entered from. Standing dead center of the courtyard was a sight so unrealistic, I thought I was dreaming again.

A glistening body of purple scales, horns of blue sitting center of cat-like ears, matching the blue tendrils flowing down its spine into its long, elegant tail. The massive beast looked intuitively at me with golden eyes. Its large wings were tucked tightly behind it as it rested on its large limbs.

"This…is…Azula?" I stuttered for the first time in my entire life. I didn't care that I sounded afraid. Anyone would be a fool not to fear a magnificent creature such as this. The dragon's gold gaze shifted from me to my right. To Cal, and then it bowed.

"Rise, Azula. I am no one special." He spoke to the dragon directly. I almost forgot that he was the son of a dragon god. So, he must be like royalty to Azula.

"Can you talk to it?" I asked.

"Yes, and so can you. All you need to do is tap into that stone embedded in your chest."

"No," I said. Last time it turned me into something dark.

"Fine. Tap into my magic," he instructed.

"How?" I asked. We forgot that we had an audience watching us.

"Why does Azula bow to Calian?" Kaliegh asked, approaching us.

"I am an Ashana," he said proudly. I saw Kaliegh's eyes grow wide and that told me she knew exactly what that meant. "Don't be frightened. I only show my true form when necessary."

Then he winked at me. I blushed at the memory of the last time he took form with us both naked.

"How do I speak with her?" I asked again. Cal reached out and interlaced his fingers with mine. Sending a feeling of electricity down the bond. Then, the gem in my chest started to surge with power. It was too much.

"It's lovely to meet you, Princess Clover," the dragon said. Her voice was almost human-like but formal.

"Thank you."

"I know you understand the power that you possess and the need for it to be released from its prison. So, I will make this quick. Trust in the queen. She will help you restore balance to this world. Release the dragons and be free from the darkness that threatens this world."

The connection was lost, and the power lessened. Almost falling to my knees, Cal caught me in his arms. My gaze shifted to Kaliegh as she appeared in deep conversation with Azula.

"What are they saying?" I asked Cal, leaning on him.

"Azula and Kaliegh are discussing the terms of our execution." I shot him a glance and then he smiled at me. Hitting him in the arm, I chuckled. "Azula is telling her to trust in you. That you mean well, and we all must work together to free the dragons."

"Are you okay?" I know seeing a real dragon was shocking to me. Almost paralyzing, and I can't imagine what this meant for him.

"Yes. It means part of my father still lives on." He never speaks about his mother. But I don't really talk about either of my parents since he asked about my scars. I cupped his face, and he leaned his forehead into mine. "I'm proud of you, my love."

"I'm proud of myself too," I said with a smile and then kissed him softly. "Cal, we can't use magic like that again. I felt that darkness within the stone trying to take me over and I think Azula felt it too."

"We need to get that thing out of you."

"I think the only way is by going to the temple."

"She's right." I heard Kaliegh's voice from behind.

"Azula confirmed the only way that stone is coming out of you is by going to the temple within the colonies and releasing it."

"How do we do that?" I asked. She paused too long, and I felt Cal growing in anger.

"No," he snarled.

"No, what?" I asked as I looked between them all. Clearly having no clue what they were silently speaking about. "Tell me."

"When we release the stone, there is a possibility of you not making it. No mortal can withstand that kind of power surging through their body and survive it." Kaliegh was serious in her tone. "I'm sorry."

"There has to be another way," Cal growled. Then I heard muttered noises coming from Azula as if she were speaking to them. I wish I could speak dragon. They could teach me if I don't die.

"You're telling me the only way to save her is by sacrificing her?"

More noises came from the dragon, and I have never felt more alone.

"Watch me," Cal said. Azula answered with more unreadable noises.

"I don't care about the laws. I am the son of the god of dragons. My father is dead, so I am now the King of dragons. I make my own laws," Cal demanded, and the dragon just bowed her head in respect.

"What do you mean?" I asked and he didn't look at me. His body was burning with rage. "Calian, look at me. Speak to me."

"I'm not sacrificing you .Not for anyone or anything." He kissed me hard and then flew into the skies. Leaving dust particles in his wake.

Chapter Nineteen

Cal was gone for hours. During that time, instead of fretting like a helpless lover, Kaliegh and I spent it strategizing.

In the multi-purpose throne hall, a large parchment with the map of our world was spread out across the auburn top.

"If I set a meeting with Tailan, the leader of our allies, we could discuss their aid when we go after the Jian stone," Kaliegh said as she pointed at the small country titled Dalaria.

"Can we release the other stones without it?" I asked, praying that we could. Going into enemy territory with the prizes that he wanted would be stupid.

"I'm afraid not. We will need to have all of them in their spots when the incantation is recited." She must have noticed the fear on my face because she placed a soft touch on my shoulder. Towering a foot taller than me, her soft blue eyes looked peacefully at me. "There will be another way around releasing the one in your chest."

"How are we going to take down this infamous wizard? I cannot tap into this magic again. Last time, I turned into something dark." She dropped her hand, keeping my gaze, and then her eyes changed color. "Are you okay?"

She didn't answer me. Panic began rising as her

body slumped over the back of a chair, words of an unknown language slipping out of her mouth. I was tempted to place a hand on her back. Before I touched her, she snapped up, a small sheen of sweat covering her face.

"Sorry about that," she simply said while straightening her blouse.

"Are you okay?" I was concerned. I have heard about certain conditions that can affect mortals. Make them convulse at random times. That is what happened to her. I didn't want to pry. She was not apprehensive about what I just saw, so I brushed it off. It was not as if I was revealing everything to her as well. Someday we could be faithful friends, but now, I walked a thin line. Betrayed by too many people. With Ziran's words playing on repeat inside my head, I wanted to be sure that the people I trusted truly earned it.

"Perfect," she said as she sipped on some water. "Where were we? Yes." She continued to point and talk, but I could sense panic wafting from her. It felt like thorns rubbing against my skin, sending a tremor down my spine. "Do you agree with the plan?"

"Yes. We travel North to Ziran, where the temple of the Dragon Colonies is found. Make that our base camp. You send word to the leader of the Dalarian Elves to meet us there. Azula will fly over Jian, scouting out the location of the Dark Wizard, and then report back. Once we know what we are up against, the plan to retrieve the stone will be put into action." I didn't know how I remembered that, and by the expression on Kaliegh's face, she approved of my memory.

"What is your weapon of choice?" she asked, a

little too excitedly. I was unwilling to confess I lacked experience in combat. Rubbing my left arm, my gaze lowered to admire the marbled floors, feeling like a little girl again about to admit the truth.

"I don't know how to fight." I swallowed hard. If she was going to trust me, help me get this thing out of my chest, I needed to reveal some parts about myself. In the middle of war, it seemed like a horrible place to reveal that part.

"I can teach you." I looked up at her. Trying to find pity, but all I saw was humility.

"Do we have time? Cal started teaching me blocking and striking techniques, but not with any weapons." Admitting that still didn't make me feel any less useless. Tempted to turn my emotions off again, Kaliegh gave me an excited smile.

"Better late than never. Come on, I will teach you what I know."

The training yard was on the outside of the castle and looked opulent. Built with silver bricks and russet brick decorations. Tall figurines, made of straw and deer hide, appearing like a target, brought the yard to life. Small holes from earlier arrows lined each chest. Kaliegh opened a wardrobe equipped with various weapons. It contained a generous number of daggers, arrows, and swords.

The space was shaped like a diamond, with multiple targets placed asymmetrically across the pavement. Above, the beautiful blue sky, and the rays from the High Sun hiding behind a fluff of white. I saw the second floor, part of it hanging over the edge of the wall, creating an overhang on one side and a balcony on the other.

Kaliegh retrieved a longbow and quiver full of arrows.

"This is Naga." I gasped at the revelation that she named her bow after one of the most important creatures in our history. She showed it to me, explaining it in detail. "It is skillfully constructed of sturdy Elkwood. Its string is made from superior Elk fur, a common material around these parts of the world."

The boughs are adorned with exquisite runes and end in slight curves shaped like talons. The handle is wrapped in hide and decorated with fine hawk feathers.

She had a sizable quiver strapped to her back, made from thick leather. The outer side is embellished with ornate golden details matching the palace crest. A beautiful stallion, or what Kaliegh calls it, the Orion Stallion Horace. The horse of her Greatest Grandfather.

"Who taught you how to shoot?" I asked as she knocked an arrow.

"His name was Sir Palmer." She released her arrow, and it buried itself in the spot that mimicked the heart.

"Did you lose him in the war?" I asked as she handed me the longbow and positioned behind me, adjusting my arms and grip. Aiding me, as I tried to pull it back, I felt weak.

"After the war," she soberly said in my ear. "You will need to work on your upper body strength."

"Right. How do I accomplish that?" Releasing my arms, the weight of the weapon caused it to slip from my grasp.

"I will get the craftsman to create one that you can use. It will be lightweight but still deadly." She smiled.

A thud in the target snapped both of us out of our conversation. A glistening dagger sits next to the protruding arrow.

"You could learn how to use these." Abby's voice came from behind us. Dressed in leather, all black, with a dagger strapped to either side of her thighs, she looked much older in her wardrobe. A beautiful long braid flowed to just above her waistband.

"Would you teach me?" I asked. Almost pleading. Walking over to her dagger, she pulled it and the arrow and strolled toward us.

"No." She sounded mean. Still angry at me for making a comment that I had no clue would have any kind of effect on her.

"Don't be mean, little sister," Kaliegh said as she took the arrow from Abby.

"If you think you can train her, fine. But from what I saw, she is as useless as a turnip." She scowled.

"I am not useless," I said defensively.

"Could've fooled me." The heartless bitch. Before my fist connected with her, a firm hand gripped my wrist, rubbing my bones together painfully.

"I know my sister can be rude, but violence isn't the solution." Kaliegh glared at me. Then snapped her attention to the smirking Abby. "Go away until you can be polite."

"You may be queen, sister, but I am death itself. You made sure of that." Then she shot me one more glare before leaving the yard. Kaliegh released my wrist, and the pain receded.

"Lesson is over for today. I will contact Tailan and see you at dinner." She left me alone in the yard with nothing but anger and rage to keep me company.

"Calian, you bastard, get back here now," I yelled to the sky. No answer. He has been gone for too long. Panic was rising. Steadying my breathing, I made my way back to my room. "Cal? Cal, are you here?"

There was no response as I looked in the bathing chambers. Sinking into the silk sheets, a rustling of parchments came from underneath me. Grabbing them with furrowed brows, there were two. One started with *My love* in Cal's penmanship. The second was in a different pen. Panic and anger fueled me as I continued to read. Running to the throne hall with the paper in hand, my heart pounded so hard it made my ears pulse.

"What happened?" Kaliegh and Rowland rushed toward me. Not trying to hide my fear, I handed them the paper. Kaliegh read it aloud.

"Thank you, Queen Kaliegh, for delivering me the last descendant of the god of dragons. Deliver me the remaining four stones and I'll ensure your people will remain unscathed when I rule the realm." Kaliegh stared at me. My heart slammed in my chest as I looked at the imprint on my hand. Placing it over my heart, Kaliegh approached.

"We will get him back," she spoke. But that was it. The betrayal that Ziran warned me about. I was a fool to trust them, and now Cal is the prisoner of the man who killed his father. Stepping back, my emotions turned off.

"Why did you do it?" I asked, glaring at them.

"You think I betrayed you?" she asked. Acting as if I just insulted her. "Honestly, I'm hurt that you think I would do that. We are on the same team, Chloe."

"If you didn't, then either he did, or your sister." No emotion in my voice at all. Matching Mother's calm, deadly, and wicked tone.

"Never. If this Dark Wizard has any kind of magic like that last bastard we dealt with, he can conjure up dark shadows to take over people." I didn't want to hear any excuses from them. It was all a lie. Since they want to play innocently, playing along should not be too difficult. I will kill them all once I get Cal back.

"Fine. We leave now," I demanded, and before they could protest, I stormed out of that hall, straight to my quarters, and packed a sack.

Chapter Twenty

How could she lie to me so easily? There was no one else who knew we were here and the purpose of our mission. Calian revealed his true form to them like a fool and they used it to their advantage.

Cal? I started, pressing my lips to the symbol imprinted upon my palm.

My love, answer me. My eyes well up with burning tears, and I don't fight them as emotions of anger, regret, and fear consume me.

My love. I felt the faintest warmth from his voice filling me. But it was not enough. Coldness soon followed, sending ice shards through my skin and into my blood, trying to suppress the fire within. *Chloe…I….love… you.* There was pain in each breathless word. He was dying. Calian, my friend, my love, my heart, my soul bound is dying and it is all my fault.

I am coming for you, Cal. Without care or diction, making my way out to the training yard, grabbing the longbow and quiver full of arrows, I started to make my way toward the path that led out of the fortress, when a gust of wind and the sound of wings knocked me onto my back. Snapping my head, I glared at the beast bearing its sharpened fangs at me. I knocked an arrow.

"Don't try and stop me." Azula snarled at me. "I'm getting him back." My arms started shaking, still not used to the strength needed to use such a weapon.

"Clover," Kaliegh's voice came from behind the dragon. With a soft thud, the queen slid down from the back of the beast and strode over to me. Without fear, her glistening blue eyes showed sympathy as she softly spoke. "I know better than anyone here what you are feeling."

"Liar," I shouted. "How could you possibly know? Your lover is safely here." Kaliegh didn't back down. She stopped, the tip of the arrow brushing against the valley of her breast. I could kill her. One wrong move and the arrow would pierce right through her thick blouse and into her heart.

"Rowland is more than a lover. He is my soulmate, my soon-to-be husband, and he was taken from me before the war even began. And Abby…" She paused. Tears were swelling in her eyes as I felt my arms starting to lower at her words. "My best friend Tristian and she were soul mates, and he was killed right before our eyes. Killed by the same man that took Rowland, destroyed my kingdom, and killed more than half of my people. He even killed my parents. Santana was an evil man that called himself an Emperor. His master was the Dark Wizard."

Gods, how could she make up a lie that is convincing? Closing my eyes, I reached out to her with my senses. I felt the truth in her words, and it melted the ice that had formed over my emotions. Fluttering my eyes open, I said, "I'm sorry." My voice trembled with the shame I was feeling.

"We didn't betray you or Calian. Azula and he are kin, which means that he is my kin. And I stop at nothing to protect my family and friends." Gods, she is a true warrior. Regardless of her youth, Kaliegh was a warrior first and a queen second. How could I not have seen this before? Blinded by the influence of my own mother. My own horrors and dark secrets. “Earlier, when you saw me convulsing, I had a vision.”

“What? Are you a seer?” How badass is this girl?

With a smile, she answered, “I am not a seer, whatever that is, but I have been blessed with the gift of sight. It means that I have visions of unknown and unpredictable futures. That’s how Rowland and I came to find each other.”

“You have this gift? And it does make you a seer, well, in my world.” Seers have been nothing but legends since I was a girl. Magic left in the past, which is now irrelevant considering what has happened in the last month.

“Yes.” She reached out to grab the bow from me, and without restraint, I let it go.

“The vision, was it a bad one? Did you see him?” I asked and pleaded for the answers. Her smile faded as her gaze dropped to the floor. That wasn’t a good sign.

Glancing over my shoulder, Azula had disappeared, which ironically gave me some relief. The last thing I needed was a dragon hell-bent on eating me for threatening her and her queen.

“What I saw…” She paused, rubbing her hand along the bowstring. She was nervous and it made me anxious. Placing a hand on her shoulder, she looked at me, thanking me silently for the reassurance.

“There was fire, screaming, and death everywhere. We were all in the middle of it. Another war with the darkness trying to seize control of the lands.” She walked over to the wardrobe and hung the bow back on the rack. I followed, hanging the quiver next to it. We turned and started walking out of the yard and onto a cobblestone path that wrapped around the fortress. Forking off to a bridge that led into the marketplace. The only noise was the chirping of birds and the crunching of the rocks underneath our boots.

"Tell me more," I said after a few heartbeats.

"Before I continue, you must know that not everything I see happens. The only visions I have had that have come true, was Rowland. I was still a novice with my gift, but now that I have mastered it, I see clearer images. Everything I see and feel is real to me. If I get hurt, in one of my visions, when I come back, the pain remains even if there is no mark." We continued walking.

"I have seen death, destruction, but nothing like this. We were all standing in an open hall. Like the inside of a temple. Each of us stood in front of a statue, shaped out of different dragons."

"All of us? Including Cal?" I couldn't help myself. I needed to know there was a future in which he lived.

"Yes. All five of us held a stone and reached out to place them in the hole that is carved into the chest of each dragon. Right in the spot where their hearts were meant to be. We were smiling at each other. Even with all the cuts and bruises, we felt like we were winning." She stopped suddenly. Turning her back to me, she picked a lily from a bush.

"What happened?" I asked.

"We were betrayed. An army of soldiers marched in with the Dark Wizard and before I could see anything else, the last thing I heard was your voice. It was full of anger when you asked why they betrayed you. You started glowing green and then I came back."

"Who was I talking to? Did you see their faces?"

Turning back to face me, the horrid flower still in her hand, she spoke. "No. But whoever it was, they hurt you so bad you started to become something else. I felt everything you were filling and then some. There was a tang of smoke and ash left over in my mouth." Magic. She felt the magic that was flowing through me. It was what I felt the last time I glowed.

"Thank you for telling me." We started walking again. A warm breeze passed over us and we were silent for a while.

"Tailan will be here soon. I know how eager you are to get Calian back, but it would be smarter if we go into this with a strategy." She was right, but could I allow myself the time to wait? "I know you are thinking there is not enough time, but from what the letter said, Calian is not going to be dead anytime soon." No, he is just going to suffer first.

"Listen to me," I started. "Cal and I can speak to one another telepathically. He is dying and I am not going to wait any longer just so we can produce a plan that you approve of. You are not my queen. I am going after him with or without your help. And since we cannot remove the stone from my chest without going to the pillars, then you need me more than I need you." It was petty and immature to bargain the stone with her, but I could see she was considering my words.

"I know that I cannot stop you. You remind me a lot of myself." She chuckled and then sighed. "Then I suppose you will be needing these." Reaching inside her blouse, she pulled out two stones. My eyes widen at the sight of them. One was a beautiful blue matching the queen's eyes perfectly and the other was the color of midnight.

"You're giving me the stones?" I asked. Still not knowing whether this was a test or not.

"You don't trust easily and if this is the only way I can reassure you of my intentions, then I am willing to trust you with the future of my people." Without thinking about it further, I grabbed the stones. Both of their pulses flowed down the palm of my hand, through my arms, and into my own chest where the other stone was.

"Thank you." She smirked at me, and I could feel that unease in her decision, but it was something I could respect. Trusting another with the future of your kingdom is difficult. But then again, it is not just her kingdom that is in jeopardy—it is the entire realm.

****

"The problem is not with the size of the armies. It is the impenetrable fortress walls," Tailan, the Dalarian Elf leader said to my right. I decided to stay, just to hear them out on the plan to attack. When Kaliegh and I arrived back in the throne hall, the elves and his generals were already waiting for us with Rowland and Abby.

I had never seen their kind before, didn't even know they existed. With pointed ears and silver tattooed bodies, it was hard to look away. I hated to admit it, but all three of them were attractive. Tailan was tall, wearing nothing but breeches and boots, showing off his chiseled torso with silver swirls of elaborate designs imprinted into his beautiful skin. Both female generals were strikingly beautiful, wearing only a chest covering, revealing their midsection, and just the skirts of a dress. It was as if the seamstress decided not to connect the two halves or ran out of fabric. Even the sides of the skirt were slit, revealing the full length of their defined legs. Baring similar silver markings.

Abby was picking at her nails with a dagger, seeming just as out of place as I felt. Rowland and Kaliegh were moving pieces of small soldiers around on the map. Trying to convince everyone of the best path to go. When tension and radiating anger started, it made my blood boil. How could I feel everything everyone else is feeling? Is it another power of the stone? Needing to clear my head, I exited the back door and went into the yard.

The White Sun was clear in the sky. *Cal, my love, if you can hear me, I am coming for you. Stay alive. Stay alive or else I will kill you myself.*

As you wish.

My heartbeat raced with elation as the tears streamed down my face. *You are still alive. Where are you?*

In a tower. They came out of nowhere, I was blinded, and there was not enough time for me to react. Forgive me.

There is nothing to forgive. I am coming to free you and to kill that bastard who dared to take you from me. Our connection went silent, and panic extinguished any remaining joy. *Cal, speak to me. Help me find you. I have the other two stones. That means all I need is the last one and...*

*Do you not mean all I need...*It was not Cal's voice nor warmth I felt this time. No, this was ice. Like death itself.

I am going to kill you. I said, sending fire back

down with my words. Dark laughter responded to my words.

You may try, but if you ever want to see your pet again, I suggest you hand over my stones. I was silent but the connection was still there. My fire fighting against his ice. *Nothing to say, little flower.* He laughs.

I am not afraid of you. You have no idea who you are messing with and for that I pity you. You may have magic, but I have something you will never have.

What is that flower? Scars from my own mother. No, you are right about that. I watched while my Mother was raped and killed by my own father and then I raped and killed him. You can try to come at me with everything you think you may have, and I would love to play along. He is taunting me, using my own past to try and sway me and it might be working. No, pull yourself together. You are not a useless flower anymore.

You are called Supreme Leader Jarhead for the antics that you love to play. But before the end of the next fortnight, your head will be in a jar put on display for all to see, that the once feared Dark Wizard was bested by a little flower. The connection snapped and the fire inside me was lit.

Charging into the throne hall, all eyes locked onto me as the room went silent except for the sound of my boots marching across the floors.

"You will all listen to me and listen closely." Kaliegh gave me a nod of encouragement. Approaching the map, I started. "Tailan and his armies will flank the eastside and wait for the barrier to come down. Kaliegh, your armies will come from the south, and the dragons will cover the skies. I have contacts back west and since we have a bit of our own magic, and a pirate captain on hand, Rob will gather a fleet from Thornwarf and flank west." During the past twenty-four hours, Rob left to go back to the harbor, which was later revealed to us as Dante's Port, to check on Petunia and the men. He was due to arrive first thing, but I plan to send a messenger to him with the plan I produced and to update him on everything that happened with Cal.

"The four of us will be a smaller, unseen unit that will break down the barrier and get inside undetected." A scoffing sound came from Abby.

"How do you suppose we do that? None of us have the ability to become invisible."

Smirking at her, I answered, "We are in possession of four Dragonhearts. Each has magic of their own. I am sure with some guidance from Azula, we can learn how to use it to our advantage."

"What about the darkness hidden within them? Didn't you say it almost consumed you?" Abby asked.

"Yes, but I won't let it get that far. The stones are strong enough to bring the barrier down. We need to be unseen, so unless you can produce another way, then I suggest you shut it." I was expecting the dagger to be thrown at me, but she just nodded, and I could sense something new from her.

"Now, once we are inside, the main goal is getting Cal out of there and finding the Jian stone."

"We have no intel. We would be going in blind," Rowland spoke this time.

"Not completely," I smugly said. All their brows furrowed with wonder. "The connection that Cal and I have allows us to see what the other is seeing. It is not perfect, but I believe once we get close enough, I can tap into his mind and get a general idea of what is going on. But there is another issue to be aware of." I paused, waiting for interjection. "The Dark Wizard managed to access our connection somehow. He spoke to me outside before I came in."

"That means he could know we are there. If he still has access to it," Tailan said. I was still getting used to his stranger dialect.

"It is a risk, but we don't have any other options." Their faces went bleak, and I could sense confusion, fear, regret, and some anger within the room. Something sparked inside of me. "I know this is asking a lot, but we are no longer divided territories anymore. United, we are one realm, one people, by the sword and shield, with honor, the first, the last, and the eternal strength above all we shall rise."

"For Dalarian," Rowland said as he unsheathed his sword and raised it. The others followed.

"For Dalarian," we repeated, and a smile came across my face and for the first time in my life, I was proud. I proved to myself that I can lead.

****

The next day, a messenger was sent to Rob with details hidden within a simple message only he could understand. Using some things, we talked about it. Or at least I prayed he would figure it out. Otherwise, that part of the plan would falter. Tailan went back that evening to prepare his armies and start their movement. Kaliegh informed me about the portal underneath the castle Tailan used to get here. There was also more than one dragon. Azula had an entire family of them.

"Verglas is Azula's mother, Xiong is Azula's Uncle. They will oversee Tailain's troop movement and communicate updates with Rowland. Azula will stay with us, and her sibling will stay behind with the other dragons as added backup," Kaliegh explained as we prepared our horses.

"How many dragons in total?" I asked, placing a saddle on top of a gray horse.

"About a dozen. They helped out with that war."

"I thought they all went extinct." She laughed at me because I was struggling with the buckles on the saddle. "I don't do much horseback riding."

"It's okay. We are all novices at some point in our lives. Anyway, the dragons went into hiding after the Dragon Wars ended. It was the only way they could guarantee survival." Makes sense.

"Are you two ready to go or not?" Abby was mounted upon a black beauty. Dressed in a chocolate leather jacket with a large V-neck, revealing an ivory blouse underneath. The cut-off sleeves reveal her defined muscles within the bronze of her skin. A long braid is brushed to the left side, hanging just below her breast. Strapped to the side of each thigh are her deadly daggers. Sheathed to the saddle is a long sword with an elegant pommel.

"We are coming," Kaliegh said as she helped me onto my horse. Still feeling embarrassed at my lack of horseback riding skills, I felt my cheeks flush. She didn't seem to notice nor care and mounted hers. The four of us stalked out of the fortress and started our journey north.

The forest was infinite, ethereal, and plush. Cedar, elkwood, and rhododendron encompassed the canopy. Their peaks allowed for short beams of light to descend for a mosaic of mushrooms to reign over the insect-riddled soils below. Twisting vines dangled from every tree, and an assortment of scattered flowers added some dull touches to the otherwise emerald forest grounds.

It was a beautiful display of nature, despite the disdain I felt for flowers. Not by their own doing, of course.

Rowland and Kaliegh occupied themselves during our stride through the forest. Abby kept to the rear, and I kept to myself. All four stones in my possession seemed like too much power, but I couldn't let myself be afraid of it all.

By the time the White Sun was rising, we decided to stop and make camp.

"How much further?" I asked.

Rowland pulled out a map from his sack and rolled it out for all of us to see. "We are here." He pointed at a spot just outside of the border between Orion and Zirian. "Once we cross into Zirian, Azula will fly over and pinpoint the exact location of the Dark Wizard's Keep."

"Are there any enemies in that territory?" Abby asked.

"No. There is nothing but wastelands. That is where a base camp will be set up. Right on the outskirts of the border," Rowland said.

"How long will it take for our reinforcements to arrive?" I asked. Looking at how far Dalaria was from Zirian. It looked like it would take a month.

"The Dalarians have their own magic. They will arrive at the base camp before we get back from rescuing Cal." Kaliegh smiled. Her confidence in them does nothing to reassure me. Tomorrow, we will set up a central command tent. Then, we put my plan into action. Gods, help us. I pray that Rob got the message and was racing to gather a fleet. If we fail, then the entire world is lost, and I let myself get distracted, just like the Cypress Queen warned. Now, I must save Cal and keep the stones safe or else the entire world is lost.

Chapter Twenty-One

"Poor little flower, lost and all alone. With no kingdom, no mate, no family to save her. Nothing but the scars to keep her company. *Mother? No, it couldn't be her. Where am I? I cannot see my hand in front of my face because it is so dark.* "Look at the fragile clover, ready to be picked."

Two red eyes appeared before me, then slowly, the green prism I was called to once before re-appeared. Standing before me is a dragon that looked like death itself. It looked more like a shadow and the solid structure of a real dragon.

"I'm dreaming," I stated.

Laughing, revealing nothing but darkness, like a giant black hole ready to suck my soul into. "No, my little flower, you aren't. I called you here."

"Liar." I started to tremble and then, without thinking, cut all my emotions off. It was the only weapon I knew I could use. Something I mastered.

"Cutting off your emotions. Clever, but there is no need. Just use your senses and you can tell whether I am lying or not." It hissed and sure enough, I obliged, and I felt nothing but truth radiating off the shadowy figure.

"What do you want?" I asked, keeping a straight face.

"To help you, of course."

"I don't need your help. Now, send me back," I demanded. It laughed again.

"You plan to free your Ashana, but you will fail. The Dark Wizard is far too powerful for you. Even with four stones in your possession." How did it know? "I can feel my brothers calling to me from the other stones, girl. Each of us is trapped in here, just wanting to be set free."

"You mean to tell me each stone has one of you inside of it, along with the souls of the other dragons?"

"Yes. We all just want our freedom, which is why I have offered to help you."

I cannot trust it.

"I don't want to, nor do I need your help." I started to turn, but there was no way out, and I don't know how to get back to my body outside of this thing.

"You can't go back until I say so, girl, so you better listen up." Sighing, I turned toward him, not hiding my ire. "Good, you need anger to help you do what is necessary for you to win this."

"Speak fast," I ordered. By the looks of it, the White Sun was starting to fall, which meant everyone would be waking soon, and that meant I needed to get back quickly.

"Using the stones will break the barrier, but it will not be enough to defeat the wizard. You must combine the magic of all the stones to defeat him."

"That will kill me. I am a mortal. Even releasing this stone from my chest could kill me." That is why Cal took off in the first place. To clear his head.

"You are not a mortal, Princess. Haven't you figured that out already?" Liar. It had to be. "Think about everything that has happened to you in your life so far. Your own mother carved into you, letting you bleed to death at times. You can control your own emotions, and others if you trained, but you can sense them. Am I making sense yet? Silence, so that is a yes." Everything he was saying was true.

"You mated with an Ashana and survived. You both thought it was because of blood magic, but no, it is because you are not a mortal. Mortals and Ashanas cannot mate. The mortal would die." My heart was racing at the revelations that were coming to life. "And you have a Dragonheart embedded into your chest. You would have died if you were a mortal woman. Tell me, Clover, what are you? Because I do," it smugly said.

"Tell me," I demanded.

"You are the Goddess of Earth and Nature. That is why Ziran forged itself to you and that is why you have survived this life. You are Emnera, reborn." Falling to my knees, my entire life flashed before me, a collage of memories from my past, present, and future. "When you combine the magic of the stones, you will become your true self, and no one, not even the wizard will be able to stop you."

"What do I need to do?" Not looking at it, it felt like my world came crashing down on top of me.

"The ice and fire stones will merge into your palms, the Heise stone will embed itself to the center of your forehead, and the Jian stone will find its way to you." Looking at my palms, the left one is plain with a small scar across it. The other, the beautiful imprint of my bond with Cal.

"What will happen to my imprint?" Keeping my head low, I raised it to my mouth and kissed it.

"Sacrifices must be made in order to win, my

dear."

"You mean I have to sacrifice my bond with Cal?" This time I looked at my imprint.

"It's a means to an end." Before I could speak on the matter further, I was whisked back into my body just as the others were stirring awake. Unaware of where I went and what happened. Oblivious to the danger that slept next to them.

I was quiet for the rest of the journey to base camp. Other than a few niceties exchanged between everyone at breakfast, we were all in a hurry to get to camp. There was nothing but orange sand for miles all around us. As soon as we crossed the border, the temperatures rose, and the forest seemed to cut off. Kaliegh and Rowland set up a large twelve by twelve-foot purple tent, with a large golden stallion emblazoned upon it. While Abby and I set up ours on either side.

The space was small enough for two. Once I set up everything, I pulled out the stones and contemplated the conversation I had. There would be no need to tell Kaliegh about what happened, because not only did the shadow dragon reveal my true self to me, but it also made me realize that I needed to do this alone.

Tonight, when they are all sleeping is when I will leave.

"Hey," I heard Kaliegh say before poking her head inside. "Can I come in?"

"Yes." I placed the stones behind me. She sat across from me.

"Only a few more hours and we put your plan into action. Are you ready?"

Trying to sound inconspicuous, I answered with a smile. "Yes." It was quiet and I started rubbing my imprint.

"We will do whatever it takes to defeat him," she said, and I looked at her. Those bright blue eyes were trying to tell me something. "Whatever it takes, you have my support."

She knows. Of course, she has the gift of sight, but this is an unspoken approval of what needs to be done, which means she has seen this and how it plays out in the end. I could ask her, I should ask her, but I don't. There is no need because, from the sorrow on her face, I already know how this is going to end.

Dinner was full of laughter and stories of how they all met. I couldn't believe what I heard about Abby.

"She was trembling when we met, but she held her sword and told me it was looking for its next victim," Rowland said.

"I never would have guessed," I said as I looked at her. She had a small smile on her face but was looking at the flames dancing in the fire.

"A lot can change in a few months. You can find the love of your life and lose him all in the same week if you are lucky. That can harden anyone." Just like that, all the joy was sucked out of the air.

"I miss him too," Kaliegh said as she reached to comfort her sister.

"How did it happen?" I asked and then retorted. "I'm sorry."

"It's fine," Abby started. "I met Tristian the same time Kaliegh did. Only he decided to fall in love with her first, until he realized who the better sister was." I heard them laugh. "Tristian was fearless, and he cared for us, even when he didn't have to. As much as I tried to hide my feelings for him by being rude, when we nearly died together, that is when I admitted how I felt. I wasn't expecting him to reciprocate those feelings until he kissed me." She started toying with the fire using a long stick. "Then we went on a rescue mission to save Rowland. Not knowing who we were dealing with at the time, Tristian's body was taken over by a shadow beast. It killed him instantly and then that bastard that controlled them converged his body with Tristian's. But that isn't the worst of it."

"What's worse than that?" I asked, looking at all their expressions, I knew it had to be despicable.

"He used my best friend's dead body to try and rape me," Kaliegh said and I saw Rowland's jaw clench. I didn't know why I said it, but I needed them to know I had scars too.

"My mother tortured me for ten years and then Cal kidnapped me, saved me, and then I was almost raped by three men, and he saved me again." All their mouths dropped and then we all laughed. As morbid as it was, we were laughing so hard we started to cry. "I'm glad I met you all. I haven't had a family before Cal, and now I have you."

"We can all be scared royals together," Abby said with a smile, and we all hugged. This moment is one I will treasure for the rest of my days. My friends, my family, and all the love that circles us.

Night came too fast, but it was time to go. Peeking out of my tent, there was no one around. Back in the tent, I placed the Death stone on my forehead and willed it to me. A sharp, burning pain shot through me as it embedded itself, and I felt an electric shock course through my veins. When it subsided, my body was drenched with sweat and I was panting. One down, two to go. Next, the ice stone burned into my left palm, but it was a fire burn. It reminded me of the pain I felt when Mother used the frost cube on my skin at once after the burning blade.

Before the last stone, I kissed the palm once more.

I love you, Cal. Until we meet again.

Placing the fire stone over the dragon, I willed it into me, and this time, it was different. The ground beneath started to distance itself from me, the tent dissolved around me, and the surrounding ambiance of each color danced in flames. I was in the air, glowing like a star, and power surged through my veins. Shooting across the sky, I was in front of the barrier in the blink of an eye. Reaching my hand out, the barrier faltered before me as I used fire and ice to dissipate it.

This was easy. A little too easy it felt, but I had no time to worry. Rescuing Cal and the Jian stone was my goal. The tower was massive, over twenty feet high, with no windows and only one door.

"Turn me invisible," I commanded the stones and only prayed it worked. Making my way down, there were two guards dressed in all black armor posted at the gate. I couldn't see any skin, to tell me whether they were human or not.

A quick prayer before darting past them. I passed right through a solid door, which thrilled me and terrified me at the same time. Scanning my surroundings, there was nothing to see except a spiraling staircase that shot right to the top. Instead of running them, I took to the air and flew in the direction of the winding stone stairs, looking for any sign of a door or life. There was nothing except solid black stone until I reached the peak. One solid steel door connected to the top of the stairs.

There was no way to see inside. Reaching out, but stopping short, realizing I could pass through solid material, I willed myself to the other side. Instantly, the weight of gravity hit me and knocked me to the floor with a hard and painful thud. Lifting my head, I stood in a room that is made of pure iron and steel. To the right, I see him. My mate was shackled to a wall by his wrist and ankles. Scrambling to my feet, I ran to him.

"Cal, Cal, look at me, love." Cupping his bruised face, he grunts. Unhealed cuts covered his body. "What happened? Why aren't you healing yourself?"

"He can't." That snarky voice came from behind me. Turning, I shielded Cal's body with mine. A hooded figure was delicately arranging jars with heads in them on a large iron shelf that lined the entire back wall. There was nothing else in the room except for them. "I see you have brought the stones just as I requested."

"Fuck off. They are mine and so is Cal."

He raised a boney black finger at me. "Such a shame, really. You are quite beautiful. Do you really think you can control those stones? You foolish girl, don't you know you can't believe a word that comes out of a shadow dragon's mouth?" Before I could protest, a familiar hand was wrapped around my throat, turning me slowly back to Cal. His once-green eyes were pure black and full of hate for me.

"It's me," I said while choking.

"You broke your bond, girl. He cannot be reasoned with, and you cannot be saved. Strip her bare and chain her up." It was an illusion. Cal was perfectly fine except the wizard had control over him. I tried to fight, but he was stronger. The stones had drained all my energy. Through misted eyes, my love stripped me bare, exposing me to the freezing air, and chained me.

"Cal, my love." I saw him trying to fight for control and hope started to rise within me.

"Cut the stones from her skin and bring them to me." I saw the dagger begin to shake in his hand. Green flashed in the blackness of his eyes.

"Calian, I love you. Please, it's me, remember the *Blood Oath*." But it was too late. The moment the dagger sliced into my forehead; my natural instincts kicked in. I became an emotionless bag of bones. The tears and blood flowed down my naked body. With each cut, I felt my life draining from me. When he got to the last one, inside my chest, his mouth was so close to mine, all I had to do was lean forward and kiss him. "I forgive you."

The dagger plunged into my chest as my lips crashed into him. Blood slid along my body, and down to the floor. It was like ice, and even as his lips broke from mine, the warmth left with him. This is how it ends. My eyes slowly close, and the last image is the face of my lover.

Chapter Twenty-Two

Calian

No, Clover, please gods. Her blood was warm on my hands. It was still spilling from the holes in her chest that were no longer rising.

"Very good, pet. Bring me the stones." Anger flashed through me. Her kiss broke the spell. Looking down at my right palm, I saw the imprint fading underneath the bloodied stones. But he doesn't realize what has happened. The spell was broken, I could use this to my advantage if I could get past the rage. Turning toward him, I kept my eyes down and slowly made my way over to him. In his hands, he held a golden box with intricate floral designs upon it.

"Place them inside." He opened it with a silver key forged into the shape of a star and revealed one single yellow stone sitting upon a velvet bed of green. I could stab him, take the box of stones, and run. But I cannot leave her here. Not with him.

"What are you going to do with the body?" I asked and received a dark chuckle.

"Are you into necrophilia, pet?" How dare he insult her? Before I knew it, my hand clamped tightly around his throat. But he didn't whimper—he was unafraid.

"I knew the moment my spell was broken, Ashana." He pried my fingers from around his slender neck with unimaginable strength. Bringing me down to my knees as I felt the ligaments in my wrist begin to strain with pressure as my bones started to crack.

"I am going to take her head and place it inside a special jar, but first, I think I will have some fun with her. You may not be into it, but I am."

"Is that the only way you can get a woman?" I sarcastically asked. Realizing I still had my dagger, I sliced it hard through his skin and bone. As black blood splattered onto my face, he let out a blood curtailing scream. Grabbing the box, I quickly ran to unchain Clover, but a gust of wind knocked me into a brick wall.

"She's mine now. Your bond is broken, so even in death she is no longer yours." Scrambling to my feet, I clutched the box tightly in my good hand. I watched in horror as Clover's eyes fluttered open. But the beautiful shimmering sapphires in her eyes were gone. Morphed into two White Suns as her body started to heal itself, the blood disappearing as she started to glow as bright as iridescent beams in the midnight sky. My heart thrummed in my chest at the sight of her ever-growing beauty.

I looked over at the wizard and all I saw was bewilderment as he clutched his bleeding limb. This was not his magic, it was hers.

"Chloe," I said as I fell to my knees. Pure white wings sprouted from her back breaking the chains that bound her.

"What magic is this?" he said.

"My magic," she answered as she knocked him into the many shelves of jarred heads. With the sound of a million screams, the glass shattered to the floor. I grimaced at the sight of all the heads thudding to the floor with the shattered glass and milky liquid, painting black stone white.

She glided over to me. Reaching out a hand, I grabbed it, and in an instant, we were gone.

On the top of a mountain range somewhere, I fell to my knees and she tumbled with me.

"Cal," she said through tears.

Her naked body embraced me as our lips collided in a passionate kiss.

"I thought I lost you. Our bond, it is broken. How?"

"It's my fault. I tried to combine the stones to free you and kill the wizard, but I failed," she said.

"I don't care—you are alive." I kissed her again, the blood in my body rushing to my cock. I needed her to know that I still loved her.

She pushed me down, tore my breeches from me, and straddled me, sinking deep into me with a groan of pleasure.

"You killed me," she said as she started moving. This was going to be rough and full of passion. We were pissed at each other, but this would re-solidify our bond.

"Forgive me," I yelled, forcing her onto her back, thrusting back hard into her. She punched me, clawed at me, and I kissed her harder with each thrust.

"I love you." She panted.

"I love you too." Captured in each other's releases, our climaxes were quick. We were sweating, but as our palms lifted, a new image appeared. White roses danced around a red dragon. Our bond was reborn.

"You have wings."

She smiled and laughed at me. “Apparently, I am a goddess or something.”

“That doesn’t make us family, right?” Gods, I hope not.

“No. My mother and father still created me; I just had the blood of a goddess inside of me. What the wizard and that shadow dragon didn’t know was that I had to die for my true self to be reborn.”

“You knew you were going to die when you came for me?” I asked, already knowing her answer.

“Yes.” She kissed my nose. We held each other close, her head on my chest, our legs tangled with each other.

“What are we going to do about the wizard?”

“Whatever we do, we do it together. We have the stones—they are the priority now.” She sat up. I could tell something was wrong as her wings dropped low. “What is it?” I asked, rubbing my hand down her soft skin.

“We can’t release the stones.” I sat up. “Each stone has a shadow dragon housed inside. We release the souls, we risk them, and they work for the Dark Wizard.”

“What do we do?” I asked.

“We need to destroy them.”

Chapter Twenty-Three

Clover

I died and came back

I died and came back reborn, but what I didn't tell him was who I saw on the other side. When the cloud of light cleared, my mother's scowling face looked down upon me. "Oh, my sweet flower, what a disappointment you are."

"I'm sorry, Mother. I failed you and our kingdom." She gripped my chin hard, digging those ever-sharpened nails into my skin. My blood pebbled beneath those talons.

"I should've pushed you more. Now look at what you did. You became an Ashana's whore, betrayed our kingdom, and disgraced the family." She was degrading me, but that is not true. None of it. I may be dead, but I died fighting for him and my people. I am not a useless, poised statue anymore.

"Get your fucking hands off me." Her eyes widened in surprise as I knocked her hand from my chin. "You think I am a whore, a disgrace, well guess what, Mother? I am none of those things. I sacrificed my freedom the day you strapped me down and tortured me. The day Calian came for me, after you and Father were killed, I hated him, but then I realized he saved me. Do you know what happened after that? I was

raped, but he saved me again. Then I got tired of being useless, like you tried to shape me into being, so I decided to fight, to love, and to be loved."

"The night Calian and I solidified the Blood Oath is the night I took my life back and I don't regret a single moment. And now that I am dead, I can be reborn into the person you so desperately tried to destroy." She crossed her arms, unafraid and untouched by my words.

"What's that, darling, a dead flower?"

"No," I laughed as I spread my arms wide. My wings sprouted from my back and my mother dissipated as Cal's shape formed in front of me. I was back, and I was a goddess.

Part Three: Shadow Light

Chapter Twenty-Four

Clover

The cheering of the crowds was the only encouragement I needed. No one expected the fight to go on this long. With her daggers in hand, the bright-eyed princess of Orion came charging at me, those shimmering sapphires full of anger and hate. She didn't notice I had anticipated her move until my right wing swept her feet from under her and she hit the sand hard with a grunt.

The feisty princess jumped to her feet, brushing her long auburn braid out of the way, glaring at me.

"No wings, Chloe," she spat.

"Apologies, Abbygale. They sometimes have a mind of their own." I smiled. It was true, to a point, that ever since I died and came back as a winged woman, I had little control over them. Flashbacks of that day kept me up at night and at times I found myself chained to the wall again. My blood pooling below my feet while Supreme Leader Rai and my mother laugh at me.

A small, wrapped fist thrust toward my face. I let her land the blow while my knee connected with her gut, earning me a wince of pain. Abbygale doubled over on her knees, clenching her abdomen while I spit my blood into the sand.

"Already done? I was hoping we could throw—"

Before another word left my mouth, Abbygale's legs kicked me to the ground with a hard blow. My wings strained, making me cringe in pain. They are quite sensitive. But that is because they are not hard like Calian's. They remind me of the wings of an ancient and majestic beast I used to read about. They were called Griffins. Although mine are pure white, I distinctly remember seeing a mix of auburn russet colors in their feathered wings.

Rolling to my side, Abbygale and I are now eye to eye. She smirks at me. "Shall we call this a tie?"

"Giving in, little sister?" the soft voice of Kaliegh, Queen of Orion, came from ahead of us. "That isn't like you at all. Shall I call the healer?"

Abbygale kicked sand toward Kaliegh, and we all laughed. Getting to my feet, I reached out a helpful hand, which could be a mistake if she truly were not done fighting, but she accepted without issue.

"We should do this again sometime. You are getting better, my friend," Abbygale says to me.

"Not without difficulty." Ever since we left the mountain range, I vowed to train harder. It was so easy for the Dark Wizard to manipulate me, just like Mother did. Although my scars are gone, the phantom pain remains. During the past month, I have learned how to block while striking, strike while blocking, mastered flying, and now I am ready to learn how to master the longbow. To be able to strike our enemies down from the skies would give us a greater advantage. I know we have the dragons, led by Azula, Kaliegh's bonded dragon, but I cannot rely on firepower alone. Our enemies are far stronger than any of us anticipated, and I know first-hand what that madman can do.

"Get cleaned up, we have a meeting at twenty. We are making the final decision on how we need to proceed with the Dragonhearts," Kaliegh said. I just nodded my response, and gave Abbygale one last pat on the back before marching back to my tent.

It was not much, but it was better than the last one I had. This one at least fit a cot big enough for the two of us to sleep comfortably—a wash basin to bathe in, and a small stationary with two chairs if we didn't want to lounge on our bed. When I walked in, Calian was already soaking in the wash basin, giving me a once-over before gesturing for me to join him.

I tossed my clothes to the side and sank deep down into the warmth of the water. I managed to glamor my wings so I could sit comfortably nestled between Calian's thighs while he lathered me up with the lavender soap. Washing the day away in silence.

This is nice.

We didn't have to always speak to know what the other one needed and at this moment, I just needed to be held.

"You are having nightmares again, my love." He rinsed the soap out of my now clean hair. I didn't say anything, just laid my head back onto his chest. "You are safe, Chloe. I promise to never kill you again."

We laughed, and although it was meant to be a joke, I know he still felt the shame for what he did. No matter how many times I have to remind him that it was necessary for me to become, well, me. The goddess of Earth and Light. I don't know much about my powers, but so far we have figured out that I can make my wings disappear and transport us anywhere I envision.

I have not done that since the incident with the

Dark Wizard.

"Cal," I started, lifting my head to look at him. "We have to destroy them."

"I know."

"But the rest of the council won't be in our favor. You know they want to free the dragons, but they don't understand the darkness that lingers within them."

"We just need to convince them."

"How do we do that when they have the influence of Azula, Verglas, and that ill-mannered beast named Xiong? They all respect you as their prince of dragons, but—"

He silenced me with a kiss.

"Cal."

"Did you know you ramble when you are flustered? I mean, it's quite cute." I smiled and then softly punched him for distracting me. "Want to play rough, my love? You know I like it."

"Never mind." Getting out of the tub, I grabbed my towel and dried off, before starting to get dressed.

"You're angry with me." I heard the water swish with his movement.

"Of course, I am. You are trying to make light of a very dark situation." Throwing my towel to the tarped floor, I started to dress but Cal turned me toward him. "No."

"I am not walking into a small tent full of people with you mad at me. We need to talk about this." Those stupid sad green eyes.

"Fine. You want to talk? We will once we have clothes on. I can't take you seriously when you look like that," I said as my hand waved up and down his dripping wet, bronzed body. He is a god in so many ways.

"Like what?" he asked, leaning down to try and kiss me. His hands wandered to my bare hips.

"All god-like." A smile formed on his lips as they landed gently on mine. I pushed him from me. "Stop trying to distract me while I am angry with you."

Turning away from him, I grabbed my ivory undergarments and adorned them quickly. Then, grabbing my violet-colored sleeveless tunic and brown breeches, with my back still to Cal, I dressed. Moving toward the small vanity, I started brushing the tangles from my hair, braiding it into two separate fishtails that sat flush with the tips of my wings.

"Okay, now I am ready to talk," I said, turning my gaze back to the still-naked Cal. "Seriously?"

"You are so cute when you are angry."

"Get dressed," I snapped.

"Just tell me what is bothering you. Is it time for your monthly bleed?" What a brave question to ask. We have not been using anything to protect us against conception. I have bled every month right on time. And we never discussed the topic of children.

"Just because I am irritated with you doesn't mean I am bleeding from my sex." He stared at me with a mix of confusion and worry in his emerald eyes. "I'll see you in the meeting."

Before he could protest, I kissed him softly as I teleported to the war tent.

The only thing that greeted me was the rounded oak table with a seat for each council member. The tent was empty. It has been four months since the fight with Supreme Leader Rai. There has been no word or sightings of him or his armies.

Azula led a scouting mission after Cal and I returned. There was nothing left except for rubble. The stones have been safely guarded by the dragons, although it was difficult for me to give them up knowing that everyone, except for myself and Cal, wanted to free all those souls.

Taking my seat, I admire the craftsmanship that went into creating a tent this large. Jian is a deserted wasteland with nothing but sand for miles all around. Azula, Cal, and the other dragons spent a week transporting all the lumber and materials from Orion.

The top has a large log that runs horizontally and extends the tent to sixty feet wide. Every twenty feet, there are logs to support each side, much like beams you can find on the top of a ceiling. Magic from the Ziran stone reinforced all the lumber.

The memory of that day fluttered in my mind. It was the third time I used that stone and when I had it in my palm again, it spoke to me. "Emnera, help us." Thousands of voices screamed to be free, causing me to feel ashamed for not wanting to liberate them.

The fabric of the tent is made from the skin and fur of Elks from the Elkwood Forest within Orion. Each time I went on a hunt with Abbygale or Kaliegh, we came back with one or two Elks. They used their meat for our food, fur for crafting, and horns for weapons.

"You are early." Kaliegh's voice broke my daze. The queen always looked ready for battle. Dressed in her crimson blouse, brown leather vest with the crest of Orion; a stallion, emblazoned right over her heart, and sword strapped to her leather breeches. Her boots are faceted tightly to her shins with a dagger hilt sticking out of each. Her beautiful, long, chocolate-colored hair was fastened in a long braid that flushed with her waistband.

"I'm just ready to get this over with." It came out cruder than I meant it to be. Her dark brows furrowed with a question. "Sorry, I didn't mean to snap, I just…" I paused, leaning forward and pinching the bridge of my nose.

"I understand you have been through a lot, Chloe, but you have to understand where we are all coming from. There are thousands upon thousands of innocent souls you are asking us to destroy."

My gaze snapped to her, anger and adrenaline coursing through me.

"And millions will be put at risk once those shadow dragons are released. You don't understand the power you are dealing with."

"And you do?"

"Have you forgotten about the fact that I was momentarily possessed by one of those things?" Nearly knocking my chair over, I got to my feet. "How about the fact that I died."

"Yet here you are."

"Here I am." Tension heated, and before we could continue our disagreement, the rest of the council flooded in. I didn't break my gaze until I felt Cal's lips caressing my ear with a whisper.

"Calm down, Princess." He nibbled my earlobe, sending a shiver of arousal through me. He picked up my chair, took my hand, and gestured for me to sit. I obliged, and he pushed my chair in before taking the seat next to me. His hand immediately landed on my upper thigh, and I dared a look at him. A small smirk danced on his sinful lips. He knew how to calm me down.

Abbygale sat to my right. Then Tailan from Dalaria, Kaliegh, Rowland, and then Azula all took their seats.

“Thank you all for coming,” Kaliegh regally stated.

“Like we had a choice,” Abbygale muttered, earning a look of disapproval from her sister.

“You all know why we are here. We need to take the final vote on what we are doing about the Dragonhearts.”

“Free them,” Tailan stated in his Eastern thick accent I still struggled to understand at times.

Easy, love. We will have our turn. Cal said through our bond, adding a caressing touch.

“It has to be a unanimous decision,” Rowland, husband to Kaliegh, stated, looking at both myself and Cal.

“Princess Chloe, what is your decision?” Tailan asked.

Quelling my anger, I took in a deep breath, slowly exhaling. “If we free the souls, I just want you all to know that you will be adding to Supreme Leader’s Rai’s forces.” Cal moved his hand up further, nearly touching my throbbing sex. A sheen of sweat formed on my brow with the added heat from his touch.

“We will be ready when the time comes,” Rowland states so matter-of-factly that my teeth clench in irritation. I grip Cal’s wandering hand, shoving it off me, and move to my feet.

“Clearly you all have forgotten the evil that threatens our world.” Scowling at them. “Free the souls if you must, but hear these words. I have seen the shadow dragon that lives within the Earth stone. Felt his power flourishing through my body. It's addicting and stronger than anything I have ever felt. We only know that there are at least five of them waiting to be freed. There could be more. What magic do you have that will kill a shadow dragon?" I watch as all their eyes land on Azula in the back.

"There is rumor of a sixth stone that will destroy Supreme Leader Rai and all his armies."

"When did this information become known? Where did this rumor come from?" I ask.

"As you are well aware of, Emnera," she starts, using my true name. I am not sure if I like hearing it more than I like the name with which I was born. "My siblings have been hunting down any information we can on Rai. We came across this information a few days ago."

"And who, pray tell, is the reliable source that told you this?" I scowl. Although Azula could end me with a blast of fire, I know she will not harm the wife of her king.

"His name is Jaxx. According to various travelers of the realm, he is a skilled craftsman," she states, her golden eyes looking earnestly at me.

"What craft does he practice that allows him to know the information he does?" I ask her.

"I believe you know him as The Hooded Mercenary."

I couldn't speak, so Cal did for me. "Where is he now?"

"In Thornwarf." I tense up. I have not been home at all since the night Cal came for me. Not once have I looked back and wanted to go home. Rob, Captain of the Petunia, has sailed across the sea numerous times sending messages to Alma. I long to see her again, but I don't know if I could stand going back to the place that is the center of my nightmares.

"Then we are all in agreement?" Kaliegh asks, and I just nod in response. "We will head to the Temple first thing tomorrow morning. May the Great Kings of the Past watch over us as we free the innocents that were taken so long ago."

Chapter Twenty-Five

Calian

I watch as everyone exits the tent except for Chloe. She sat back down, lost in her own head. Reaching my hand to her face, I cupped her chin and turned her toward me. "My goddess, my queen, tell me what I can do to ease your worries."

"Cal, something doesn't feel right about this. Since when does Azula, an honorable dragon, trust the words of a notorious criminal?" Her body turned slightly toward me, making her honey-colored braids sway slightly. I will never get used to seeing how beautiful she is. The way her sapphire-colored eyes look at me. Each time they change with whichever mood she is in.

"Do you want to leave?" My question appeared to have shocked her.

"Would you really leave here with me?"

Leaning in, I placed my hand on her hips, my lips caressing her neck, then her ear. "All you need to do is ask." Her hands wandered up my thighs as I sucked on the tender spot of her neck.

"Cal," she stated breathlessly as my cock hardened. She didn't let me have her before we came in, and now I wanted her so badly, but like always, I wait for her permission.

"Tell me what you want, Princess," I say against

her lips. In an instant, we are teleported back to our tent, and she has me pinned down with a dagger to my throat.

"I want you to stop trying to seduce me during important meetings." She tried to cover her arousal with anger, but I knew better. Heat radiated off her sex.

"As you wish, Princess." Those words got her every time. Leaning down, the blade at my throat, she kissed me deeply. I let her take the lead as her tongue mingled with mine in an intimate duet. She tasted so sweet, and I wanted more. Gripping her hips, I flipped us over so she was under me. I felt the warmth of my blood trickling down my neck from where the dagger had sliced ever so gently.

I pinned her wrist together above her head with one hand, while the other cupped her breasts. "What do you want, Princess?"

"You to fuck me so hard I forget about everything." Releasing her hands, I tear her blouse from her, clamping my mouth on her right breast, nibbling on her hardened peak, and revel in the moan leaving her lips.

"As you wish." Her hands travel to my trousers, fumbling with the string as I sucked harder, leaving my mark on each breast. When she failed to untie my breaches, I felt her scrambling to tear my blouse free. I assist her, my blouse landing on the floor. I kissed her again, grinding my hips into her. Her nails scratch my back as I continued to tease her with anticipation.

My lips trailed along her body, kissing every spot that used to have a scar. I do this to show my admiration for her strength in enduring a life of torture, knowing she still experiences those feelings. Getting to the top of her breeches, I rip them from her body and place my head between her legs. I love the sight of her glistening sex.

My eyes locked onto hers as she arched her back, her fingers raking through my hair. She pushed my face into her sex. I start with one lick; she tastes so sweet. I suck on her nob as my two fingers thrust inside her wetness. Her back bows as she thrashes from her building climax.

"Cal, don't stop. Gods." Her hips moved in rhythm with my tongue and fingers. One last moan—she released her climax onto my tongue, and I licked every bit up. Rising, I remove my breeches, releasing my erection. She sat up, wrapping her hand around my shaft, her eyes locked onto mine as she licks the cream from the tip and then takes me whole. But I cannot wait. I need to be inside her.

"Get on your stomach." She kissed the tip once more and then got on all fours at the edge of the cot. I placed my tip at her entrance and then eased myself in, wanting it to be slow.

"Fuck me," she ordered, and like always, I slammed into her. Gripping her two fishtails, I pulled on them and she released a moan. Pumping into her, I felt her stretching, clenching, and another climax released from her as I pumped harder. With one hand gripping her braids, I take the other and find her swollen bundle of nerves. Circling it, she arched her back. "Faster."

"As…you…wish." With everything I had, I pumped faster until my release couldn't be held back. I filled her with my seed. We both collapsed on the cot, sweaty, spent, and happy. She curled herself into my arms.

"I love you," she said, turning over and kissing me softly.

"I love you, my goddess." She gave me a wayward smile. "Does it bother you when I call you that?" One of her hands found its way to my chest. Swirling her fingers through my hair, her eyes wandered down.

"I have only known one name my entire life, until I died." She paused to look up at me. "And I hated it since the moment that first blade touched my skin."

"And now?"

"Now, I have a choice. I can claim the name Emnera, or I can keep the name given to me by the woman who tortured me." I rubbed a comforting hand along her spine.

"You are also my queen."

"I don't feel like a queen or a goddess." Hovering over her, she shifted onto her back as I planted myself between her legs.

"Shall I worship you again?" I asked, kissing her softly.

"I'm not opposed to the idea of you worshiping me."Her breath hitched as my hand cupped her still-wet sex. Our releases mix along my fingers. I lifted them to my mouth and sucked them dry, watching as her eyes alight with lust.

"Tell me what name I shall call you so that when that pretty little mouth is around my cock, I know what name to roar when I fill your throat with my seed." She smiled and her sex clenched as I entered two fingers inside her.

"I don't know if I have earned the title of being a queen or a goddess." I stopped moving my fingers, cupping her face.

"You have earned the title of being my queen. I am the only heir to the god of dragons. That makes me a king. You are my wife, my heart, my queen. I will not have it any other way. If you choose to denounce the title of Emnera, then I will support your decision, but I will not sit here and allow you to berate yourself. You are Queen Chloe. My queen." With that, I buried my face into her sex and showed my queen just how much I praised her.

Morning came with the light of the High Sun's rays peeking through the slit in our tent, and a warm breeze blew through. As I gazed upon my queen, sleeping in the crook of my arm, I admired her beauty. She didn't have a nightmare last night. We don't talk about them, and although I have tried to persuade her, she just waves me off like they are no big deal. But I can feel the terror surging down our bond when she has them.

I can only assume they are memories of what her mother did to her. When it happens, I do my best to hold her tight and send soothing warmth down our bond.

"Calian." A distant whisper of my name filled my head. Looking around, I don't see anyone else. "Come home to me, pet."

"Who's there?" I rise to my feet, grabbing the hilt of my sword. I still don't see anyone.

"Your Master calls to you." I felt it in my head, the voice that ordered me to kill her. Long, bony fingers claw at me, digging their sharpened ends into my brain.

"Cal." Chloe's voice rang in my ears and through blurred vision, I saw her. I felt her touch on my face and the memory of her bloodied body chained to the wall flooded my mind as my dagger pierced her heart. "Cal, wake up."

Opening my eyes, something firm was in my hand. It was her neck. Releasing my grip, she coughed and sucked in a sharp breath as I backed away in horror. "I'm sorry."

She walked over to me, wrapping me in her embrace. "Where'd you go?"

"I don't know. One second I was here, and you were sleeping, the next I was stabbing you again." Looking up at me, she kissed me softly.

"I'm alive, Cal, and I'm not going anywhere." Her beautiful white wings wrap and mingle with my dark dragon-scaled ones.

"I heard him."

"Who?"

"Supreme Leader Rai. He was calling to me."

"Has this happened before?"

"No."

"Do you think this means he's back?"

"I don't know, but, Chloe…" I backed up from her, putting on my shirt. "He was trying to get control of my mind again."

"Can he do that?"

"I'm not sure. We don't know the extent of his powers," I answer while pulling my breeches on. She begins to dress as we continued talking. "All I know is, my hand was wrapped around your throat. I could've killed you, *again*."

"Cal, you just had a flashback. I get them too."

"When? You have never told me this before." I don't hide the irritation in my voice.

"It's no big deal. They have only happened once or

twice."

"Chloe, you can't hide things like that from me. I'm your mate." She is fully dressed, walking over to me, pouting her lips, and placing her hands on my hips.

"It usually happens when we are sleeping. Anyway, don't turn this conversation around on me. We need to figure out if Rai still has some hold over your mind. And if he does, we need to kill him sooner than later." As we exit the tent, I know she is not acting like it right now, but she was scared. I saw the terror in her eyes when I came back.

The entire army is here in Jian. What started as just a couple of tents here and there, has turned into a large campsite for three armies. Rob and his crew stay on the seas, and I have gone back to see him every so often to check on the communications between him and Alma.

Prince Eli has agreed to team up with Alma in the fight against the Dark Wizard, which is great if I trusted the bastard. I still want to kill him for what he did to Chloe. As I follow her to the War tent, I look out upon the vast pavilions spread out, the soldiers sharpening their swords and sparring with one another.

There are a few I know by name, but I am not a general. That is Rowland and Abbygale's position in the ranks. Chloe and I are the guardians of the skies. Flying with the army of Ice Dragons.

As we enter, I feel the tension in the air with the argument going on between the two sisters. From the months we have spent here, Abbygale Orion is a stubborn young lady, who on one hand, opposes anything her sister says. And on the other, will cut down anyone who threatens her family.

"Because I said so, that's why," Kaliegh stated.

"For someone who never wanted to be like our mother, you sure do try, and act like her," Abbygale spat. My gaze landed on Rowland, who was always posted at Kaliegh's side. I have respect for him. As her husband, he was entitled to the position of being the king, but he never demanded it.

"Sorry, are we interrupting something?" Chloe asked.

"No, Abbygale was just leaving." I watched her eyes roll as she exited the tent, muttering curses under her breath. "What's wrong?"

"Calian and I have come to ask for a favor." Not a favor really.

"Anything," she says eagerly.

Chloe gestured for me to take the lead. I stepped up next to my queen. "Is it possible that Supreme Leader Rai could still have some control over my mind?"

She appeared to ponder the question. "If you would permit me, I would like to reach into your mind and see if he remains." Kaliegh is a Seer. They have many undiscovered powers, but she and Rowland get visions or prophecies sent to them by the gods. She can also see into the mind of another with just one touch.

Nodding my approval, she placed both hands on my temples and closed her eyes.

I felt nothing, but as I watched her body convulse before me, Rowland wrapped his arms around her body to support her. In a heartbeat, she stilled, opened her eyes, and wiped the sheen of sweat from her brow.

"What is it? What did you see?" The look of terror in her blue eyes revealed it was bad.

"I felt him inside you. It was dark, cold, and I felt like I couldn't breathe. His magic still lingers inside of your mind and if we don't destroy him soon, he will destroy your mind. Making you his slave once again."

Chapter Twenty-Six

Clover

Sweat gleamed off my head as I dodged another punch from Abby. For someone smaller than me, she packed a lot of muscle.

"What's with you today?" she asked, keeping her bandaged fists in position. We learned from a healer that to protect our knuckles from cracking, we needed to wrap the thick fabric around to add a layer of protection.

Abby and I started this friendship off on rocky ground when we first met. Lately, I find myself spending more time with her than anyone else, except for Cal. We started training together after I told them about what happened when I went rogue, as Abby puts it, to save my mate.

Taking a swig of water, I swallowed hard, contemplating if I should tell her everything, or just a synopsis. "We think the Dark Wizard still has magic inside Cal's mind."

"What are we going to do about it?" Sometimes I don't understand her nonchalant attitude. I watched her sip her water, admiring the hardened nature that is this young woman. Only at the age of seventeen, she has experienced the sorrows this life can bring you.

"We haven't discussed it yet, but I think we are

going to pursue Jaxx." Her brow rose with wonder. "What's that look for?"

"Nothing." She paused, stepping closer to me. "It's just usually you and the lover boy over there have decisions made before you talk to anyone else about them." She was right. Something was slightly off between us, but it could be the flashbacks, the nightmares, or maybe that we don't talk as much as we used to. If the Dark Wizard still has magic inside Cal, I need to make our bond stronger, not weaker.

"This time we want to include all of you."By the look in her eyes, I knew she didn't believe me, yet she didn't pry.

"When do you want to leave?"

"I will let you know at tonight's meeting."

"You know what I would love more than anything?" I cocked my head to the side; I could guess it had something to do with her sister. "For Kaliegh to stop being such a stuffy person. I thought that after she married Rowland, she would finally have sex and relax a little."

"Has she always been so regal?"

"No." I sensed a tone of sadness in her voice. We walked around the grounds. Several soldiers moved out of our way, averting their eyes as we passed. I don't hide my wings, not when I am out of the tent. It didn't feel natural to keep them hidden.

Passing by the blacksmith's tent, he kneeled, stopping his hammering on the blade of a sword. We have told the soldiers numerous times that when they are in a non-formal setting, kneeling is not necessary. The older generation will kneel regardless.

"I hate it when they do that," I said, interrupting

Abby's babbling.

"Get used to it. You're a goddess and a queen."

"Would it be shameful if I told you I'm not sure I want to be either of those?" The sand kicked up with a warm gust of wind. Using my wings, I shielded us from the particles that tried to pelt our skin.

"For someone who doesn't like those titles, you sure do love to use those," she stated after the wind died down and I lowered them.

Avoiding that conversation, I revert to the plan. "I'm going to suggest to Kaliegh that a small squad finds this Jaxx character and get his assistance with taking down Rai."

She stopped, causing me to do the same just before her tent. "I'm going to say this because deep down in the pit of despair that is my heart, I might like you. Be careful when dealing with criminals. They can take the thing you love most and destroy it."

"You speak like you know from experience. Is this about Tristian?" Silence filled the space between us.

"Just be careful." She turned and entered her tent. She was too young to know the heartache that haunted her.

Soaking in the bath, I sipped on a chalice of plum wine. A delicacy to this part of the realm and I loved it. *What bothers you, my Queen?* Cal's voice entered my mind along with the faintest of touch.

Everything, I responded. Then phantom fingers are felt on my shoulders, followed by the movement of pressure.

You are tense. Let me take your stress away.

Where are you? I asked as those hands dug deeper, making my sore muscles ease further.

Scouting out Jaxx with Azula. I will be back soon.

When you come back, be ready to fulfill your promise of relieving my stress.

As you wish, my Queen. I can help you right now if you wish.

I am scared and intrigued to ask. *Show me.*

Those phantom hands made their way to mine. One moved down to my sex and circled that throbbing bundle of nerves, while the other pinched the raising peaks of my breasts.

I felt the faintest caress of his lips on my neck. *You don't know how badly I want those to be my hands. Can you feel how badly I want you?*

Yes. I rasped as he guided my hands, building pleasure in my core. The water splashed with each movement of our fingers as my thumb circled my knob and two fingers thrust inside of me. As my release rushed through me, his touch was suddenly gone.

Getting out of the bath, I dried off and began to dress. Another meeting with the council that wanted to risk freeing a vast shadow across our world. Running my fingers through my hair, I fastened it into a braid before adorning my crimson blouse, brown breeches, and boots. I couldn't remember the last time I had worn a corset or dress.

The same leaders were sitting in their wingback chairs by the time I entered. Cal and Azula were the only ones absent. *They must still be on that mission.* I take my usual seat, with Abby sitting next to me.

"Chloe, you may take the lead," Kaliegh so graciously offered.

"Cal and I have decided to seek out Jaxx. To gain information on how to kill the Dark Wizard." Tailan and Rowland exchanged looks, but since Kaliegh and Abby already knew what happened, they didn't act surprised.

"If the council is in agreement, it will be allowed." Out of my peripheral vision, I saw Abby's eyes roll with annoyance.

"Will it just be you two?" Tailan asked.

"No," Abby stated before I could. "I will be accompanying them along the way."

"Very well. We will free the souls," Kaliegh stated matter-of-factly. I bit my inner cheek to avoid speaking my mind. It will do no good. They all knew how I felt about their plan. Making Cal a priority might be selfish, but if Rai gained control of him again, I might lose him.

"Since Abby doesn't have wings, how will you all travel?"Rowland asked.

"I can teleport myself and her to The Petunia while Cal transports himself. Captain Rob will be expecting us. From there, we will journey back across the Great Sea and make port in Thornwarf."

"Are you ready to go back home?" he asked. I never warmed up to Rowland Kawthorne. His demeanor and willingness to side with everything Kaliegh said, just breathed snitch. Cal has never liked him ever since we met him. Yet, he has done nothing to make us not trust him.

"Yes." I lied with a convincing smile on my face.

"Meeting adjourned. Stay safe and we will see each other again on the battlefield." I didn't wait for anyone to leave until I was back in my tent.

"You are getting stronger my love."

I flinched at the sound of Cal right behind me.

"You scared me."

"I told you I would come back soon."

"That was faster than I anticipated." He wrapped his thick arms around me, careful not to squish my wings. "Did you find him?"

"We did." He kissed my neck. "But we can talk about that tomorrow."

"We leave tomorrow." Spinning me around to face him, he planted a kiss on my lips.

"I know something is wrong, so tell me what it is."

"Going back there, preparing to face the wizard, freeing the souls, it all frightens me." He cupped my face, those two pools of green filling with warmth and desire. Planting a kiss on my brow, he turned away from me.

"I have something I know will cheer you up," he started, scrimmaging through his bag.

"It isn't another flower, right?"

"You hate them, remember," he teased and then pulled a small box out, turning it toward me. "I have had these since I was a child." Opening the small black box, two golden bands shimmered as bright as day.

"They're beautiful."

He picked up the one with a dragon emblazoned upon it, then held my left hand. "If you will allow me, these are the bands my parents wore when they were married."As he held it up, I noticed an engraving written on the inside.

"What does it say?"

A smile formed on his lips. "You are the shadow light that guides me through the darkest of times." He slid it on my ring finger. "It's true, Chloe. No matter what happens, I know your light will guide me back to you."

The tears flowed before he wiped them away.

"And yours?" I asked.

"You tell me."He smiled, handing the band to me.

"You are the heartbeat to my very soul. Cal, these are beautiful, but they belonged to your parents. Are you sure you want—" He kissed me so deeply, so tenderly, that my breath caught.

"You are mine. That band around your finger and the symbol tattooed on your palm, represent our union to others. But here,"—he points to his heart— "is where our blood beats together. I will never regret that day our bloodied palms joined, and you became mine. From then and to eternity we will do everything together." I kissed him softly as he walked us to the cot. "And tomorrow, we will face Thornwarf and the wizard together."

"Cal."

He placed a finger over my lips.

"Tonight, we won't talk about our worries, because tonight, I am fucking you until you forget about all the bad dreams you have ever had."

Chapter Twenty-Seven

Calian

"You're mine, Ashana. When I tell you to kill Emnera, you will not hesitate to please me. I am your master, and you will bring her to me so I can take her power for my own.``

"As you wish, Master." I feel my hand wrapping tightly around her taut throat. Those two sapphires gleam with sorrow as I choke her into submission. Iron clasps her wrists and ankles as I take my dagger, slicing each wrist, watching with glee as the crimson liquid pools into the buckets below her.

"You promised," she croaks. "You are stronger than this, Cal. Fight him."

"I only take orders from my master. You are nothing to me."

"Look at your hand, remember me." She is trying to manipulate me. Feeding me lies about my master, about me and her. "Cal, please, I love you."

"Kill her." My master gives me the final order. I approach her, I notice the beauty that is her hair, those wings, the curves of her body. I steady my blade at her chest.

"Goodbye," she whispers before my dagger plunges into her chest as her lips crash onto mine.

"Cal, wake up." My vision cleared once I see her

below me, my dagger pressed into her throat.

"Shit. Chloe, gods." Jumping out of the bed, I dropped the blade to the floor.

"It was a nightmare, Cal. It isn't your fault."

"I killed you. He made me kill you again." She followed me, her soft hands caressing my bare chest.

"I'm here. I'm alive." My gaze landed on the healing graze on her neck.

"I cut you."

"I'm fine, Cal."

"He's going to make me kill you for your power." I stepped away from her. I'm supposed to be protecting her, not hurting her.

"Don't you dare pull away from me."

"I almost killed you."

"You can't kill me, Cal. I am a goddess, remember?"

"It doesn't matter, Chloe. The fact is he can get inside my mind and make me do things. I have to leave. You can't be near me." Before I could teleport away from her, she tackled me to the floor, pinning my wrists, and using all her strength to hold me down.

"No." She glared at me. Her naked body pressed into mine. "You said *together* last night. I will not let you run away because of a nightmare."

"Using your goddess' strength isn't fair."

"I don't give a fuck, Cal. You are mine. You belong to me, and no one can make you do anything except me." Her stare was intense, and her eyes began to glow with power. "I am your queen, your Goddess Emnera, and I will not allow you to push me away."

The power radiating from her was intoxicating, alluring, arousing.

"I don't want to hurt you."

"Shut the fuck up with that bullshit. You know you cannot. Do not let him wedge his way into our bond. We are stronger than him." She moved her hands to my face, and I flipped us. She wrapped her legs around me, holding me to her.

"Let me go."

"No," she growled. I know she felt the anger and lust flowing through me.

"Fine." Without another word, I slammed myself into her, both of us groaning in ecstasy. "You are going to have to let me go."

"Fuck you. Gods, fuck me," she moaned as her nails dragged down my back. "You are my Calian." Hearing her say that eased the fear within me.

"Say it again," I demanded as I thrust harder.

"You are mine." She moaned her pleasure.

"Together," I said as my lips crashed onto hers.

"Always and forever," she whispered, as our tongues danced and we both climaxed at the same time. Panting, she pulled me into her.

"I'm sorry.

"You can't push me away, Cal. We are in this fight together. All of it."

"I know." I kissed her deeply. Neither of us wanted this moment to end. We both knew once we released each other, our ultimate battle will begin.

****

The trip to Helm's Harbor was quick. Chloe transported herself and Abby. I am amazed at how powerful my queen is.

As we walked onto the deck of The Petunia, Chloe gave me a flirtatious wink while educating Abby on the nomenclatures of the ship.

"Nice to see you again brother." Rob's deep voice caught me off guard.

"Rob, have you lost weight?" I joked, a smirk forming across my lips.

"How is she?" His concern for Chloe was endearing. They have become great friends over the past couple of months.

"She's having nightmares again," I whispered. My Chloe, just as strong as ever. Not wanting to talk about them. "She is good. Her powers grow stronger every day."

"You think she will get sea sickness again? If so, she should just fly."

"I will be fine," Chloe stated from behind me. "But thank you, Rob."

"Shall we meet in the cabin?" he asked. Heat flashed across her body and down our bond at the memory of the last time we were in there together. I fucked her on top of that table right before we set sail. Afterward, we both felt slightly guilty for it. Only because we were trying to make plans with Rob.

"Yes," I answered and then felt the invisible caress of her hand on my cock.

Are you going to behave this time? she asked while thrumming it up and down.

Me? You are the one rubbing me. Going into that meeting wanting to fuck you is not the way you make me behave.

She released her hand, but not before I grabbed her wrist, spun her into my arms, and crashed my lips onto her. "I prefer the real thing, love, but this meeting is important."

A sinful look flashed in her jeweled eye. "I'll behave if you do." She blinked her thick lashes innocently.

Releasing my hold on her, we walked hand in hand through the wooden doors and took our seats at the round table.

"Princess Abbygale, it's a pleasure to have you aboard my ship." Rob was being extra polite to her. She is an attractive woman, and no doubt he wanted her pinned under him. He will learn that she wants nothing to do with him. At least in that manner.

"I'm not going to fuck you, Rob, so you don't need to be so nice," she hissed and then plopped her feet onto the table, took one of her daggers, and picked at her nails.

"Do you really have to be so crude?" I say. She always sat like that. No matter how important a meeting is, Abby sat like she had no one to answer to. Chloe tells me to back off her.

"Aren't you a demi-god?" she asked, and I raised a brow with inquiry. Where was she going with this? "I mean, if you are an all-powerful being, then why do you have to be so,"—she circled her dagger, trying to figure out her words— "uptight. No?"

"Enough." Chloe interrupted. "If Rob is fine with the way Abby sits, then it isn't our place to speak about."

"Thank—"

"And you have no right to speak to him like that." The blue sapphires flickered with the anger I know she felt. "No one insults him. You are my friend, Princess, but Calian is my mate. I will not stand by and let anyone, let alone a spoiled brat, offend him. Do you understand me?"

My cock hardened for her. The power, the beauty—if she could see herself as I do, I know she would see the goddess I do. I should fall to my knees for her. Everyone in this pathetic universe should worship her.

I looked between Abby and Rob, noticing the slight tremor of fear radiating from them. I placed my hand on hers, and she felt hot to the touch, the kind of heat that comes with a fire roasting boar. Her head snapped to me, and then her glow simmered as she realized there was no real threat here.

"Before you arrived, I received another message from Alma," Rob stated, breaking the tension within the room. I noticed Abby adjust her position.

"Is everything all right?" Chloe asked.

"They have captured the Hooded Mercenary."

"Excellent." She smiled, but soon it faded at Rob's worrisome expression.

"What else?" I pried.

"The message stated that he isn't human." Rob paused, gauging our reaction. At the mention, Abby stopped her nail digging to look at him. "He is an Ashana, and he only wants to speak with you." He pointed a thick finger at me.

"Impossible." I knew I was the only Ashana alive. I was a baby when my parents died, and I was handed off to a stranger in Greveil. That woman never told me anything.

"Cal, are you sure?" Chloe asked.

"I don't speak about my childhood, but I grew up with a human couple until I reached the age of seventeen. I left and became a guard to the court of

Greveil." I paused for a moment. "Get the rum. If I am going to give you a synopsis of my younger self, I need a drink."

Rob got up, went to his desk at the back of the room, and pulled off a bottle of liquid amber and four glasses. "I didn't know how to glamorize my wings when I was a child, so naturally, the couple I was living with, hid me away. Cecil was a soldier's wife. She told me about the Dragon Wars and how I was an orphan.

"When I asked who gave me to her, she stated one of my father's last remaining soldiers did. The bastard only gave her a note and two golden wedding bands." I noticed Chloe ran her finger over hers. "She was instructed to keep me safe until I learned how to control my powers. When that day came, I was recruited by the King at the time to join his court.

"I took a vow to protect the court for the rest of my life." I paused and took a sip, welcoming the burn as the liquid flowed down my throat. "I never once broke my vow. Never had a reason to. Until I met my mate." I looked at Chloe and I saw a glaze of tears whelming in her eyes.

"I was told that I was the only living heir of my father. There are no other Ashanas alive. And if he claims to be, how was he so easily captured? Nothing and no one has that kind of magic. Except for Supreme Leader Rai."

The room was so silent, I could hear the faint whizzing of a bug across the room.

"Cal," Chloe started, but couldn't find her words.

"It's not possible." I heard the croak in my own voice as my throat suddenly went dry. Rising, the chair smashed to the floor as I stormed out of there.

I don't know why I was feeling worked up over this. I am the only Ashana alive. I would know if I had a sibling. Why would I be given up if I had one? Why would we be separated? The cool salty air hit my heated skin as I took flight.

Everything was calmer while in the skies. No complications. Nothing. From above, I saw the tiny figures of the crew doing various jobs. Rob made his way back to the helm, while Abby appeared to be yelling at a deckhand who tried to grab her ass.

Where is my queen?

"Cal." Looking over my shoulder, I stopped, flapping my wings every few seconds to keep myself from falling. "Are you okay?"

The rays of the High Sun glowed upon her, making the beautiful flecks of electric blue shine. Her loose ivory top fit her body perfectly, showing the plumpness of her breasts. My eyes trailed the curves of her thick thighs, yearning to tear those breeches off and plunge my cock into her.

"We can talk about it." She moved closer. I didn't want to talk about it. Not with the anger mixing with the need to have her. Gripping her waist, I pulled her into me. My tongue danced with hers. A moan escaped her lips as I trailed mine across her neck to the tops of her breast. "Cal, talk to me."

"I don't want to talk right now." I peered down at her, trying to make her understand all I needed was a release. A distraction from this new revelation. "Turn around."

She did. I had to dodge her beautiful wings. I pulled her back to me, rubbing my cock along her ass. One hand trailed under her blouse, down to her waistband. Lifting her breeches and the lace undergarment, I felt her wet heat coating my fingers. "You are always so wet for me."

"You're always so hard for me," she breathlessly stated, turning her head to kiss me. I undid her breeches, pulling them to the tops of her knee-high boots.

"Bend over," I commanded. I get the full sight of her glistening sex. I tasted her again and then eyed the puckered hole. Placing my finger over it, I asked, "I want to fuck you here."

"Cal, I've never."

"Will you let me?" She nodded. "Not today. Today I want you wet on me. But I will play." The adrenaline we both felt was high. We had to make sure our wings didn't falter. Pulling my breeches down, I freed one leg. Placing my tip at her entrance, I swirled it around. Plunging into her, I sucked on a finger before entering.

"Fuck." She moaned as her head kicked back. I upped the pace with each thrust. Adding another finger. Her walls clenched as she climaxed. I didn't slow down. She moved a hand to her bundle of nerves, adding more stimulation as I added another finger and continued to thrust into her.

My balls drew up and I felt my release coming.

"Cal, I'm going to…"She screamed my name as another climax surged through her and I roared with mine. We began to fall when we both stopped moving. Before we plunged into the sea, I gripped her tightly and soared into the air again.

Panting, spent, and relaxed, I turned her toward me and kissed her. "I love you."

"I love you too." Bending down, I pulled her

breeches back up. "Cal, are you ready to talk?"

We were still mid-air, but I grabbed her hand and gestured for us to fly together.

"I don't want to talk about the possibility of me having a sibling. You are the only family that I have and need."

****

We made it in time to wash and change before meeting the prisoner. Alma was escorting him. Clover had me in her embrace, comforting me and giving me strength. The struggle to maintain my emotions was as difficult as the struggle to fight off Rai's power. I got a moment of reprieve as soon as the throne hall doors swung open and I saw him.

"Don't stop the party on my account," he quipped as Clover and I broke apart. "On second thought, I believe the party has just begun." The sound of scratching echoed against the floor and I looked to find the bone tips of his wings dragging slightly across the tiled floor.

I kept my tone calm as I said, "Hello, brother."

"Kneel before your queen," Alma said, followed by her staff knocking the back of his knees in. With a hard thud, he winced as his knees hit the floor.

"I like it rough, but you could at least buy me a drink first," he spat and then she moved to strike him, but Abbygale quickly gripped her wrist.

"I don't think it is wise to strike him while he is defenseless." Their eyes locked for a moment, and something formed between them that reminded me of the moment I first laid eyes on my mate.

"Jaxx." Clover demanded his attention, breaking the fog between them. "Do you know why you are in chains?"

"Because I was attacked, drugged, and kidnapped by your guard." He gestured his head toward the white-haired warrior.

"You are in chains because you are a criminal." She stepped closer, and I watched as my mate began her interrogation, feet cemented to the floor, my eyes never leaving him. "I would like to remove those chains, but first you must give me your word you won't cause problems or flee."

"I don't usually make deals with royal scum, but,"—he paused, looking at me— "for the sake of my baby brother, I will give you my word."

As Alma approached him, I added a condition. "I want her to do it." He pointed at Abbygale. Reluctantly, she grabbed the keys as the guards forced him to his feet. He stood a foot or two over her. "I don't like how interested he is in our young princess," I whispered to Clover. She didn't respond as we watched the scene play out.

As the chains were handed over, he gripped her wrists and pulled her into his embrace. His chest to her back, a hand quickly wrapped around her slender neck, while her arms are pinned.

Idiot.

"Halt," the queen ordered as the guard charged toward him. "You went back on your word."

"As your guard put it earlier, I'm a criminal. Now let me go, or I snap her neck." None of them moved, his brow furrowing in confusion until Abby had them flipped, pinned beneath her with a dagger to his throat. A smile broke free as I sustained my laughter. "Aren't you a wicked little thing."

"If you think I won't slit you from ear to ear, you are mistaken," she warned. I couldn't help but notice the burning heat in his eyes as he assessed her.

"Abby, I think you have proven your point," the queen stated.

"Are we going to have a problem, Jaxx?" Abby asked. He shook his head side to side, and she slowly removed the dagger before standing, offering a hand to help him up.

"Abbygale Orion is a princess and will be treated with respect," I growled.

"Beg pardon, Princess." He feigned a bow.

"Enough. My name is Chloe. You are here because we received word that you know the location of the shadow magic we need to destroy the Dark Wizard."

His gaze shifted from Abby to Chloe. "I might know the said information."

"Tell us," I snarled, growing impatient with these games.

"So primal. I thought when you finally fucked a whore, you wouldn't be so angry." He was trying to goat me into an attack but the fool didn't know that Clover didn't need my protection to defend her honor. In a shimmering light of gold, Chloe had pure white wings, and her sapphire-colored eyes were now white, her hand raising him into the air with a feral growl vibrating in her throat

"You will not insult him."

"Isn't this a twist. My, my, you didn't just fuck a royal whore. You fucked a goddess. I must say that I am pro—" She thrust him into the wall. I heard the crunch of his wings as his breath caught on impact. "You will understand that you have no power here.

Whether you agree to give that information up willingly or not, we will get it out of you." Chloe's threat had his body quaking for a moment. Getting to his feet, he spat blood onto the ground.

"It won't be easy to obtain the materials required for the spell," he warned.

"What spell?" I asked.

"You need magic to destroy magic." He slowly closed the distance between us. "To create the dagger of Vertumnus, we need elements from each species of dragon."

"Why does it have to be dragons?" Abby asked.

"Because the Dark Wizard committed the ultimate sin to become who he is today," he answered. We exchanged glances. "He wasn't always a murderous bastard. He was a human once upon a time.

"Before the war started, he was an advisor to one of the human kings. An adversary between dragons, elves, and humans. Somewhere along the way, he lost his position. Like any typical pathetic human, he sought out revenge. He searched the deepest, darkest parts of the world and found the colony of Shadow Dragons. They all became excellent friends and thus began the Dragon Wars."

"What was the ultimate sin?" Abby asked.

"Killing my father. Tika, God of Dragons."

"What are the ingredients?" I challenged, avoiding his stare.

"Blood from each leader of each colony. Ice, fire, earth, nurture, and shadow," he replied.

Silence sliced through the air. A coldness overcame the room.

"Alma." I watched as the queen's guard

approached her. “Contact Queen Kaliegh. I need them to wait to free the souls. Tell her why and that we will once we head back.”

“Yes, Your Majesty.” Alma left and I watched as a wicked grin spread across her mind-night-colored face and a flash of black crossed over the whites of her eyes.

“Are you sure you can trust her?” I stated.

“I would trust her with my life,” Chloe stated.

“We just got here and now we are heading back?” Abby stated.

“Your sister is heading to the Temple to free those souls. If we are not there to get the blood, then we will have to travel around the entire world and we don’t have that kind of time. Cal doesn’t have that kind of time.” At the mention of my name, I snapped out of my daze.

“What’s wrong?” Jaxx asked.

“Nothing that you should concern yourself with,” I spat. “How do we know he isn’t lying?”

“You hurt me.”He feigned a gasp, clutching my chest. “What reason would I have to lie to you? I want revenge for our parents’ murder.”

“I can tell he isn’t lying,” Chloe stated.

“Thank you, Chloe.” He smirked.

“We should contact Azula,” Abby stated.

“For now, we need to rest and eat. Tomorrow we can go back to the docks,” Chloe said.

“Should this be an opportune time to mention the other ingredients?” We looked at Jaxx. “You need to retrieve the dagger itself. Last I heard, some queen up north has possession of it.”

“You bastard.”

He charged toward me, but Chloe stepped between

us.

"Queen Iliana is in possession of the weapon we need to kill the Dark Wizard? How do you know this?" Chloe asked.

"Well, Your Majesty, I have been the *Hooded Mercenary* for over a decade. My many transactions with royal donors gave up more than their coin." He paused, shifting his gaze to Abby, who seemed unaffected by him at all. "Secrets can be just as heavy as money."

"Chloe, are you seriously going to believe him?" I hated him.

"I believed you after you kidnapped me," Chloe stated.

"That was different," I said defensively.

"Was it, Cal? Because I seem to remember after you kidnapped me, you kissed me, then I found myself chained to a wall. Should I remind you of that?" My fist curled and anger rose as her words cut me to the core.

"Fine, but I warn you, Jaxx. You betray us and I will take a dragon bone dagger and stab you in the heart," I threatened.

"So territorial. Makes me wonder how much of you is mortal, and how much is dragon," he stated.

"Thank you for your cooperation, Jaxx. I will have my guards escort you out," Chloe stated.

"Before I go, I should warn you that your precious guard has concocted some type of serum that suppresses the powers of an Ashana. She isn't to be trusted."

"Liar!" I yelled.

"Fine. Do not believe me. But if the fact that I can be pinned down by a little woman doesn't back up my statement, then I don't know what will. I don't have any of my powers, except I still have my wings." The anger was difficult to hide, but my patience was running thin. He didn't like being accused of lying. I hated being lied to even more.

"We will look into it, thank you," Chloe said. "Now, please get out of my throne room before I have you tossed out."

"As you wish, Your Majesty." He feigned another bow, stealing a glance at Abby before exiting.

Chapter Twenty-Eight

Clover

The throne hall was vacant except for me, and Cal. Abby went off to ensure Jaxx actually left the castle grounds. I didn't trust him enough to let him roam about my palace freely.

"That was interesting." I tried to make light of the way Cal was feeling. Finding out he had family out there that knew him and didn't try to reach out to him. That had to hurt.

"I don't trust him," Cal snarled, causing me to roll my eyes.

"That much is obvious. Like I said, I sensed the truth in each word he spoke." I locked my hands into his. "Talk to me. I can sense great turmoil within your heart."

"He knew about me and didn't even attempt to make contact. It took him being taken prisoner for me to find out about him." Cal let go of my hands, pinching the bridge of his nose in frustration.

"You are hurting and that is to be expected. We don't have to worry about him any longer. He told us what we needed and left." I knew part of that was just me trying to cheer him up. I felt he wanted to get to know his brother. A part of him had always longed to know his true heritage.

"I doubt he is going to just stop his path to vengeance just because you told him to go away. You are the Goddess Emnera and High Queen of the realm, but Jaxx doesn't take orders from you." His tone was full of hate. Although not directed at me, it still hurt. "Forgive my tone, it's just I just don't understand why."

He paused a moment, turning away from me. Placing my hands on his shoulders, I began to knead the tension, using my powers as an empath to send a calming sensation through him.

"Thank you."

"Cal, I know this is going to be an adjustment, but you cannot hide from your feelings. Jaxx is not going away, and now that you have a brother, are you sure you want to go on hating him? He probably has an explanation for what he did."

"Did your mother have an explanation for why she cut you?" he snarled, turning his green eyes at me, now pools of black. "Tell me, Emnera, what good reason did she have for making you bleed?"

"Cal, this isn't you talking. Snap out of this. Fight him."

"What are you going to do, Emnera?" he snickered, and beyond Cal's voice, I heard him. The man that has been haunting my dreams. I will not let him take Cal from me. Calling upon my light, my wings spread wide, eyes alight, I blasted my light at him, willing the darkness away.

Cal plummeted into the back wall, making the room shutter. Guards rushed in, but I held them off. "You will not take him from me."

Cal rose off the floor. A wicked grin formed on his face. The man I shared my heart with was no longer in front of me. Shadows began to spill around him, like tendrils of black ribbons.

"Come now, Emnera, you can do better than that."A ball of shadow magic forms in his hand. "Or are you afraid of hurting your dear Ashana?"

Another light formed in my hand. There wasn't much I could do without hurting Cal. And he knew it. "You know, I can hear him screaming inside of here. Fighting me to gain control again. It's funny, really, since all you are good for is someone to wet his cock."

"Shut up." My light crashed with his shadow, and the entire palace trembled. The blasts knocked everyone to the ground. Getting to my feet, I searched for Cal as the ceiling started to crumble. "Cal. Cal."

A ball of darkness rose from the rubble, and in the center was my mate on the ground. I didn't fight the tears flowing down my cheeks. A pair of thick, warm hands gripped my waist and pulled me away from him. "No, I can't leave him."

"It's too late." Jaxx's deep tone filled my ears, and I turned to see him. His eyes are so much like Cal's, only they are full of the pain I now felt. Like the first time my mother cut my skin but multiply that by a million burning stars and instead of on my thigh, it was my heart.

"Cal, I *will* save you." I think of the training yard and teleported us right before a large piece of ceiling crushed us. A blood-curtailing scream erupted from my throat as a blast of light shattered through the entire realm.

"What the hell happened?" Abby rushed out.

As she reached out to me, Jaxx says, "Don't touch her."

Abby glared at him. “What did you do?” she asked.

“It wasn’t him,” I stated, getting to my feet. “If you touch me right now, you will be incinerated where you stand.” The first glimpse of fear flashed in her eyes. “I am a fully embraced goddess now, Abby. Touching me will kill you until I simmer down.”

“Where’s Cal?” she asked.

“He took him,” Jaxx answered for me as I watched my palace crumble to a pile of rubble, and the faintest glimmer of a shadow shoots away from us. Cutting my heart in half.

“Supreme Leader Jarhead?” she asked. “How?”

“Cal lost control of his emotions. I tried to help him, but it was too late.” I shook my head. “Something corrupted him the moment his brother entered my throne room.”

“Placing the blame on me when I had no clue what was going on inside his head, to begin with, doesn’t sound right to me. Think, Your Majesty.” He was right. Jaxx had no clue of what had been happening. But something he said before he left seized my heart again.

“What did Alma do to you?” I asked him, hoping that my doubt is misplaced.

“She drugged me with some type of suppressant before throwing me in jail.”

“Why did you say I shouldn’t trust her?” I asked. “Knowing I wouldn’t believe you?”

“Because, Emnera, you are a goddess with the abilities of an empath, which means, you can tell when someone is lying to you. I knew that you felt the truth, but your own heart didn’t want to believe a friend could betray you.” He paused for a moment and I felt my powers settling down. “When you dismissed her, I saw a black flash across the whites of her eyes along with a wicked grin. That is what told me she was compromised."

"Why didn't you say that?" Abby scowled. "Why be all cryptic?"

"Would you have believed me if I said it outright?" he asked. She crossed her arms and huffed in frustration. He winked at her, which made her roll her eyes. The attraction between them eased my anger.

"What is the plan?" Abby asked.

"Get the ingredients for the dagger, make it, and kill the wizard," I said matter-of-factly. I was done being the nice, naive shadow of my former self. I am Emnera, Goddess of Earth and Light, and I will not yield.

The energy emitting from the Earth shifted. New souls entered into our world. Shooting to the sky, I can see the vision of Kaliegh releasing the souls. The Ice Dragons were first, flying to settle down into the Ice Caves within the Snow Forest.

The Fire Dragons, with scales of red, orange, and amber, soared through the skies, turning the green plains of Huo to ash before settling down. A volcano rose with the combined powers of every beast.

Third, the Nurture Dragons flew into the skies, all varying colors of the sunrises. Settling in the mountain range of Jian.

Fourth, the Nature Dragons. The one at the head of the fleet was familiar to me. Ziran, the leader of these magnificent beasts.

Behind them all, my vision shifted to the mass of shadows seeping out of the Temple. All Shadow Dragons dissipated, no doubt flocking to their leader.

My heart skipped a beat as black eyes with the faintest shade of green locked onto me. Calian was leading them to their master. Reaching out, I tried to speak to him, but my vision blurred and everything went back to normal.

"Your sister is a fool," I snarled, landing next to Abby.

"I could've told you that." She didn't even try to defend her. "What did she do this time?"

"She released the souls," I answered.

"That's a good thing, right? I mean, don't we need their blood to make the dagger?" she asked.

"She was meant to wait for us!"

"Clearly, the message wasn't received in time." She stepped closer. A scowl and dare crossed her face. She knew I could kill her, but didn't care when it came to family. I admired her and even respected her for the way she acted. That was a mask she donned for what she truly felt internally. That is something she cannot hide from me.

"Step away, Emnera." Jaxx came between us. His eyes were two green flames warning me to make a move. The desire he felt for Abby reminded me so much of what I have for Cal.

"I didn't ask for your help," Abby spat. I stepped back, a smirk playing on my lips.

"Ziran is heading this way with the rest of the colony. We will make plans once they arrive. For now, we just need to be grateful everyone made it out before they were crushed," I stated.

"Not everyone."

At Jaxx's words, I snapped my head toward the pile of stone. Blood ran in pools over the white stone and my throat tightened.

"Help me clear this," I ordered him, and together, with our combined strength, we cleared the rubble. Piece by piece, until I saw the catastrophic death of a dozen men and one servant girl who was with child. Their clothes swam in a combined pool of blood and crushed bone fragments. It was so horrid I couldn't tell what belonged to who.

"What are your orders?" A guard approached me. They deserved a proper burial, but I couldn't give them that.

"Jaxx," I asked, turning to look at him. "Is your magic replenished?"

"Not completely."

"We will burn them, but I need to replenish your magic. Rid the shadow magic used to suppress your powers."

"How? Can you do that?" He genuinely seemed interested.

"Yes, but you have to let me in." He nodded. Placing my hands on either side of his head, I walked him through the process. I don't know how I knew how to do this, but since I had fully embraced my title, knowledge, and power started to imprint on my brain. Like it was there, but I just needed a key to unlock it.

"Close your eyes." I looked around. "Everyone." They did as instructed. Once more, my hands are on either side of his head. I felt the shadow magic dancing along his veins. Pushing my light into him, he winced in pain. "Don't fight me. You must relax yourself to see past the pain. Become numb to it."

As I pushed my magic into him, finding each tendril of shadow magic and washing it out with my light, his body relaxed. When I cleaned out the last of it, I felt the dragon sleeping within him. Jaxx had no clue of the untouched power he has within him.

He opened his eyes, letting out a breath, and his large dragon-like wings flex wide. "Thank you."

"Burn them." He nodded and within his hand, a fireball formed as he set all the rubble and dead ablaze. It took incredible amounts of heat to burn stone, but with the light that I gave him, he could burn through anything. "The shadows cannot harm you or corrupt you ever again. If I would have known this before, I could've saved Cal."

"You didn't know," Jaxx stated.

"All this heart-to-heart crap is kind of wasting time," Abby stated.

"Don't worry, Princess, I will still let you pin me down with a dagger to my throat. It'll be more fun if we are both naked." He grinned.

"My Queen." Ziran's voice rang out as a thousand thuds shocked the earth with every landing of each dragon. "You have saved us all.

"Good to see you again, Ziran, but this greeting will be short," I said, looking up at her.

"I know. I am here to help you." I looked at all the newly freed souls. "We all want to help our queen," she stated.

"We three are heading to Shulong to get the dagger of Vertumnus."

"You wish to kill the Dark Wizard. Then you need my help indeed," Ziran stated with conviction.

"You know about the ingredients?" I asked.

"Yes. You need the dagger itself, plus the blood of each colony leader. Which means, you need my blood,"

Ziran stated, then her eyes immediately fell upon Jaxx, and she lowered into a bow. "My king."

"Now this is more like it," Jaxx stated.

"You may be the son of the god of dragons, but you are no king," I spat at him.

"My queen, you shouldn't address him like that. You two must work together in this quest for freedom." I caught Abby's eye roll, and I almost wanted to follow her lead. "Let me help you with this journey."

"I need this palace rebuilt. Do you have a warrior you trust to lead this task?" I asked her. She perked up at this request.

"Absolutely. Drocono." As she spoke the name, a dark green dragon with yellow eyes approached us. "The queen needs her palace rebuilt. Can I trust this task to you?"

He nodded and I wondered why he didn't speak. "He lost his tongue during the war."

The beast opened his mouth, and sure enough, there was no ligament inside.

"Good, we leave at once," I stated.

"What about humans? She has no wings," Ziran said, and my eyes fell on Abby, waiting for a snarky remark.

"She can fly with me." Jaxx winked, placing an arm around her.

"I would rather walk." She shrugged him off.

"I could take you all on my back," Ziran offered.

"I have my own wings, thanks," Jaxx said. "Last chance Princess. Fly with me and get the full experience of soaring with an Ashana. Or fly on the back of a scaly green beast?" He teased. She approached him and I started smiling because I knew this was going to be funny. Jaxx clearly didn't understand who he was messing with.

With a hand on his shoulder, Abby leaned in. "Not interested, Dragonboy." Her knee thrust up right into his cock and he doubled over in pain.

Ziran sucked in a sharp breath.

"It's okay, Ziran."

Abby turned and headed over toward me. "Do I have your permission to hop on the back of Ziran?"

Leaning closer to her ear, I whisper low that only she can hear me, "I know what you feel toward him, Abby. And I know why you will not act on those feelings, but don't rob yourself of happiness because you can't let go of the past."

She acknowledged my words, knowing she cannot lie to me, and then climbed up Ziran's lowered wing before holding onto one of the fine tendrils.

"Well, Dragonboy, coming, or are you too good to fly on the wings of a real dragon?" I teased as he continued to rub out the pain from his balls.

"I think I will fly a little. See if she can keep up." He winked before taking to the sky. I looked back at Ziran and she nodded before flying after him. I heard a squeal of excitement leave Abby before I followed suit.

Placing my left hand over my heart, with his mother's band directly over the thrumming beat, I sent a silent prayer to Cal, down our bond that I knew was balancing on a fine thread. *Hold on, my love. Your Shadowlight is coming. You are the heartbeat to my soul, and I will not lose you to the shadows.*

Chapter Twenty-Nine

Calian

The faintest memory of the girl with the honey-colored hair keeps resurfacing in my mind. Her lips are painted red, soft fair cheeks are coated with tears. My master says she is the enemy. If she gets too close, she will kill us.

My eyes take in the vast sight before me. Thousands upon thousands of Shadow Dragons encircle us around an amphitheater, made of obsidian and amethysts. Ten platforms are raised housing rows of dragons, orcs, and manticore beasts. All loyal, all under suspicion.

In the very middle, on a raised platform, six-feet high, my master stands to my left, a crown of steel balancing on his hairless head. Our bond is strong, steadfast, and I know I will do anything to protect him.

Using his powers to amplify his voice, the crowd settles down. "For two centuries you have been locked away. Your souls were stolen from you."

"You're the one who took them," one creature yells. A crowd of agreements goes up. I don't bother correcting him, just bask in the knowledge knowing my master will do it.

He snaps his fingers and in a flash, the creature appears before him. It is a ghastly-looking beast, with yellow tusks coming out either side of its fur cover head. The top half of its head is that of a beast, torso of an average person, and legs of a bull. I will never understand why the gods created such useless creatures.

"What's your name?" Rai asks.

"Voltak, Master." I see no fear in Voltak's brown eyes. An error.

"And do you feel as though I have done a disservice to you and your comrades?" Rai feigns guilt by gesturing to the crowd.

"You took their souls and trapped them from us. Our families are dead while we have to fight another war for you." Voltak just made a mistake yelling at Master Rai. Drawing my swords, I start to approach him, but I am halted by my master telling me to stop.

"Does anyone else feel that I have wronged you? Your king has failed you?" I let myself bask in his pretenses, waiting until he gives the order for bloodshed. My fire urges for release as the crowd cheers in agreement. They are all scum. Master Rai raises his hand to quiet the crowds again. "Then let me pay you the compensation you deserve."

Without saying another word, my blades alight, taking my leg, I kick the beast's hackles as he falls forward unaware of the death approaching him. Placing my blades on either side of his head, his brown eyes full of fear and regret. "Ple—"

The feeling of flesh and bone crushing and burning beneath my blades fuels the shadows within me. Humming with new energy and bloodlust. The blasphemer's head rolls itself perfectly in front of Master Rai's feet, while I incinerate the rest of the body.

I watch with honor as he conjures a crystal jar with a golden lid. He bends down and scoops the head inside before summoning the milky liquid he uses to preserve it. Once it is full, he places it somewhere inside his many layers of black robes.

The crowd is in an uproar, but I don't care. I will slaughter each and every one of these vile...*Cal.* What was that? *Cal, I love you.* Palming my head, the faint familiar voice with warmth and light fades with her face.

"Silence." Master Rai's voice echoes throughout the entire arena. "If you choose to defy, question, or even look at me with malice, I will have my pet kill you where you stand." Pet? What is a pet? Surely he cannot be addressing me in that manner. "I am your king, your master, and the ruler of this realm. And we have work to do." Rai turns to me and says, "Come, pet. Summon the generals. We have plans to discuss."

"Yes, my Master." I watch as he jumps from the raised platform and lands on the sand surface below. Looking at the crowd, I let my voice be heard. "All generals report to the council room immediately. Failure to comply will result in death."

Flexing my wings, I take flight. The warm air kisses my skin as I glide over the crowds before landing in front of the vast metal doors leading into the Dark Tower. The Fortress of Rai is guarded by magic, making only the single tower visible to outsiders.

If anyone were foolish enough to attempt a break-in, the force field surrounding us would incinerate them. Only magical signatures and loyalists to Master Rai are safe from death. Master Rai informed me the tower was recently rebuilt after he was attacked by our enemies.

When I find out who did that, I will make them suffer and bleed for the assault on him.

On the other side of the doors lies a single spiral stone staircase that leads to ten distinct levels. Each level has a different purpose. Master Rai's personal quarters are at the top level. Five levels are for prisoners and interrogations. The rest are quarters. The tunnels below the seating area of the amphitheater are used for masonry, training, and metalworking.

The council chambers are on the ninth level. Stepping off the stairs, I take the corridor to the left and enter through another singular metal door. Within, my master is already sitting upon his stone throne. Kneeling, I greet him.

"The generals should be arriving soon, Master."

"You have done well, pet." That name strikes anger through me. It's degrading, humiliating, and I deserve it. I think about telling him about the voice earlier. My master knows all things and could help me. Before I speak my mind, the doors open.

General Scarr, the Manticore regiment commander, General Jakhem, Orc commander, and General Krall, leader of the Shadow Dragons. All three kneel before taking their place in the barren room.

"Generals, we need to move the plans forward," Master Rai states, his long black talons scraping against the stone armchair of his throne. "Dalaria is being desecrated without me sitting on the High Throne. Humans with their greed, manipulation, and filth, should be turned into the slaves the gods meant them to be."

"What about Emnera?" General Krall asks.

Shadow Dragons are black tendrils that can reform their size. The only thing seen is the hollow holes for eye sockets.

"The goddess?" General Scarr questions. "She has been gone for centuries."

"She has recently been re-born," Master Rai states. "As powerful as she may be, I have plans for the golden-haired beauty."

"What about him?" General Jakhem asks as he gestures his thick green finger toward me.

"Calian, son of Tika, God of Dragons, where do your loyalties lie?" Scarr asks me.

"Master Rai is the one true King of the Realm," I state matter-of-factly.

"Rumors within the regiments state that an Ashana and the goddess are mated through blood magic. They struck a *Blood Oath* and solidified the bond." General Jakehm's accusatory tone infuriates me. I would never mate with an enemy of my master.

"I would never betray my master," I argue.

"Show us your palms," General Scarr demands. Master Rai has always made me wear gloves and ordered me to never take them off. Looking toward him for guidance, I see a smirk forming at the corner of his mouth.

"You are mistaken, generals. Calian is mine and no one else's. There is only one Ashana in all of existence and he is mine," Master Rai states.

"Show—" General Scarr starts but is cut off when Rai starts choking him with his magic.

"I am your king; you will not question me and my decisions. If I say Ashana is mine, then he is mine. Understand?" His voice thunders off the walls, making all of them cower before him. He let the Manticore General breathe again. "We have a vast enough army to start the siege of the west side of the continent. General Scarr, you will lead your regiment into those territories. Everyone who doesn't bow down will be struck down."

"The human usurpers will be subjected to interrogations. Each one will bend the knee or face execution. Ashana,"—I look over toward my master—"you and I will travel to Morte. There is a relic there I will need to destroy that goddess."

The steel doors shut behind Generals Scarr and Jakehm. General Krall and I await further instructions.

"Krall, I am aware that your time spent in the Ziran stone gave you the opportunity to invade the mind and body of the goddess," Master Rai states.

"And what a body to be in. Wouldn't you agree, Calian?" I give the beast an inquisitive look, but he laughs it off. "She wasn't difficult to manipulate, for a human that is. Now she has powers that I am not strong enough to overcome," Krall commented.

"That is why we three are traveling to Morte," Master Rai states.

"You have uncovered the sixth stone," Krall states with a feline grin forming across his hollow face.

"There is another Dragonheart? I thought there were only five," I ask.

"There are only five. The sixth stone is a myth, a legend meant to scare little beasts into submission," Krall states.

"If Master Rai says it exists, then it exists," I bite back.

"Calian, Krall, enough. We leave for the stone at once." I watch as the master leaves us to head to his quarters.

"Tell me, son of Tika, have you thought about her?" Krall asked, floating in front of me.

"Thought of who?" I inquire.

"Your mate," he hisses.

Gripping the hilt of my sword, I glare at him. "I don't have a mate. I am duty-bound to serve my master."

He sneers at me. "Is that so? Look at your right palm." Then he disappears to meet the master. Looking down, my gloved hands are trembling before me.

What is happening? It is not true, it cannot be. Pulling my glove off slowly, I notice the edge of a red, white image appear. Ripping my glove off entirely, my heart drops as visions of a woman with honey-colored hair and painted red lips flash through my mind.

The first time I laid eyes on her, she was surrounded by guards in her room. My heart beats faster with the thrumming I felt with the feel of her hand in mine. Our warm blood mixing with the *Blood Oath* that changed our lives forever. She was the most beautiful woman I had ever seen in my entire life.

The vision shifts to the first time we kissed. I lifted her into my arms, pushing her back against a wall. Her tongue dancing with mine. I knew she had me then. Those sinful, addictive lips mixing with mine. Flash forward to the first time I made love to her.

In the middle of a forest of green. Her body was littered with scars, but I didn't care. I worshiped her strength, her beauty, and her honor. The bond solidified when we came together. Making her mine and I hers forever more.

Blinking, my mind becomes as clear as my vision.

Our bond resonates within me. I feel the warmth of her love radiating down to me. The emblem imprinted on my skin, white roses dancing around a red dragon, proof of our bond.

Pulling my glove back on, I rush out to meet Krall. "Krall," I snarl.

He snickers before turning to me. "Welcome back, son of Tika."

"Why did you help me?" I ask. Shadow Dragons are evil. Krall is no better.

"You are the son of dragons, heir to the throne of my people. My loyalty lies with you primarily." I sense the truth in his confession.

"I killed that Orc." I try to feel remorse, but none comes.

"He was as evil as any other soldier out there," Krall states.

"And what about you? You are a beast of shadow magic; you are not innocent," I growl.

"True, but I am a servant of my true king." Drawing my swords, my fire dances along the blade. "If you wish to intercept Master Rai and ensure your dearly beloved doesn't die, then I suggest you wait until after we steal the stone to kill him."

"Why should I trust you?" I ask, pointing my blade at his throat.

"Because…I may be a villain, but I believe in honor. Rai has no honor." He watches me closely.

"Chloe controls the power of light. She can destroy you and your colony—why would you help me save her?"He lets out a snicker.

"I am well aware of what the goddess is capable of. I don't fear death," he states. "You are my king, and I will follow you to the end."

There has to be more to it. I will uncover the truth one way or another, but for now, I need to keep the facade up.

"I will trust you, but if you double-cross me, I will personally see to it that your death will be a slow and painful process," I state, seething my sword.

"You are not completely free of Rai's control over your mind. Use the bond image imprinted on your palm to remind you. I will help keep the master believing you are still his, but when we get to Morte, the goal is to take the stone and find your goddess," Krall states before leaving for the amphitheater.

I follow suit and we meet Rai at the center. "Come, pet, time to transport."

As I am whisked away into a portal of darkness, I focus on the bond, praying I can send a message before the connection is too strained.

I am coming, Shadowlight.

Part Four: Emnera Reclaimed

Chapter Thirty

Emnera

Cal has been gone for two weeks, but it felt longer. Our bond was strained, and I felt the darkness surrounding it. Pushing back with my light had only been met with more force. Throughout our time apart, we made our way to Greveil to seek out assistance for our negotiations with the Queen of Shulong.

"So, Chloe, are you really a goddess?" Eli asked me. His golden eyes examined me from head to toe. Searching for something. "You look like you did the last time I saw you."

"Nothing has really changed," I stated.

"Except the wings," Abby stated.

"And the powers," Jaxx added.

"We didn't come to discuss with you—we have come to ask your assistance with the Queen in Shulong. I am told you know the layout and her son, Prince…"

"Prince Alaric," Eli finished my statement. "Yes, we trained together as squires and knights."

"Good. What can we expect when we arrive?" I asked him. Sitting at the wooden table in the dining hall, my mind flooded with the memory of our meal together. The dagger he held to my throat, Calian coming to save me.

"You shouldn't expect anything but a formal

greeting from her. You are a queen, and she is a queen."

"Yes, well, this is also the queen who paid an outlaw to kidnap and rape me." The incredulous look in his golden eyes told me he was not aware of that truth. "You didn't know?" He shook his head. "Then perhaps you could accompany us. Since you and her son are so close."

I noticed a faint blush appearing just below his dark skin. My empath abilities made me sense the longing and desire he had for Alaric. Something I would not have expected since his advances toward me, but not unheard of.

"As much as I would love to assist you with your diplomatic issues, my place is here. My father has passed on and the kingdom is now in my hands." I sensed discomfort and anxiety.

"Do you not have an advisor or council you trust?" I prodded further. I wanted to push him like he tried to push me. Grudges are not very ladylike, but this man chained me to a wall and exposed my darkest truths.

"I do, but—" He fidgeted with the hem of his crimson tunic. I could practically see the beads of sweat forming on his brow. It was amusing that he found me intimidating.

"Eli, have you ever heard of an empath?" I asked, crossing my right leg over my left. Jaxx and Abby remained silent but were ready to fight if necessary. Eli's eyes shifted between the three of us. I asked Jaxx to hide his wings, not without argument. He agreed, with Abby's help.

"Yes, but there hasn't been one around for generations," he stated.

I hummed with the answer. "Eli, do you know why

I came here?"

"You need assistance with seeking an audience with the queen in Shulong. But as I said before, I—"

"Cannot leave," I interrupted. "Yes, I know that. You see, you have yet to mention her name. You know the prince, since you two were close, I figured you would at least know his mother's name." The anxiety had increased, but I was prepared.

As the blade pressed to my throat, Jaxx's wings burst from his back while Abby aimed her daggers at him. Holding my hand up, I halted them.

"Tell them to stand down or I slit your throat," he threatened. A weak one.

"Stand down," I calmly stated. Confusion clouded his eyes.

"Stand up." I rose to my feet as he held the dagger to me from behind. His chest caressed my hidden wings, the bulge in his pants pressing to my back.

"Still a sadist?" I teased.

"Shut up. You are just as I remember you." His hot breath kissed my ear.

"And what exactly do you remember?" I asked him.

"You and that traitor, Ashana, attacked me. Did something to my mind. It comes in flashes, but you were my prisoner. And your body, it was hideous. Tell me, did you finally spread your legs for him?" All of his words would have hurt my former self. Possibly added to my insecurities, but not now.

"I am going to give you one opportunity to lower your dagger and bend your knee before me," I warned him. Just as I expected, he pressed the blade hard enough for it to split my skin, while letting out a dark laugh. "Is that your definitive answer?"

"I should've killed you last time I had you in my chains. I won't make that mistake again." As he pressed harder, my wings burst from my back, knocking him backward into the stone wall behind us. While he remained disoriented, I knocked the blade from his hand, gripped his throat, and raised him to the wall.

"You should know better than to threaten me." Blood dripped from a cut on his forehead. His eyes glazed over with fear.

"Not possible." He took in the full sight of me. His eyes drifted to Jaxx. "How?"

"Jaxx is the long-lost brother to Cal. The man you just insulted, and I told you, I am no longer a human." He looked back at me. Fear was no longer housed in his gaze, but pure hatred. "Tell me everything you know about Shulong, and I might just let you keep your cock."

"Never." He spat in my face.

"Wrong answer." Throwing him to the ground, I grabbed the rope from Jaxx, not sure where he got it from nor did I care. I tied Eli's wrists behind him. Carrying him forward, I threw him down on the table. Jaxx held him down as I began unfastening his breeches. The bastard still had a hard-on.

"What are you doing?" There was now fear in his voice.

"I told you what was going to happen if you didn't cooperate." Pulling his breeches down to his ankles, I gripped the base of his cock in one hand, and took the blade he threatened me with in the other. Placing it, I pressed it to the base.

"Wait, you can't." I started to move my hand in

slow movements. He tried to squirm as he screamed in pain. "Stop, I'll tell you."

"You had your chance, Eli. Besides, a sadistic bastard like you doesn't deserve to know pleasure. You've threatened me and my mate for the last time."In one swift movement, I sliced his cock clean off. Then used my power of light to burn the bleeding wound.

His scream of pain and humiliation echoed throughout the castle walls. Guards tried to barge in but were unable to get past the shield outside the doors I placed just as we had entered.

Looking at Jaxx, his face had a grimace as he guarded his own cock.

"You are such a badass," Abby stated. Eli was almost unconscious from the pain, but I slapped his face with his own cock.

"You bitch." His weak insult had no effect.

"Now you know that I am serious with my threats. Tell me everything you know, and I won't shove this down your throat and make you choke on it." I smiled.

Jaxx pushed him to sit up. Eli looked at his cock in my hand, then down to see the burned mark where it used to be. His eyes fixed back on mine. Anger, regret, humiliation, and fear are the emotions he felt. Did I go too far? Not in the least. Eli would have raped and killed me if the roles were reversed.

"I hate you and I will kill you for what you have done. Greveil and Thormwarf are now at war." I let out a small laugh at his empty threat.

"You have no idea what is going on outside your own territory. Tell me what you know, last warning." I put the head of his cock to his lips.

"Alaric and I practically grew up in Shulong. Their

palace is a fortress. You will not be able to get past their army of soldiers posted outside the gates. You have to send a request through the general, who then sends it to the next general at the gate, until it reaches the queen." He paused for a moment. A soft wince escaped him as his eyes fell on his separated adulthood again.

"A message like that could take months to hit the Queen's desk and then even longer before an answer is received." He stopped.

"Keep going." I glared at him.

"If you can get past the region of soldiers, then within the palace there are several traps laid out for trespassers. They can only be secured when the visiting dignitary is escorted to see the queen." He swallowed before continuing. "There are too many to tell you, but I could draw the semantics of each location."

Eying him, I sensed truth and defeat coming from Eli. Good, he knew he was defeated. "I just want to know where the dagger is."

"What dagger?" he asked. "The queen has many."

"Where does she keep all her daggers?" I preferred not to reveal the specific one we were searching for.

"In the east wing. But you won't be able to get in there without her."

"Elaborate," I demanded.

"There is a series of five doors. Each one has a specific key to open it."

"And let me guess, the queen keeps all five keys on her person at all times." He nodded.

"I can get in without those keys," Jaxx stated. Eli looked toward him with intrigue. "My reputation as an outlaw would be tarnished if I couldn't simply break through five doors and steal a dagger."

"Outlaw?" Eli questioned.

"Eli, meet Jaxx, also known as the Hooded Mercenary, and as I said before, Calian's older brother."

"You have your information. Now let me go." He winced as he leaned forward. Before I could answer his plea, a large blast of cannon fire shot through the side of the castle, breaking through the shield I had placed. Eli's guards burst through the doors.

Jaxx and Abby readied their weapons. "Kill them," Eli shouted. I watched as Jaxx and Abby engaged in fights, slitting throats, and slicing heads. As I rushed to join them, another guard ran inside.

"Greveil is under attack." The fighting in the room died out with his statement.

"What do you mean?" I asked.

"An army of beasts marches on, slaughtering any who won't surrender." He glances around, assessing the room before pointing his blade toward me. "Unhand my king."

Before I could move, Jaxx was on him, knocking the blade from his hand and holding a dagger to his throat. "Threaten her again and I won't hesitate to slit you from ear to ear," Jaxx snarled.

"Didn't know you cared so much?" I teased.

"You're my brother's mate, which makes you family, and no one threatens my family."

The next moment, I heard Ziran's dragon roar. She was soaring the skies, keeping watch from above.

"Let the rest go."

Jaxx and Abby released the guards.

"Are you going to flee like a coward?" Eli taunted

from behind.

"No, because then that would make me like you." I gestured to Jaxx, and he freed Eli's wrists and Abby followed me outside.

Screams of terror echoed in my ears as I watched the horror unfold. Beasts of green skin, adorned in black steel armor, slaughtered innocents before me as Eli's soldiers fought them off.

"Jaxx, Abby, save as many innocents as you can. I want their general on his knees before sundown." Without protest, they joined the fight. The familiar figure of a woman formed in my line of sight.

Running toward her, I gripped her wrists. "Alma, what are you doing here?"

As she turned to face me, her once golden irises were now pools of darkness, the feeling of warmth and love replaced with hatred and disgust. I barely had enough time to react before her blade connected with mine.

"Traitorous whore," she spat at me with such venom, it took me aback.

"Alma, this isn't you." She swung again, which I blocked before she swept her legs undermine. I caught her waist as we tumbled to the ground. Our blades dropped in the roll. I found myself pinned beneath her.

"My master says we must take you alive."A ringing sound filled my ears as her fist made contact with my face. "But he didn't say you didn't have to bleed first."

"Alma, stop this. Fight him." Another punch, and another. Blood trickled down my nose and I could feel my lip swelling. I could hurt her if I tried to banish the shadows. Instead, I take flight, knocking her off me.

Her shouts of anger are drowned out by the bloodshed I see before me.

"My Queen," Ziran called out from behind me.

"There are too many of them. This kingdom was lost before the fight began," I stated.

"You have to leave. It's the only way to ensure we defeat the Dark Wizard." Her words made sense. Leaving innocents at the mercy of beasts filled me with remorse. I searched the ground for Jaxx and Abby, finding them fighting side by side.

"That's ten for me. What number are you at, Princess?" Jaxx teased. They appeared to be having some sort of competition for the most kills.

Chapter Thirty-One

Calian

Hot burning coal overwhelms my senses before my feet thud into the soft ash that coats the ground. The surrounding area is foreign to me. Scattered ruins of a fortress show evidence of a battle fought not too long ago. Black crows pick at the charred remains, while starved coyotes gnaw on scattered bones.

"What happened here?" I ask. Letting my curiosity get the best of me. Krall's ribbon-like body circles us, while Rai leads us toward the center of what used to be a courtyard. The broken-down framework of the fortress is clear despite the black scorch marks painted on all the stones that remain.

"This was the Fortress of Morte," he answers while using his magic to clear a path for us. Stone, armor, and bones are swept to the side like the filth they are. "One of my most loyal soldiers oversaw this prison."

"Prison?" I asked, curious to know why a man like him would need a prison.

"When you have power like mine, there are those that will try to cease it for themselves."

"You mean enemies? Master…" I calmly state. He stalls to look at me with narrowed eyes. "The traitorous fools who try to undermine your rule," I finish, trying to ease his suspicious glance.

"Yes." He continues our journey into the ruined courtyard. It is clear he is looking for something in particular. Taking in my surroundings further, I cannot make out where everything was except for the cratered pool of lava not too far off the right side of the rubble.

"What are you looking for?" Krall growls, sounding particularly annoyed at being dragged here.

"If you were important enough to know, you wouldn't need to ask that question," Rai replies, earning another growl from Krall. I realize Krall shares no true loyalty to Rai, which makes me believe his intentions of helping me are honorable.

The further we walk, the wider the path gets until we approach a wall. The only one that is untouched in this entire place. There is a sort of symbol imprinted upon it. A five-point star with a ring around it.

"What is this place?" I ask.

"This,"—he pauses before tracing a long black nail along each line until he completes the star. The wall begins to move, sending tremors across the ground—"is my destiny."

Through the darkened space behind the secret door, a stone of pure gold sits on a bed of crimson velvet.

"Is that what I think it is?" Krall asks.

"What is it?" I ask them again. It looks like a stone, but it feels like so much more. "A dragon stone?"

"The stone of Valentini," Rai replies while delicately picking it from its bed of green.

"What exactly is that?" I am curious about the power I feel radiating from it.

"I am surprised that the son of the dragon god doesn't know this powerful relic and its history," Rai states while turning toward me. I didn't exactly grow up with my father, so the history of dragons, or anything to do with them, is what I learned through the study of lore.

"No matter," Rai continues as he walks toward me. "That just means I can put it to the test without protest."

"Test? What do—"

Rai thrusts the golden stone toward my chest, and I instantly feel my life draining from me. Only, it was not my life, but my magic. My knees buck as a vortex of power consumes my own, turning the golden stone into a burning ember in Rai's hand.

"Yes, give his power to me," Rai's twisted laugh echoes through my ears.

"Stop this," I beg as I fall to my hands and knees. The strength in me is fading like the brittle leaves during a winter storm.

"Don't you see?" He laughs again as the relic continues to drain me of my inner fire. I feel the brisk cold of frost on the edge of my skin. "With the power of an Ashana, I will command all dragons, new and old. They will be loyal only to me—their new god."

I give a quick glance to Krall, but I don't see him until I am knocked to my side, and I hear the thunderous roar of a beast.

"You will not harm him." My weak brain tries to register the words and the voice that spoke against Rai. As my head clears from the fog, the earth settles before my feet, and my gaze lands on the shimmering figure of a Krall. The black wisps have been transformed into glistening golden scales from the tip of his nose to the end of his tail.

"What is the meaning of this?" Rai angrily demands. I look over at him, the once golden stone is now a purely clear crystal floating in the air between them. Although I am still weak, I stumble toward Krall, placing a hand on his smooth scales.

"Grab the stone and get on my back." Krall growls. Rai and I reach for the stone at the same time, but he is knocked backward a few feet by some invisible force field. "It won't stay up for long, we need to move."

Without another moment to spare, I grab the stone, tuck it inside my tunic pocket and climb onto Krall's back. We take flight immediately leaving Rai unconscious on the ground of the crumpled remains of a once great fortress.

My own wings try to flex at the feel of the wind against them, but I am far too weak to hold them up. As they drape over my shoulders, they shield my body from the new-found cold of the night air. My inner fire is gone.

"Do not fret, my Prince, your powers will be restored to you." Krall's voice thundered through my ears as we shot across the sky.

****

"Calian," Chloe's voice echoes in my head. I try to find her, but I cannot see past the darkness. "Kiss the imprint on your hand, and your shadow light will guide you home."

Moving my hand to my face, I can barely see the faint outline of the white roses dancing around the head of a dragon. Pressing my lips to the mark, a wave of warmth washes over me, melting the frost covering my bones. A bright white light begins to shine all around. I blink twice, and she appears before me.

Dressed in nothing but a white lace gown that stops just above her knees. Those beautiful white feathered wings cast an iridescent shadow behind her, making her shine like the goddess she is. Those mesmerizing honey-colored curls are like painted waves dancing around her body.

"Chloe." I gasp at her overwhelming beauty and power. I move to close the distance between us, but my feet are cemented to the surface below me. "Let me hold you."

"Soon. Soon you will be reunited with Emnera," she states, using the nomenclature of the goddess of Earth and Light. I move to ask her a question, but her soft finger presses to my lips. She closed the distance before I could blink. A smile forms on her face, and I wrap an arm around her waist, pulling her into me.

I move her hand from my face and crash my lips to hers. Soaking in the sweet scent of her; earth and honey. The taste of her is a mix of ash and sugar. Power and beauty send a surge of desire through me. My throbbing cock rubs the inside of her thigh as both my hands grab her rear, hoisting her up so she can wrap her legs around me.

"Gods," she moans as I begin to trail my lips down her body, her nails digging into my back. I suddenly realize I am bare before her. The warmth of her skin touching mine is too real.

"Chloe," I groan, and her hips buck against my throbbing cock. The need to be inside of her is too much. I gently lay her on her back, pushing the hem of her gown up and over her head, freeing her bountiful breast. Clamping my mouth on one of her breasts, her head tilts back as I suckle it, moving my fingers to the pooling dampness at her core.

"Fucking perfect," I growl. Her hands find the tip

of my erection, running a finger over the pearly white moisture of my arousal, coating it. I dip my fingers inside her wetness, pumping relentlessly until I can feel her clamping down and screaming my name.

"Fuck me, Cal." She didn't have to ask me twice. I line myself up at her core. The wet heat coating my tip. With one powerful thrust, I fill her to the hilt, making her back bow.

"Too fucking long," I groan, my mouth finding hers again. She moans into my mouth the harder I move. Those thick thighs wrap around my hips, moving me deeper. Her tightness makes it difficult for me to stay in control and I need this to last. I need her to know how much I love her.

Her nails rake down my back as I move my mouth to her neck. Sucking and biting, leaving my mark on her. "You're mine," I growl.

"Yes, I'm yours." She moans and I move faster until I can feel her clenching around my shaft, screaming my name, and I growl hers as I finish.

Panting, sweat dripping off our joined bodies, I look into her electric blue eyes and see nothing but love.

"If I am never to wake again," I start, while cupping her face, "this is what I will dream about for all eternity."

"Us having sex?" She chuckles. I narrow my eyes, showing her I am serious about my next statement.

"Making you completely and irrevocably happy until the end of time."

Chapter Thirty-Two

Emnera

Sitting up, I wipe the sweat from my brow. That was the most realistic dream I have ever had. Even more so than the ones of my tortured past. This dream makes me want to attempt something.

Cal? I wait for a response. A feeling, anything from the bond. *Calian, are you back?* Looking around, the rays from the High Sun are just peeking over the horizon and my companions are still sleeping. Getting to my feet, I opened my water sack and gulped down the refreshing flavor.

The moist air smells like rain will come soon. Walking down to the stream, I used the light of dawn to ensure I am alone. Stripping bare, the pool of my clothes neatly piled to the side of the bank while I step into the ankle-deep water. Using my wings as a shield, I splash the warm water over my body.

You look divine. Cal's voice vibrates down the bond.

Cal? Is that really you?

Yes, Shadowlight, it is me. With the truth of his words comes a gentle caress.

Where are you? I ask with a sense of urgency.

On the back of a dragon, he answers and then sends an image showing golden scales flying through the clouds.

A golden dragon? How? I ask in disbelief at the sight he has given me.

I will explain it all once I have you in my arms again…well, after I have had my fill of you, he answers. The humor in his tone confirms it is truly him. My heart will be returning to me.

We are headed to Shulong. Meet us at the border, I replied.

I will see you soon, Shadowlight. A wisp of a kiss caresses my cheek as the bond goes silent again.

With newfound motivation, I quickly dry myself and dress in clean clothes. My blonde curls flow down my back, flush with my wings. Back at camp, I see Abby and Jaxx are already having their typical flirtatious dispute.

"Believe me, Princess, once my mouth is on you, you'll never want for anyone or anything else," Jaxx says smugly, making Abby rear back to punch him.

"If you two are finished." I try to stop the fight, but it doesn't seem to work as Abby's fists move forward. Jaxx grips her wrists, turns her around, pinning them to the small of her back. "I have received a message from Calian."

That catches their attention. "He will meet us in Shulong."

"Is he…you know…back?" Abby asks, still pinned to Jaxx's chest.

"Yes," I replied. "Jaxx, let go of her so we can get a move on." He lets her go but not before earning a punch to his gut.

I look around. "Where did Ziran go?"

"She was gone by the time we were up," Abby

answers while packing up her bedroll. Staring at the skies, I try to see her, but I still cannot find her.

"I'm here," her voice reaches us before she reappears. "I was just receiving this for you."

She opens her large claw. Inside, upon her palm, is a vile of crimson.

"Is this what I think it is?" I ask.

"You need my blood to create the dagger," she replies. "I need to give it to you before I leave."

Snapping my gaze to hers, my face scrunches in confusion. "Leave? But we just got word Cal is back, and you're never going to believe who is with him."

"I must return to the colony. We need to prepare for war. Especially since Greveil is lost. I will send word to the Queen of Orion that we need reinforcements now," Ziran states.

"Are you well enough to travel? What if those shadow dragons attack you again?" I place my empty palm on her claw.

"Jaxx healed me. It will take more than three of them to take me down." She growls. I look over to my two other companions, and with a sigh of defeat, place my forehead against her lowered head, giving her my blessing.

"Be safe, my Queen," she softly states before taking flight. I watch another friend of mine leave me to join in a war that could kill us all.

"Should we fly?" Jaxx eagerly asks.

"I don't have wings, Dragonboy," Abby states.

"You can ride me." He winks, making bile rise in my throat. Gods, when are those two going to fuck? I keep that thought to myself, knowing the true reason they are both hesitant to act on their obvious attraction.

"No, thank you," Abby replies, then walks over toward me. "I would rather fly with you."

Leaning in, I whisper in her ear, "Then you would have to avoid him. Where is the fun in that?"

I chuckle and then head to my sack, tossing it over my right shoulder.

"Traitor," Abby murmurs while putting her sack on.

"Flying would be faster," I said, pulling out a map from my sack. "We have to cross the Great Sea and into a mountain range before we enter Shulong. That is where we will meet Cal." I started rolling the map back up and placing it back in my bag.

"What about teleporting?" Abby suggested.

"It could work," I state, and she smiles. "But we might end up in the middle of the sea."

"What is the point in you having those powers if you can't use them for good?" she scoffs.

"I've never been to Shulong. If I were familiar, then I could do it, but I am not."

"So, it's settled then. Princess, you are coming with me." Jaxx grabs her waist. Before she or I could protest, he takes off with her. Flexing my wings, I follow suit. Hearing the distant protest of Abby cursing him.

The wind swirls around me like a hug from an old friend. Ever since I got my wings; this has been my favorite part. Being in the clouds feels like freedom. There are no rules, no regulations, no enemies to defeat. Just pure bliss.

Chapter Thirty-Three

Calian

My body is still weak from the power that was taken from me. As I lay down on the back of the beast I knew to be a legend; the leader of the purest form of dragon; Krall, Golden Dragon of Unity.

It seems cliché that the dragons dedicated to unity and honor would be cursed to become Barringers of death and distraction. I know only what the scholars of old wrote in the books about dragons. The history of the Dragon Wars was recorded, and it has been believed that all dragons were extinct. That they all perished when their god did, my father.

Now I know that was false.

In the last year, I have met Ice Dragons, Shadow Dragons, and now a Golden Dragon. Seems to me either the scholars got it wrong, or the text was manipulated somehow. But what I don't understand is why? Why go through such links to discard history? Why hide the truth of what occurred?

There are at least two people that could answer that question and one of them is currently sitting next to my mate, deep in conversation atop the mountain range below.

I feel Krall start to descend, and I immediately lock onto the two bright sapphire eyes staring deep into my soul.

Shadow Light.

My heart.

The only words we are able to speak through the growing tether of our bond. It was silent and non-existent while I was under the influence of Rai. Now, as I draw closer to her. To the scent of her, the feel of her soft skin touching mine, I can already feel the power returning to me.

Jumping from the back of Krall, I can no longer wait to embrace her. Closing the distance in three quick strides, my lips instantly find hers in an all-consuming, earth-shattering, and possessive kiss.

“I can’t believe you’re here,” she says through kisses. Her tears of joy coat our lips, adding to the flavor of her. I don’t want to stop. I want to prolong this moment. But a small cough catches my ears. Making my tunnel vision expand ever so slightly.

“Good to see you too, brother.” Jaxx’s teasing tone makes a smile break out on Chloe’s face and a slight blush rise in her cheeks. Making me smile right back. Turning, I walk over to him, holding out a hand to offer a truce. A silent thank you for keeping my mate safe. Although I know she can take care of herself.

Knowing he didn’t abandon her like he did me when I was a baby almost makes me want to forgive him. Almost.

“What’s this?” he asks, eyeing my outstretched hand.

“A hand.” My brow raises. “You’re supposed to shake it.”

“And why on earth would I do that?” Taking my hand back, I roll my eyes, ignoring his question, while turning my attention to Abbygale.

Before I could move, she tugs me into her warm embrace, thanking the gods for bringing me back to them safely.

“Missed you too, Abby,” I state while returning her embrace. “Has my brother behaved?”

“Of course not. He is an egotistical male. What would you expect?” She glares at him. If I didn’t think it was impossible, she would gladly throw her daggers at him with just one look.

Turning back to him, he just shrugs and then turns his attention to the giant beast speaking with Chloe.

“How is this possible?” I hear her ask Krall.

“There is a lot to discuss, but I would like to rest,” he answers her.

“Of course, it must have been a long journey.” She bows her head in respect. Sauntering over to her, the tension between us grows with the unsaid words, the need to feel each other. The need to worship her and taste her sweet juices on my tongue.

“Gods, Abby and I will occupy ourselves while you two can fuck your brains out in privacy,” Jaxx mutters, making Chloe’s cheeks flush again.

Without protest, I grab Chloe’s hand and try to take flight. But I didn’t realize I was not at my full strength until I couldn’t raise a wing.

“What’s wrong?” she asks with a creased brow, worry coating her features.

“Nothing. I am just tired.”

“Then you should rest.” She cups my cheek. As much as I need to be inside her, I don’t think I have the strength to do it.

Abby, Jaxx, and Krall are gathered around the

campfire, while Chloe is tucked into my arms at the far end of the mountain range. Giving us some much-needed privacy. A single bedroll for us to share, my hand gently circles along her bare stomach, while I just breathe in her scent.

Her wings are glamoured, making room for us to be as close as possible, and I cannot help but push my hardened cock against her.

"Cal," she warns.

"I can't control my cock when it's rubbing against your rear," I whisper, nipping her ear, loving the way her body shutters with my touch.

"You need your rest. I know you have been through a lot these past couple of weeks. And as much as I want to reconnect with you,"—she pauses to turn over—"to feel your skin pressed against mine." Gods, this is not helping. My cock is throbbing against the fabric of my breeches.

She gently presses her lips to mine, making a groan hum in my throat. "To feel what it means to give you pleasure. To give you my body." Fucking hell, woman. Her hands find the strings to my breeches. Pulling them to free my length.

"Chloe," I growled. "You said we are—"

"I said 'you' need your rest." I take a gulp at her insinuation. She kisses me one last time before saying, "Relax," and begins licking the already beaded cream at the top.

I cannot help but thread my fingers through her honey-colored curls, pressing her down, not forcing, but permitting. Her lips part as she takes me to the back of her throat, swirling her tongue around my cock, making me want to cum right then.

"Fuck," I growl, gripping her head tighter. As she moves her mouth up and down, finding the perfect rhythm, I feel the need to give her the same release. Without physically moving, I travel invisible fingers down our bond, under the waistband of her breeches, finding her soaking folds.

She moans around my shaft, making me thrust up, hitting the back of her throat. Finding her clit, I press down while slipping two fingers into her, matching her rhythms.

As our movements pick up pace, the need, lust, and desire for each other take over our senses, and darkness starts to invade. Trying to snuff out the light, the love, the intimacy of this moment.

"No," I shouted, making her jerk away from me. A humiliated and confused look coats her face.

"What's wrong?" she asks. Hurt fills her features.

"Nothing." She scowls, and I know I cannot lie to her.

"It's the shadow magic, isn't it?" she asked while prowling back to me, still on her hands and knees. She moves to straddle me. Her wet heat directly over my hardened cock.

"Yes." My hands grip her hips. "But I don't want to talk about them. I just want to get lost deep inside you. Want your voice pushing out his." She looks at me, sorrow filling her eyes.

"I can help you," she says, cupping my face. "Let me help you."

"I don't think you can, Shadowlight." She doesn't respond with words. Getting to her feet, she strips before me. The light from the White Sun makes her radiantly beautiful. "So perfect."

She moves to straddle me again. Gripping the base of my cock, moving the tip to her wet center, before sinking herself onto me.

"So, fucking tight, gods, you feel fucking amazing." I groan as her head falls back when she is filled to the hilt. Moving to sit up, she plants her hands on my chest, shaking her head.

She wants this to be about me. To give me the release and distraction I asked for. That is what our bond is. We know what the other one needs, and we give it to them.

As she moves slowly at first, I want to move my hand to her. To touch her and give her just as much as she is giving me.

"No, you don't get to touch." She growls, swatting my hands away. "Just watch and let me worship you." I didn't think I could get any harder, but I feel myself throbbing inside her with those spoken words.

My eyes trail over her bountiful breasts, my hands curling into the wool of the bedroll to resist the urge to touch. She wants to be in control. To worship me.

"Touch yourself, Shadowlight," I command. And she obeys. One hand palming her breast and the other teasing that sweet bundle of nerves I am aching to taste again. "Beautiful. My Queen. My Goddess. My Shadowlight. Mine."

Our eyes lock on one another as she moves faster. Bouncing up and down, bringing me closer to our release. The distant shadows try rising again, but as I look at my mate, her fair skin begins to glow the faster she moves.

Completely mesmerized by her, I don't move, don't speak. The shadows come forward again. But her hands land on my chest, and her mouth closes out mine. I feel warmth spreading over me, through me, where our bodies are joined.

A flash of the past comes into view. My hands are painted red and my eyes land on my mate chained to a wall. The images changed to the present. My release is here and my hips begin to buck, my balls draw up, and with a roar so loud it shakes the mountains, I fill her with my seed. She screams her release. Glowing and pushing magic into me at the same time.

My vision fades to black for a few seconds before she slumps over me. Our breaths come in quickly. Our slick bodies press together.

"Wow." Is the only word that seems to spill from my lips

"Yeah." She looks at me. "Your shadows are gone."

"What?" I am stunned by her confession.

"Hi, my name is Emnera. Goddess of Earth and Light. I have the ability to banish shadow magic from people." I look at her and see the difference. Her pure white wings seem larger. The light shines around her, and her scent is no longer floral. But earthy and warm.

"My goddess. My Queen. My Shadowlight."

Chapter Thirty-Four

Emnera

I told Cal last night about how I embraced my true self the moment Rai took him from me. He was remorseful again for betraying us. But I did my best to convince him that it was not his fault.

"If only I was powerful enough," he protested. I still didn't want him to feel that guilt. So, after another earth-shattering orgasm, or three, he finally fell asleep.

"Good morning," I say as I stir awake. He touches me. Searching for an illusion that is not there. "I am here. You are here. We are together again, my heart."

"The shadows are gone," he states more than questions.

"Yes." I pressed my lips to his.

"Thank you, my love," he murmured against my lips, pressing his forehead to mine. "You really are light within the darkness."

I inhale the spicy scent of my mate being close to me again. The warmth of his body heat caressing mine. I cannot get enough.

"If you two are done fucking." Jaxx's growl interrupted our moment. "We should get moving."

Looking down, Cal has already moved his wings to cover my naked body. His chest is pressing into my back, a low growl of possessiveness humming in his throat spreading through my body and straight to my sex.

"Get the fuck out of here so we can get dressed," Cal growled at his brother, who snickered and then marched away.

"We should really go wash up," I stated as he curled an arm toward me. His fingers brushed the still tinder bundle of nerves within me.

"No," Cal growled, then cupped me, sinking two fingers inside me. "You were in control last night and now it's my turn. You don't get to cum unless I say so. Understand?"

All I can do is nod and slink back against him as he brings me close to my climax.

"I missed you and I told you to let me worship you. You took advantage of me last night and I let you. You saved me from the darkness and now I get to reward you. But not until I have had my fill of you first." His words left me breathless and moaning. Begging for more.

"Cal, please." He pumped faster and I am so close until he suddenly pulled out, leaving me panting. Before I could do anything, he moved those fingers and pushed them into the puckered hole, using the arousal from my sex to coat it.

"You are mine. All of you. And this is mine just like your pussy." All I can do is nod. Cal is different. Stronger. Powerful. Commanding. "Tell me, goddess. Are you mine? Is this all mine?"

I didn't speak, just nodded my head as he pulled those fingers out before lining his tip up. "Relax, Shadowlight." His tone was gentle as he whispered in my ear. "Are you ready?"

"Yes," I practically moaned. He slowly pressed inside me. Stretching and filling me completely. His hand moved to my clit.

"So, fucking perfect," he growled and then circled my clit while pumping inside of me. He started slowly, allowing me to adjust to this new feeling. But then the pace picked up speed. He groaned and cursed. "You feel so fucking good."

His thrusts increased, and I held on as he roared through his releases. Once done, he pulled out, turning me around to face him before crashing his lips to mine and hoisting me into the air. I wrapped my legs around his waist as he laid me down.

His lips moved down to my neck, nipping and biting as his fingers continued to pump in and out of me. Licking and biting, marking me as he traveled down my body. His tongue circled my clit; I thrust my hips and began riding his face while searching for my release.

"I forgot how fucking good you taste," He growled before licking my pooling wetness. I didn't care that the others surely knew what was going on from the moaning and roaring. Because right now, my mate was here. And nothing else mattered.

I screamed his name in ecstasy as I orgasmed into his mouth. Panting through the end and then reveling in the sight of his swollen, glossed lips.

"I love you, Shadowlight," he said while crawling back up to face me. "And I will never leave you again. I promise."

"I love you too." He held me in his arms, and I imagined the flowing stream we passed on our way here and teleported us there so we can clean ourselves.

After drying and dressing in new clothes, we made our way back to camp. Cal had to borrow some from Jaxx, who grumbled again about the time we wasted fucking, but he didn't understand what it meant to be mated to someone. At least, not yet.

"We will breach the south wall while you distract the queen. I know a few tricks to get around any magic locks or traps," Jaxx smugly stated.

"And while you are playing with magical trinkets, I will be snatching the dagger with ease," Abby stated with a glower. There was something going on here, and it was more than just sexual frustration. I knew something happened on the way here. From the panic I sensed from Jaxx, I thought something bad would happen, but they showed up unscathed.

"You aren't coming," Jaxx growled.

"Yes, I am," she growled back, crossing her arms and stepping closer to make sure she was toe to toe with him.

"I don't need some frilly princess getting us caught. Especially a human girl." Ouch. Insult much? I mean, I am not human anymore, but still. I gave a sideways glance at Cal, who seemed to be amused at the situation.

"And we don't trust a known criminal with the relic that is meant to save our realm from darkness," Abby spat back. Then a stare-off started, sending my senses into overdrive.

Hate. Anger. Regret. Lust.

"You will both be going," I stated.

"What?" they both say with a look of incredulity.

"You will produce a plan to retrieve the dagger and not get caught. Then meet us back here." I simply stated.

“Emnera, I love you, but come on. It is bad enough you made me fly with him, and now I have to go on a covert mission with him? It will be like watching an infant,” Abby argued. Her blue eyes pleading.

“Infant? Really, Princess? Is that the best insult you have? Because take one look at my co—”

“Enough,” Cal growled. And I am thankful he stopped Jaxx from finishing that sentence. “Do as my mate says or get the fuck out of here.”

Abby and Jaxx looked stunned at his aggressive behavior, but it only turned me on more.

“Guess you didn’t work out all your aggression. Emnera, I need a word with you. Alone,” Abby asked, and with a nod, we walked far enough away from the Ashana brothers that they could not hear us.

“Look,” she said. “I am so happy Cal is back. I mean, it is him, right? Did you do that light magic thing on him?”

“Yes.” I chuckled. She was worried. “It’s him.”

“He seems different.”

“I noticed it too, but whatever I banished from him, freed him of more than shadows. I don’t know what exactly but, he feels like his true self.”

“You mean a total asshole? Oh, gods, please, for your sake, I hope he isn’t like his brother.” I shot her a knowing smirk.

“What happened between the two of you?” I prodded.

“Nothing. I just don’t trust him.”I could tell she was telling the truth. But I sensed something else. But then again, there was always something else with her. An emotion that she didn’t want to address or overcome.

Gripping her shoulder, I pushed some calming magic into her. Jumping back, we both realized what I had just done.

"Holy goddess, did you feel that?" she asked.

"I didn't know I could do that," I confessed.

"Do it again." She reached out to me.

"No, what if I hurt you?"

"You won't," She reassured me. Touching her hand, I let out a breath before focusing on the serenity of the atmosphere, pushing the feeling into her. When it reached her, I saw her relax completely, but then she began to sway.

"Too much. Shit. Cal," I yelled. She passed out, but it wasn't Cal who caught her, but Jaxx.

"What did you do?" he growled. Anger and worry hit me with full force. Tasted like acid on my tongue.

"She…I…" I'm at a loss for words, but Cal's presence calmed me.

"You discovered a new ability," he proudly stated.

"I guess so." I waited for Jaxx to find her pulse. "It was just supposed to calm her down, not knock her out."

"You shouldn't be using your powers on a human," Jaxx growled. Gods, he didn't just feel an attraction for her. I could see it. A small glimmer of light trying to fight the darkness around his soul. Around his heart.

"Didn't know you cared, Dragonboy," Abby muttered.

"Thanks, the gods." Jaxx started helping her to her feet before letting go. "I mean, this is no time for naps, Princess."

Abby rolled her eyes before reassuring me she was

okay. “Maybe you should use your powers to ease the stick out of his ass.” She pointed at Jaxx.

“Oh no, sweetheart. The only ass that will have anything in it, is yours.” Jaxx winked at her. Back to his crass smugness. “If you are done resting, we need to move.”

The plan was set in motion. I had forgotten all about the big Golden dragon until he showed up after we made our final plans.

“A shiny thing like you will be spotted easily,” I stated.

“Right. I will stay up here. If you need me, just call out.” He nodded respectfully toward Cal.

Since we didn’t have time to send word of my arrival, Cal and I decided to just show up at the front gates. I just pray we weren’t stepping into another trap.

Chapter Thirty-Five

Emnera

"Do you think they made it?" I asked Cal as we prepared to approach the front gates of the shimmering steel palace.

"Yes," he answered, while assessing the surrounding area. Always plotting the next move. If the need to escape arose, Cal would have a plan. "Abby is smart and Jaxx…" He stopped for a moment.

"Jaxx is an outlaw, so those two together could do anything," I finished for him, and he smirked. I didn't like to use my gifts on him, but I was getting the feeling that something was up. "Cal, please tell me what's wrong? What happened when you were with Rai?"

"Not right now." He gave me a quick peck on my cheek and then marched forward.

I will find out the truth, Calian, so you better stop shutting me out. I stepped up to him. We locked arms like any happily married royal couple would and proceeded toward the large iron gate where we were greeted by two gilded guards. Both adorned in golden-plated armor from helm to toe. Even their arrow-tipped spears were golden.

"Good evening," I said. Waiting for some type of warning or greeting. I gave a sideways glance to Cal, who grasped my arm tightly. *What's wrong?* I ask, down the bond.

There is something in the atmosphere. I can feel my magic locking down on me. It is as if the air is made ofiron. I sucked in a sharp breath, but I couldn't taste or feel anything that suggested iron was in the air.

"What business do you seek at this late hour?" one of the guards asked. Unmoving.

"I seek an emergent audience with your Queen," I stated as regally as possible. Remembering all the times Mother spoke so formally. A phantom pain crossed my abdomen at the memory of her. But I quickly shook it off and gave the guards an innocent smile.

I adorned myself in a crimson gown with black lace for the arms and a plain silver tiara set upon my golden curls. Calian wore his usual attire of all-black. We were mated but we had yet to do any official ceremony or even a coronation for either of us. We have been just too busy fighting and strategizing the downfall of Rai.

"High Queen Chloe of Thornwarf," I stated formally. Although it felt like a lie rolling off my tongue. I was no Queen. Especially now that I knew who I was.

"There is no 'High Queen' anymore." A sultry woman's voice came from somewhere beyond the bars. "Tell me who you really are, and I might let you leave with your heads on your shoulders."

A feral growl rumbled low in Cal's throat. In response, the guards placed both hands on their spears.

"Call off your guards," I firmly stated. I preferred not to hurt humans, but if it came down to Cal's life or theirs, I would kill them. I watched and waited. Listening to the sounds of everything around me. Night owls hooted greetings through the noise of the whispering winds.

If they don't stop threatening you, I will rip their hearts out," Cal growled down the bond.

"Bring us to your queen," I demanded, but they remained still. Did not speak. It was as if they turned into statues. A figure in the shadows moved forward as the bars of the gate rose. A female, adorned in a black hooded cloak that flowed over a sheer black gown, approached us.

"There is no High Queen. Tell me who you are," the woman demanded. I could see a plump face hidden behind the shadows of the hood. When I remained quiet, I saw the hint of a smirk form at the corner of her blue-painted lips. "I was told that the entire High Royal family was killed by some shadow man. Yet, I see you standing here before me claiming to be the queen. Tell me, are you willing to risk execution for impersonating a Royal Queen or are you going to tell me the truth?"

"I will only speak with your queen. You may let me in the effortless way, or I can come inside by sheer force. You choose." I placed the fate of her people in her hands. But I might have spoken too soon because Cal doubled over in pain. "What's wrong?" Looking at the woman, I felt my power pushing at the edge of my skin, begging to release. "What did you do to him?"

"I have done nothing. This is merely a test, and I can see that your guard has failed, and he isn't human." She seemed amused. "Iron is every magical species' weakness. I coat the atmosphere of my entire kingdom in it. The chimneys breathe the iron into the air. Even my walls are infused with it."

"You're the bitch that sent those rapists after me," I

snarled. Her hood fell, and I saw the face behind the voice. Two deep brown eyes, a plump mid-night colored face and bodice. Pure black curled hair flowed from the top of her round head. A metallic and sugar-sweet scent wafted from her clothes.

With Cal unconscious in my arms, I looked straight into those pools of darkness, knowing this will be the exception. "You hurt my mate," I started by placing one palm on the earth before me. Power surged through my veins as I connected with its power. My wings burst from my back as the white of my light engulfed not only me but Cal. "And now," I saw the look of fear on her face. "You will die."

Roots burst from the ground, wrapping themselves tightly around the necks of my three victims. Their protest was nothing but garbled choked words.

"We….have…the…others," the queen choked out. I loosened the root ever so slightly.

"Repeat that!" I ordered.

"We have the human woman and other magical men. If I die, so do they." A look of triumph tried to replace the fear in her eyes. But I sensed the truth of her words.

"Clearly you don't understand who you're messing with." I rise to my feet after gently lowering Cal to the ground. "Your iron doesn't affect me. Your presence doesn't scare me. There is only one thing that can stop me, and you are not it." I snapped the necks of her guards with the swift jerk of my wrist controlling the roots.

"Who the hell are you?" she asked in a shaky tone. Stopping right in front of her, I wrapped my roots all around her body. Immobilizing it.

"I am Emnera, Goddess of Earth and Light. And you will release my friends, or I will kill you." I threatened, baring my teeth. The stench of urine invaded my nose, and I knew I had scared the piss out of her.

"We must go to the palace dungeons," she states.

"Do you have something to cure him?" I asked, pointing at my poor mate lying on the ground.

"No," she stammered. "He will surely die if he ingests too much iron. It is like poison. Or so I have been told."

"Who told you this? Do you know what he is?" I asked her.

"He is an Ashana. They are weak against iron. My master told me." That word is one I have heard before. "My master is going to kill you all."

"No, he's not." With the jerk of my wrist, I snapped her neck too. Running back to Cal, I placed my palm with our insignia on his chest, relishing in the steady beat of his heart. I reached into the earth and gave a silent command. *Take him to a safe enough distance from here. Have food and water waiting for him.*

Not that the earth could talk back, but I could have sworn I heard it say, 'As you wish.' As the roots do what I commanded, I ran through the gate, across a wooden drawbridge, and through the archway into a courtyard full of armed soldiers.

"All right, boys. Who's ready to die?" I asked, smirking, as the twenty of them surrounded me.

"Stand down."A male voice rang out from a balcony atop stone steps on the right side of the yard.

"Your queen is dead," I yelled. Probably should

not have said that, but at this point, I just wanted my friends and the dagger. Iron and human weapons don't affect me.

"And I have your friends ready to hang with a rope around their necks." He pointed to a spot I didn't see at first. A woman and a man with wings stood with their arms bound behind their backs and black bags over their heads. They had wrapped rope around their necks while their feet remain planted upon wooden stools above drop doors.

"Let them go," I growled. This must be the prince. He was quite handsome. Beautiful midnight-colored skin adorned in a long black tunic with golden lacey. Eli does have good taste in men. "And I might let you live."

"I don't think you are the one with the upper hand here, goddess." He moved down the steps, two guards on either side, toward me. "Because I find it interesting where we found these two."

"Oh, you mean behind your secret magic door?" I scoffed. "You really need to update your security system if a human woman and Ashana could get through."

"You know what, I think you're onto something because I warned Mother about the same thing," he stated with his hands directly behind his back. Relaxed and unaware of the threat standing right in front of him. "Do you think I fear you, goddess?"

"I think you'd be foolish not to," I answered. Closing the distance between us, he smirked at me.

"Tell me something, goddess. When your friends and lover are dead, who will you blame?" His question baffled me. But I have been through mind tricks before.

"Will you blame me? Will you blame Lord Rai? Or will you blame yourself? Because you have the opportunity to save them all if you just surrender yourself to me and to my master."

"Don't do it." Cal's weary voice echoed through the yard, and I instantly turned to see him in iron shackles on his knees with blood coating his face.

"Ahh, the prodigal son joins us at last. Do you see that blade resting across your lover's neck?" I looked over and saw the white color of a bone connected to the golden hilt. "It's humorous, really. A simple shard of a dragon bone can kill the son of a god."

"What's your name?" I asked him. It appeared my question and calm tone surprised him. You would not know it unless you were standing right in front of him.

"Alaric, Prince, well, now that Mother is dead, King Alaric of Shulong," he smugly stated. *He thinks he has won, but he has not.*

"You think I will surrender myself, my power to a traitor like you?" I snarled.

"Well, yes actually, be—"

"Because what? You have my lover? My friends? No, Alaric. I will not give myself or my power to any man. You see, the problem with men is that they think women are fragile. They think we are the lesser species and so by default, underestimate us." I gave him a knowing smirk.

"Kill them," he yelled, and just like that…my world stopped. My throat tightened as rope strangled the life out of Jaxx and Abby. My heart split in two as the dagger slit Cal's throat, but I didn't cry. I didn't fall to my knees and beg. No, I fought.

Calling on all my power, I focused on the ropes

first and used my light to sever them like a dagger to a chord. Floating to the air, I felt arrows piercing my skin, but I didn't stop. The earth aided me in my fight as roots broke through the stone floor, killing the soldiers that threatened me.

"Your lover is dead, goddess." I heard those words Alaric spoke, but they didn't register. Because right now, he was my target. Forming light in my hands, I shot a beam at him, which he blocked by a shield of shadows. "You can't harm me. I am invincible."

"Not against me." Jaxx brought the false king down to his knees in a chokehold.

"Don't kill him," I ordered. "We need the dagger." As my body drains, my head feels heavy, and I tumbled to the ground.

"Emnera," Abby screamed, and my head snapped in her direction. The direction that Cal was in when that dagger slit his throat. Stumbling over to them, the tears flowed and my heart broke. "He's dead," Abby cried.

"No. No. No. Calian." I cradled his head in my lap. His blood stained the ground, staining our clothes, and my hands. "Cal, don't leave me. You cannot leave me. I don't have a soul without you." *You promised.*

I know. His voice fades as I try to feel for our bond, but it's not there. Silence. Darkness. Ice. Death.

"Look at me," I yelled as I tried to wake him from his eternal sleep. "Please, I can't do this without you." My heart felt like an anvil shattered it. The grief was all-consuming. I kissed his cold lips. The ones that captured my heart the first time they claimed me. His green eyes were still open, but the life that was once there was gone. The eyes that made me feel like the only woman that ever existed in this world were now closing.

"I'm sorry," Abby whispered through her cries. And I knew she understood this pain. "What…what do we do?"

I contemplate those words. My grief turned into rage. Because now, the world will pay.

"Jaxx," I called over to him, "beat the traitor until he has one last breath. If he doesn't give us the dagger, he will die. If he doesn't deliver the location of Lord Rai, he will die." I turned toward them. "You will die, Alaric. Your blood will coat my hands as I rip your black heart from your soulless body."

"You cannot harm me, goddess. Good girls are not cold-blooded killers," he scoffed. Marching toward them, I stepped up to him, reveling in the fact that my face would be the last he will see. Placing my right hand over his heart, I pressed my fingers in, adding some light to them.

"What are you doing?" Alaric winced in pain. I pushed harder, breaking through cloth and skin. "Stop. Please."

"Looks like you underestimated a woman," Jaxx hissed. I sensed the anger, grief, and pain wafting off him at the loss of his brother. But he was giving me this death.

"The dagger is in a safe in my private quarters," Alaric cried out.

"And the location of Rai's base?" I growled, pushing harder. His blood was slowly coating my fingers. I felt the rapid beating of his heart.

"It's in the Jian Desert. Hidden by magic. But you cannot get in without me. It requires a magical signature."

I paused a moment. “Where is this magical signature?” I asked.

“If I tell you, you’ll just kill me,” he muttered.

“I’m going to kill you, anyway. So do something good for once in your pathetic little life.”

“My blood. You need my blood,” he stated in defeat. I removed my hand and Alaric’s shoulders relaxed.

“Looks like you get to breathe a little while longer. But only until I have something to put your blood in.” I wiped my blood-coated fingers on him. “Tie him down. I don’t need him running off before we have the dagger in our hands.”

“I don’t take orders from you, Emnera,” Jaxx growled.

“Oh really? Hmm, seems to me like you would do anything to avenge your family unless I got that all wrong?” Jaxx narrowed his green eyes at me. It made my broken heart shatter more at the familiarity of them. “Go find the dagger so I can prepare my mate for his descend into the Realm of Immortium.”

Even saying the words, considering the fact that Cal was gone. His body was still here, but his soul, the very being that made him, was gone. Walking over to Abby, I trailed my gaze over her grief-ridden face down to the red mark around her neck.

Reaching out, I gently touched it. She winced in pain, but I couldn’t help but push light against it. Not the same light I used to cut the ropes. Or the ones that could slit throats. But light that was full of all the emotions I felt for her. Friendship. Sister. Love. Warmth.

The red receded as I healed the wound. Her once

hoarse voice, now normal again as she spoke.

"How? Thank you." She sobbed while pulling me into her embrace.

I returned the gesture before whispering into her ear, "Go with him. I don't trust him not to do something foolish."

"What makes you think I have any influence over him?" she whispered back.

"He has feelings for you. He trusts you. If you have to, use it to your advantage." I pulled back at my last words and she nodded in understanding. I gestured for her to go with him while roots raised Cal's body. Every time I called on my powers, I got stronger. I made a raised bed of roots for my love.

"I failed you." I placed my forehead against his blood-stained one. "I will love you for all my life. I vow to avenge you. To seek justice for the wrong that has been done to you. The world will know my pain as I burn every last shadow to the ground."

Gently placing a kiss upon his lips, I closed the roots over him to form a coffin, then placed my palms against it to push everything I ever felt for him into it. Hate turned to lust. Lust turned to love. Enemy turned into a lover. Stepping back, I let the last of my tears flow before lowering my love to the ground. I then covered the hole with dirt.

Turning around, I walked over to Alaric, gripped his hair so he met my eyes and gave him one last look at the woman who defeated him. "You killed my mate, and now…" I formed a ball of light in my hand and pressed it directly into his cock. "You will never know the touch of a lover again."

His scream of pain felt in my ears was the joyous

sound of triumph. As he blacked out from agony, I let him fall face forward on the concrete ground. Turning my back toward him, I didn't realize I was dropping until my hands and knees impacted the floor.

Too much power. Too much pain. The world spun as I tried to catch my breath. My life collapsing in on itself as flashes of what could have flooded my mind. A beautiful baby boy with bronzed skin, bright eyes the color of the sea, and raven-colored hair; looking at me with love and filling the hole in my chest.

But that was an illusion. A dream. A wish because my mate was dead. Nothing and nobody can come back from that, not even me. Chloe died and Emnera was reborn. But Cal—Cal was not a god reincarnated, he was the son of one. An Ashana. I will never be whole again.

Chapter Thirty-Six

Emnera

Blood. Death. Searing pain.

The only thing I felt within the darkness of my mind. "Your Ashana is dead, my flower. Time to come home." Mother's voice sounded in my ears.

"No. You're wrong," I spat back, looking around to see nothing but a single-lit scone attached to a torch along a brick wall. There was something familiar about where I was.

"Time for another lesson, my flower," she stated, and I felt restraints all along my body.

"No. You're dead. This…this is not real. I am a goddess." A cackle escapes her as she comes into view. Only it wasn't the woman I saw standing there. It was much worse.

"Look at us, Chloe. You think you're a goddess, but you are not. You are nothing but a cold-blooded bitch, just like our mother was." It was my own reflection talking to me, only it was the old me. The scars littered her body where mine were gone.

Snapping awake as the ice hit my veins from my own words, I noticed the High Sun had already peaked. Was I out all night? I must have burned myself out using all that power and Cal, gods, I can't.

I tried to move, but my body was immobilized by a

thick iron chain wrapped around me from neck to ankle.

"I see she has finally awakened." The scratchy voice that has haunted so many, one that I have heard only a small number of times but still made its mark on me. Turning my head, I see him standing in his all-dark robe attire. Right next to the two bastard princes that have either tried to kill me or assault me.

"I see your pet has called you while I was incapacitated. No doubt the only way he could get away with it." I smirked. "Did he tell you what I did to him? How I burned his cock right off his disgusting body?" I chuckled, then heaved when two boots connected with my sides..

"Kicking a woman when she is down, not very gentlemanly," I huffed out. My wings were aching from being anchored down, but as the roots of the earth began to intertwine themselves with the chains, I inwardly smiled. Knowing all I needed was to give my dear friend time to work.

"You aren't a woman, though. Are you a goddess?" Rai asked. I rolled my eyes at him. "You may have a cunt and breasts, but you are just a sick, seductive killer."

"Oh, you're going to make me cry." I feigned tears. I watched as Rai walked over to Eli and Alaric, petting their hair as if to tell them 'good boy.'

"Should we have some fun with her first?" he asked them rhetorically. They both smirk and turn to look at me, unsheathing their daggers.

"Is this about your dicks? Because I mean, really, I did you both a favor. Now you can't spread your little demon seed to any unsuspecting woman." When the first punch connected with my jaw, I laughed at the taste of my blood. Which was foolish because they both started punching me.

"Enough," Rai ordered, and like two domesticated animals, they stopped. "Lift her up. I want to look into her eyes as I drain all that power from her." They hoisted me to my feet and the roots instantly stilled.

"Your mate is dead, goddess. What are you fighting for?" he asked me. His hot breath caused acid to rise in my throat.

"Have you ever heard of mint paste? Or even attempted to chew on some mint leaves?" I asked him. He feigned a smirk forms right before he landed a few punches. They are more powerful, ten times more painful than human hits. I spat blood onto the ground and held my chin up high.

"I am going to give you the opportunity to save yourself, goddess." He sneered. "Tell me where the dagger is, and I will grant you a quick death."

"Fuck. You." I spat in his face. If Jaxx and Abby succeeded and returned to this shit show, then I pray they were smart and ran off with the dagger. Although, knowing Abby, she will more than likely try to kill these bastards.

"Don't test me, girl. I've been around for centuries; you are just now reborn. An infant. You haven't even gained your truest form yet." He laughed before nodding to Eli and Alaric next to me. "Do you know what it feels like to have your wings cut?"

As he asked, the first blade cut across the inside of my right wing. My knees buckled instantly, and I screamed in pain. *It's too much.* As he continued, it felt like a part of me was being cut off. A part of my soul. Bone and flesh. I refused to let the tears fall, but allowed numbness to envelope me.

An instinct that became natural after all the years my mother tortured me. As my eyes fluttered closed, boney fingers gripped my chin. “Now, now, Emnera, we don’t want you turning off your emotions now, do we?”

Another searing pain penetrated my right shoulder as he slammed a shadow blade directly into it. Filling my body with shadow magic. It was like death was moving through my body. Snuffing out the light that was there to warm me. As uncontrollable tears tumble, I see the end.

I had nothing left to fight for. Nothing and no one left to live for. Calian was gone. My parents were gone. And Alma, poor innocent Alma, was under the influence of this man. The only thing I could do before my light was completely out was to pray to any god and goddess listening that Abby and Jaxx succeed. All the dragons remain free, and Rai is killed.

“That’s it, Emnera, give your power to me. Give it to me and you will finally be free. Your dear Ashana awaits you,” Rai stated as my death sat at the edge of my vision. I didn’t feel the dagger as they cut my wings from me. The two princes, who were once allies to my father, now laughing and tossing my tattered wings to the ground.

My chains and clothes fall from my body, so I was now naked before them. I didn’t fight. I didn’t resist their touch, the running of the blades as they dragged it over my body. Forming new scars.

“I remember where each one was,” Eli stated with a look of hunger in his eyes. “You made your mark on me and now I will do it to you.” With Alaric at my back and Eli at my front, I knew I couldn't win. My light was almost gone, but it left the moment Cal was taken from me.

Fight, a phantom voice growled in my ear.

Fight for me. Not a phantom voice. Cal's voice. *Fight for me, Shadowlight.* I knew he wasn't here but the feel of him flooded through my body. *Don't give up on me. On them.* Tears flowed down my body, mixing with my blood. It wasn't from the assault. It wasn't from the pain. It's from him. My mate reached out to me beyond the veil of life and death.

My eyes snapped open and saw the neck of Eli close to my mouth. I felt two fingers in my sex and two in my ass as they moved in sync with their assault. Moaning came from them as they kissed each other and rubbed their remaining nubs against my body.

"Fuck," Eli groaned and I let them have just another second before I slaughtered them. The rays of the High Sun hit me and refueled my body. Heating it to unbearable temperatures. They didn't have time to react. To scream. Before I turned them into ash.

"Impossible," Rai yelled as he blast shadows at me. But a shield of roots blocked it as I felt myself lift from the ground. My body was healing itself as I fought back.

"And now, you die," I stated in a calm tone. A ball of light appeared in my hand and immediately aimed at Rai. An explosion of black and gold formed a large ball of smoke. I growled as I charged through it.

"Emnera," Abby's voice broke through my concentration. Turning, I see the two of them hand in hand with a golden chest clutched to Abby's side.

"Give it to me," I commanded, but she flinched.

“Not until you calm down.” She angered me further. Jaxx must have noticed because he placed himself between us.

“Cool off, Emnera. Just because you’re my brother’s mate doesn’t mean I won’t kill you.” He snarled.

“Move aside or you both die.” I couldn’t believe those words were uttered by me.

“Rai is gone and from the dried blood all over you, I think you are in amped-up mode,” Abby stated from behind the wall of muscle that was Jaxx.

Looking into Jaxx’s eyes, I see the familiarity in them. The same green eyes that have looked at me with love and passion. I simmered down as I looked into my own reflection. My hair was no longer the color of honey, but pure white like my wings once were.

My beautiful white wings—broken and blood-stained. Naked and humiliated, I fall to my knees. Two strong arms catch me before I hit the floor, and my emotions invade me again. The floodgates of a damn opening up to all the pain, all the grief, all the shame I felt.

“Get her something to wear,” Jaxx mutters to Abby. Who do I assume listens because a moment later she is handing me a silk robe and dressing me in it? I try to stand my knees wobble and Jaxx lifts me into his arms. Cradling me like a Mother to her babe.

“I’m sorry.” I sob, burying my head into Jaxx’s chest. “I’m so sorry. I failed you all.”

“No, you didn’t,” Jaxx mutters. “We have the dagger and from what we walked into. You killed two pathetic assholes. I mean I was going to save you and all, but then you decided to kill them with burning beams of light."

The corners of my mouth lifted as he looked down at me with a genuine smirk. My senses reached out and I feel the shift in him. A wall no longer blocks me.

"Thank you," I whispered as exhaustion took over and I slowly drifted to sleep.

"You don't need to thank me. We're family and family doesn't end in blood."

****

As I wake up, my body rocked side to side. The roof above me seemed familiar, just as the salty smell in the air. I moved to sit up and discovered I was dressed in a simple ivory blouse and black trousers. I was in Petunia. God, I hate sailing.

On a small round table next to the bed I'm in is a plate of seaweed. Looking around, I recognized the cabin as mine and Cal's. The one we had shared many times. At the end of the bed is a pair of leather boots. I tried to stand but instantly fell back down as nausea overcame my stomach.

"Fuck sea sickness," I muttered.

"You're awake." Abby all but ran to hug me. "How are you feeling? I know you get seasick, but I mean you're a goddess so, I just figured it might not affect you but then again you still bleed, so I thought she might still be part human."

"Abby," I say to cut her rambling off, "what happened?"

"Oh, right. You almost died, but you did blast Rai away."

"I know that. I mean, where is the dagger? Where is Jaxx? Where is—" I reached behind me. Searching for them but only felt jagged edges of bones sticking out of my back where my wings used to be.

"I'm so sorry. We couldn't save your wings."I saw the tears swelling in her eyes.

"It's fine. It just proves that goddesses can be killed," I state, trying to hide my own sorrow. My wings had become a part of me. Something that I relied on as I took to the skies. The times Cal and I spent flying together. But I guess since I can't have him, I shouldn't care about my wings anymore.

"Are you hungry?" Abby asked.

"Not really. Where is everyone?"

"In Robb's quarters. Let's just say you woke up in time. Everyone is here and pissed."

"Everyone except you?" I smirked.

"No, but that's my secret. Being pissed all the time is how I get away with everything." We both laughed as we made our way out of the cabin and onto the deck. The White Sun was high in the sky, and I could see only a few deckhands at the top of the deck.

Rob's First Mate is at the helm, while others are standing port and starboard watching with their hands on their weapons. Ready for any attempted assault.

As we walked through the double doors, the room went quiet and all eyes landed on me. Everyone except the dragons was here.

"Chloe, I mean Emnera, I'm so glad you are okay," Kaliegh states while rushing to hug me.

"Thank you." Tailan, Rowland, Jaxx, and Robb were on their feet. Eyes full of emotion—anger, sorrow, lust, and grief.

"I assume you all are discussing the dagger and the plan of attack?" I asked.

"Yes, come sit down." Kaliegh and Abby walked

me to a chair perched between them, but before I could sit, Rob had me in his embrace.

"Calian was like a brother to me. I'm sorry I wasn't there to save him," Rob muttered in my ear. I felt his grief at the loss of his friend.

I didn't respond, just gave him a peck on the cheek before taking my seat.

"So, where are we?" I asked, but no one responded. They all just glanced and my gaze found Jaxx leaning back in a chair with his boots propped on the table. Just like Abby.

"We have all the vials of blood, but we can't get the damn box to open," Lord Rowland stated, pointing at the golden item in question.

"It's sealed with magic," I stated. "Blood magic."

"Whose?" Tailan asked.

"Doesn't matter," I muttered.

"Emnera, if you know who it is, you must tell us," Kaliegh said. When I remained quiet, that's when the anger irrupted. The frustration. The yelling. The demands. When my eyes locked onto Jaxx, he silently told me to say it. Say the phrase I knew would shut them all up and shatter their hope of winning this war.

"He's dead," I said, and the voices slowly died. "It doesn't matter because the man that sealed it is dead."

"How do you know?" Tailan asked. As the flashes of Eli and Alaric's assault flooded my brain, my tears burst forward. I trembled. Hating myself for regressing back to my former self. The one that didn't fight for her body. The one that just gave up.

"Because I killed them," I said at last. And there it goes. The death glares. The shame. The disappointment. It started to suffocate me.

"You are a fucking idiot. Do you realize what you did? You doomed us all!" Tailan yelled. I didn't move, but Jaxx does. In a blink of an eye, Tailan was pinned to the floor. Rob and Rowland tried to pull Jaxx off him.

"They raped her," He growled. The air in the room and the breath in my lungs hitched. "I don't give a fuck about some magical seal when she defended herself. She killed those bastards for what they did to her. Turned them into ash before they could get off."

Kaliegh tried to reach out to me, but I flinched at the contact. "Oh, I'm sorry. I didn't know."

"If there is anyone in this room who deserves a fucking break, it's her," Jaxx growled. "And if I hear any of you insult my sister again, I will kill you."

Sister? Jaxx accepted me as family? But why? Calian was gone. Without looking at anyone, I got to my feet, placed my palms on the table, and let out a breath before speaking.

"Blood magic is tricky, but it can be broken. Just like a *Blood Oath*, the bond can be severed if the vow is broken." I allowed myself a shaky breath before continuing. "I will make a *Blood Oath* with the chest. It should open itself to me." This next part came out without me even thinking. "I will vow my heart to it."

"Out of the question," Jaxx stated.

"Not possible," Kaliegh murmured.

"Your heart belongs to Cal. Not some inanimate object," Rob said.

"Calian will always have my heart, but he's…" I choked as the words come out. "…dead. I will not allow his sacrifice to go without vengeance. That's final."

"No," Jaxx growled.

"It isn't up to you," I growled back.

"Everyone, leave this room, *now*," Jaxx commanded, flexing his wings in a threatening gesture.

"They don't take orders from you," I snarled.

"Get. The. Fuck. Out." Without a single protest, everyone but Abby leave. "That means you, Princess."

"You may think you're all powerful, Dragonboy, but if you think for one sec—"

"It's okay. I'll be fine," I tell her and she gave me the are-you-sure-because-I-can-kick-his-ass look. I nodded. Once the doors closed, Jaxx and I entered into some kind of stare-off.

"Since when am I your sister?" I asked.

"Since you became my brother's mate." He placed his palms on the table in front of him.

"Cal is gone. I am going to do this because I am the only one who has a heart to lose. As much as it pains me to think about giving my heart up, I just can't stand the weight of it anymore. It belonged to Calian, but now it doesn't belong to anyone, not even me." I waited for him to interject, and I tried to reach out to sense what he was feeling, but I felt a mix of love and sorrow.

"You aren't the only one with a heart to lose." Before I knew what he was doing, Jaxx's bloodied hand was on the chest, and he muttered the vow.

"No!" How did he cut his hand so fast? "What have you done?"

The doors swung open, and my eyes caught the sight of Abby placing a hand over her heart. Falling to her knees, she appeared to be gasping for air. I looked at Jaxx, who was roaring in pain as he fell to the deck with the chest connected to his hand.

The boat rocked hard with the power of magic. Ash and acid overwhelmed the flavor in my mouth. Sorrow, betrayal, loss.

Once the boat steadied itself, I ran over to them. The chest was open and inside on the velvet bed of crimson was a beating heart. Looking at Jaxx, I noticed in his hand he wielded a pure gold-plated dagger.

"What have you done?" I looked over at the unconscious Abby.

"I saved us," Jaxx stated.

"By sacrificing your heart?"

"It was the only way."

"You're an idiot. Now you can never solidify the mating bond with her. You have bound yourself to a chest."

"It's what I deserve. I'm not worthy of her."

"You're a damn fool. When this war is over, you will fix this. I will not have Abby suffer for the rest of her life because of you."

"When this war is over, she'll never see me again," he stated. "My heart is gone. I no longer have boyish emotions impeding my mission."

"What do you mean?" I asked. As he rose to his feet, I watched him walk over to a cupboard and pull out five vials of liquid crimson.

"I mean," he started by opening all of them. "My revenge." I stood there like a statue as he poured the dragon leader's blood on the dagger, reciting the incantation, creating the Dagger of Vertumnus; Shadow Killer.

Chapter Thirty-Seven

Calian

Darkness surrounds me as I try to figure out where I am. My body is cold, and I'm standing unclothed. The pain against my neck reminds me of how I died at the hands of a dragon bone dagger. The last glimpse was of my beautiful mate fighting against a traitorous prince.

Although I know she survived, I can't help but feel panicked. Something is wrong with her. I know my death hit her hard, but what I don't understand is how I can feel her. Feel that something is off about her.

"Calian, son of Tika, god of dragons, how very nice of you to join us here," a high pitched voice says from somewhere beyond the shadows.

"Who's there?" I ask, scanning the surrounding area.

"That's not the question you wish to ask."

"Okay, where are you?"I almost felt delusional for speaking into nothing.

"Wrong again, son of Tika, god of dragons."

"Stop saying that," I growl.

"Is it not true? Are you not the son of a god? The one who reigns over all the dragons," it asks.

"Reigned. My father was killed when I was a babe," I say, frustrated. It lets out an obnoxious laugh. "Does my grief humor you?"

"No, but your ignorance does." Confused, I try to think of what it could mean. "Gods and goddesses can't be killed. Not completely, however. Their souls just pass on and wait in limbo. Waiting for the perfect vessel to merge themselves with."

"Like Emnera and Chloe?" I ask.

"So, you do have some wits about you." It sounds pleased. "When your father died, who took his place as the god of dragons?" it asked.

"No one. There isn't anyone."

"Correct. Until now."

I still don't understand what it could mean. "You're not saying…it's not possible." Running its words in the back of my head, trying to figure out if it meant me.

"An heir with the same bloodline is the perfect match. It's just unfortunate for you that you died before your big brother," it stated. "Although, he may join you sooner rather than later."

"What?" Jaxx is with Emnera and if he is in danger, then so is she.

"Calm your scales. I'm just saying your big brother is very spontaneous. Acts without thinking about the consequences."

"Tell me what you mean to say and stop wasting my time."

"Touchy. Fine. You, if you choose to accept it, will become the new god of dragons, taking on the name of Darius. Your older brother, however, has just made a *Blood Oath* with a magical chest. Destroying practically any chance for him and his mate to be together." It sounded annoyed.

"None of it makes sense. Why would Jaxx make a

Blood Oath with a chest?"

It scoffs. Sounding almost like a real person. "Out of all that, you worry about the semantics?" I swear I could see a head shaking in disappointment. "Accept the position and go back and ask him yourself."

"Just like that? Say yes and I go back to them?"

"Yes, but as a god." I thought about the impossibility of the scenario. The possibility of going back to them. To my family.

"If I do this, will I have the power to kill Rai?" Not that I wouldn't be saying no. I would go back and aid in the war.

"They will not be able to win the war without the god of dragons," it spoke. And I wonder how something, a voice at that, could know all this.

"What are you?" I ask, and with the answer, I see the being behind the voice. A skeleton adorned in black robes, holding a scythe.

"I am the God of Death."

"Are we family then?" I ask, feeling a smile twitch at the corners of my mouth.

"No. You need to understand that we are only gods because of the power we inherit. It has nothing to do with familial bloodlines."

"Who created the gods and goddesses?" I ask, crossing my arms.

"I'm not answering that question, boy. Are you ready to accept your new position or not?" Death sounds impatient, which, to me, is ironically humorous. My mind races over all the information he told me. Am I ready to take my father's place? What would Jaxx think? Isn't it his birthright? "Whatever your questions are, you will get the answers by making a decision. And make it soon."

"This isn't like deciding what breeches to wear—it's a major life decision," I argue, and I could've sworn I saw a brow raise. Without further protest, I made my decision. "Tell me what to do."

Death didn't respond with words or gestures. He simply raises his scythe and with the force of a roaring storm, slams it into the ground beneath us. My mouth is filled with the flavor of magic. My body is engulfed in golden flames. But I feel no pain.

Looking at my hands, black scales begin to cover my skin. My bones crunch as my body shifts.

"Welcome, Darius, God of Dragons," Death says as he gestures toward a looking glass. The reflection shows a pure black dragon with electric green eyes. I try to speak but all that comes out is a roar. "You're very welcome. Bring justice to the realm, Darius. I do hope to never see you again."

Before I could roar something, he slams his scythe again, and I am whisked away into a swirling vortex of darkness. Emnera flashes through my mind as my heart begins to beat with the anticipation of seeing her again.

My eyes squint with the approaching rays of light cutting through the shroud of shadows. I flex my wings, trying to get used to my new form. I can feel the rush of the warm air coming over me as I continue to drop.

The sky is painted blue, and the High Sun is at its highest peak. Turning over, I flex my wings and, with a large forceful flap, stop myself from plunging into the Great Sea. Looking around, I try to pinpoint the black banners of the ship I spent a lot of my life on.

How do I shift out of this form? Maybe I want it? As the thought crosses my mind, my body begins to crunch and shrink as my mortal form takes over. My wings shrink down to the size they were before I became a dragon. Something I am sure I will get used to.

As I try to orient my location, I breathe in the familiar salty air drifting from the sea. Looking down at my palms, I notice the gold band is there, but the rose and dragon imprint is gone.

Panic floods my mind as I try to search for a reason it is gone. Searching for a solution but the only thing that comes to mind is our bond broke when I died and became a god. Something that will be corrected once I have her in my arms again.

With the High Sun on my back, I follow the flow of the sea. I will either end up in Orion or Thornwarf.

After an hour of flying, I spot the banners of the Petunia and aim to land on the deck. The closer I get, the harder my heart beats. As I land dead center, I go unnoticed by the deckhands. Most likely due to my family.

Taking steps toward Rob's quarters, I wait and listen by the doors.

"He took off with the damn thing," Abby states. But I don't care to hear her voice.

"Once a criminal always a criminal, you should've never trusted him." That posh voice comes from Lord Rowland. Who are they talking about?

"Abby, what else happened while you were gone?" Queen Kaliegh's concern for her sister is evident in her tone. Where is…

"It doesn't matter. If he kills Rai, we win. Which is what he is going to do." Her voice sings in my ears. I can't wait a moment longer. I push through the door and step in.

"Shadowlight," I say as my eyes only look upon her. To me, the rest of the world disappears. She looks slimmer. Her color is gone from her hair and her wings. I rushed for her, taking her hips into my hands. "Gods I've missed you."

"Cal? Is it…" she asks.

"I'm here. I'm really here." I wipe away the tears flowing from her eyes.

"How?" She grips me. Running her hands all over me ensures I am not an illusion.

"It doesn't matter. What matters now is us," I tell her and press my lips to hers. A cough sounds from behind us, but I don't give a fuck. I deepened our kiss by slipping my tongue through her soft lips and entangling it with hers.

"Cal," she says, breaking the contact. "We are kind of in the middle of something," she whispers as red rises to her cheeks.

"Tell them to go away. I'm sure whatever it is can wait until after I have made love to you," I growl, and she smiles.

"Actually, it cannot," Lord Rowland's voice states from behind me. I clench my jaw in irritation.

"Calian, is it really you, brother?" I don't have time to answer Rob as he pulls me into his arms. Crushing me against his rounded belly. "Gods, I thought you were dead."

"I was," I said as he released me. Looking over all the faces in the room, I catch onto Abby's. A memory of her holding me, crying over me as the final light faded from my eyes, comes to mind. I walk over to her and hug her.

"Thank you," I whisper, hoping she knows what I mean.

"I'm sorry I couldn't save Calian," she whispers back as pain laces her words. I pull back and see the heartbreak in her eyes.

"You missed a lot when you were dead, mate. But you're here and we can give you a brief synopsis," Rob states.

"Where is my brother?" I ask them, but all their faces turn to either sorrow or rage. "Tell me where Jaxx is."

"Gone," Abby states.

"What do you mean?" I look to my mate, and she reaches out a hand to me. Not wanting to go without contact any second longer I take it.

"After you," Emnera swallows. "Everything went to chaos after you died. Abby and Jaxx went for the dagger, and I used up a lot of power and I blacked out. When I awoke, Rai was there, and I was defenseless." Rage pulses in my veins at the thought of her being vulnerable. "Rai, Eli, and Alaric,"

"Eli? As in Prince of Greveil? I ask.

"Yes," she answers.

"What happened?" She wouldn't meet my eye and dread entered me. "Did they fucking touch you?"

I was growling with rage because she didn't have to say it. I knew from the look in her eyes that they had assaulted her.

"They will die for touching what is mine," I growl.

"They are already dead," Abby states. "Your girl here turned them into ash. Should have seen it. Totally badass."

"And my brother?" I ask, still not taking my eyes

off my mate.

"He took off with the Shadow Killer before giving his heart to the chest," Abby sums up. She shrugs it off, but her eyes said more. He betrayed her. Betrayed everyone. All for his selfish revenge plot.

"Everyone needs to leave this room *now*," I order in a deadly calm tone. When no one moves, I emphasized my next phrase. "I will be speaking with my mate alone."

Emnera gave them all a nod. As the last one left, I calmed my breathing before stepping toward her.

Chapter Thirty-Eight

Emnera

When Calian walked through those doors, I thought I was seeing a spirit. As he kissed me, I knew it was him. He was here. Reaching out with my sense confirmed it to be him, but something changed within him. His soul was different.

Now that we were alone in this room, I didn't know whether to give in to the desire of having him in my bed again. Or run.

"Stop. We can't do this," I said. It hurt, but I'm not worthy of him.

"Yes, we can." He didn't move forward. That's the thing about Cal. He doesn't take it without asking.

"Look at me." I gestured down the length of my body. From my white hair to my broken wings. "I'm broken again."

"Are you kidding me?" he asked, and I knew he didn't care about my scars before, but this was different.

"I was raped!" I had to say it and make him understand my torture. "My body is ruined and I did nothing to stop them. I couldn't do it."

I began to fall, but Calian caught me and pulled me onto his lap.

"Do you think that makes me love you any less?"

he asked. Gently, he tilted my chin up to look at him.

"But our bond broke again. Why does it keep happening if we are fated to be together?" I asked, frustrated. Knowing he wouldn't know the answer to that.

"Do you think I fell in love with you because of an imprint?" he asked, and I just shrugged. Feeling defeated. "If you don't know that answer, then I have failed you in more ways than one."

"Never," I said, cupping his jaw. "You have never once failed me."

"I fell in love with you because of the strength of your heart and the fierce nature of your being. You captured me the moment I laid my eyes on you. This,"—he held my hand and placed it over his heart.—"belongs to you. In life and in death."

I didn't know what to say to that. He pulled my hand with the golden band on it to his mouth and kissed it.

"I am broken. There is no way to fix me," I say as a sob tore through my throat.

"You are beautiful," he said, and I knew what he wanted. He wanted to show me. To prove his words to me through actions.

"I'm afraid to be touched again," I admitted. "I don't think I am ready."

"Then I will wait until you are, my Shadowlight." My heart fluttered at the truth of his words.

"What if I am never ready?" I dared to ask.

"Then I will be whatever you need me to be. A shoulder to cry on. An ear to listen. A voice of reason. I am yours, Shadowlight. If I never get to fill you with my seed again, I will be happy knowing that I was still yours." I knew at that moment, those words, that fiery look in his eyes, that I truly did have my soul mate.

I was in his arms and his hands never once strayed from my back. I may never fly again, but I know time will heal me.

"Kiss me," I whispered, and he only responded with the three words that captured my heart every time he recited them.

"As you wish."

****

We lay in each other's arms the rest of the night. My thoughts surrounding everything that had happened to us this last year. Cal's chest rose and fell softly, his heart beating strong beneath my ear, reassuring me that he was alive. Words danced at the tip of my tongue, instead of suppressing them, I spoke them. "There is no place I would rather be than right here in your arms. No matter what has happened to me, you are alive. We are alive and together. And if anything is reassuring me that we will get through this—it's that we both defeated death and found love in the strangest of ways."

I sat upright to look deep into his eyes and make one final vow to not only him, but to myself. Gripping his hand and placing it over my heart, I said, "In this life and in the next, there is nothing that will ever separate us again. We will heal together and we will fight together, and if the gods demand it, we will die together"

He sat up, his hand moving to cup my cheek, his warmth spreading through me as I felt the vibration of his magic coursing through my veins, bringing me back to life. "There is nothing that I want more than that. Everything that I am means nothing without you. If you wish, I would like to make you my wife, officially."

"Yes." I didn't hesitate as my lips met his. The flavor of him already erasing the evidence of what happened to me.

Calian flew us to the temple of the gods while the ship was still sleeping. A sash wrapped around our hands, a knife to slit each other's palms, and then something unexpected happened. When our blood blend for the second time since the *Blood Oath*, ash filled my mouth as heat coursed through my body. Pain forced a scream to escape me as I felt my back begin to tear. My muscles stretched, and I glanced over my shoulder, watching in agony and amazement as my bones began to mend.

"Your wings…" Cal's breathing was fast, and my heart was pounding and tightening as I felt burning in my throat. An explosion of fire and light came from inside of me, pouring out of my mouth and eyes. The blast separated us and my vision faded for a few heartbeats until the pain subsided. I stood.

"Beautiful," Calian whispered as he approached me. I looked over my shoulder and saw fire-covered feathers attached to me. Looking down, a gown of white scales covered me from bosom to foot, and my hair had copper tips.

"You healed me?" It was a question for both of us.

"It must be my new power," he admitted. "When I died, I was reborn as the god of dragons. Being that you are a goddess and my mate, the mixing of our blood must have healed you."

"That is correct." Our heads snapped in the direction of the voice, and out of the shadows entered a group of five different beings, all dressed in white gowns. Power emanated from them. “We are the council of the gods. The monarchy, if you would, and when two gods perform a hand-fasting ceremony along with mixing their blood, they share their power. Since Emnera was weakened, Darius’ blood healed her.”

“Darius?” I asked, looking over at my husband.

“It is my new name. Since I was reborn.” He smiled.

“You both have completed your task on this earth. It is time to join us,” she says, her golden irises gleaming.

“What about Rai? We need to stop him,” I stated.

“That task has already started,” she answered. “The Ashana with no heart and mortal princess will be the ones to defeat him. That is what the fates have decided.”

“Won’t they need us?” I inquired.

“They have everything they need with them. It is their job to figure it out. You two must come before the dawn breaks and the portal closes,” she insisted.

Cal intertwined his fingers into mine, non-verbally telling me that whatever I choose, he will stand by me. I turn toward him, gripping his other hand, mimicking his move, and pressing my forehead against him. “This is our chance at happiness. Is it selfish to want to leave knowing that we have this power?”

“We will watch over my brother and Abbygale. If they need us, we will return, but we’ve done so much for this world that this is our chance at eternity. If you wish, then so be it,” he whispered.

There was nothing I wanted more than to be with him forever. To leave at peace without fear of looking over my shoulder with every turn.

"Our fight is finished," I whispered. "Take me home and love me for all time."

I lifted my head to meet his burning gaze, our lips colliding in a shroud of heat and light as the world around us faded away into nothing.

"As you wish."

A word about the author…

C. M. Hano is a Fantasy Romance author who aspires to write strong female-driven characters, hot and magical adventures, and being a good mother. She lives in Louisiana with her husband and two daughters.

Thank you for purchasing
this publication of The Wild Rose Press, Inc.

For questions or more information
contact us at
info@thewildrosepress.com.

The Wild Rose Press, Inc.
www.thewildrosepress.com